AMERICAN LITERATURE READINGS IN THE 21ST CENTURY

Series Editor: Linda Wagner-Martin

American Literature Readings in the 21st Century publishes works by contemporary critics that help shape critical opinion regarding literature of the nineteenth and twentieth century in the United States.

Published by Palgrave Macmillan:

Freak Shows in Modern American Imagination: Constructing the Damaged Body from Willa Cather to Truman Capote
By Thomas Fahy

Women and Race in Contemporary U.S. Writing: From Faulkner to Morrison
By Kelly Lynch Reames

American Political Poetry in the 21st Century
By Michael Dowdy

Science and Technology in the Age of Hawthorne, Melville, Twain, and James: Thinking and Writing Electricity
By Sam Halliday

F. Scott Fitzgerald's Racial Angles and the Business of Literary Greatness
By Michael Nowlin

Sex, Race, and Family in Contemporary American Short Stories
By Melissa Bostrom

Democracy in Contemporary U.S. Women's Poetry
By Nicky Marsh

James Merrill and W.H. Auden: Homosexuality and Poetic Influence
By Piotr K. Gwiazda

Contemporary U.S. Latino/a Literary Criticism
Edited by Lyn Di Iorio Sandín and Richard Perez

The Hero in Contemporary American Fiction: The Works of Saul Bellow and Don DeLillo
By Stephanie S. Halldorson

Race and Identity in Hemingway's Fiction
By Amy L. Strong

Edith Wharton and the Conversations of Literary Modernism
By Jennifer Haytock

The Anti-Hero in the American Novel: From Joseph Heller to Kurt Vonnegut
By David Simmons

Indians, Environment, and Identity on the Borders of American Literature: From Faulkner and Morrison to Walker and Silko
By Lindsey Claire Smith

The American Landscape in the Poetry of Frost, Bishop, and Ashbery: The House Abandoned
By Marit J. MacArthur

Narrating Class in American Fiction
By William Dow

The Culture of Soft Work: Labor, Gender, and Race in Postmodern American Narrative
By Heather J. Hicks

Cormac McCarthy: American Canticles
By Kenneth Lincoln

Elizabeth Spencer's Complicated Cartographies: Reimagining Home, the South, and Southern Literary Production
By Catherine Seltzer

New Critical Essays on Kurt Vonnegut
Edited by David Simmons

Feminist Readings of Edith Wharton: From Silence to Speech
By Dianne L. Chambers

The Emergence of the American Frontier Hero 1682–1826: Gender, Action, and Emotion
By Denise Mary MacNeil

Norman Mailer's Later Fictions: Ancient Evenings through Castle in the Forest
Edited by John Whalen-Bridge

Fetishism and its Discontents in Post-1960 American Fiction
By Christopher Kocela

Language, Gender, and Community in Late Twentieth-Century Fiction: American Voices and American Identities
By Mary Jane Hurst

Repression and Realism in Postwar American Literature
By Erin Mercer

Writing Celebrity: Stein, Fitzgerald, and the Modern(ist) Art of Self-Fashioning
By Timothy W. Galow

WRITING CELEBRITY

Stein, Fitzgerald, and the Modern(ist) Art of Self-Fashioning

Timothy W. Galow

WRITING CELEBRITY

First published in 2011 by
PALGRAVE MACMILLAN®
in the United States—a division of St. Martin's Press LLC,
175 Fifth Avenue, New York, NY 10010.

Where this book is distributed in the UK, Europe and the rest of the world,
this is by Palgrave Macmillan, a division of Macmillan Publishers Limited,
registered in England, company number 785998, of Houndmills,
Basingstoke, Hampshire RG21 6XS.

Palgrave Macmillan is the global academic imprint of the above companies
and has companies and representatives throughout the world.

Palgrave® and Macmillan® are registered trademarks in the United States,
the United Kingdom, Europe and other countries.

ISBN: 978–0–230–11271–1

Library of Congress Cataloging-in-Publication Data

Galow, Timothy W.
    Writing celebrity : Stein, Fitzgerald, and the modern(ist) art of
    self-fashioning / Timothy W. Galow.
        p. cm. —(American literature readings in the twenty-first century)
    ISBN 978–0–230–11271–1 (hardback)
    1. American literature—20th century—History and criticism.
    2. Modernism (Literature)—United States. 3. Celebrities—United
    States—History—20th century. 4. Fame—Social aspects—United
    States—History—20th century. 5. Fitzgerald, F. Scott (Francis Scott),
    1896–1940—Criticism and interpretation. 6. Stein, Gertrude,
    1874–1946—Criticism and interpretation. I. Title.

PS228.M63G35 2011
810.9′112—dc22   2010048453

A catalogue record of the book is available from the British Library.

Design by Newgen Imaging Systems (P) Ltd., Chennai, India.

First edition: June 2011

10 9 8 7 6 5 4 3 2 1

Printed in the United States of America.

*To the professor who made me want to do this work
in the first place and the one whose tireless
efforts made it possible*

CONTENTS

ACKNOWLEDGMENTS

Looking back over the course of this project, I realize that it would take another book to thank all the people who have helped along the way. So I will be far too brief here, leaving out the names of literally hundreds of people who provided intellectual, emotional, and economic support as *Writing Celebrity* developed. Your help, I assure you, is not forgotten.

My first debt of gratitude is always to my mother and father, without whom none of this would have been possible, and I mean that in the broadest possible way. I also wish to single out Fran Ratzburg. I mention the unsolicited support that put food on my table during graduate school, but it was your generosity of spirit that mattered most. You are much missed.

Friends, colleagues, and students at the University of Chicago, the University of North Carolina, and Wake Forest University have supplied invaluable assistance at all stages of this project. I have received significant institutional support from each school as well. Without the graduate fellowship from the University of Chicago, I would have missed out on many opportunities. At the University of North Carolina, a Frankel Dissertation Fellowship, a John R. Bittner Fellowship in Literature and Journalism, and a Smith Research Grant all provided economic support at crucial junctures. An Archie Research Fellowship at Wake Forest University enabled me to conduct research at several libraries around the country. The Bentley Historical Library at the University of Michigan provided research support for work on *Esquire*, which figures into the later chapters of this book. I want to express gratitude to *Modernism/modernity*, which published a piece of this book under the title "Literary Modernism in the Age of Celebrity," © 2010 The Johns Hopkins University Press. This article first appeared in Volume 17, Issue 2, April 2010, pages 313–29. Grateful acknowledgment is also given to the *Journal of Modern Literature*, in which an earlier version of chapter 4 appeared under the title, "Gertrude Stein's *Everybody's Autobiography* and the Art of Contradictions," © Indiana University Press. This article first appeared in Volume 32, Issue 1, Fall 2008, pages 111–28.

I cannot finish this woefully insufficient expression of gratitude without mentioning my son, Calvin, who is now only three, but may some day grow curious about his father and pull this dusty old book off the shelf. You will have no memory of the hours we spent throwing stones on the path in front of our apartment building, or the afternoons we went down to the lake to talk with ducks. But these are the things that I remember most about writing this book. You make the work worth doing.

Lastly, and a bit sheepishly, I address the one person whom I could not possibly thank enough: my wife, Amy. You gave up more for this book than your stupid husband will ever realize. And you did it with more humor than I had any right to expect. Please know, my only regret about this project is that I had to spend so many nights away in my office, when I could have been home with you.

PRELUDE

Writing Celebrity outlines the rise of a national celebrity culture in the United States and surveys the impact that this culture had on "literary" writing in the decades before World War II. Then, it examines how two authors, Gertrude Stein and F. Scott Fitzgerald, negotiated with this new landscape while constructing their public personae during the 1920s and 1930s. Each part can be treated as a self-contained analysis, but all three parts were designed to communicate with one another and support a number of larger arguments that emerge over the course of the book.

Chapter 1 examines several important changes in U.S. culture during the latter half of the nineteenth century. Print technologies evolved and markets expanded so that, by the turn of the century, magazines and newspapers were able to help lay the groundwork for a culture that was truly national in scope. As this new "mass" culture began to emerge, the literary field split into two highly visible sets of institutions for producing and promoting texts, a situation that encouraged people to speak about books in binary terms. High/low, elite/popular, and serious/light are just a few of the labels that have historically been used to distinguish between texts.

While aspects of this discussion may seem familiar to American literary or cultural scholars, much of the previous work done on these developments has neglected one crucial and related change: the emergence of a national celebrity culture. In order to convince readers of the important role that celebrity media played during this period, I argue against two positions that feature prominently in contemporary writing on the subject. First, critics continue to treat star coverage as if it were a degraded offshoot of "serious" journalism. Second, some literary scholars, despite the recent explosion of studies on celebrity, continue to marginalize the topic in discussions of modern authorship. In order to challenge these views, I argue that celebrity coverage has long been a part of American media and that it played an increasingly prominent role in the press over the course of the nineteenth century. By 1900, this form of journalism had become important enough that it influenced the way in which a number of cultural products, including literary texts, were produced and marketed.

Some elite authors railed, at least occasionally, against these developments. They also implicitly disparaged the realm of mass culture by associating it with femininity, a move that helped reinforce the distinction between so-called popular writing and the elevated masculine world of "serious" letters. Such attitudes led many subsequent scholars to characterize highbrow authors at the turn of the century as antipathetic to the marketplace. This critical appropriation of the high/low dichotomy quickly transcended the rhetorical function that it served for many authors in the early 1900s, and dislike for mass/popular/light culture subsequently came to be seen as one of the principal characteristics of the modernist movement. In the process, the terms "high" and "low" have come to stand in for a wide range of social and institutional developments in a way that obscures the relationship between modernist authors and their world.

While many scholars over the past several decades have worked to correct the oversights of these theoretical formulations, more consideration needs to be given to the effects that an expanding celebrity culture had on the profession of authorship. In chapter 2, I argue for the value of "celebrity" as an interpretive paradigm in modernist studies, both from a historical perspective and as a unifying concept for textual analysis. Celebrity culture helped transform all aspects of the literary field, from the production and marketing of a book to the way in which it was received by consumers and professional critics. It also changed how authors presented themselves to the reading public. A careful examination of these developments can expand our knowledge of textual production and consumption in the early twentieth century while also revitalizing analyses of a wide range of texts produced during this period.

The remainder of the book builds on these claims by examining how Gertrude Stein's and F. Scott Fitzgerald's writing positioned them in the market. I have chosen these two authors because they represent, by contemporary standards, "oppositional" career paths. F. Scott Fitzgerald received national recognition with the publication of his first novel and spent much of the next two decades struggling for critical respectability while writing for smaller and smaller audiences. Conversely, Stein spent decades generating cultural capital and cultivating relationships with influential patrons in the hopes of finding a publisher for her large collection of manuscripts. It was not until she was in her 60s, with a best-selling memoir to her credit, that she was finally able to secure a long-term publishing arrangement with Random House.

Despite these different paths, both authors shared a remarkably similar set of concerns about the potential effects of promotional efforts on their reputations. Moreover, Stein and Fitzgerald responded to their concerns in somewhat similar ways. Each writer invoked the high/low divide, but not simply to adopt the pose of an elite writer who despised the literary market. Instead, they attempted to bridge these two poles, creating an imaginative fusion that would allow them, at least on the page, to operate in both fields simultaneously.

In chapter 3, I trace Stein's immediate response to fame by examining a series of publicity pieces and literary texts that she produced after the publication of *The Autobiography of Alice B. Toklas.* Taken together, these texts reveal Stein's attempt to publicly theorize an authorial identity that exists only in the very instant of creation but is still capable of instilling texts with permanent value. The literary work, then, becomes an isolated and inviolable object with inherent qualities that exist independently of readers, critics, or even the author herself. The current critical consensus positions Stein as a protopostmodern theorist of the "open" text, that is, as one who believes *readers* create textual meaning and value. I argue instead that Stein, in response to the pressures of public exposure, cultivated a theory similar in many ways to that of contemporary New Critics.

Yet, in opposition to some forms of New Critical philosophy, I contend that Stein did not ultimately work to isolate the subjective consciousness and locate aesthetic value in the text simply in order to "escape" personality. On the contrary, she uses her own subjective isolation from the completed text as grounds on which to freely engage in market activities. Just as this formulation allows Stein to cross the high/low divide, it also allows her, despite her gender, to maintain allegiance with the masculine world of high art. Stein's authorial identity, which, she claims, exists only in the act of creation, lets her downplay overt signs of difference—including femininity, lesbianism, and Jewishness—in her textual persona without altogether rejecting them as constitutive elements of her consciousness.

Chapter 4 reads Stein's second major autobiography, *Everybody's Autobiography,* as both the development and embodiment of these theories. The book as a whole generates tension by highlighting the play of contradictory impulses, many of which revolve around the seeming opposition between Stein as elite author and Stein as popular memoirist. In terms of the "great divide," then, I read this book not as an attempt to mediate between high and low so much as to occupy both poles at the same time.

The final part of the book focuses on F. Scott Fitzgerald's promotional activities. Chapter 5 examines the public persona Fitzgerald cultivated during his two decades as a professional writer. Unlike Stein, who worked for thirty years before producing a bestseller, Fitzgerald was heralded as the voice of a new generation almost immediately after the publication of his first novel. During the early years, he represented himself as a young genius who could produce timeless masterpieces in the few spare moments he had between parties. By the end of the decade, however, Fitzgerald's stream of fiction had slowed to a trickle, and he attempted to reposition himself as a sedate and reflective author.

The final chapter examines Fitzgerald's "Crack-Up" essays, a series of confessional articles he wrote about suffering a nervous breakdown, in light of his larger publicity aims during the decade. The canonical reading of these articles, which has been rehearsed by innumerable critics since the author's death in 1940, suggests that Fitzgerald wrote them in an effort to make a clean break with his alcoholic past and press on with his writing. In contrast, I read these pieces not as a confession of a "real" breakdown, but as a meditation on the process of breaking down, one that could potentially bolster Fitzgerald's image as a fearless artist. This positioning also helps to situate these essays as important "literary" reflections that are somehow different from other tawdry and effeminate public confessions. Fitzgerald's narrative persona, then, cultivates a site for "serious" masculine authorship within the confines of a traditionally feminine mode of discourse.

Many critics have speculated, without reaching anything like a scholarly consensus, about the overwhelmingly negative response that the "Crack-Up" essays received when they were first published in early 1936. I conclude chapter 6 with an examination of specific responses to these pieces in order to demonstrate that many of the male respondents took issue precisely with the gendered subtext of the articles. Ultimately, I argue that it is Fitzgerald's attempt to position himself both within and against reigning notions of masculine authorship that led so many men, including *Esquire* readers, male writers, and men working in the literary field, to condemn the pieces.

Taken together, these parts provide a glimpse of one often-overlooked aspect of authorship in the early twentieth century. Part I briefly surveys the expansion of celebrity culture in the United States in order to suggest its relevance for literary analysis. It also provides a broad assessment of some of the theoretical and methodological challenges that a study of literary fame would entail. By underscoring the complexity of the system in which writers such as F. Scott Fitzgerald and Gertrude Stein had to operate, this part also provides a backdrop for the subsequent analyses. The later chapters, in turn, demonstrate how a focus on "celebrity" can provide valuable insights into literary texts and the larger cultural field. Both authors engaged with and struggled against emerging promotional outlets. In the process, they created texts that positioned them in an increasingly complex literary marketplace. These works constitute one important element in the dynamic process that generates public identities, and they suggest something of the struggle that took place around popular personae at the time. Critics have only just begun to address the convoluted exchanges that produce particular personalities and their connection with efforts to dictate the parameters governing aesthetic value, but such interactions have long influenced attitudes toward literature. As such, they deserve more serious consideration from scholars seeking to understand both recent literary history and the changing contours of twentieth-century American culture.

PART I

Contexts: Literary Modernism in the Age of Celebrity

When F. Scott Fitzgerald submitted what would become his first novel, *This Side of Paradise,* to Scribner's for the third time in late 1919, the young editor Maxwell Perkins had to deliver an impassioned speech to the board, effectively resigning over the book's repeated dismissal, before *Paradise* was finally accepted for publication.[1] Fitzgerald had only one story published in a commercial magazine at this point in his career and was largely unknown outside the coterie of literary friends he had made during his undergraduate years at Princeton. Within a year, the novel became an essential text for many teenagers in the United States, and Fitzgerald himself was heralded as the voice of the younger generation.

Gertrude Stein labored for nearly three decades to find a major publisher for her output—labored, that is, until writing *The Autobiography of Alice B. Toklas* in the fall of 1932. Much like *Paradise,* this book was an immediate success. After excerpts appeared in *The Atlantic Monthly, The Autobiography* sold its entire first printing, more than 5,000 copies, nine days in advance of its official publication date.[2] The immense popularity Stein achieved as a result of the book allowed her to begin publishing pieces from her massive collection of manuscripts. It also laid the groundwork for a successful tour of the United States in 1934. Stein's trip from France was front-page news in nearly every New York newspaper, and she was flocked by interviewers and curiosity seekers the moment she stepped off the boat.

While such stories of near-immediate national renown might seem commonplace today, the speed with which Fitzgerald's and Stein's names traveled across a continent and the extensive opportunities that such sudden fame afforded them were relatively new phenomena in the early decades of the twentieth century. These phenomena were made possible by the massive restructuring of the U.S. cultural landscape in the late nineteenth century. The rapid development of new resources and technologies that have come to be lumped under the general term "modernity" brought many people physically and imaginatively closer together. It also gave rise to processes that enabled the widespread consumption of relatively homogeneous products and messages. Thus, F. Scott Fitzgerald, three weeks after the publication of *Paradise*, could script an "interview" with himself and send it to his publishers in hopes that it might be reprinted simultaneously in newspapers, literary inserts, and book reviews around the country. He could, for the first time in history, anticipate submitting his opinions almost immediately to millions of contemporary readers across the continental United States.

* * *

The early twentieth century has been studied extensively by celebrity scholars.[3] Part of the reason this period has received so much attention is because it marks both the emergence of independent public relations firms and the film industry's earliest forays into star promotion. For all the consideration that has been given to these significant developments, more attention needs to be paid to the changes in U.S. print culture that helped to make them possible. The gradual formation of national media during the latter half of the nineteenth century established many of the circuits through which promotional accounts would have to pass and helped to dictate the terms under which new forms of reporting would operate. Moreover, celebrity accounts themselves had a long history that helped to shape the methods employed by later journalists. Gossip pieces and personality profiles, for instance, have existed since the earliest days of the republic, and notable individuals received an incipient form of "star" treatment well before the mid-nineteenth century. As publications with a truly national scope became increasingly common, coverage of notable figures, and the figures themselves, only increased in prominence.

In what follows, I briefly trace these developments to demonstrate that the turn of the century not only marks a crucial point for contemporary media but also represents an important moment in what could now be referred to as the "history of celebrity." The growth of national outlets for star promotion transformed the ways in which people engaged with larger publics and laid the groundwork for increasingly sophisticated publicity campaigns in the 1910s and 1920s. As noted above, film has received a prominent place in studies of these years; however, the effects of earlier changes can be seen in many different forms across a wide range of media. Literary texts in particular were inflected by the expanding scope and range of celebrity journalism. Authors acquired many new channels for constructing public personae, and they gained the ability to communicate rapidly with audiences all around the country. As markets grew and publicity mechanisms became more complex, they were also able to call on a growing body of business intermediaries, such as literary and press agents, to assist them in these efforts. Conversely, readers' engagements with literary texts were increasingly mediated by new sources of information about books and authors.

Despite this seemingly rich area for study, the impact that celebrity culture had on the formation of modernist literature remains largely unexplored. One obvious reason for this oversight is that some authors at the time reacted to the increasing interpenetration of business and art by positioning themselves, at least nominally, in opposition to the market. Another reason is that scholars and writers alike have long treated celebrity reporting as if it were little more than a symptom of contemporary cultural decline. This dismissive attitude needs to be reconsidered. Rather than thinking of gossip columns and human-interest journalism as a parasitic offspring of "real" news or "serious" culture, these forms of reportage were a constitutive part of a developing national media, one that became increasingly important to the publishing industry in the early decades of the twentieth century. Furthermore, as personality promotion became more common, authors from all "brow" levels were forced to engage in some form with these new publicity mechanisms.

I conclude by arguing for the potential usefulness of "celebrity" as an interpretive paradigm in modernist studies. In order to demonstrate the value of this concept, I briefly examine how studies of textual production and reception after the turn of the century could benefit from a more systematic examination of personality promotion. This survey is intended to show how celebrity can be used to generate new interpretations of, and provide fresh perspectives on, the literary field in the early decades of the twentieth century. It also suggests ways in which valuable insights made under other scholarly rubrics can be expanded through the study of celebrity. For example, much useful work has been done exploring the ways in which modernist writers rhetorically distanced themselves from the concerns of the marketplace. Without disregarding the imaginative appeal that such an antagonistic stance had or the rhetorical force writers generated by occasionally railing against "the market," it is necessary to go beyond simple oppositions in order to account for the ambivalence many authors expressed over issues of personal promotion.

CHAPTER 1

Critical Histories: The Changing Face of Literature, 1870–1920

PRINT MARKETS, POPULAR CULTURE, AND MASCULINITY IN THE LATE NINETEENTH-CENTURY UNITED STATES

The rapid expansion of print markets in the last decades of the nineteenth century greatly increased not only the number of people who could be reached by the press but also the speed with which a single message could be distributed. Urban dailies, for one, began to reach wider audiences at this time after a series of technological and institutional developments modernized the news industry at midcentury. The invention of the telegraph in the 1840s provided the means for distributing news beyond the confines of written text. Within a decade, the United States had developed one of the most complex telegraph networks in the entire world. The Associated Press (AP) formed in 1846 and shortly thereafter began disseminating stories to a handful of papers in New York. The AP service quickly expanded to cities such as Boston and Philadelphia and eventually to regional press groups throughout the country. Articles from the major urban dailies were often picked up by other papers and magazines, a trend that only increased during the Civil War. By the 1880s, syndication had become common.[4]

Along with the increasing availability of standardized news stories, developments in printing presses and typesetting technologies after the Civil War allowed publishers to increase copying speeds while also cutting costs. The invention of the halftone process, which reproduced photographs by transforming them into small dots of varying sizes and densities to replicate the black and white shadings of a photograph, also allowed newspapers to become a more visual medium in the latter decades of the nineteenth century. In 1880, the *New*

York Daily Graphic became the first paper in the United States to run a halftone; within a decade, most major newspapers were regularly using photographic reproductions along with pictorial comic features and advertisements that had an increasingly visual focus. This format was far more accessible than previous print-dominated arrangements. Pictures also enhanced the effectiveness of more sensational news stories, which became increasingly prominent with the advent of Joseph Pulitzer and William Randolph Hearst's "yellow" journalism in the 1890s.[5]

New production technologies, increasingly readable formats that emphasized photographic reproductions and splashy headlines, and a growing urban middle class all contributed to dramatic increases in newspaper sales. In 1892, ten papers in four cities had circulations higher than 100,000. In 1914, more than thirty papers in twelve cities reached the same number. By way of contrast, total national circulation was only about 300,000 in 1840, a number that rose to over 15 million by the turn of the century.[6]

Alongside the rise of newspapers, mass market magazines became a dominant cultural force during the so-called magazine revolution of the 1890s, a decade in which total monthly magazine circulation nearly tripled. In the years immediately after the Civil War, about 700 different magazines were published in the United States. By 1885, there were more than 3,000. Up to this point, the most popular magazines had circulations of just over 100,000. By 1900, there were over 5,500 magazines in total, at least 50 of which were national, and the *Ladies' Home Journal* alone had nearly 1,000,000 subscribers. The *Journal* would surpass the million mark in 1903. By this time, there were almost a dozen magazines with circulations that exceeded 500,000.[7]

Though some commentators cite a few publishers' names or the success of specific magazines to explain this change in the industry, the explosion in magazine circulations resulted from a series of historical shifts. Physical distribution of magazines became easier after the U.S. government granted 131 million acres to railroad companies in the 1850s and 1860s. The transcontinental railroad was completed in 1869, and by 1871 companies had laid over 19 million miles of track, an expansion project that continued steadily through the turn of the century. Moreover, in 1885, the Post Office dropped rates for all second-class mailings from three cents per pound to one cent per pound. As a result, publishers focused more attention on subscription sales. Most major magazines had mechanized subscription and renewal systems in place by the turn of the century.[8]

Along with developments in mail-order operations, most publishers continued to seek out new venues for direct sales. Chain and department stores, which began appearing with greater frequency between 1876 and 1900, became important outlets for the industry.[9] Newsstands, which had originally supported only daily papers, also expanded to support magazine sales. By the turn of the century, there were between 3,000 and 4,000 newsdealers in the country, most of whom dealt with periodicals.[10] The role that advertising played in periodicals also shifted during the 1880s and 1890s. Almost all magazines contained some ads prior to this point. Even the highest-quality volumes, such as *Harper's New Monthly Magazine, Scribner's Monthly, Century Magazine,* and *The Atlantic Monthly,* carried both ads and reviews. In the final decades of the century, however, advertising became central to the operations of most magazines. A wide range of businesses greatly increased their marketing efforts during this period in order to maximize expanding production capacities. At the same time, consumption of mass-produced goods was on the rise. People moving to cities for industrial jobs found themselves in positions where home production was inhibited or marginalized by new urban conditions. Demand greatly increased for prepackaged goods and day-to-day necessities. In addition, the subset of professionals who emerged to meet the managerial demands of expanding businesses sought new kinds of goods as a marker of their elevated social status. These increases in production and consumption helped periodicals to swell with new pages of ads both for home goods, such as razors, pens, and oatmeal, and for the most modern leisure goods, such as phonographs, cameras, and bicycles.[11]

In conjunction with this expansion of advertising, ad agencies, which largely functioned as space brokers earlier in the century, began to take on more tasks, from copywriting to market analysis to media selection. As Jennifer Wicke points out in *Advertising Fictions,* "Advertising remained a congeries of loosely allied practices, a crossroads between newspaper, coffee-house, freelance writer, and the firm with the product until the latter half of the nineteenth century."[12] N. W. Ayer & Son was founded in 1869 and is often cited as the first agency to assume responsibility for advertising content.[13] The J. Walter Thomson Agency, started as Carlton & Smith in 1864, began expanding its role in the process during the late 1870s. By 1890, there were a dozen major agencies offering services in the largest American markets. This new group of professional advertisers was faced with the challenge of differentiating products from a rapidly growing field, a situation that led to the expansion of advertising techniques such as branding, which both differentiated specific items and functioned as a quality guarantee for newly standardized products.[14]

Businesses' need for more advertising space, and the increasing ease with which ads could be placed, led to a wholesale shift in the way periodicals functioned during the 1890s. Instead of relying on sales for income, a practice that led to relatively high cover prices and low circulations, publishers slashed prices to increase sales and began relying on the influx of advertising revenue to offset production cost losses. As a result, the prices of most magazines fell from around thirty-five to ten cents an issue, and the number of advertising pages expanded rapidly between 1893 and 1900. Magazines that had only a decade before included a dozen pages of advertising expanded to carry forty or fifty pages. General-interest magazines contained even more. By December 1895, *McClure's* had 150 pages of ads. In 1905, it had 200 pages.[15]

Editors and publishers, in turn, were forced to consider the specific constitution of their audience in order to tailor content and create more coherent periodicals. The refined product images could then be used to court specific advertisers, a process that required a significant shift in the scope of business operations. Most major publishers were conducting in-house market surveys by the early twentieth century and, in 1911, the Curtis organization hired the first market research director, Charles Coolidge Parlin.[16]

Part of the reason periodical production has proven so important for recent studies of mass culture at the turn of the century is because the industry provides a direct link between major trends in the emerging corporate business environment and shifting patterns of consumption. On one hand, publishing houses began to develop increasingly complex organizational structures and they required more information both to regulate internal processes and to situate products in the marketplace. On the other hand, monthly magazines' emphasis on periodicity and rapidly changing content supported and validated the desire of a newly emergent middle class to remain in touch with developments outside their increasingly narrow fields of specialization. Professionals who had been taught to value knowledge, and whose knowledge secured their position in the marketplace, could remain culturally relevant in part by dabbling in the major periodicals of the day.[17]

Such trends continued into the Progressive Era at the beginning of the twentieth century, which was, most historians agree, the point at which American culture transformed from distinct communities into a regulative bureaucratic order. This shift depended in large part on public faith that an emerging group of technical experts could organize society in a way that would prove beneficial to all people. Yet the increasingly complex social and economic structures that were forming throughout the latter half of the nineteenth century meant that most people were left with a limited understanding of larger institutions and forces that were coming to play an increasingly central role in their lives. As Robert Wiebe notes, for many in the United States the shift toward "nationalization, industrialization, mechanization, urbanization...meant only dislocation and bewilderment."[18]

In addition to this more general difficulty, the shift raised distinct challenges for working men, for whom employment increasingly meant routine intellectual or physical labor tied to a monotonous schedule. Not surprisingly, scholars have located a general "crisis of masculinity" in the nineteenth century. The traditional places in which men had affirmed their manhood were beginning to disappear from bourgeois life, necessitating the rise of compensatory spaces in which new versions of masculinity could be staged.[19] The rise of organized sports in the latter half of the nineteenth century is one such space. Collegiate sports, for instance, were becoming increasingly popular at this time. These events not only celebrated (male) physical prowess but also reaffirmed spectators' connections with particular universities and the upward mobility that these institutions were increasingly coming to represent. Boxing also became a popular attraction, and John L. Sullivan, the heavyweight champion from 1882 until his loss to James Corbett in 1892, attracted a larger following than any sports hero to date. As John Kasson notes, it was largely Sullivan's popularity that transformed boxing from a disreputable pastime to a mass entertainment appropriate for middle-class audiences.[20]

These emerging male sports also reflect two major cultural shifts in the latter half of the nineteenth century: the turn toward larger and more spectacle-oriented forms of entertainment and the increasing organization of American cultural life. Boxing transformed from an underworld pursuit for gamblers and criminals to a respectable display of male prowess. Similarly, collegiate athletics changed from disorganized intramural activities disparaged by university officials in the first half of the nineteenth century to highly organized, and well-attended, events by the turn of the twentieth. An intercollegiate football association, which united Columbia, Rutgers, Princeton, and Yale, was formed in 1873. The first intercollegiate track and field association formed two years later, in 1875. Baseball also evolved from an amateur pastime to a profession in the years immediately following the Civil War, as the Cincinnati Red Stockings became the first team to pay its players a regular salary. The National League was founded in 1876, with the American Association forming as a rival in 1881.

In addition to these male-heavy spectacles, vaudeville emerged in the 1880s, combining the variety show format popular in theaters through much of the 1800s with stricter moral standards. Antebellum theaters, though attended by people of all classes, often carried the taint of disrespectability, not only because they served as workplaces for prostitutes and criminals but also because the economically varied audiences often behaved unpredictably. In contrast, vaudeville theaters were clean and respectable. Performers were even known to chastise the crowd, encouraging respectful and civilized behavior.

"High" Art and the Emergence of Literary Modernism

Alongside the spectacle-oriented mass culture that emerged in the decades immediately following the Civil War, critics have traced the rise of an alternate, and often oppositional, form of culture. Richard Brodhead argues that the upper classes consolidated after the war in part by identifying with cultural forms and practices that were not embraced by the masses.[21] This effort at class consolidation led to increasingly regimented cultural spaces—including museums, libraries, and concert halls—and modes of appreciation. Contemplating art for these patrons became something that required concerted effort and experience, if not yet formal training. Thus, the eclecticism that characterized American culture in the early decades of the nineteenth century, when museums exhibited plants alongside paintings and music halls mixed concert pieces with popular show tunes, gave way to a process of segregation. Not only were "legitimate" artistic productions isolated and linked with more rigorously defined modes of spectatorship, but these distinctions were also institutionalized in centers funded and frequented by patrons seeking cultural distinction.[22]

A similar divide became more apparent in the literary field as well. Though many critics have described the emergence of a "great divide" between high and low art in the latter half of the nineteenth century, Janice Radway's survey of these years in *A Feeling for Books* is particularly useful for its emphasis on institutional transformations. A distinction between quality literature and frivolous writing certainly antedated the U.S. literary scene of the nineteenth century. Yet, as Radway trenchantly argues, these distinctions were "reified during the latter half of the nineteenth century and erected into two distinct sets of institutions and practices for producing, disseminating, and controlling books."[23]

One form of text was linked with the immediate desires of the reader, who engaged in reading to fulfill particular needs. Whether pursuing pleasure or information, these consumers sought books as utilitarian objects that lacked long-term value. Accordingly, most of these texts were produced cheaply by specialized publishing houses that dealt primarily in disseminating a particular kind of information or low-cost fiction. The explosion of paperback publishers in the 1870s and 1880s, including Street & Smith, Donnelley, Lloyd & Company, and Beadle & Adams, represented a new kind of business that sought not widespread but repeat sales of their various pulp series. Accordingly, these works were not written by reputable "authors" but "hacks" whose names did not often appear on the finished texts.[24]

In contrast to these assembly-line works of fiction, another form of text was conceived as the product of a gifted author, whose message could only be grasped through focused attention and rigorous scrutiny. Again, this conception of literature existed long before the latter decades of the nineteenth century, but the rise of a new and what many saw as a degraded form of literature generated much anxiety about the status of the book at the turn of the century. These anxieties led in part to the emergence of new arenas in which "quality" books could be preserved.[25]

Developing English curricula in universities and public schools, both of which were in formative stages during the latter half of the nineteenth century, worked to formalize specific reading practices and elevate particular types of books as worthy of study. As businesses demanded more skilled workers to fill technical and managerial positions, higher education became an increasingly central part of white middle-class life in the United States. In 1870, only one in sixty men between the ages of eighteen and twenty-one was enrolled in college. By 1900, that number had risen to one in twenty-five.[26]

Many of these institutions began to develop generalist approaches that accorded with Matthew Arnold's idea of literature as the best that had been thought and said. Such a stance allowed literature to be conceived as a transcendent repository of human value, in contrast to both the utilitarian values of an industrial age and the pressure for specialized education being exerted by business. As generalist approaches slowly gave way to more specialized forms of literary study, the new modes of analysis retained this sense of the literary text as a distinct, and inherently valuable, form of writing that rewarded close scrutiny.

These attitudes toward literature were also apparent in quality magazines of the day, notably *Harper's, Century, Scribner's,* and *The Atlantic. Harper's,* in particular, which the Harper brothers started in 1850 to maximize the use of their press when they were not printing books, emerged as a vehicle to market their volumes to an elite, educated audience. All four magazines also employed or published many of the major genteel academic critics who emerged before the turn of the century, such as E. C. Stedman, Barrett Wendell, Henry Van Dyke, and George Woodberry.[27]

In addition to the consolidation and institutionalization of distinct aesthetic spheres, the literary field also shared a sense of masculine crisis with other cultural arenas. The tension between a feminized mass culture and a masculine elite culture was already quite apparent at midcentury, when Nathaniel Hawthorne famously wrote his publisher to denounce the "damned mob of scribbling women." Hawthorne's disdain arose in part from the notable success of many female authors. Harriet Beecher Stowe's *Uncle Tom's Cabin,* first serialized in 1851, was the most popular book of the nineteenth century, selling over 300,000 copies in the United States alone during its first three years of publication. Susan Warner's *The Wide, Wide World* sold over a million copies in total. E. D. E. N. Southworth, who wrote perhaps as many as fifty novels, was probably the best-selling author of the nineteenth century.

Yet the link between elite literary products and masculinity was distinct enough that many of these female authors viewed their success apologetically and often described their work not as intellectual labor but as an emotional outpouring. Stowe, who had already refracted her politics through the supposedly feminized sentimental novel, famously attributed the authorship of *Uncle Tom's Cabin* to God. Caroline Howard Gilman likened the emotion that accompanied seeing one of her poems in print to being caught in men's clothing.[28]

In this context, Andreas Huyssen's argument that male intellectuals at the turn of the century assumed that "mass culture is somehow associated with women while real, authentic culture remains the prerogative of men" seems far less radical.[29] Loren Glass, in *Authors, Inc.,* usefully notes that Huyssen's argument, based on a study of European art, is "even more applicable to U. S. modernism, where Emersonian self-reliance and frontier individualism contributed to a modernist image of the hypermasculine male author."[30] The rise of this image in the early twentieth century, through figures such as Jack London and Ernest Hemingway, suggests that its emergence also had much to do with the United States' larger transition toward a consumer economy and the emergent regulative, hierarchical, bureaucratic order of the Progressive Era. Both changes led to a view of society that de-emphasized the distinct individual in favor of discernable market groups and standardized "sets" of people based on characteristics such as income, age, intelligence, and ethnicity.

Hence, by the turn of the century, many of the ideas that would become central to interpretations of the modernist period had already begun to germinate in emerging literary and critical institutions. Distinct publishers, critical organs, and a growing class of literary scholars all reinforced the idea of "high" literature as a distinct, and transcendent, object requiring its own formalized procedures of study. In addition, this field, developing out of a literary tradition that associated the masculine with concentrated study and "serious" thought, was coded in opposition to both a feminized mass culture and the "low" sphere of popular writing, the domain of nameless hacks writing formulaic stories to publishers' specifications.

THE RISE OF A NATIONAL CELEBRITY CULTURE

While some aspects of this story will certainly be familiar to contemporary modernist critics, one important element that has received relatively little attention is the concurrent development of a national celebrity culture. As might be expected, the roots of this culture existed well before the turn of the century. One needs to look no further than P. T. Barnum's spectacles and oddities in the mid-nineteenth century to find a strikingly contemporary example of self-promotion. Barnum was a quintessential showman, emphasizing his name in every endeavor so that each success not only benefited him financially but also expanded his renown. The self-proclaimed "prince of humbugs," a title that suggests both his own commitment to the art of deception and his skill at public manipulation, took every opportunity to generate controversy around his projects. In 1835, for instance, Barnum learned of a woman named Joice Heth, who was supposedly 161 years old and claimed to have been the nursemaid of George Washington. Barnum took the woman on tour as a scientific curiosity of national significance. Then, when crowds began to dwindle, he planted a newspaper article that claimed she was actually a robot. In the process of debunking his own exhibit, he effectively created another attraction and encouraged audiences to come back for a second look.[31]

Figures such as Barnum who acquired national renown early in the nineteenth century were generally people who found ways to overcome the difficulties of living in a time of limited information flows, most frequently by touring, cultivating informal social networks, engaging in widespread publicity campaigns, or by disseminating their works, often times quite slowly, on a broad scale. Such limitations did not mean that "celebrities," with their attendant armies of journalists and fans, began to appear only in the last decades of the nineteenth century or, later still, in the emerging film culture of the early twentieth century. When Charles Dickens first arrived in the United States in 1842, journalists leapt on board his ship as it was docking in hopes of getting the first exclusive interview.[32]

The shifts in American culture around the turn of the twentieth century, however, led to significant changes in the U.S. celebrity landscape. As newspapers and magazines became national in scope, developments in transportation and the growth of spectacle-oriented entertainments late in the nineteenth century allowed an increasing number of individuals to figure more prominently in public conversations. Theatrical productions, for instance, which had relied on the appeal of major actors and actresses since early in the century, became more dependent on the personae of performers when traveling shows increased in prominence during the 1870s and 1880s. In 1871, there were about fifty theatrical companies attached to specific theaters in larger cities throughout the country. By 1880, only about ten remained. These independently operated outfits were gradually replaced after the Civil War by "combination companies," which spent the season touring local theaters with a single play. By 1886, almost 300 combination companies were touring the country.[33] This transformation greatly increased the visibility of particular theater performances and individual performers as well as the demand for information about both. Three different papers devoted to the theater appeared in a seven-year span: the *New York Dramatic News* (1875), the *New York Mirror* (1879), and the *Dramatic News* (1881). Many major newspapers also began employing reporters as "dramatic paragraphers" to cover entertainment news and write feature stories about the stars of the stage.[34]

Similarly, vaudeville acts, burlesque shows, and gradually professionalizing forms of sport all depended heavily on popular figures, and publicity stunts, to draw audiences. Boxer John L. Sullivan not only went on a coast-to-coast tour with five other boxers in the early 1880s to promote the sport but also offered to fight anyone at any time for $250. He supposedly knocked out eleven men during the tour. By the late 1880s, Sullivan was so popular that his last bare-knuckled fight against Jake Kilrain in 1889 became something of a media circus. Newspapers carried a notable amount of prefight coverage, reporting on the fighters' training regimens and their thoughts about the upcoming event. Journalists also speculated extensively about the outcome. After Sullivan won the seventy-five-round fight, his name appeared in papers across the country.[35]

While such a spectacle is certainly reminiscent of more contemporary sporting events, Sullivan, as a famous public figure, was never subjected to the intense personal scrutiny that would become characteristic of twentieth-century celebrity journalism. The absence of such systematic scrutiny, however, does not mean that the press avoided revealing intimate details about people. Gossip was an important part of newspaper journalism from the earliest days of the republic. Prior to the 1830s, many papers functioned as organs for political propaganda and occasionally printed scandalous, or even libelous, details about public figures.

Though the tone of such information began to change with what many historians consider the advent of modern journalistic methods in the 1830s, gossip continued to play a role in newspapers. Reporters were sent out on beats to capture news as it happened, which helped to direct attention toward the day-to-day events that have since become the staple of daily news. These beats also meant that reporters continued to keep track of crime and court orders, popular subjects in earlier newspapers, as well as the activities of important members of high society.

Additionally, throughout much of the century there were scandal "sheets," generally short-lived papers that printed any degrading detail the public might find interesting. An 1842 issue of *The Weekly Rake,* for instance, teased audiences with a mention of "a man in town that requested another to shave his legs." The piece concludes, "We have received a detail of the whole affair. Shall we publish it??"[36]

While these early gossip papers do bear some resemblance to more contemporary incarnations of the genre, the scandalous anecdotes they contained were far from the systematic and repeated explorations of individual lives characteristic of much twentieth-century media. Moreover, any salacious details that did happen to emerge were still read, more often than not, by a limited and local public. The most notable gossip magazine in the nineteenth century was *Town Topics,* which rose to prominence in the 1890s after it had been taken over by the so-called godfather of gossip, Colonel William D'Alton Mann. Under his ownership, the magazine printed fiction, verse, and criticism. It also contained lots of gossip bought from anyone who might be willing to provide inside information about New York's elite society, including disgruntled servants, telegraph operators, and delivery men. The scandals Mann and his network of spies uncovered implicated figures of national significance, from the Vanderbilts and J. P. Morgan to Alice Roosevelt, and they were remarkably accurate. As a result, the magazine frequently gained national attention and sold copies all around the country.[37]

Besides moving gossip onto the national stage, Mann also popularized techniques that would become staples of early twentieth-century scandal magazines, mainly for their ability to keep publishers out of court. With the rapid spread of media and the continuous expansion of urban areas, which brought people into increasingly close proximity to each other, much anxiety surfaced over the eroding boundaries between public and private at the turn of the century. Perhaps the most influential legal opinion of the period, Samuel Warren and Louis Brandeis's "The Right to Privacy," came out just one year before Mann began running *Town Topics*. In their analysis, Warren and Brandeis posit an "inviolate" right to both privacy and "one's own personality" as a way of coming to terms with a world in which "gossip has become a trade."[38] In such an inhospitable legal environment, Mann partnered with an attorney to ensure that nothing he printed was actionable. He frequently, for instance, ran the most defamatory pieces without including the subject's name. These anonymous pieces would then be followed by a seemingly innocuous reference that linked a specific person with the incidents previously mentioned, making the unnamed subject clear to readers.

Gossip rags certainly had a devout readership, but they were not the only outlet for information about famous personalities during the last decade of the century, nor were they the most widely read. Mass magazines consistently profiled recognizable figures, both alive and dead, through biographical sketches, portraits, and autobiographical recollections. These pieces proved to be immensely popular and, as a result, came to play an increasingly prominent role in national magazines at the time. For instance, when S. S. McClure cut the price of *McClure's* from fifteen to ten cents in 1893, the magazine initially struggled to expand its audience. The first issue sold only 8,000 copies. It was not until the next year, at about the time when McClure began running Ida Tarbell's "Life of Napoleon," that these numbers began to rise. By the end of 1894, circulation had increased by 150 percent.[39] Similarly, the first installment of Tarbell's "Life of Lincoln" raised sales by 50 percent in one month.[40]

While these magazine features did often share a revelatory impulse with their gossipy counterparts, they tended to provide more sympathetic portraits of their subjects. As Richard Ohmann describes it, depictions of famous individuals were not designed "to heroize a mortal, but to humanize a hero." Accordingly, when McClure gave Tarbell the assignment to write on Lincoln, he instructed her to bring the former president back to life for readers.[41] A similar comment has been attributed to Joseph Pulitzer, who supposedly instructed a manager to "impress on the men who write our interviews with prominent men the importance of giving a striking, vivid pen sketch of the subject: also a vivid picture of the domestic environment, his wife, his children, his animal pets, etc. Those are the things that will bring him more closely home to the average reader."[42] These statements accord with the dictum of another media magnate of the day, William Randolph Hearst, who operated under the principle, "names make news."

The detailed discussions in the monthly magazines proved that more expansive pieces on individuals' private lives could captivate a national audience. These articles also provided a foundation for later reporting on celebrities. While much attention has been paid to the public treatment of movie stars, mass market magazines cultivated the personalizing approach that the film industry would borrow and expand upon in the first decades of the twentieth century. Such a point does not diminish the impact that film promoters had on the U.S. celebrity landscape. By putting significant amounts of money into publicity, for instance, the industry helped to underwrite a burgeoning market of "fanzines" and film-centered periodicals that both fed and encouraged audiences' desires for "inside" information about performers. Still, many of the techniques that journalists employed had been developing throughout the end of the nineteenth century, long before actors and actresses were promoted individually.[43] It was not until 1909 that studios began regularly publishing the names of performers in publicity materials or in credits at the end of films.

Other studio efforts at star promotion, as Richard deCordova argues in *Picture Personalities*, were also quite tentative at first. In one of the first instances of individual marketing, the Imp company simply ran a photo of Florence Lawrence, who is widely considered the first film star for her early publicity treatment, in the corner of a movie poster. Over the next decade, more and more information appeared about stars, but much of it was tailored to emphasize a performer's on-screen persona. This task was particularly easy given that most narrative films relied on idealized characters, and performers tended to play similar roles across a range of projects. Nevertheless, articles were often couched as intimate revelations, and they employed a conversational tone that would appeal to readers seeking inside information.[44]

Such "news" dominated coverage in film magazines until the early 1920s, when a series of scandals, beginning with Roscoe "Fatty" Arbuckle's alleged murder of Virginia Rappe in 1921 and William Desmond Taylor's mysterious murder in 1922, shattered the illusion that performers lived the relatively pristine lives that were represented in the press. This is not to say that audiences naively believed everything they read in publicity spots prior to the early 1920s, but that in an emerging climate of scandal, including increasingly common reports of drug use and adultery, industry press could no longer maintain credibility with their readers if they chose to ignore such matters. As a result, in deCordova's words, "the star became a site for the representation of moral transgression and social unconventionality."[45] Film star reportage, in short, began to offer up salacious details as a way of authenticating publicity, a hybrid approach that draws on the appeal of both human interest journalism and gossipy "scoops."[46]

CELEBRITY AND THE LITERARY FIELD

The joint development of print and celebrity cultures in the United States at the turn of the century had an enormous impact on the profession of authorship. The expanding geographical range covered by newspapers and mass market magazines promoted national conversations about books and authors, conversations that became an important part of most major news publications in the early twentieth century. The increasing amount of space devoted to texts meant that columnists and writers kept a close eye on literary developments and almost any event or interesting detail could receive mention. Literary supplements, which provided a direct source of information about books and authors, also became increasingly popular. Inserts such as the *New York Times* literary section expanded early in the century to meet the increased demand for such information, and several prominent reviews were formed not long after. Both the *New York Herald Tribune's Books* and the *Saturday Review of Literature* first appeared in the 1920s.[47] Gossip columns and literary reviews were so important in the years after the First World War that press agents who could develop relationships with columnists, and occasionally influence copy, often received significant advances for their services.

In addition to these new conversations about the literary world, authors became more prominent public figures. During the early decades of the twentieth century, it was more common for writers of all levels of sophistication to participate in interviews, go on book tours, make public appearances, and give lectures. The increasing importance of the author figure can also be seen in the number of writers' autobiographies being produced around the turn of the century. According to Louis Kaplan's bibliography of American autobiographies, between 1800 and 1880, only forty-two autobiographies were written by journalists or authors. From 1880 to 1920, that number increased by 400 percent to 168. In the next twenty-five years, the number doubled again.[48] Figures who were prominent in the literary establishment, including publishers and editors, began receiving more attention for their stories as well.

The increasing diversity and complexity of publicity mechanisms, rapidly expanding new venues for literary talents, and the growth of both the U.S. and the international book trade all made authorship an increasingly complex occupation after the turn of the century. Not surprisingly, the same period also saw a rapid expansion of business intermediaries, namely, those professionals whose job it was to help authors and other performers navigate the complexities of the marketplace. By the early 1900s, clipping services, which helped authors track their publicity, literary agencies, and press agencies had all become viable businesses.

While these changes raised challenges for everyone involved in the book industry at the turn of the century, they proved to be particularly problematic for writers and publishers committed to the idea that art could possess an inherent, and transcendent, value not dictated by the operations of the marketplace. Some publishers, such as George Doran, an early partner of Frank Doubleday, complained that good literature could not be successfully promoted. By the mid-1930s, when even "high" modernist authors such as James Joyce and Gertrude Stein had published bestsellers after notable publicity campaigns, Doran ruefully commented in his memoirs: "The great profession of publishing has measurably degenerated into a business of mass production where each highly enterprising publisher of the era seeks by advertisement and other ultra-modern methods to outsell his contemporaries."[49] Doran's fear that advertising led directly to the degradation of literature was not uncommon at the time. Henry Holt, for instance, had made a similar complaint thirty years earlier in a review of Walter Hines Page's *A Publisher's Confession*: "Books are not bricks, and...the more they are treated as bricks, the more they tend to become bricks."[50]

These complaints were taken up even more forcefully by writers in the early decades of the twentieth century. Authors on both sides of the Atlantic often couched their opposition to the market in highly inflammatory language designed to shock bourgeois sensibilities. Wyndham Lewis, for instance, in a larger rant about how family "reconstitutes itself in the image of the state," stops at the end of his argument to attack "this unreal, materialistic world, where all 'sentiment' is coarsely manufactured and advertised in colossal sickly captions, disguised for the sweet tooth of a monstrous baby called the 'the Public.' "[51] Ezra Pound brought the charge more directly in his famous lines, "Nothing written for pay is worth printing. Only what has been written against the market."[52]

Other writers displayed a more subtle form of antagonism. Both F. Scott Fitzgerald and Gertrude Stein, for instance, often attributed economic rather than aesthetic motivations to pieces of writing when they wanted to speak dismissively of them. Fitzgerald regularly disparaged his short story writing by describing it as a means of support for his "real" work: crafting novels. In one interview given in 1927, the year after he published his short story collection, *All the Sad Young Men,* Fitzgerald said, "I keep myself pure in regard to my novels. I have written only three of them. Each one takes two or three years. Of course, there are my short stories—but, then, you have to live."[53] Stein similarly distinguished between what she referred to as her "moneymaking style" and her "really creative one."[54] She invoked this distinction most frequently in the mid-1930s, as a way of differentiating between her accessible and immensely popular memoir *The Autobiography of Alice B. Toklas* and her often obscure experimental writings.

The appeal of this rhetorical stance should be clear given the transformations in American culture after the Civil War. The rapid expansion of print markets and the fissures it created in the literary field generated much debate about the status of literature in the early decades of the twentieth century. Authors, critics, and a whole host of business intermediaries were forced to reassess their roles in a changing marketplace, and their heated comments reflect a wide range of anxieties about both the processes at work and the transformations that were taking place. The force of this rhetoric has had a significant effect on subsequent histories of early twentieth-century literature, but, as many recent critics have shown, authors' attitudes toward, and engagements with, the market are far more complex than the above comments might suggest. When viewed in context, such remarks can be seen as local tactics in particular authors' ongoing struggles within the literary marketplace.

In the next chapter, I will revisit the early twentieth century in order to argue that the emergence of a national celebrity culture was a significant factor shaping these struggles. The increased visibility afforded by expanding media outlets, the development of new strategies for promoting individuals, and intense public interest in star figures all helped to transform the way texts were produced and received. By surveying the influence that these developments had, I will demonstrate how a more systematic examination of celebrity can alter prevailing histories of modernism and provide a new perspective on cultural and literary texts before the Second World War.

CHAPTER 2

Critical Reassessments: Celebrity, Modernism, and the Literary Field in the 1920s and 1930s

Writers' occasional, though certainly striking, outbursts about the literary market led many early scholars of modernist literature to suggest that some authors were opposed to operating in the marketplace. While this extreme generalization can still be found occasionally in criticism today, many contemporary scholars, attentive to postmodern critiques of totalizing systems and poststructural disruptions of binary oppositions, have been highly critical of such a simplistic dichotomy. Most critics reflecting on this shift, in what is now a well-worn story of the historical development of modernist studies, claim that the transformative figure was Fredric Jameson. Jameson, in his widely cited article "Reification and Utopia in Mass Culture," proposes that high culture and mass culture are interrelated and can only be understood through a historical analysis of their joint emergence under the conditions of capitalism.[1] While some scholars have expressed unease with the wide acceptance of such a simplistic and linear narrative,[2] few would deny either the influence of Jameson's work or the transformative effect that materialist critical approaches have had in the sphere of what is now called "modernist studies." The last three decades have witnessed an explosion of volumes examining the various ways in which canonical authors, despite their occasionally strident rhetoric, have engaged with and been implicated in the marketplace.[3]

Much as this work has complicated the traditional opposition between high culture and the mass market, many important developments continue to be subsumed into the more general operations of the marketplace. The increased cultural emphasis on celebrity personae in the early twentieth century is a particularly notable omission. By the 1920s, there were enough products devoted to disseminating the images of, and information about, celebrities—from sports cards to gossip columns to fan magazines—that many historians and cultural scholars have unreflexively referred to the existence of a distinct "celebrity culture" during the era. Yet in Douglas Mao and Rebecca L. Walkowitz's recent survey of studies devoted to "the marketing of modernism" in *PMLA,* celebrity did not even merit a mention.[4] While this omission does not necessarily reflect a lack of interest in the topic, it does suggest the relatively unsystematic nature of some contemporary approaches to literary celebrity. Much work, from biographical scholarship to media analyses to institutional surveys, could potentially be brought to bear on the subject; yet very little has been done to bring these often disparate forms of analysis together. The following sections lay the foundation for this kind of project by examining the creation of literary celebrity in the early twentieth century as a complex recursive process that involves authorial actions, the production of specific works, the promotion of texts and their authors, and audience reception. Subsequent sections briefly examine each of these forms of activity in order to demonstrate the impact that they could have on the image and reputation of writers. By emphasizing the potential effects that a wide range of figures had on the production of authorial personae, this chapter seeks to complicate unreflexive conceptions that figure a writer's reputation as a static object readily discerned through the analysis of specific literary or critical works. In the increasingly media-saturated environment of the early twentieth century, public renown seems more usefully approached as the outcome of a dynamic process, a contested value that is continually renegotiated in multiple contexts by stars, fans, and a wide range of intermediary figures.

CELEBRITY AND TEXTUAL RECEPTION

Many studies of the modern marketplace suggest the relevance that a systematic analysis of celebrity would have for the field as a whole, from Jennifer Wicke's work on the dialectical relationship between advertising discourse and literature to Lawrence Rainey's examination of the material conditions underwriting modernist textual production. Rainey's study in particular foregrounds the new strategies of authorial self-fashioning necessitated by economic and cultural developments in the early twentieth century. What these and many other works suggest, on the most general level, is that celebrity discourse, even in the earliest decades of the twentieth century, functioned as an important site for constructing meanings around texts.

Part of the reason this point has not been made more forcefully by scholars is that it stands in direct opposition to conventional theorizations of modernist textuality. Aaron Jaffe usefully elaborates these ideas in his study of modernist literature's "promotional logic."[5] Jaffe argues that avant-garde writers were not removed from the scene of the mass market, but instead instantiated themselves in it by creating literary objects that bear a specific "stylistic stamp." This stamp, or "imprimatur," served the dual purpose of distinguishing a text from others in the marketplace and of sanctioning that text, particularly as the specific name attached to it began to accumulate value in the literary sphere. The endpoint of this "logic," then, is that modernist authors successfully operated in the marketplace by turning themselves into "formal artifact[s]."[6]

Jaffe's book provides a useful account of one way in which writers accumulated cultural capital while at times remaining overtly opposed to the market. His focus on this particular form of "promotional logic," however, moves his study away from any direct evaluation of the influential publicity efforts that such a logic dismisses as secondary. It would be difficult to argue, for instance, that T. S. Eliot, a major figure in Jaffe's study, gave public lectures in order to promote himself as a formally dispersed textual object. Yet, as Jaffe would assert, both Eliot and the New Critics would have considered any publicity generated by the lectures irrelevant to the study of Eliot's work. It is in part by dismissing these activities and focusing attention on the "masterpiece," theorized as an autonomous repository of literary value, that many authors and critics were able to cultivate an air of objectivity and supposedly insulate their work from the corrupting influence of promotional activities.

One important consequence of these theories is that they help to deter questions about the potential influence of marketing efforts on readers and critics. A brief look at the publicity surrounding F. Scott Fitzgerald in the early 1920s will demonstrate how useful such an analysis can be. Much of the publicity surrounding Fitzgerald's early career fashioned the author as both a brilliant writer and a representative example of the impetuous young adults that populated his early work. Advertisements, interviews, and Fitzgerald's own autobiographical essays all emphasized his youth, his fast-paced lifestyle, and his literary talents. Over the next few years, as Fitzgerald's antics kept his face in the newspapers and reinforced his image as a debauched young man, many of the articles written by and about him reiterated other aspects of his persona. Fitzgerald himself was quite fond of emphasizing how effortlessly he produced his popular stories. In one piece, he uses his experience writing the short story "The Ice Palace" to explain his "theory that, except in a certain sort of naturalistic realism, what you enjoy writing [and thus write quickly] is liable to be much better reading than what you labor over."[7] In another autobiographical article, he implicitly applies this theory to all of his early short stories, claiming, "The quickest [was] written in an hour and a half, the slowest in three days."[8]

The success of these publicity efforts can be seen in highbrow critics' responses to Fitzgerald's first two novels. Reactions to *This Side of Paradise* (1920) were incredibly diverse in tone and content, ranging from the lavish praise of H. L. Mencken, who calls the book "a truly amazing first novel—original in structure, extremely sophisticated in manner, and adorned with...brilliancy," to the ambivalence of R.V.A.S., who applauds *Paradise* as "fundamentally honest," but finds "the intellectual and spiritual analyses...sometimes tortuous and the nomenclature bewildering."[9] By the time *The Beautiful and Damned* was published in March 1922, however, many highbrow critics had reached a consensus about Fitzgerald's work: the always-lively Fitzgerald certainly had talent, but he had not worked hard enough to master his abilities.

Gilbert Seldes, writing in *The Dial,* asserts that Fitzgerald's flippant attitude toward art overrides his considerable skill as a writer and severely damages the book.[10] Similarly, Henry Beston, in *The Atlantic Monthly,* writes, "The present endeavor marks no advance [over *This Side of Paradise*] in either method or philosophy of life," though "the book is alive, very much alive."[11] John Peale Bishop, an established poet and friend, wrote a particularly scathing review of the book in the *New York Herald*. He begins by claiming that the protagonist, Anthony Patch, is "a figure through whom Mr. Fitzgerald may write of himself." He then launches into a series of attacks on Patch/Fitzgerald, mentioning, among other problems, his "inherent laziness" and his "illusion that he is rather superior in intellect and character to the persons about him." This belief, however, is not true according to Bishop because Patch/Fitzgerald is merely the sort of man who "spent his time among many books without deriving from them either erudition or richness of mind." Finally, after listing a series of more general problems with the book, he concludes, "These are flaws of vulgarity in one who is awkward with his own vigor."[12]

The uniformity of these reviews is startling, especially given the wide variety of responses to *This Side of Paradise*. In just two short years, this particular group of critics, many of whom railed against the ever-expanding celebrity media outlets and bemoaned the credulity of undereducated audiences, had come to an implicit consensus about Fitzgerald based in part on his media-generated persona.[13] The only significant difference between Fitzgerald's self-presentation and reviewers' depictions of the author was the standard they used to assess his persona. These critics all seemed to agree that Fitzgerald did, as he repeatedly claimed, have a natural talent for writing. Yet, for men who used education and an aura of sophistication to garner both cultural and financial capital, Fitzgerald's supposed gift was not something, in and of itself, worthy of praise. They valued instead the industrious learning and knowledge of tradition that set them apart from more popular and, in some circles, less respected writers. Fitzgerald's public disdain for just such labor, then, is precisely what prevents his work from being considered "true literature," a title that highbrow critics considered themselves uniquely able to confer.[14]

Critics, of course, were not the only ones influenced by such large and increasingly sophisticated marketing campaigns. Public personae could help to guide general readers' interpretations of texts and, in more extreme cases, they could even be said to replace the need to read altogether. Janice Radway has demonstrated how some texts in the 1910s and 1920s were promoted as objects of knowledge rather than as literary works that contained inherent value. As a result, educated middle-class readers who were anxious about remaining "current" could potentially reap social benefits by knowing about fashionable literary titles rather than actually reading them.[15] Authorial personae functioned similarly, as an important site of knowledge production that could ultimately displace the texts upon which a writer's fame supposedly rested. For instance, when Gertrude Stein came to the United States for a lecture tour in 1934, newspapers tracked her movements and some of the major papers even ran extended commentaries on the trip. Yet the focus was not often on Stein's writing or on the content of her speeches, which had at least nominally occasioned the notices in the first place. Her clothes, her appearance, and her effect on audiences regularly took precedence.

In addition, while people came in surprising numbers to hear Stein's lectures, very few of them demonstrated a desire to learn more about Stein's ideas. In one oft-told story, the author fired her tour organizer, Marvin Ross, shortly after arriving in the United States because over 1,700 people had tickets for one of her opening lectures at Columbia University, far more than the 500-person limit she had specified. Yet the transcripts of her talks, subsequently published as *Lectures in America,* sold poorly. In other words, this bold and mysterious woman who had long been a topic of conversation in the American press, gaining such nicknames as the Mama of Dada, Mother Goose of Montparnasse, the high-priestess of the Left Bank, the Mother of Modernism, and the queen bee of the expatriate hive, had managed to generate a significant amount of interest in her persona without drawing audiences to her ideas. At the beginning of *Everybody's Autobiography,* Stein's memoir about the lecture tour, she explains this phenomena to her publisher, Alfred Harcourt: "Harcourt was very surprised when I said to him on first meeting him in New York remember this extraordinary welcome that I am having does not come from the books of mine that they do understand like the *Autobiography* but the books of mine that they did not understand."[16]

CELEBRITY, TEXTUAL PRODUCTION, AND PROMOTION

One danger of focusing on the reception of texts is that it often leads critics to oversimplify the production process and place an inordinate emphasis on the agency of particular individuals. It would not be difficult to take Stein's quote as an indication that her difficult texts were conceived as part of a larger effort to convince readers that she was, as she so often claimed to be, a "genius." By extension, the high/low aesthetic divide can seem like little more than a tactical move perpetrated by authors trying to find a space in a thoroughly commodified literary marketplace. The complexity of a text certainly did have an impact on the way writers were categorized by readers; moreover, writers of all dispositions did attempt to shape the way they were perceived by audiences. The efforts of individual authors, however, always exist within, even as they contribute to the formation of, a complex system of institutions and practices. The image of Stein that appeared in conjunction with the publication of *The Autobiography of Alice B. Toklas,* for instance, was affected by prevailing conditions in the publishing industry, a field that had long struggled with the gradual commodification of literary texts.

If, as noted previously, the United States' emergent consumer culture was already a concern for some established publishers at the turn of the twentieth century, the situation became far more problematic for those who attempted to form new houses in subsequent decades. Catherine Turner has demonstrated how, during the 1910s and 1920s, Donald Brace, Bennett Cerf, Alfred Harcourt, Donald

Klopfer, Alfred Knopf, and Horace Liveright were all forced to mediate between the increasingly complex demands of an intensely competitive literary marketplace and the genteel notions of traditional publishing houses. A new firm could secure its reputation by supporting quality literature, that is, texts whose value did not, at least in theory, depend on sales. Yet, to remain competitive, the new firms had to employ the latest marketing techniques in order to promote both themselves and their books.[17]

The contradictions that arose from such a position are readily apparent in Alfred Harcourt's massive publicity campaign for Gertrude Stein's *The Autobiography of Alice B. Toklas*. Ads appeared in all of the major literary supplements proclaiming Stein's role as an "eminent American woman" at the forefront of contemporary artistic production. She had, many ads proclaimed, the knowledge to explain "why modern literature *is*." By implicitly constructing "modern literature" as something difficult, a phenomenon that needs explicating, Harcourt could draw on Stein's reputation as an avant-garde author as well as on the gradually accumulating cultural capital of "modern literature." Yet the ads also emphasize both the readability of *The Autobiography* and its sheer entertainment value. This memoir will be, the ads promise, both a major part of modern literature and a straightforward guide to the rarefied world of high art.[18]

Such an ad campaign reveals the complex interrelations among public personae, market conditions, and aesthetic theory in the early decades of the twentieth century. It also suggests how figures in the book industry helped to shape the images that emerged before the public. While interactions among publishers, editors, and authors have been explored at some length in recent scholarship on the "marketing of modernism," the impact that these people had on the cultivation of celebrity personae has received relatively little attention. Many other figures crucial to the process have also fallen outside the purview of much contemporary scholarship, including literary agents and journalists.

If the previous example suggests one way that Stein's image may have been inflected by external forces, Fitzgerald's attempt to refashion his persona during the 1930s demonstrates how little control writers often had over their own personae. As noted above, Fitzgerald cultivated the image of an impetuous genius during the early years of his career and he was regularly characterized in the press as the voice of a new generation. By the end of the decade, however, Fitzgerald's situation had radically changed. Alcoholism, ongoing problems with *Tender Is the Night,* which would take him the better part of a decade to complete, and troubles with his wife Zelda, who was hospitalized in April 1930 and subsequently diagnosed with schizophrenia, all began to take a toll on both the author and his career. Work became increasingly difficult for Fitzgerald and he spent considerably less time in, or seeking to be in, the public eye. In part as a result of these factors, Fitzgerald's name retained its connection with the Jazz Age long after the Great Depression had redirected the public's attention.

To counter the perception that he was a washed-up alcoholic, Fitzgerald began consistently adopting the persona of a sober, reflective literary man in his work during the 1930s. His autobiographical writings, his literary commentaries, and even many of his interviews portray a thoughtful and committed artist that stands in sharp contrast to the crass young genius of his early publicity pieces. Sedate literary reflections, however, written by an author most associated with what was seen in retrospect as the unsavory glamour of the 1920s, received relatively little attention and did not go very far in rehabilitating Fitzgerald's image. For many people, then as now, he remained simply the "voice of the Jazz Age."

Celebrity and Authorship

Fitzgerald's ongoing struggle with his public persona reflects the increased importance of promotional activity in the early decades of the twentieth century. Over his twenty-year career as a professional writer, Fitzgerald wrote dozens of autobiographical, or seemingly autobiographical, pieces for popular magazines, gave numerous interviews, scripted several "interviews" of his own, and participated, particularly during the early years of his career, in many well-publicized spectacles that made good copy for the gossip columns. He worked with his editor and agent on the production and promotion of his texts, and he suggested marketing tactics that would maximize the sale of his books.

Stein was also an ardent self-promoter who spent several decades circulating her work among artists, writers, publishers, and editors in three different countries. She worked to cultivate relationships with those who might be able to get her work into print. She even incorporated important figures into some of her texts, both as a way of getting their attention and of attracting a larger audience for her work.

Such preoccupations with artistic self-fashioning were not uncommon in the early twentieth century. As Ann Douglas summarizes, "The dangerous business of attention management and exploitation fascinated all the writers of [this] generation, whether as subject matter or life-style or both."[19] Figures as diverse as T. S. Eliot and Marianne Moore, Willa Cather and Ernest Hemingway, F. Scott Fitzgerald and Gertrude Stein all wrestled with the new media apparatus and forms of promotion. Given the struggles of influential writers, it is necessary to consider the rhetorical strategies they employed in their attempts to come to terms with an emerging celebrity culture. To give just one example, I will return to perhaps the most frequently cited text in discussions of modernist authorship, T. S. Eliot's "Tradition and the Individual Talent." In this piece, Eliot makes his famous quip about poetry as an "escape from personality," a claim that would seem to align the author with traditional conceptions of modernist author- ship, at least until he ironically concludes: "But, of course, only those who have personality and emotions know what it means to want to escape from these things."[20]

Similarly, Eliot advocates "divert[ing] interest from the poet to the poetry"; yet the essay as a whole is preoccupied with detailing the proper relationship between an author's "personality" and a "signifi- cant" work of art. The impersonal process of creation, Eliot argues, requires the creative mind to function as a catalyst, in that it recom- bines elements from the world into something new while itself remain- ing "inert, neutral, and unchanged."[21] The author, consequently, is irrelevant to the analysis of a work of art because the complex emo- tions and situations that appear in texts have nothing to do with the "real" experiences of the author.

Still, Eliot cannot totally remove authorial consciousness from the scene of creation, as he also wants to insist on the "responsibil- ity" of a poet to "develop or procure the consciousness of the past" through "great labour."[22] So not only does the whole article revolve around the larger irony that a poet must cultivate impersonality, but Eliot also admits in passing at the end of his argument, "there is a great deal, in the writing of poetry, which must be conscious and deliberate."[23] Though Eliot does insist that such choices be made in the interest of impersonality, he does not examine the distinction between conscious choices and unconscious formations, nor does he acknowledge how such a backdoor admission, made in the last sen- tences of his argument, might affect his larger goal of removing the author from the scene of the completed poem. In short, Eliot posits the ideal scientist/author figure familiar to much modernist scholar- ship while also allowing for a "real" author who must both aspire to appear scientific in relation to any given work and actively participate in the construction of that impersonal appearance.

Given the proliferation of celebrity outlets, the spread of the mass market, and the increased commodification of literary products in the early decades of the twentieth century, all of which threatened to erode the authority of the autonomous writer, Eliot's anxiety over authorial agency is not surprising, nor was it uncommon at the time. Writers and critics regularly localized value in the work of art, thereby removing the author from the scene of textual evaluation. Yet the same critical apparatus always retained, as scholars such as Jaffe remind us, a privileged space for the godlike author/creator whose genius could be everywhere seen but never directly discussed.

This reading of Eliot and what scholars have come to see as the modernist impulse remains within conventional understandings of modernist authorship, in that the figure of the poet is finally cultivated through the medium of the poem itself. Eliot's concern with the relationship between an artist and his or her audience, however, did regularly extend beyond the medium of the artwork, especially in his writings on mass culture. Much recent scholarship reminds us that Eliot's notions of cultural hierarchy are far more complex than the stereotypical caricature occasionally found in discussions of the "great divide." At times, Eliot even figured a direct relationship between high and low, as in an essay on Marianne Moore where he insists, "fine art is the refinement, not the antithesis, of popular art."[24]

Important as such dialogues are for examinations of Eliot and for modernist studies more generally, they again neglect an opportunity to broaden the discussion into the field of celebrity, particularly in the places where public renown plays a direct role in Eliot's theoretical formulations. For instance, in a eulogy for famous music hall singer and comedienne Marie Lloyd published in *The Dial,* Eliot figures her popularity not just as a mark of achievement but as a function of the particular accomplishment of her art. Lloyd, he claims, was beloved throughout England because of "her capacity for expressing the soul of the people." In order to stress her organic connection with this audience, Eliot goes on to mention the working-class neighborhood where she was raised, and he repeats a popular story about her first performance. At age ten, Lloyd reputedly sang a song entitled "Throw Down the Bottle and Never Drink Again" for a local crowd and "is said to have converted at least one member of the audience." By replaying these elements of Lloyd's persona, Eliot shows how central her image was to her art and, in the process, makes a case for the potential value of popular personae.[25]

Again, such preoccupations with artistic self-fashioning were not uncommon in the 1910s and 1920s, when both "tradition" and the

eulogy were written. The claim that many modernist authors deliberately engaged in some market activity, however, is not necessarily
as radical in its implications as some contemporary scholars might
contend. Such a position does not mean that earlier work done on
writers' disdain for the market, or on the high/low binary that these
studies frequently posit, must simply be discarded. It would be difficult to argue, for instance, that an underlying conception of "pure"
art, existing outside the reach of a degraded and degrading mass
culture, did not have imaginative appeal in the early decades of the
twentieth century. Thus, as Michael Nowlin points out, Ann Douglas
presses the point a bit too far when she applies Charlie Chaplin's term
"high lowbrow" as a general descriptor for a wide range of artists
simultaneously seeking fame and critical acclaim in the 1920s. The
situation was never quite as open or liberatory as this phrase suggests.[26] Many authors participated in promotional activities while, at
times, rhetorically distancing themselves from their own efforts. The
year after Fitzgerald's first novel, *This Side of Paradise,* made him a
household name, he wrote his editor, "My one hope is to be endorsed
by the intellectually elite & thus be forced on to people as Conrad
has."[27] This statement is a striking bit of posturing for a best-selling
author who had begun sending self-promotional blurbs to his publishers as soon as his first book was released.

Gertrude Stein also regularly downplayed her own promotional
efforts, particularly when communicating with aesthetes. She frequently gave acquaintances the impression that she had no concern
for publishing or selling her work, as when she wrote Henry McBride,
a critic who saw success as a corrupting influence on artists, to deny
that she had any intention of writing a popular autobiography. This
particular letter was written just a few years before Stein began *The
Autobiography of Alice B. Toklas* and, when she wrote to McBride,
she had already given literary agent William Aspinwall Bradley the
explicit directive to make her rich and famous. At the same time, she
was advising Paul Bowles about the importance of cultivating large
audiences, advice that certainly contradicted her own supposed commitment to noncommercial art.[28]

"Modern" Authorship: From the Late Work of Stein and Fitzgerald

The previous examples show the importance that a particular conception of high art had for authorial self-presentation. They also
suggest that Stein and Fitzgerald cannot be characterized as either

stereotypical populist figures or traditional literary modernists opposed to "the market." Instead, these two writers often employed the rhetoric of both sides. They made this stance more explicit late in their careers by foregrounding contradictions and, in the process, cultivating a mode of authorship that does not exist in between poles as much as it encompasses both sides simultaneously. This approach aligns Stein and Fitzgerald with histories that read some early twentieth-century literature in terms of an impulse toward contradiction and integration. Daniel Joseph Singal provides one of the most expansive forms of this argument. Singal defines modernism as an "integrative mode" that attempts to "reconnect all that the Victorian moral dichotomy tore asunder—to integrate once more the human and the animal, the civilized and the savage."[29] Yet, Singal argues, modernists' desire to create a new synthesis is always tempered by the awareness that such a goal is unattainable in an unpredictable and ever-changing universe. The result is a "paradoxical quest for and avoidance of integration" that results in the ongoing production of unstable and contingent fusions of culturally entrenched oppositions.[30]

While such a definition might seem best suited to analyses of the themes and forms of modernist texts, saturated as they often are with paradox and ambiguity, other studies tie these attitudes more directly to the transitional character of early twentieth-century culture. Lawrence Rainey, responding in part to traditional conceptions of modernist authors, argues that "modernism marks neither a straightforward resistance nor an outright capitulation to commodification but a momentary equivocation that incorporates elements of both in a brief, necessarily unstable synthesis."[31] Robert Scholes, in *Paradoxy of Modernism*, adds to these formulations by foregrounding the productive aspect of modernist theorizations. He suggests that authors and critics contributed to the contradictions they faced through the application, at least in theory, of a series of binary oppositions, such as high/low, old/new, and hard/soft.[32] Scholes's point is important for writers such as Stein and Fitzgerald who did utilize some of these terms, but often employed them in rhetorically complex ways. As a result, their efforts suggest new ways of conceptualizing these binaries even as they recall old divisions. Both authors also chose to structure their personae around oppositions at important moments in their careers, a move that, again, redeployed old terms and ideas in ways that produced striking literary results.

In order to understand the importance of these complex operations, it is necessary to keep in mind the shifting institutional bases of the high/low split in the United States. Unlike in Europe, where a much older set of institutions undergirded aesthetic hierarchies, the widespread development of such organizations and structures in America began primarily in the latter half of the nineteenth century. Moreover, by the early twentieth century, the marketplace had already developed to the point where any simple dichotomy, if it could be said to have acquired a dominant cultural position at all in the United States, was already becoming inadequate to the demands of an emergent consumer society.

The most obvious sign of these shortcomings is the appearance of a new stratum of products and institutions in the 1910s and 1920s that scholars have subsequently come to call the "middlebrow." This new cultural formation was supported by consumers who sought an alternative to both crass lowbrow art and the deliberately confounding highbrow products of the avant-garde. They were people for whom culture was important but who did not have the time or inclination to devote themselves to it. So, over the course of the 1910s and 1920s, products that promised the allure of culture in readily consumable forms began to emerge.

One of the earliest such instances came in the form of Dr. Eliot's Five-Foot Shelf of Books, which was first published by P. F. Colliers & Son in 1910. The Shelf, a collection of supposedly essential works selected from a range of academic disciplines (history, philosophy, science, politics, literature, and the arts), combined the notion that a corpus of great texts could serve as the foundation for a cultivated citizen while also trading on the reputation of long-standing Harvard President Charles W. Eliot and presenting these important works in a readily displayable form. So a purchaser could acquire some cultural capital simply from owning and displaying the books.

New commodities that promoted the allure of culture appeared throughout the 1920s and 1930s, including history and philosophy "outlines," slick magazines such as *Vanity Fair*, and book clubs.[33] All these new products suggest that the traditional high/low dichotomy was inadequate to encompass the needs and aspirations that were being created by consumer culture for a growing American middle class. Yet the split did retain its imaginative appeal for many artists and scholars, even as marketers were subdividing the "general public" into more refined target markets, critical outlets were proliferating in the press, and new methods of book distribution were helping to reshape the publishing industry. For some, the binary allowed for relatively simple, and rhetorically powerful, discussions of textual production and reception in the context of an increasingly chaotic literary field. For others, these terms represented ideological or material restrictions that needed to be transcended.

One common solution was to propose a third term that could embody, synthesize, or mediate the entrenched opposition. Van Wyck Brooks provided a particularly influential form of this argument in *America's Coming-of-Age* (1915). Brooks claims that the United States can be characterized by a divide between "Highbrow" and "Lowbrow," that is, between theory and practice, culture and the market, and, for authors, "literature" and "bestsellers." He emphasizes the need to overcome this divide, which diminishes the modern writer, and proposes to follow Walt Whitman in cultivating "a middle tradition, a tradition which effectively combines theory and action."[34]

Stein and Fitzgerald adopted an alternate approach late in their careers, one that utilizes opposition itself. Contradiction became a tool for both authors and was employed at crucial moments to challenge the restrictions implicit in common conceptions about literary production and reception. With respect to the high/low divide, both authors suggest that, particularly in the mobile media environment of the early twentieth century, the two options are not necessarily mutually exclusive. It is possible, at least in the imaginative context of their literary and promotional texts, to fashion a persona that can acknowledge differences without being entirely bound by them.

Modernism in the Depression

While such an approach might seem fitting amidst the radical experimentation that characterized some aesthetic circles in the 1910s and 1920s, much of the analysis in subsequent sections involves work produced during the Great Depression, a period not typically associated with speculative self-fashioning or traditional debates about aesthetic value. Scholars examining the 1930s have gravitated toward the populist forms of literature that were taken up by many writers during the decade. This focus on what seem like radical new modes of writing implicitly sets up a divide between previous decades, which are often characterized as the period of so-called high modernism, and the folk-infused documentary efforts of the 1930s. In addition, an emphasis on the staggering economic and social difficulties during the decade has often led scholars to downplay some of the larger continuities between the Depression era and the historical periods that surround it.

The difference between the 1920s and 1930s, however, is, in a few notable ways, more of a progressive change than the sharp break that some studies suggest. Several scholars, for instance, have persuasively argued that consumer culture made significant leaps *forward* during the 1930s, in part because the perceived need to revive market demand shifted attention from the producer to the consumer.[35] As Roland Marchand points out in *Advertising the American Dream,* marketers, perhaps out of sheer necessity, tended to characterize the Depression as a change in consumer attitude, a resurgence of thrift, rather than as a change in economic conditions. Hence, methods and theories were refined, advertising taboos fell away, and product promotion became an increasingly subtle and pervasive part of American life.[36]

Alongside this development in the consumer marketplace, the growth of suburbs continued and the market for leisure goods expanded, as technology freed up more time for industrial and domestic workers alike. Moreover, spiraling unemployment, limitations on work hours, and increasing supplies of consumer credit over the decade all encouraged people to find new ways to occupy themselves. Books on how to fill leisure time saw dramatic increases during the decade. According to Warren Susman, between 1910 and 1919, only about fifty titles devoted to leisure appeared. From 1920 to 1929, the number increased to about 200. In the period between 1930 and 1939, 450 different titles were published.[37]

Finally, mass media continued to expand and dominate the public's attention over the course of the decade. Both broadcast radio, which replaced the local programming of the 1920s, and talking films became cultural institutions during the Depression. A wide variety of magazines also entered the national consciousness, from comic rags such as *Ballyhoo* to consumption-oriented periodicals such as *Esquire* to the visually stunning pictorial magazine *Life.*

Book publishers faired far less well and many underwent notable changes in their efforts to remain viable. Traditional houses, for instance, began promoting new genres, such as the detective novel or proletariat fiction, in an attempt to produce profits. This change marked a shift in policy for some publishers and, from one perspective, exacerbated the gradual fragmentation of the industry that had been encouraged by both new publishing houses' embrace of market operations and the emergence of middlebrow literary outlets.

Yet, as historian John Tebbel points out in his seminal study of book publishing in the United States, during the Depression, "Jobs were lost, and a few small houses disappeared, but in the end the structure of the trade was relatively intact." It was not, Tebbel claims, until after World War II that relatively autonomous, and often family-owned, publishing houses became more directly engaged in the corporate world, a move that led to radical changes in the industry over the next half century.[38] The lingering conservatism of the industry is perhaps best summed up by an article in a 1939 issue of *Fortune* magazine that concluded, "Any ordinary businessman coming in cold to take over a publishing house would be driven mad in no time."[39]

So, one prominent institutional base for the aesthetic divide remained, if in a somewhat less stable form, throughout the 1930s. Similarly, difficult economic conditions tended to foster, at least in business matters, a reliance on established forms and products. Publishers and marketers were far more likely to employ traditional aesthetic categories than they were to cultivate new approaches. As with Harcourt's campaign for Stein's first autobiography, publishers often reinforced the notion that highbrow art was a distinct type of cultural product requiring its own critical practices.

These continuities in the book market were also supported by a certain degree of stability in "highbrow" writing. As Linda Wagner-Martin trenchantly argues, writers who had produced avant-garde literature in the 1920s did not radically alter their approach during the Depression. The themes that figures such as William Faulkner and John Dos Passos engaged may have shifted, but many aspects of their technique proved to be far less malleable. In addition, many writers beginning work in the early years of the Depression retained a typically modernist self-consciousness about form and borrowed important stylistic traits from earlier writers, such as the use of direct and simple language, an emphasis on concrete visualized detail, and the absence of overt editorializing.[40] Alfred Kazin, an emerging literary figure in the early 1930s, aptly summarized the situation for a group of young writers when he said that "[we] wanted to prove the literary value of our experience, to recognize the possibilities of art in our own lives, to feel we had moved the streets, the stockyards, the hiring halls into literature—to show our radical strength could carry on the experimental impulse of modern literature."[41] Kazin's emphasis on the "literary" shows just how relevant traditional aesthetic dichotomies still were during the 1930s. His invocation of stockyards and hiring halls also suggests the degree to which, even as the focus of much literary writing began to shift with the onset of the Great Depression, high literature continued to be associated with male experiences and perspectives.

Again, writers' continued reliance on traditional aesthetic conceptions does not mean that they refused to engage with the mass market or the expanding mechanisms of celebrity culture. In this regard, my work challenges the claims of Marc Conroy, whose study of twentieth-century fiction and "mass publicity" is notable for engaging directly with conditions in the 1930s. Conroy asserts, "It is really in the thirties that the fragile partnership between literati and mass culture is most dramatically frayed."[42] This claim is surprising, given that, as Conroy himself notes, so many writers were employed by Hollywood and/or engaged in journalistic endeavors during the decade. Conroy dismisses such complicity by suggesting that there is a psychological distinction between using print and electronic media, a gap that supposedly allowed writers to imagine themselves involved in "an entirely different enterprise."[43] Not only does this explanation fail to account for many of the nonliterary print projects in which writers engaged during the decade, but such a generalization is a clear distortion of the wide array of attitudes writers expressed toward electronic media. Fitzgerald, for one, ran the gamut from admiration to disgust with talking pictures during the course of his career, depending in part on his momentary level of involvement with the major studios.[44] It would also be hard to explain the reasonably well-funded marketing campaigns that accompanied the publication of books such as *Ulysses* and *The Autobiography of Alice B. Toklas* if the "literati" had in fact begun a wholesale revolt against mass culture during the Great Depression.

Many authors, despite their occasionally heated rhetoric, engaged with popular media and general audiences during the 1930s. Stein and Fitzgerald did so in a way that produced new personae capable of reconciling the conflicts generated by the reception of their works. At the same time, both authors, in a typically modernist fashion, establish these fusions as contradictory, a move that reinforces the divides they are purportedly traversing while at the same time elevating the literary text as a space where such contradictions can be imaginatively unified.

One particularly interesting aspect of these claims is that the forms they are written in contribute to the literal tensions they construct. Both authors produced significant amounts of work during the 1920s and 1930s in genres that many of their contemporaries would have considered of minor significance (formal autobiography, fictionalized biography, public lecture, and publicity blurb). Yet several of these texts, in addition to making forceful arguments about what should be considered high art, implicitly or explicitly position themselves as significant works of literature. So these pieces can be seen as both theoretical and practical interventions in the literary marketplace, textual spaces that work to mediate aesthetic, literary, and market demands simultaneously.

The following sections will analyze each author's work at some length, focusing on the texts they produced in conjunction with major changes in their public reputation. These studies shed light on how two major American authors attempted to navigate the turbulent cultural waters of the 1920s and 1930s. They also demonstrate how an examination of celebrity media and authorial self-fashioning can both expand our historical knowledge of the literary field after the turn of the century and revitalize analyses of a wide range of texts produced during this period. The latter point is particularly important for scholars attempting to push beyond earlier binary approaches to the same material. My previous examples should make it apparent that traditional oppositions between "high" art and the marketplace do not sufficiently account for some of the major strategies of self-representation employed by Anglo-American writers in the early decades of the twentieth century. Authors who aspired to acquire cultural capital often found themselves negotiating between the supposedly degraded aesthetic forms of the mass market and the dictates of an increasingly prominent celebrity culture. Such writers did not want to be associated with the often anonymous hacks creating so-called production-line pulp novels, nor did they want their output to be controlled by either the whims of the marketplace or publishers' marketing machines. These conditions necessitated a distinct authorial presence to ensure the integrity of a given work. Yet authors could not simply market themselves and allow their personae to propel sales, as that would ultimately undermine claims about the autonomy and the supposedly transcendent value of "true" art.

Even a basic understanding of the modernist author represented through "style," as the selective consciousness suffused throughout a work but never directly represented in it, requires a tacit acknowledgement of the importance of public personae in aesthetic theories and practices during the early twentieth century. When put in these terms, it seems plausible to argue that the changing strategies of authorial self-representation at this time were as much a function of developing celebrity media and increasing public fascination with famous personalities as they were of changed epistemologies or the expanding circuits of consumerism. Pressing such discussions further could also allow them to intersect with other contemporary critical conversations about representation, the relationship between modernism and postmodernism, the status of authorship, the regulation of aesthetic categories and hierarchies, the relation of print media to visual media, and the space of the "literary" within the larger cultural field. In all of these areas, "celebrity" could function as a useful interpretive paradigm, both from a historical perspective and as a unifying concept for textual analyses. On more traditional grounds, it provides a basis for rethinking key elements of modernist culture even as it points to new ways in which previous binary models can be expanded to better reflect the complex position of writers in the early twentieth century.

The emergence of a whole subset of cultural artifacts devoted to disseminating information about stars, both real and potential, raised many challenges for people working in the literary field. Yet the complex ways in which writers and other intermediary figures responded to these difficulties, and the ways in which their efforts were received by an increasingly fragmented reading public, suggest many fruitful areas of inquiry that remain underserved by contemporary modernist scholarship. Such work will help us gain a better understanding of both the vocational sphere of authorship after the turn of the century and the texts produced at that time. It will also provide benefits that extend well beyond the field of modernist studies. A more systematic engagement with celebrity during this period could offer valuable insights into the subsequent restructuring of the cultural field in the latter half of the twentieth century. Understanding the shifting values associated with certain types of public personae might even help to explain the seemingly diminished space afforded to popular authors' personae in recent decades. Therefore, through a more sustained analysis of modern celebrity, we can not only come to a better understanding of a world where Stein's public appearances and Fitzgerald's drunken antics were prominent news items, but we can also more readily approach a culture in which writers are rarely afforded such attention.

PART II

From Toklas to Everybody: Gertrude Stein between Autobiographies

GERTRUDE STEIN AND HER CRITICS

In the fall of 1932, Gertrude Stein, at the age of fifty-eight, began work on what was to be her first bestseller, *The Autobiography of Alice B. Toklas*. After thirty years of writing, Stein had managed to publish only four books in the United States, none of which sold particularly well.[1] *The Autobiography*, in contrast, sold its entire first printing, more than 5,000 copies, nine days in advance of its official publication date and inspired a tremendously successful six-month lecture tour in late 1934. The tour was pivotal for Stein not only because it marked her ascendancy to a new level of literary significance, but also because it occasioned her first trip to North America in nearly three decades. The following year, she began to write *Everybody's Autobiography*, an account of her recent experiences as a celebrity that centered on the U.S. tour.

Between these two autobiographies, Stein wrote a series of pieces reflecting on her career, aesthetics, and the nature of contemporary celebrity. These texts include "The Story of a Book," a blurb she wrote for the Literary Guild in 1933 when *The Autobiography* was chosen as a fall selection; *Four in America,* an obscure biographical exploration of four famous Americans composed during 1933 and 1934; a series of lectures she gave on her American tour, subsequently published as *Lectures in America* in 1935; and the book-length philosophical meditation, *The Geographical History of America or The Relation of Human Nature to the Human Mind,* published in 1936. Given the relative obscurity of Stein's early poetic experiments and her own resistance to direct explication, several of these later works have proven to be invaluable for critics. Yet, despite the centrality of these pieces to discussions of Stein's oeuvre, very little work has been done exploring the relationships among the texts. Many scholars have been content to borrow Stein's language without considering either the context in which statements first appear or their larger implications for Stein's work.

One negative consequence of this tendency is that critics have taken many of Stein's statements at face value and circulated them as if they were simple facts, not part of a complex process of self-historicization. For instance, most critics dealing with Stein's work in the 1930s discuss the writer's block Stein claims to have suffered after writing *The Autobiography*; some celebrity scholars have taken this episode as a seminal moment in Stein's supposedly tortured transition to literary fame. Such accounts are by now quite familiar: the avant-garde artist struggles in obscurity for years until an unexpected bout of popularity challenges his or her self-conception and forces a radical reassessment of aesthetic principles. In Stein's case, however, this basic story becomes much more complex when her work during the period is taken into account. Laurel Bollinger, relying on the Yale Catalog of Stein's manuscripts, claims that the actual number of texts Stein generated in the months after finishing *The Autobiography* compares favorably to her production in other years. The primary difference, Bollinger says, is that many of these texts were letters or short articles and not the experimental literary pieces Stein valued most.[2]

Ulla Dydo, in *Gertrude Stein: The Language That Rises*, concludes that Stein suffered from a block of sorts; she then provides an assessment of the period that is similar in many ways to Bollinger's analysis. Dydo asserts that Stein did produce little new literary work between December 1932 and April 1933, but she also points out that, in addition to any other writing that may have been done during this time, Stein was both preparing *The Autobiography* for publication and working on the typescripts of pieces she had written the previous summer.[3] So, while Stein did seem to be producing less of a certain kind of work, it is not entirely clear whether the slowdown was caused by psychological difficulties, changing circumstances, or simply the practical demands of mass-market publication.

To complicate matters further, Stein's own claims about her writer's block are contradictory. In "And Now," a short article published in *Vanity Fair* just before Stein left for the United States, she discusses her inability to write and attributes it vaguely to "success."[4] By the time Stein submitted this article for publication in mid-1934, she could certainly consider *The Autobiography* a "success," but what this word means in an earlier context, at the time of her supposed writer's block, is not quite so clear. Did "success" come when Stein finished writing, perhaps because she was personally satisfied with her work or, more directly, because she was aware of the potential popularity of the book? Or did "success" come only as a result of outside approval? Her agent, William Aspinwall Bradley, read and praised the book in late November 1932, which would accord with Dydo's analysis of the manuscripts. Yet Alfred Harcourt, who was ultimately to become the publisher, did not receive a copy for another month and did not agree to publish it until January 1933, well after Stein's supposed writer's block began.[5] Stein would have had to wait until May of 1933, when *The Atlantic Monthly* began serializing the book, to assess the general public's response.

In an equally obscure passage, Stein claims that her writer's block ended when the "dollar fell and somehow I got frightened."[6] Again, this statement could be made to accord with the extant manuscripts. The United States abandoned the gold standard in the spring of 1933, a move that led to a series of unpredictable fluctuations in currency values. It was at about this time, Dydo claims, that Stein began producing new work again. When Stein repeats her claims about writer's block in *Everybody's Autobiography*, however, she says that she did not resume writing again until starting her play *Blood on the Dining Room Floor* at the end of the summer.[7]

Such vagueness, not uncommon in Stein's writing, reflects her tendency to prioritize theoretical and formal concerns over historical ones. Accordingly, Stein employs the trope of blockage similarly in "And Now" and *Everybody's Autobiography*. ("And Now," while published as an independent article, is actually the remnant of Stein's effort to write what she referred to as the "Confessions of the writer of the Autobiography of Alice B. Toklas," an early precursor to *Everybody's Autobiography*.) Stein does not attempt to show, as F. Scott Fitzgerald did in "The Crack-Up," the psychological effects of a breakdown on her writing process, nor does she attempt to detail her own tentative steps toward a resolution to the problem. Instead, she emphasizes the act of *reflection*, which is to say she depicts herself, in a characteristically even tone, as someone who has overcome the problem and not as someone still consumed by it. This position allows Stein to navigate between what Pierre Bourdieu has called "the field of restricted production," in which artists produce for a coterie of elite consumers, and "the field of large-scale production," in which artists produce for a more generalized "public."[8] On one hand, Stein is crafting pieces that are intended for a mass audience. On the other, her supposed psychological difficulty with this process reflects a commitment to the values of the avant-garde, even as the posited state of resolution implicitly assures her audience that these issues have no bearing on the piece at hand. Put more simply, the trope of writer's-block-overcome allows Stein to emphasize her status as an elite artist who has strong reservations about the literary marketplace while she is simultaneously writing pieces that will be marketed to a broad reading public.

So, regardless of whether or not Stein actually found herself unable to write in the wake of "success," she seemed to be well aware of the complexities of her situation and, before leaving on her U.S. tour, had already begun tailoring her self-presentation to fit the image of a celebrity genius. This depiction of Stein contrasts with the image of the author that emerges from most contemporary celebrity studies involving Stein, which take her writer's block as an historical given and depict her as someone searching for the terms to define her predicament. As one scholar puts it in his study of American literary celebrity, "[Stein] felt strangely as if she had become someone other than who she had been before."[9] I do agree that Stein's "celebrity" raised serious theoretical and practical concerns for her, and, in the remainder of this section, I will argue that the texts Stein wrote immediately after *The Autobiography of Alice B. Toklas* develop an aesthetic theory that confronts the legacy of her first major success. Yet Stein is hardly an innocent artist lost in the wonderland of modern celebrity culture. She had spent the previous two decades promoting her work in three different countries through a wide variety of means. She cultivated relationships with famous artists, writers, publishers, and editors. She sent copies of her books to popular reviewers and critics. She even began writing "portraits" of famous or influential acquaintances, in part to help her work gain wider visibility.

As G. F. Mitrano points out, when Stein began writing portraits in 1910, she was attempting to move beyond her reputation as a supporter of avant-garde artists and secure patronage for her own literary endeavors.[10] In 1911, for instance, she wrote her well-known portrait of Mabel Dodge, a wealthy patron of the arts who had visited Stein's studio the year before. Dodge liked the piece enough to have it published in a private edition, which she circulated among her friends in Europe and New York. Dodge also wrote the first major explication of Stein's writing in conjunction with the Armory Show, an art exhibit designed to increase the visibility of contemporary French, German, and Spanish artists in the United States. Dodge's essay, entitled "Speculations, or Post-Impressionists in Prose," was first run in the March 1913 issue of *Arts and Decoration* and then rerun, along with Stein's portrait, in the June issue of Arthur Stieglitz's *Camera*

Work. Stein had similar success a few years later with her portrait of art critic Henry McBride, who also had the piece printed in a private edition and helped to secure its publication in *Vanity Fair*.[11]

Though Stein would continue to have difficulty finding a publisher for her work until she wrote *The Autobiography*, her efforts at self-promotion were in other respects quite successful. Her salon was an essential stop for writers and artists visiting Paris throughout much of the early twentieth century, her work appeared in a variety of little reviews, and her name frequently circulated in the popular press. Numerous parodies of her writing appeared throughout the 1910s and 1920s, and many major literary figures felt compelled to notice her, even if only to dismiss her efforts as insignificant.[12] Both H. L. Mencken and Elinor Wylie, for instance, listed her as one of the "ten dullest authors" in a 1923 *Vanity Fair* symposium, and T. S. Eliot, reviewing Stein's lecture "Composition as Explanation" in 1927, said, "her work is not improving, it is not amusing, it is not interesting, it is not good for one's mind....If this is of the future, then the future is, as it very likely is, of the barbarians. But this is a future in which we ought not to be interested."[13] The fact that a writer who was commonly considered unreadable could enter discussions of literature in a wide range of newspapers and magazines is a testament to the cultural capital Stein had begun to generate early on in her writing career. And these public pronouncements did not escape Stein's notice. She employed a New York clipping service to help keep track of the various discussions about her and her work in the press.

So, while some celebrity theorists follow Stein's own self-representations in the mid-1930s and depict her as a media ingenue, such a characterization hardly seems appropriate for the woman that publisher Bennett Cerf referred to as "the publicity hound of the world."[14] In fact, much of the confusion over Stein's attitudes toward celebrity can be accounted for by addressing the context of her various statements on the subject. Stein not only understood the profound difference between the fields of large-scale and restricted production, but, as noted earlier, she also strategically altered her attitude toward her work in different circumstances. It is precisely this rhetorical savvy that makes decontextualizing Stein's claims so problematic.

The problem is only compounded by Stein's own tendency to make seemingly universal proclamations about her life and work. In the lecture "Portraits and Repetition," for instance, she characterizes her career as the search for an art form appropriate to the "composition" of her time period and concludes the discussion with a sweeping generalization: "It is true there is something much more exciting than anything that happens and now and always I am writing the portrait of that."[15] While it might be tempting to cite such a statement as defining the trajectory of Stein's career, her previous lecture, "The Gradual Making of *The Making of Americans*," retraces the same ground only this time emphasizing her early desire to create a history of everyone. She concludes, "When I was up against the difficulty of putting down the complete conception that I had of an individual . . . I was faced by the trouble that I had acquired all this knowledge gradually but when I had it I had it completely at one time. . . . And a great deal of *The Making of Americans* was a struggle to do this thing, to make a whole present of something that it had taken a great deal of time to find out. . . . That then and ever since has been a great deal of my work and it is that which has made me try so many ways to tell my story."[16]

The view of Stein's work presented in "Gradual Making," written at approximately the same time as "Portraits and Repetition," helps to demonstrate what Stein referred to in an earlier lecture as "beginning again and again."[17] Her goal in these lectures is not to uncover one overarching telos for all of her previous writing, but to describe and rearticulate the various interrelated processes that, in retrospect, can be seen operating in her earlier books. Thus, the reader is provoked to understand the major currents of her thought while also considering the potential contradictions and discrepancies that arise among her various accounts.

Given the complexity of Stein's method and the intricate portraits of her thought that emerge, the tendency among critics to employ Stein's statements selectively has led many to misrepresent her claims or, more problematically, to misread the texts themselves. In their more innocuous forms, such readings simply misconstrue Stein's ideas or extend them beyond their relevant context. For instance, Neil Schmitz, in an important piece that examines the "mode" of *Tender Buttons,* claims, "In *Four in America* [Stein] herself distinguished two primary modes of composition: 'writing what you are writing' and 'writing what you intended to write.' These modes were not absolute; they represented a bias, an intention, but in her distinction she placed herself emphatically within the former."[18]

Contrary to Schmitz's assertion, Stein's tendency to prioritize one pole over the other becomes most apparent during her American lectures, which were written several months after *Four in America*. In the later work, she discusses a new dichotomy between an author's serving God or Mammon, and the positive emphasis is clearly placed on serving God.[19] In *Four in America,* as Charles Caramello points out, Stein does not lean "emphatically" in either direction, but openly declares her desire to write in both modes at once.[20] Despite his more detailed reading of Stein's later theories, Caramello ultimately makes the same incorrect generalization as Schmitz, only he does so by extending his argument in the opposite chronological direction. He implies that Stein continued to embrace both poles equally through-out her critical analyses in the 1930s and, without accounting for Stein's shift in terminology, equates writing what you are writing/writing what you intended to write with the God/Mammon split. Both critics, then, dehistoricize Stein's aesthetic theory and ultimately leave readers with the impression that she adhered to one stable set of ideas throughout her career.

While these interpretations tend to misconstrue Stein's larger theoretical project in the 1930s, other uncontextualized readings go as far as to misread her specific formulations. In one of her first books, *The Making of Americans,* Stein famously declared, "I write for myself and strangers."[21] This claim has been important for critics who want to read Stein's work from the 1930s as radically inclusive. Juliana Spahr, for instance, claims that Stein's multilingual environ-ment inspired her early grammatical experimentation and, at least in part, led her to create "multivalent" texts, which is to say texts that do not lead readers "to a neat box of a conclusion" but instead "encourage dynamic participation" in the process of meaning cre-ation.[22] Spahr then attempts to read *Everybody's Autobiography* as an openly inclusive work and a defense of this earlier approach, a claim she links with Stein's earlier declaration: "In this section I examine Stein's claims that her writing is for everybody. Or as Stein phrases it, 'I am writing for myself and strangers.' "[23] Barbara Will, while exam-ining ambiguities in Stein's use of the term "genius," makes a similar connection: "Stein writes in *The Making of Americans,* 'I write for myself and strangers.' Thirty years later in *Everybody's Autobiography,* she states that her story, the story of a 'genius,' is potentially the story of 'everybody.' "[24]

What both these critics neglect to notice is Stein's changing atti-tude toward this phrase, and her audience more generally, during the 1930s. Stein cites the passage from *The Making of Americans* with approval early on in the decade, in *The Autobiography of Alice B. Toklas* (1932) and "The Story of a Book" (1933). By the time she delivered the lecture "What Are Master-pieces and Why Are There So Few of Them" at Oxford and Cambridge Universities in February 1936, however, she had come to disavow her earlier claims, saying, "I once wrote in writing *The Making of Americans* I write for myself and strangers but that was merely a literary formalism for if I did write for myself and strangers if I did I would not really be writing because already then identity would take the place of entity."[25] I will discuss Stein's attempt to theoretically isolate herself from her audience later; here, it is sufficient to say that Stein is renouncing her previous formulation because it suggests a form of writing based on "identity." She uses this term to represent modes of self-knowledge that are tied to the recognition of others. In contrast, "entity" is a form of self-awareness that contains its own essence, which is to say it is not dependent on the opinions of others. Creating a text that is linked to "entity" then—the ideal text for Stein—is to be true to one's own essence without submitting to the expectations or desires of others in the writing process. In short, Stein no longer wants to write for strangers but only for her true self.

After dismissing the theoretical importance of the audience in "What Are Master-pieces," Stein began editing her previous claims in *Everybody's Autobiography* (1937). Several years earlier, in "The Story of a Book" (1933), Stein talks about the process of having her manuscript enthusiastically accepted for publication. She not only quotes "myself and strangers" from *The Making of Americans*, but she also says that having finally reached these strangers leaves her feeling "unburdened."[26] This article is incorporated almost verbatim into *Everybody's Autobiography*, except for the reference to "myself and strangers," which has been omitted.

Moreover, when Stein does directly address the topic of her audience in the second autobiography, she is openly dismissive: "In writing *The Making of Americans* I said I write for myself and strangers and then later now I know these strangers, are they still strangers, well anyway that too does not really bother me, the only thing that really bothers me is that the earth now is all covered over with people and that hearing anybody is not of any particular importance because anybody can know anybody."[27] Stein suggests that her previous conception of writing as a means of communication with other people is irrelevant in the contemporary era where people are free to travel almost anywhere and communicate with whomever they want. As a result, Stein is less interested in her own relationship to her audience and instead focuses her attention on an abstracted view of human interactions, interactions that constitute one important element of, to use Stein's term, the contemporary "composition." She even directly attributes her change in attitude to shifting historical conditions, claiming, "At that time [of writing *The Making of Americans*] I did not realize that the earth is completely covered over with everyone.

In a way it was not then. . . . but now since the earth is all covered over with everyone there is really no relation between anyone and so if this *Everybody's Autobiography* is to be the Autobiography of everyone it is not to be of any connection between anyone and anyone because now there is none."[28]

So the critical tendency to appropriate and decontextualize Stein's theoretical claims, a tendency encouraged by her own powerful rhetoric and sweeping historical scope, has led to numerous complications in recent studies of her work. In particular, critics have understated the degree to which Stein's ideas developed throughout the decade, especially with regard to the nature and function of literature itself. Part of the difficulty is that, as with "myself and strangers," Stein repeats key words, phrases, and anecdotes throughout her career, often, but by no means always, recalling their original context and meaning in her later works. Thornton Wilder, in his introduction to *Four in America,* first suggested that future critics take up the challenge implicit in such a technique: "There are hundreds of [locutions] which may strike a first reader as incoherent expressions thrown off at random; but they are found recurringly distributed throughout her work. The task of her future commentators will consist in tracing them to their earliest appearances embedded in a context which furnishes the meaning they held for her. Thereafter they became bricks in her building, implements in her meditation."[29] While I agree with the spirit of this statement, I would add the caveat that commentators must be equally sensitive to both the changes that occur in Stein's usages and the particular moments at which various elements recur. As with the story of her supposed writer's block, Stein is especially sensitive to rhetorical context and is attentive to the circumstances in which she operates.

In short, Stein's work in the 1930s is not simply a public declaration of long-held theories or a historical account of her past work, but a deliberate self-historizicization that, in part, responds to the market pressures initiated by the widespread success of *The Autobiography.* Stein's ideas are particularly difficult to trace in any straightforward, linear way, both because of her own technique, which employed repetition as a fundamental principle, and because she spoke insistently in the present tense, emphasizing her current knowledge over the historical contours of her own shifting positions. I intend, however, to read Stein against her own grain, as it were, and trace the theoretical changes that preceded and ultimately paved the way for her second major memoir, *Everybody's Autobiography.* My approach will also help to counteract the ahistorical tendency present in much Stein criticism and place some of her most important works from the mid-1930s into dialogue with each other.

In the following chapters, I argue that the texts Stein wrote between her first two major autobiographies develop a theory that ultimately isolates both authors and their work from external influence. By privileging interiority, Stein constructs a mode of authorship that is dedicated to high art ideals while also remaining free, as a direct result of its metaphysical isolation, to operate in the marketplace. This theoretical work established the grounds on which Stein constructed her second memoir, which purports to solve her difficulties by incorporating the structural contradictions of the contemporary marketplace into the work of art itself. In other words, Stein does not choose to pursue the aesthetic, and ascetic, purity of the avant-garde or the ample rewards associated with modern celebrity. Instead, she embraces both goals at once and, in the process, attempts to create an autobiographical masterpiece that is simultaneously easy and difficult, a memoir for her popular fans as well as a profound philosophical meditation on the nature of contemporary life.

CHAPTER 3

The Celebrity Speaks: Gertrude Stein's Aesthetic Theories after *The Autobiography of Alice B. Toklas*

Many biographers and scholars have commented on Stein's struggle, in the early years of her career, to secure a publisher for her difficult literary experiments. Critics have expanded these discussions by showing the various ways in which Stein's hopes and anxieties surface in the often-opaque texts she was writing at the time. Yet, no one has attempted to systematically examine how Stein's attitudes or her aesthetic strategies changed after the publication of *The Autobiography of Alice B. Toklas* (1933), a time when she began to reflect, in ways that she never had before, on the nature of her writing and its relationship to a larger public.

Some of Stein's more direct texts from this late period, such as *Lectures in America* (1935), have drawn much commentary, but this criticism has rarely considered the larger tendencies apparent in Stein's work. Moreover, many other pieces Stein wrote in the mid-1930s, such as the unusual biographical experiment *Four in America* (finished in 1933–34) and many of the supposedly less "serious" pieces that were published in popular magazines, have gone almost unnoticed by critics. Taken together, these works document Stein's evolving responses to her fame and present a very different picture of the author than the one that emerges in much literary criticism.

The texts I will examine were all either published or intended for immediate publication and thus constitute a crucial aspect of Stein's self-presentation during the 1930s. They also all reflexively examine this process of self-presentation and comment both directly and indirectly on the complex web of relations among author, text, and audience. In the following chapter, I examine some of the texts Stein wrote shortly after finishing *The Autobiography*. Her earliest pieces draw on the now-familiar language of the aesthetic divide and, in typical Steinian fashion, attempt to bridge the gap between high and low or, more directly, critical and popular success. As she faced the prospect of lecturing to a live audience, however, always an anxious affair for Stein, her formulations became increasingly exclusionary as she strove to erect a theoretical barrier between the creative mind and the audience. It was only after Stein returned to Paris that she could begin to re-reconcile the oppositions that characterized her thought and dispel the potential dangers of writing another popular memoir.

THE FIRST YEAR OF FAME

One of the first articles Stein wrote after *The Autobiography* was "The Story of a Book," a short piece she was obligated to produce for the Literary Guild when *The Autobiography* was chosen as a fall selection. While this short introduction to her famous memoir might seem like little more than a standard publicity release, it is interesting for being one of the first published pieces in which Stein directly discusses her own writing. It also contains a slightly different perspective on the author than that which typically appears in discussions of her work during this period.

Stein begins by telling the now-famous story about the way beautiful fall weather in Bilignin, the French province where Stein and Toklas spent their summers, kept the women there through early November, thereby giving her enough time to write *The Autobiography*. She then goes on to discuss her agent's response to the book, employing a dichotomy between "real" art and mere popular literature. Bradley, she claims, had always liked her work, but was disappointed that none of her books had been more than "what the French call a success d'estime." He assures her, though, that her new memoir will be both a "conspicuous success d'estime" and a bestseller, to which Stein responds, "I was pleased."[30]

Stein's desire to have this book be both a popular and an artistic success should not be surprising given my previous sketch of Stein's opportunistic attitude toward such distinctions. She could proclaim a high-minded apathy toward selling books to people such as Henry McBride while at the same time employing a well-known literary agent and starting her own publishing house, the Plain Edition, to release books that could find no other publisher. In other words, Stein's bold declarations about her art are easy to take out of context. During the last decade of her life, for instance, Stein occasionally made dismissive remarks about her first autobiography. The most frequently cited

comment comes from "A Transatlantic Interview," an interview conducted shortly before her death in 1946. Stein says, "I had a certain
reputation, no success, but a certain reputation, and I was asked to
write a biography, and I said 'No.' And then as a joke I began to write
the *Autobiography of Alice Toklas*."[31] While such an attitude would
seem to be just one more piece of evidence supporting a depiction of
Stein as a hardened modernist dismissing popular literature, this attitude does not reflect her only assessment of *The Autobiography*, and,
as will become apparent, it is a perspective that does not fully emerge
in her writing until later in the 1930s.

In "The Story of a Book," Stein avoids the "either/or" implications
of a traditional high/low aesthetic split by simultaneously embracing
both popular success and critical esteem. She also shows herself to be
deeply concerned with the reception of *The Autobiography*, a position that an elite artist would be loathe to adopt.[32] Stein claims that,
while writing her previous books, she spoke openly to everyone about
her new projects, a reflection of the confidence she typically showed.
Stein admits, however, that she mentioned this book to only two people and simply told them that she "was doing something and perhaps
it might be interesting." Then, with the manuscript finally finished,
she eagerly asks Toklas, "Do you think it is going to be a best seller,
I would love to write a best-seller," a question that Toklas prudently
avoids answering. It is not until the manuscript has been typed and
submitted to her agent that Stein, "to [her] delight," finally receives
the affirmative response from him that quells her anxieties.[33]

After Stein's work has received Bradley's approval, the reader,
originally a potential customer in the Literary Guild, is immediately
reassured, through testimonials from Stein's agent, her publishers,
and the editors of *The Atlantic Monthly*, that *The Autobiography* is
both brilliant and entertaining. The fact that she shows herself to
be in need of such reassurance is particularly striking, especially
given Stein's egotistical reputation and the large body of scholarship
devoted to exploring her confident assertions of genius. Stein is not,
for once, telling people what to think, but is anxiously awaiting their
assessment of her work.

While such posturing might be dismissed as purely a function
of marketing her book, both Stein's attempt to bridge conventional
artistic categories and her traces of uncertainty reappear in her next
book, *Four in America*. According to Ulla Dydo, much of *Four in
America* was most likely written throughout the fall of 1933 and the
spring of 1934, which places its composition roughly between the
book publication of *The Autobiography* in September 1933 and the

composition of Stein's lectures for the U.S. tour during the summer of 1934. It is the first new full-length work Stein attempted to have published after the widespread success of her memoir and, despite its repeated rejection by publishers, she hailed it as one of her "major" works.[34]

Four in America examines the lives of four famous Americans in relation to four potential lives that they might have lived. Stein juxtaposes Ulysses S. Grant, the general, with his fictional counterpart Hiram Ulysses Grant, the religious leader. She then examines Wilbur Wright as both the inventor of the airplane and a painter, Henry James as a novelist and a general, and, finally, George Washington as a general and a novelist. While these difficult meditations cover a wide range of topics, Stein uses the lives of famous men in part to interrogate celebrity in America; she repeatedly questions how people are represented in larger cultural economies ("Think not only of why he has a name but why name does rhyme with fame.... Think only of how to think of nothing else"). She explores the ways in which fame might reflect or even create internal difference ("The thing always worries me is how you whose name everybody knows is different from those whose name nobody knows").[35] She also uses a self-conscious reflection on her own reconstruction of these "lives" to explore the creative process and the relative value of such "biographies," which are parallel in some ways to Stein's previous endeavor, *The Autobiography of Alice B. Toklas.*

The larger dualities that run throughout this book (real/constructed lives, famous/nonfamous people, and internal/external identities) are most directly brought to bear on the craft of writing in the third chapter, "Henry James," where the discussion revolves around two different kinds of writing, exemplified for Stein by the difference between Shakespeare's plays and his sonnets. Works that were "written as they were written," including Shakespeare's plays, are spontaneously constructed and so, she claims, have a "lively" sound. Such writing is opposed to pieces such as the sonnets that are "written as they were going to be written." This latter category covers writing that is planned or otherwise prepared in advance and, as a result, has a smooth sound.[36]

One crucial element of this distinction is that the split is located in the mind of the writer. Much as Stein has chosen to explore a decidedly social phenomenon such as "celebrity" by retreating into a reflection on her own idiosyncratic examination of the lives of famous men, she suggests that "writing as it is written" and "writing as it is going to be written" are differentiated by the author's creative process. "Writing as it is written" represents a form of spontaneous work while "writing as it is going to be written" depends on prior planning. "Planning," a word not clearly defined in the text, is employed in several different forms. It is often associated with Henry James and refers both directly and indirectly to the forethought that went into creating his intricately structured texts. The word is also used to refer to forms of writing that have been written, in various other ways, *in advance*. Stein claims to have discovered the distinction between planned and spontaneous writing while transposing Georges Hugnet's poem *L'Enfances*, a situation where the model for her own text was quite literally created beforehand. Yet, in all of its various usages, the word "planning" provides a clear opposition to spontaneous writing and affords Stein a basis for the other, less familiar distinctions she draws between planned "writing as it is going to be written" and the spontaneous "writing as it is written." "Writing as it is going to be written," for instance, makes a smooth sound because planning eliminates the unexpected from the writing process. As a result, "writing as it is going to be written" is figured as the form that, through its very familiarity, leads to immediate audience satisfaction.[37]

While Stein does introduce the idea of "value" in her discussions of these two forms of writing, she does not attempt to make this value distinction absolute. More specifically, she claims that Shakespeare's plays, her example of spontaneous "writing as it is written," are *seen* while his sonnets are *heard*, and "anything seen is successful. A thing heard is not necessarily successful." It is important to note that the accomplishment of the spontaneously produced plays does not preclude the sonnets, despite their being planned in advance and "heard," from being successful too: "Any sound heard well any sound heard is heard. Any sound heard if it is heard is successful."[38]

So, despite the fact that Stein seems to be favoring spontaneous writing by claiming that it is always successful, she is far from setting up a clear opposition between the two forms. She even goes so far as to say that *both* are "common" types of writing employed by many authors. This claim is particularly important in that any distinction she might claim for her own work cannot come from employing one mode of writing or the other. For works of art that are truly distinct, she must posit an alternate form, one not widely used by others. Thus, she says, "I did not choose to use either one of two ways but two ways as one way."[39] This position, in its deliberate melding of smooth and lively sounds, planned and spontaneous writing, echoes Stein's earlier claim from "The Story of a Book" that *The Autobiography* could ultimately be both a bestseller and a "success d'estime."

It also represents part of her theoretical effort to bridge the gap between popular literature and successful writing, even as critics and reviewers sought to differentiate her best-selling memoir from her more enigmatic works. For instance, Ellery Sedgwick, the editor of *The Atlantic Monthly*, supported excerpting Stein's book in the magazine despite having repeatedly rejected her earlier work. He wrote, "During our long correspondence, I think you felt my constant hope that the time would come when the real Miss Stein would pierce the smoke-screen with which she had always so mischievously surrounded herself.... Hail Gertrude Stein about to arrive."[40]

At the time of writing *Four in America,* Stein had not yet given up hope that her memoir might one day be read alongside books such as *Tender Buttons* or *The Making of Americans*, a point that many critics have overlooked when considering *Four in America*. Given Stein's blithe statements about *The Autobiography* in subsequent years and the strict dichotomies that emerge in some of her later theoretical writings, many readers have been quick to dismiss the subtle distinctions that Stein makes here. Even Thornton Wilder, who, in his introduction to the first edition, openly acknowledges Stein's lack of "disapproval" for "writing as it was going to be written," evinces a need to qualify her assertions: "She appears to be reconciled to [writing as it was going to be written], it is the way in which the majority of all books have been written."[41] Again, this statement directly contradicts Stein's formulations in the book. "Writing as it was written," while it may always lead to successful texts with lively sounds, is no less common or, for Stein's purposes, more important than "writing as it was going to be written."

Stein's attempt to theoretically distinguish her work depends on more than her claim to mediate this dichotomy. It is important for Stein that the determining factor behind the two different forms of writing depends on the author's creative process.[42] In this way, a writer can determine what type of effect his or her text will finally have simply by changing the approach used in writing it. Stein, by extension, is free to categorize both her economically unsuccessful texts and *The Autobiography* however she sees fit, because her "success" depends on how she constructed the particular piece in question.

Still, it is not enough for Stein to assert her own authority over texts without also accounting for the role that readers might play in such a process. Stein, in accordance with her larger effort to internalize value, deftly avoids many complications by isolating her consciousness, in a fairly typical modernist fashion, from the minds of all others. In this way, she does not have to consider potential interpretations of her work because others' readings will always remain fundamentally distinct from her own ideas. She says, "Clarity is of no importance because nobody listens and nobody knows what you mean no matter what you mean.... But if you have vitality enough of knowing enough of what you mean somebody and sometime and sometimes a great many will have to realize that you know what you mean and so they will agree that you mean what you know, what you know you mean, which is as near as anybody can come to understanding anyone."[43] Bob Perelman reads this passage as a reflection of Stein's attitudes toward her own genius and suggests that Stein believes her work to be, on some fundamental level, inaccessible to the nongeniuses of the world.[44] Yet there is nothing in the context of this statement that suggests Stein means it so selectively and, in light of her larger aesthetic aims in this book, it makes more sense to read Stein's claim as a general statement about the human condition.

In fact, Stein made similar statements about the radical isolation of the human mind throughout her career in a variety of different contexts. In the March 1933 issue of *transition,* for instance, cofounder and editor Eugene Jolas printed a statement about the suppression of individuality along with various artists' responses to it. Stein replied, "I don't envisage collectivism. There is no such animal, it is always individualism, sometimes the rest vote and sometimes they do not, and if they do they do and if they do not they do not."[45] What distinguishes this response from many of the others as well as Jolas's own dramatic assessment of what he calls the "crisis of man" is Stein's matter-of-fact tone. Her statement is not an impassioned defense of the individual, or even a reasoned assessment of the realities of group identification. It is a rather blunt dismissal of the very idea of collectivism. For Stein, each person is unavoidably trapped within the confines of his or her own consciousness without any ability to escape or truly reach "the rest," a term that, in itself, reflects Stein's sense of distance from other human beings.

Stein would reiterate this claim in an equally forceful manner thirteen years later, during the final interview of her life: "Nobody enters into the mind of someone else, not even a husband and wife. You may touch, but you do not enter into each other's mind."[46] As a result of this view, Stein frequently used the term "contact," as opposed to a word like connection, to suggest the limited way in which two people, even in the most intimate of relationships, could interact. "Contact" is precisely the term Stein used in "The Story of a Book" to describe her relationship with the reading pubic,[47] who, as she would say several months later in *Four in America,* could come to know, at best, only that Stein understood what she said.

One important consequence of this formulation for Stein is that it precludes evaluating art based on meaning. Since, according to Stein, no one can ever know what other people are thinking, much less what ideas they derived specifically from a work of art, it is impossible to generalize any particular interpretation beyond the individual consciousness that generated it. It then follows that, as an author, she does not have to be concerned with "clarity." Yet Stein had no intention of keeping manuscripts piled up in a drawer for her own personal assessment either. It is for this reason that "vitality" becomes a crucial term in the previous quote. For Stein, acknowledging a text's vitality, in opposition to the "clarity" of its expression, does not require a reader to understand the particular "message" of the work. Instead, it appeals to some aspect of cognition that operates outside of logical "understanding," existing at an undefined pre- or arational level, and can thus be used as a basis for aesthetic valuation in a world populated by distinct consciousnesses.[48] From this perspective, Stein's refusal to define "vitality" or directly examine its presence in particular texts can be seen as more than willful ambiguity on her part; it is a reflection of the necessarily impossible task of putting into language something that cannot ultimately be subject to direct "understanding."

Stein reasserts the limited role of understanding and connects it directly to her own text when, shortly after presenting the concept of "vitality," she stops to entreat the reader: "There are two ways to write, listen while I tell it right. So you can know I know."[49] Stein, quite ironically, can expect no more from her readers than that they be convinced by the sheer force of her words on the page. If she is able to construct her texts through the proper procedure, that is, through her rare ability to fuse "writing as it is written" and "writing as it is going to be written," then she will ultimately be able to convince "a great many" of her knowledge, even if that knowledge is ultimately uncommunicable.[50] The end result of these formulations, then, is a creative process and an aesthetic system centered on the mind of the author itself.

Of course, the lack, from a metaphysical perspective, of any specific "content" in Stein's texts radically transforms the nature of the interpretive process, an implication she readily, and paradoxically, acknowledges in the "Wilbur Wright" section of her work: "An interlude. This does not really distract my mind from the very great the very vital subject of what is a painter not only while he paints but when he has painted and how would Wilbur Wilbur Wright have this in common. Nobody need yield to that in not making a mistake. There is no mistake, not anything is a mistake in which they mean I mean."[51] Readers, Stein suggests, can impute any meaning they want to her text, and nothing they say can be considered, in Stein's sense, incorrect ("not anything is a mistake in which they mean I mean"). Moreover, though the exact referent for "that" in "nobody need yield to that" is not clearly defined in the text, the word certainly refers to some element of Stein's previous text, which means that she has interrupted her own writing in order to invite readers to ignore what she has just said. The process of interpretation, that is, readers' "not making a mistake," can proceed "correctly" even beyond the confines of the primary text itself.

Many critics take the seemingly "open" nature of Stein's texts as a reflection of her desire for communion through textuality. I have already suggested that Juliana Spahr and, to a lesser extent, Barabara Will, rely on such a concept, but the most comprehensive argument in this line is Harriet Scott Chessman's *The Public Is Invited to Dance*. Chessman argues that Stein's works employ various dialogic forms in part to "ask for the active and intimate presence of a reader" in the text. Chessman goes on to suggest that these open dialogues are intended to "shape us into readers who come to her writing as equal lovers or intimate acquaintances, separate but always open to the possibility of 'coming together.'"[52] As previously noted, Stein explicitly argues against the idea that two people can cognitively "come together" through her work. She certainly does not lament the fact that readers can and will freely interpret her texts in an infinite number of ways, but such readings can never form the basis of any intimate connection. Instead, it would probably be more apt to characterize each reader's engagement with a given text as an isolated and internal process, a process that never engages Stein herself or creates any shared "meaning" in the text, even on a level of pure potential. The only real possibility is "contact," a word with implications that are very different than Chessman's "coming together."

Stein's effort to distance the audience from the scene of value creation, however, is not absolute in *Four in America*. Even though Stein places the final authority for creating "interesting" texts in the mind of the author, she does introduce some uncertainty into the process. The two different forms of writing both sound different once they are on the page, Stein claims, but "the words next to each other that sound different to the eye that hears them or the ear that sees them...do not necessarily sound different to the writer seeing them as he writes them."[53] So, despite the fact that the author's approach to writing determines the "vitality" contained in the final text, the writer is not entirely in control of this process and requires a subsequent analysis of the completed text in order to truly assess its value. Such a view does not require any particular audience, as Stein herself can presumably reread her own words to determine their impact, but even such a small degree of uncertainty, evident also in "The Story of a Book," decenters the authority Stein is seemingly bestowing upon herself as the creator of vital art.

This gap also reflects Stein's larger commitment to the autonomy of the aesthetic object in *Four in America*, a position indirectly evident in the other aspects of her theory. When Stein is discussing the relationship between "writing as it is written" and "writing as it is going to be written," she wonders whether the difference between the two forms results solely from the author's intentions or if those different intentions are actually evident in the words on the page. She finally concludes that the words on the page contain some notable mark of the creative process: "If the writing and the writer look alike...the words next to each other make a sound. When the same writer writes and the writing and the writer look alike but they do not look alike because they are writing what is going to be written or what has been written then the words next to each other sound different."[54]

This distinction is crucial because, given Stein's perspective, readers could not be trusted to impute motives to an author based on textual evidence, regardless of how much information is available. For any detectible distinction to exist, it must be located in the words themselves. The emphasis here is not only on the type of writing an author is attempting to do but also on the sound that a particular mode of authorship produces in the words themselves, which, Stein repeatedly says, does not have anything to do with meaning or "sense." It is the particular "intensity" of the words on the page that matter.[55]

Stein's uncertainty about the effect of her words as she writes them reveals a similar commitment to the autonomy of the art object. If vitality is located inside the words themselves and meaning is wholly relative, then the work of art, once it is completed, is presumably independent from anyone who might read it, even its creator. Though Stein does not elaborate on this idea in *Four in America,* as she would later during her lecture tour, she does seem to believe that the words on the page, and not anything in her particular consciousness, somehow determine the degree of intensity present in a text. While Stein does not allow herself total control over the process, she has erected a theoretical apparatus that positions the author as the ultimate determiner of aesthetic value. If that value ultimately resides in the art object itself, free from the constraints of interpretation and, presumably, historical change, it is finally a result of the particular mode of writing used to create a text. Yet taking these theories from a relatively dense, highly philosophical work and implementing them in the form of a second, potentially popular, autobiography raised another issue for Stein. She had repeatedly stated that her own consciousness was irredeemably distinct from other minds, but what if the creative process could be altered by her own subjective awareness of potential readers?

At the same time Stein was working on *Four in America* in late 1933 and early 1934, she was toying with the idea of writing a second autobiography.[56] She knew the potential market value of another book, and, in her private correspondence, she attempted to use the promise of a new memoir to get her other finished works published. William Heinemann was offered English publication rights for the new book provided he put out reprints of *Three Lives* and *The Making of Americans*. Stein also insisted that her agent offer the memoir to Alfred Harcourt, who had published the first autobiography, only as part of a package including both *Four in America* and an unspecified book of portraits. No contracts were drawn up at the time for either *Four in America* or Stein's second autobiography.

Yet Stein did begin writing the book at some point during late 1933 and the early spring of 1934: a notebook from that time bearing the title "Confessions" still exists. The project was ultimately abandoned, probably around the time Stein committed to doing an American tour and needed to begin preparing her lectures. She did send one heavily revised excerpt to her agent in May 1934, shortly after she finished work on *Four in America*.[57] The short piece, retitled "And Now," was published in the September issue of *Vanity Fair*, just one month before Stein arrived in the United States.

"And Now" is interesting in part because it shows what *Everybody's Autobiography* might have looked like if it had been written several years earlier. It also provides an interesting theoretical transition between *Four in America* and Stein's lectures, which, with the exception of "The Gradual Making of *The Making of Americans*," were written in the summer of 1934. As might be expected of a piece revised shortly after the completion of *Four in America*, "And Now" picks up on many of the ideas she circuitously explored in that text. Stein, however, changes the focus of her position in the latter article by problematizing fame—a shift that anticipates the new direction her theories would take in subsequent years.

The article begins with a brief description of what is supposedly Stein's new memoir, which covers, she says, "what happened from the day I wrote the autobiography to today." She then immediately proceeds to explain the challenge posed by her sudden "success": "I lost my personality. It has always been completely included in myself... and here all of a sudden, I was not just I because so many people did know me. It was just the opposite of I am I because my little dog knows me."[58] Here, Stein sets up the central distinction operating in this essay, between her autonomous "inside" and "the rest," and suggests that fame had eroded the boundary between these two categories.

This perspective provides a strong contrast to *Four in America,* where Stein's position relied on a relatively stable internal sphere. Ulysses S. Grant, Wilbur Wright, Henry James, and George Washington would all, according to Stein's assessment, continue to express the same characteristics regardless of their particular profession. By extension, the reader is led to infer that Stein herself remains essentially the same person regardless of whether she is producing bestsellers or "successes d'estime" or not writing at all. She can focus on different approaches to writing because the mind that creates ultimately remains inviolable behind the text.

In contrast to the independent, self-governing mind of *Four in America,* "And Now" suggests that it is not enough to isolate the artistic consciousness from other minds because the mere awareness of an audience can alter an author's approach to writing. Such an awareness can, in Stein's words, "cut off your flow" so that "the syrup does not pour."[59] Stein must now secure the boundaries of her own consciousness before returning to a discussion of the mechanisms by which that consciousness produces art.

Contrary to some contemporary criticism that characterizes Stein as an arrogant elitist, she does not simply opt for the position of the aesthete and declare herself immune from the potential corruptions of the outer world. Instead, she admits, "I could not write and what was worse I could not worry about not writing." The attention she received, combined with the sudden influx of money, displaced writing from the center of her life, she claims, for the first time in thirty years. Yet, when the value of the dollar suddenly dropped, Stein was reminded of the ephemerality of economic value and she put aside the joys of earthly fame for the lasting pleasures of artistic creation: "There is no pleasure so sweet as the pleasure of spending money but the pleasure of writing is longer. There is no denying that."[60]

While it is tempting to take Stein's recommitment to her work as a proclamation of allegiance to so-called high art, such a distinction would misrepresent her primary focus in the article. One of the major purposes of structuring her aesthetic theory in the way she has is precisely to avoid such distinctions, which are invariably tied to external market conditions. If Stein can accurately be said to "re"-commit to anything, it is here a turn back to her own internal creative process, a move reflected in the way she characterizes her choice. Her final decision is not between inside and outside, but between two different forms of pleasure. Once she chooses writing, the choice between inside and outside, as we have seen from her previous statements about art, has already been made. Her own internal process is what instills vitality in the work of art. In this way, Stein can insist that both critics and popular audiences should, in theory, like her work because she has constructed her texts in the correct frame of mind and has accordingly filled her words with vitality.

As noted earlier, Stein also rhetorically mediates between these two aesthetic camps by employing the trope of writer's-block-overcome. The acknowledgment of her past anxiety reinforces her modernist credentials; however, her commitment is also the ground on which she can freely enter the marketplace. Nothing she does outside of the creative process can disrupt the value that is located inside her texts, and so there is no reason why she should not go on a lecture tour promoting her work or appear in publicity photos. For this reason, Stein does not need to disavow her enjoyment of wealth nor does she need to adopt a condescending attitude in order to reinforce her distance from the marketplace. Moreover, by suggesting that she has overcome these difficult issues without overtly proclaiming allegiance to either elite or common taste, she implicitly reassures both audiences that any anxieties they have over her recent work are baseless, despite the potential difficulties elite and popular audiences might have had reading her short autobiographical piece in a slick middlebrow magazine.

As a result of her choice to recommit to her internal process of art, Stein claims that she has moved past her writer's block: "I write the way I used to write in The Making of Americans, I wander around. I come home and I write.... Just at present I write about American religion and Grant, Ulysses Simpson Grant, and I have come back to write the way I used to write and this is because now everything that is happening is once more happening inside.... And so the time comes when I can tell the history of my life."[61] Initially, Stein is speaking of the physical process of writing, but her repetition of the phrase "write the way I used to write," especially in conjunction with a difficult book such as *Four in America*, suggests that she means to connect her present work with the past texts that established her standing as an avant-garde writer. Moreover, by claiming that she has returned to her original state of self-containment, the driving force behind aesthetic value for Stein, she can implicitly claim that her work is no less valuable now than it used to be.

This position implies, of course, that there is no significant difference between her popular writing, such as "And Now," and her supposedly more complex works, such as *Four in America* or *The Making of Americans*, both of which she links with her current piece. Similarly, because *The Autobiography* was itself written before the confusion that disrupted her creative process and her second memoir is going to be written now that she has regained her composure, both of these pieces can also be numbered among her important works. So, though Stein clearly understood the conditions of the literary marketplace and was willing to operate under the prevailing system in order to secure the publication of her many books, she seems to be working out a theory, in both her so-called popular and difficult works, that will allow her to attribute value to all her writing. It is an attitude that would gradually begin to change in Stein's next major work, *Lectures in America*.

The Lectures

By mid-July of 1934, Stein had committed to going on the six-month lecture tour, and she wrote the bulk of her talks over the course of the summer.[62] These pieces, published together at the end of her tour as *Lectures in America*, have proven to be an invaluable source for critics exploring Stein's work and her larger aesthetic goals. They are the most widely discussed of Stein's theoretical texts from the mid-1930s and, as such, deserve far more attention than can be given to them here. In order to keep my discussion focused, and to avoid redundancies, I will discuss the aspects of these texts that take up the concerns of her previous works, placing particular emphasis on the development of her thought. I have already indicated several facets of Stein's theories that remain relatively constant, such as her belief in the fundamentally isolated nature of individual consciousnesses, and, rather than produce examples or lengthy reiterations to show the stability of these ideas, I will leave them aside unless they are significantly developed or challenged in the lectures.

As in each of Stein's texts discussed above, the first lecture in this collection, "What Is English Literature," sets up a new dichotomy between "serving God" and "serving Mammon," to help explore the predicament of the contemporary artist. This new set of terms is particularly interesting because, unlike in "And Now," Stein uses it to revisit ideas from her previous texts. She recasts, for instance, her consideration of the difference between having an internal and an external focus during the creative process: "When I say god and mammon concerning the writer writing, I mean that anyone can use words to say something....he may use those words directly or indirectly. If he uses these words indirectly he says what he intends to have heard by somebody who is to hear and in so doing inevitably he has to serve mammon....Now serving god for a writer who is writing is writing anything directly it makes no difference what it is but it must be direct, the relation between the thing done and the doer must be direct."[63] On its most basic level, these new terms codify the split Stein discusses in "And Now." Writers must commit either to writing indirectly in hopes of pleasing an outside audience or to addressing their own creative productions directly. This choice will finally determine the type of writing that emerges.

Later in the piece, Stein also incorporates terms that would seem to approximate those she used in *Four in America*: "The writer is to serve god or mammon by writing the way it has been written or by writing the way it is being written....If you write the way it has already been written...then you are serving mammon, because you are living by something someone has already been earning or has earned."[64] Stein strengthens the connection between the two works by referring her audience to the "Henry James" section of *Four in America* and then introducing this final distinction after a discussion of James's contribution to literature. These references, given that Stein's earlier book was not yet available for publication, can be seen in part as a fairly overt marketing tactic. The conflation of the two texts also allows Stein to appropriate the ideas of the earlier work for her present concerns.

The difference between Stein's earlier formulations and the two types of writing outlined here is aptly characterized in the shift from her earlier phrase "writing as it is *going to be* written" to the expression used above, "writing the way it *has been* written." In the previous book, Stein focuses on the way in which an author addresses the writing process. Accordingly, "going to be" emphasizes the future product that is yet to emerge from the writer's mind and refers directly to the "planning" that will secure a particular textual effect.

Part of the reason for this perspective is that the split Stein focuses on in *Four in America* arose, she claims, from her translation of

Georges Hugnet's poem *L'Enfances*. She attributed her insight about "writing as it was going to be written" to the process of transforming another writer's completed work into her own words. In "And Now" and the lectures, however, she begins to take seriously the possibility that her own motives might be compromised by an internalized sense of the audience's expectations. If her own motives could be compromised, Stein might be tempted to write, consciously or not, in ways that had been proven to appeal to her audience, which is to say "writing that has already been written."

While this distinction might seem trivial, the implications of Stein's shift in focus lead directly to several larger differences between *Four in America* and the lectures. Stein's use of a more traditional inside/outside split to characterize the fear of contamination anxiety places her within a deeply entrenched set of modernist aesthetic values that valorize individual creativity over market success. Plus, her own somewhat uncharacteristic use of biblical terminology marks one choice, "serving Mammon," as clearly negative. So Stein is pressured through the rhetoric of her own formulations to avoid the combination strategy that she employed in *Four in America*. She even criticized her good friend Bernard Fäy in personal correspondence for attempting what she sees as a similar maneuver. She writes, "What bothers me is that you to me use your lectures to make you, and in doing so, if you did it completely well alright but doing it partly is again serving god and mammon which cannot be done."[65]

The shift away from "choosing both" is not the only distinction between *Four in America* and the lectures. In *Four in America,* Stein figured the distinction between "writing as it is written" and "writing as it is going to be written" as an authorial choice, and both forms of writing were depicted largely in terms of intentional processes, even if the author was forced to consult the final text to see how effective he or she had been. Conversely, in "What Is English Literature," Stein claims that the so-called choice of positions is itself foreordained: "And now about serving god and mammon...really there is no choice. Nobody chooses. What you do you do even if you do not yield to a temptation."[66] Again, this position serves to insulate Stein from both charges of market contamination and aesthetic failure because it takes the choice entirely out of her hands. Even if *The Autobiography* was to be categorized as a "popular" book, distinct from Stein's other writing, and its style read as some type of concession to public tastes, this notable shift in form could not be dismissed as a product of her own desire for fame, at least not according to the position she describes in "What Is English Literature."

While this formulation provides a strong defense against critics who would impugn Stein's intentions, its implications for revaluing Stein's work are less clear. Stein could use this larger mandate, as she did in "And Now," to stress the cognitive unity that produced her works and proclaim that she is simply predisposed to serving God. As such, *The Autobiography,* despite any appearances to the contrary, could be nothing less than another brilliant Stein text. Stein, however, seems to take another approach in the lectures, one that begins to move her away from the implied acceptance of *The Autobiography* in both *Four in America* and "And Now."

Critics have noted that Stein talks very little about *The Autobiography* in her lectures, which is surprising given that the success of this book was one of the forces behind her lecture tour. Instead, she uses her talks and the publicity afforded to her on the trip to promote less popular books, works that might otherwise have been overshadowed by the runaway commercial and critical success of *The Autobiography.* As Bryce Conrad points out, Stein chose to illustrate her lectures with passages selected almost exclusively from works that were then available in America, including the libretto of *Four Saints, Portraits and Prayers, Geography and Plays,* and *The Making of Americans,* which Harcourt released in an abridged version during Stein's tour.[67]

While Stein's silence by itself is difficult to interpret, one reference to *The Autobiography* in the lecture "Portraits and Repetition" suggests that she has come to consider her memoir as something less than a masterpiece. In this lecture, Stein traces her various efforts throughout the 1910s and 1920s to capture the essence of existence in her portraits. After two decades of pursuing this project in a wide variety of forms, Stein says, "I got a little tired, all that had been tremendously exciting, and one day then I began to write *The Autobiography of Alice B. Toklas.* You all know the joke of that, and in doing it I did an entirely different something...that had come out of some poetry I had been writing, *Before the Flowers of Friendship Faded Friendship Faded.* However the important thing was that for the first time in writing, I felt something outside me while I was writing, hitherto I had always had nothing but what was inside me while I was writing."[68]

This statement marks a significant shift in Stein's discussions of the period. She had previously addressed her translation of Hugnet's work, which was given its wry title after the collaboration led to a falling-out between the two writers, in *Four in America,* where she claimed the translation process first made her aware of two different modes of writing. While this process certainly changed her perception of writing, the account in *Four in America* does not dwell much on the external value of the two texts produced from this collaboration. As such, the translation simply marks an interesting development in Stein's thought and is not treated in an explicitly negative fashion. When she went on to problematize her writing from this period in "And Now," she passed over the episode with Hugnet altogether and linked her internal confusion directly to "success."

In "Portraits and Repetition," Stein shifts her assessment again and blames the earlier work for her confusion. *The Autobiography* has become a product of, rather than the catalyst for, the difficulties that disrupted Stein's writing process and, presumably, also ruined the quality of her work. Stein continues, "I wrote the *Autobiography of Alice B. Toklas* and told what happened as it had happened.... what happens is interesting but not really exciting.... It is true there is something much more exciting than anything that happens and now and always I am writing the portrait of that."[69] Stein not only distinguishes *The Autobiography* from much of her other writing, including the work that she is "now and always" doing, but also suggests, without repudiating the work altogether, that it is not as good as her other efforts. Her own exhaustion and confusion ultimately led her to create a work that retold the past without being able to extract any of the inner vitality that would make the work truly "exciting."

So, by the time she writes the lectures, Stein has come to focus on an inside/outside dichotomy and is insisting that in order to "serve God" writers must commit to their own internal process of creation, a step she had taken for granted in *Four in America*. She also extends her previous formulations, in a way not inconsistent with them, beyond the process of writing itself: "Now serving god for a writer who is writing is writing anything directly.... the relation between the thing done and the doer must be direct. In this way there is completion and the essence of the completed thing is completion."[70] The idea of completion, absent from the previous works under discussion, appears throughout the lectures and, as in the above quote, takes on several important meanings. First, "completion" refers to the creative process itself, meaning that an author must work without considering an external audience so that the mind can be directly expressed in writing. It becomes, in effect, a closed process whereby the writer pours his or her thoughts onto the page.

Second, the "completed thing" refers to the final product of this closed process, the autonomous artwork itself. While Stein had previously removed any impact a reader might have on one of her texts and had embedded vitality in the words themselves, she did not specifically address the relationship between a text and the objects it necessarily depicted. Stein returns to this issue in her lecture "Pictures" and brusquely severs all connection between art and the world. Though this sentiment is not uncommon among modernist authors, Stein's widely quoted formulation of the idea is certainly one of the most emphatic statements from the period. In a discussion of her early experiences with paintings, she says, "there is a relation between anything that is painted and the painting of it. And gradually I realized...that the relation was so to speak nobody's business....It could be the oil painting's business but actually...after the oil painting was painted it was not the oil painting's business and so it was nobody's business."[71] Stein's resolute dismissal of the relevance of signification leaves the painting as a formally contained object that embodies the painter's mind at one particular point in time, which is to say that, after the oil painting is completed, it does not even bear a direct connection to the artist.

One benefit of this formulation becomes apparent in "What Is English Literature," when Stein digresses to consider the implications of completeness: "You cannot explain a whole thing because if it is a whole thing it does not need explaining, it merely needs stating."[72] Stein, who has refused the relevance of interpretation for a work of art, pushes her point one step further here to suggest that a work of art does not need commentary or, by extension, criticism. Echoing the major New Critical doctrine that Cleanth Brooks would later call the "Heresy of Paraphrase," Stein suggests that a complete object cannot be transposed into any other form without becoming a completely different entity. It is for this reason that critic Michael Szalay, in an apt characterization, claims that Stein is ultimately committed to "the self-defining autonomy of identity."[73]

Of course, Stein's lectures are themselves a form of criticism or, at the very least, commentary on her work, a potential logical contradiction that she both acknowledges and attempts to address. In most of her discussions, she avoids explicating specific works, instead limiting her discussions to abstract ideas and personal experiences. In this manner, her approach largely coincides with some of Brooks's own writing. He often eschews discussions of "meaning" through a focus on what he calls "essential structure," tension, and balance. In addition, both writers frequently employ comparisons with nonverbal arts to de-emphasize the importance of content to aesthetic discussion.

Yet, even with this carefully modified approach, Stein still acknowledges the relative unimportance of her own critical formulations. She concludes "Pictures," the first lecture given in the United States, by directly qualifying the significance of everything she has just said: "All this is very important because it is important. It is important not for the painter or for the writer but for those who like to look at paintings."[74] Since an artist who is "serving God" must not be influenced by the comments and interpretations of others, her theories can do little more than educate other aestheticians considering the nature of contemporary art. As such, they are of value only outside the active moment of creation itself.

Such an attitude differs markedly from Stein's earlier statements in *Four in America,* where she held out the possibility that her analysis could be of use to writers: "If you know these things and you can know these things then you can write as if you knew...if you do not know these things although the time will or will not come that you will know these things, then you write as one who has been allowed to know these things without knowing them."[75] Again, Stein's approach in this text, written long before she had to come face-to-face with her audience, does not evince the same need to safeguard the internal purity of the artist and focuses primarily on the mode of writing used to create a text. As a result, knowing the difference between "writing as it was written" and "writing as it was going to be written"— two distinct processes that, at this point in her theorizations, depend more on the actions a writer takes to create a text than on less tangible forms of intellectual commitment—can help writers to approach their own process differently.

Despite this larger change in attitude, Stein redeploys "vitality," her crucial term for denoting value in "Henry James," in the lectures. This term, again, allows Stein to circumvent her own dismissal of interpretation, criticism, and even commentary by positing an a- or prerational quality by which a text can be judged. Stein had long been interested in the idea of human nature and, in her 1926 lecture "Composition as Explanation," had suggested that beneath contemporary "composition," people share a common humanity: "Composition is the difference which makes each and all of [a generation] then different from other generations and this is what makes everything different otherwise they are all alike."[76] "Vitality," then, allows Stein to tap into some aspect of this nature. It opens the way for her not only to evaluate individual works of art but also, by suggesting some constant form of human response, to theorize about the existence and qualities of masterpieces. In her lecture "Pictures," she says, "The oil painting once it is made has its own existence this is a thing that can of course be said of anything. Anything once it is made has its own existence and it is because of that that anything holds somebody's attention. The question always is about that anything, how much vitality has it and do you happen to like to look at it."[77] Stein distinguishes between the vitality of the text and personal taste, acknowledging that not everyone will like every text no matter how vital it may be. Yet, distinct from the question of subjective preferences, vitality is the one pertinent characteristic that can be assessed in all art, and assessed, presumably, without deforming the work itself through explanation.

Stein developed the ideas from her lectures a bit further when, late in the tour, she was invited to teach a two-week course on narration at the University of Chicago. These talks, later published under the title *Narration,* were written shortly before the course began on March 1, 1935, and, in terms of her theoretical approach to art, they primarily recast her ideas from the lectures. In the last lecture, however, Stein's focus changes slightly and, anticipating her famous lecture on masterpieces, she openly wonders how to determine what books will "last" before history has elevated them to the status of classics.

In approaching an answer to this question, she chooses to focus on the audience, an unsurprising move given the centrality of the audience to her previous formulations ("And anyhow what has an audience to do with it. Well in a way everything").[78] Stein begins by reiterating that "no one really not any one knows what any one means by what they that is that one is saying," a point she applies not just to "saying" but also to writing, as "any one can say that they do not write for an audience and really why should they since anyway their audience will have its own feeling about anything."[79] While this position is nothing new for Stein, she presses the implications further in *Narration* and suggests that the only true audience an author can have is herself. In addition, since a work of art becomes an independent entity after creation, writers can only truly be their audience during the process of production: "The writer writing knows what he is writing as he recognizes it as he is writing it and so he is actually having it happen that an audience is existing...As he is a writer he is an audience."[80]

Stein's attempt to usurp the audience function for the writer seems like a logical outgrowth of her previous ideas. Yet such an absolute insistence on removing the audience from the scene of production also makes the process of lecturing in front of a group of people potentially problematic. Stein had long been aware of the difficulties of theorizing about public performances and, as early as the "Wilbur Wright" section of *Four in America,* she began grappling with what it meant to be an actor producing art in front of a group of people, though such considerations were not brought to bear directly on the process of lecturing.

In her lectures for the U.S. tour, Stein broached the issue of her own performances several times, but, again, she did not attempt to untangle the implications of her work. For instance, she opens "The Gradual Making of *The Making of Americans*" by saying, "I am going to read what I have written to read, because in a general way it is easier even if it is not better and in a general way it is better even if it is not easier to read what has been written than to say what has not been written. Any way that is one way to feel about it."[81] Her unwillingness to clarify the distinction between speaking spontaneously and reading prewritten texts reflects her general attitude throughout the lectures, where, even in a lengthy lecture on acting, she does not extend her ideas to the lectures themselves. Such a lack of consideration is surprising given that Stein had serious concerns about the effect her physical environment would have on the speeches. In order to mitigate any potential distractions, she ultimately insisted that her audiences be capped at 500 people and that she be alone on the stage while speaking.

It was not until after Stein had been traveling around the country for several months that she finally stopped to directly reflect on her own activity as a form of performance. In her final lecture to the students at the University of Chicago, she claims that speaking is a different situation than writing because of the "physical exciting" involved, which is to say a speaker is forced to hear his or her own voice (he "hears what his audience hears," to use Stein's gendered terminology) and, as a result, cannot focus on the essence of the words themselves ("[there is no] real recognition...of what you talk as you talk"). As such, speaking "destroys the physical something that a writer is."[82]

Stein then goes on to claim, both as a response to her initial question about timeless art and as an implicit denunciation of public speaking, that true literature can be created only by focusing the creative part of the brain and its reflective capacities—here characterized as the "audience" function—on the process of creation itself: "That audience [for literary works] has to be there for the purpose of recognition as the telling is proceeding to be written and that audience must be at one with the writing, must be at one with the recognition, and can that be true of the historian or the newspaper man. No."[83] At this point, very near the end of her argument, Stein has advanced to speaking of author and audience as one entity, a point underscored by her reference to historians and journalists, that is, to the people creating texts and not actual audiences.[84]

One implication of Stein's insistence on the author's concentration during the act of writing is that the entire mind is focused on the present. No part of the brain should yield to outside influence or be caught up in the process of remembering, which is the challenge that historians face. Stein says, "An historian who knows everything really knows everything that has been happening how can he come to have the feeling that the only existence the man he is describing has is the one he has been giving him. How can he have this feeling, if he cannot then he cannot have the recognition while in the process of writing, which writing really writing must really give to the one writing."[85] This passage clarifies two important elements of Stein's theory. First, it reveals that "really writing," as a consequence of the author's total concentration on the immediate present, comes to be felt by the writer as a wholly *original* creation. If he or she admits external influences or incorporates the reconstructions of memory, then the pure creation will presumably give way to an indirect, planned, or derivative product.

Second, the above passage draws attention to the feeling the author receives during the process of writing, which marks a major shift from Stein's earlier works. In *Four in America*, Stein insists that authors cannot know what kind of writing they are producing while they are working. She now eliminates that slight uncertainty from the process and allows the author herself to have direct awareness of the success or failure of her texts.

This formulation clarifies some of the ambiguities in Stein's previous theories. It also provides the grounds for her last major defense of *The Autobiography* before she dismisses it as a misguided effort in later writings. At the end of her lecture, Stein says, "You see that is why making it the *Autobiography of Alice B. Toklas* made it do something, it made it be a recognition by never before that writing having it be existing."[86] Here, Stein attributes the aesthetic success of this book precisely to her displacement of perspective, that is, her "making it" the autobiography of another person. By putting her own history in the mouth of this textual Toklas, Stein was able to create a new story that did not attempt to reconstruct her own knowledge of the past from the present moment, and she was thereby able to attain a recognition of her words as they were being created in the process of writing.[87]

Stein's roundabout argument, praising the present moment of writing at the expense of fidelity to historical details, also provides her with an implicit defense against charges of inaccuracy, such as the ones leveled against her by many of her former friends and acquaintances, including Matisse, Braque, Andre Salmon, and Tristan Tzara, in a special issue of *transition*. Published in February 1935, at approximately the time Stein began writing her *Narration* lectures, the "Testimony against Gertrude Stein" criticizes her for misrepresenting aesthetic conditions in the early part of the twentieth century. Stein's position, couched in a larger exploration of timeless art, implies that considerations of historical accuracy are irrelevant to the creation of "real" writing and that they are consequently of little significance to her. Moreover, her increasingly emphatic insistence on the hermeticism of artistic creation provides her with protection not only from the encroachment of the public but also from those who would attempt to use her work as a conduit to the author herself. This pattern of internalization would continue in Stein's work, though in a distinctly modified form, long after the lecture tour had ended.

Gertrude Stein and Her Critics Revisited

The analysis of Stein's theories up to this point stands in stark contrast to the most common interpretation of Stein's work, which places her in a direct relation to postmodern poetics, particularly the form embodied by the so-called L=A=N=G=U=A=G=E movement of the late 1970s. Though the link owes much to the poets' own invocations of Stein, academics working in this vein most frequently return to Marjorie Perloff's analyses both in *The Poetics of Indeterminacy* (1981) and, more recently, in *21st Century Modernism: The "New" Poetics* (2002). The essential link between Stein's work and that of more contemporary poets, Perloff argues, is that both "use material form...as an active compositional agent, impelling the reader to participate in the process of construction."[88] Jennifer Ashton divides this statement into two major tenets that run throughout Perloff's analysis.[89] First, Stein's poetry deliberately disrupts the referential function of language in order to open up the text as a space of indeterminate meaning, thereby emphasizing the intractable materiality of the signifier itself over some supposedly essential meaning that the text conveys. Second, given that a poem can be read in an endless number of ways, the reader in effect adopts the role of author and "creates" the text by constructing one specific meaning configuration for the poem.[90]

While Perloff's larger argument is certainly more complex than I have made it here, these two crucial elements—the emphasis on the materiality of words over their referential function and the necessity of active reader participation in meaning creation—have been taken up by many other critics and writers, including, as we have seen, Juliana Spahr through her conception of "multivalent texts." Stein herself, according to my previous reading, also seems to agree with both these points, at least as independent ideas. When Charles Bernstein, a poet whose name comes up repeatedly in discussions of L=A=N=G=U=A=G=E poetry, writes in his 1992 book *A Poetics*, "the poem said any other way is not the poem," he could very well be paraphrasing Stein's claim that an artwork "does not need explaining, it merely needs stating."[91] Similarly, Stein openly and repeatedly acknowledges that readers can make whatever meaning they want out of her texts. Yet, as Ashton rightly asserts, Stein is not committed, as many postmodern poets are, to art as an object of experience, which is to say an art object that takes on value only through each individual reader's experience of it. Instead, Stein believes that an essential value exists in the language of the autonomous work, a position more akin to the "closed" poem theorized by New Critics than supposedly "open" postmodern texts.

Ashton's disagreement with Perloff rests in part on her belief that Stein's theories are "at odds" with several major tenets of the New Criticism. She claims that Stein's commitment to the autonomy of art comes into conflict with two other common New Critical views, namely, "that the poem must not mean but be" and "that paraphrase is heresy." Ashton argues that if a New Critical poem is to be considered an autonomous object or, to use Stein's term, an "entity," it must contain its own essential meaning, but, following the "Heresy of Paraphrase," the poem has no meaning. It is simply an object to be experienced, which means that all a reader can do is revel in the phenomenological experience of the poem. Any attempt to interpret or understand will simply distort the pristine object on the page. The trouble is that everything about the phenomenological experience resides in the reader and not in the poetic object itself. As Ashton puts it, "Everything that constitutes the text's objecthood—the 'sound' and 'feel' of its constitutive syllables—belongs entirely to the experience of someone—exactly what Stein insists it cannot do and still be a masterpiece." In order to posit a poem as an entity rather than an object, then, critics confuse the effects it produces in the mind of readers with something inherent in the poem. As Ashton puts it, New Critics mistakenly "equat[ed] objecthood with autonomy."[92]

However, as demonstrated above, Stein does explicitly ascribe to the view that a true work of literature "merely needs stating." She manages this potential difficulty through her concept of "vitality." This term allows her to disconnect the value of art from the production of meaning and the subjective experiences of readers. As a result, she can declare that an artwork is beyond criticism while saying that it is also capable of being judged by a universal standard, even if that standard itself cannot be put into precise analytic terms. And this "vitality" is finally contained in the words on the page.

The distinction that I would like to draw between my own reading of Stein's position in the lectures and Perloff's interpretation of her poetry then lies in the relationship between the two major tenets Perloff has explored. While, as Ashton says, "indeterminacy would...seem to be a necessary consequence of...'anti-absorptive' poetics," Stein sidesteps this issue by employing a third term that is connected to the words but lies outside the interpretive process. It is for this reason that she can espouse both tenets of one form of postmodern poetry while not herself ascribing to the "objecthood" of art that is foundational to that view.[93] It is also the reason Stein can espouse the "Heresy of Paraphrase" with such seemingly divergent figures as Bernstein and Brooks.

This position does not simply mean that Stein should be labeled, in Lisa Siraganian's words, "an expatriate New Critic in avant-garde clothing, promoting the autonomous poetic object."[94] Siraganian challenges the label of New Critic for Stein because her theoretical focus is different from that of most critics of her time. For instance, Wimsatt and Beardsley's formulation of the "affective fallacy" posits that a poem's meaning "disappears" in the presence of readerly emotion. Conversely, for Siraganian, Stein's lectures suggest that "the meaning of a poem is entirely indifferent to the reader's emotion, or, for that matter, indifferent to any type of judgment the reader could deliver."[95] As should be apparent from my previous discussion, I both agree and disagree with this statement. While I concur with Siraganian's central point that Stein disregards the reader in her conception of the artwork, I would argue that Stein is equally dismissive of the concept of "meaning" in relation to art.

I also believe that Stein's theoretical focus is not the only grounds for eschewing such a loaded label as "New Critic" when it comes to her work. The theoretical position I have outlined above stems from a consideration of works done, in part, as a response to her sudden celebrity in the early 1930s. Though Stein shared many of the theoretical commitments mentioned above earlier in her career, she had by no means formulated a single coherent theory of art before embarking on her major theoretical projects in the 1930s, as can be seen through the development of her thought in these works. So it would be historically inaccurate to pull a statement from one of Stein's lectures and use it to govern interpretations of her early writing without any further consideration of context or external circumstances.

Nor do I mean to suggest that interpretive procedures for Stein's work should be constructed out of a contextualized account of her own theories. As astute critics such as Perloff have shown, Stein's early poetry does employ devices, forms, and ideas that could accurately be termed, or easily modified to encompass the term "postmodern." The problem I would like to address arises when critics mine Stein's later writings for statements and ideas that seem to correlate with their analysis of her work so that they can claim that Stein explicitly agrees with their interpretations.

Given this caveat, Stein's work in the early 1930s evinces a clear tendency to isolate the creative process and, in turn, to separate the text from the outside world. By the time of writing the lectures, she has not only isolated herself from the psychological pressures of being a famous author but also extricated audience interpretation from the "essence" of the artwork. She does acknowledge readers' freedom to construct meanings and, at times, even seems to revel in the creative freedom provided to her audience, as when she playfully invites them to interpret *Four in America* without regard for her text. Her primary emphasis in both *Four in America* and the lectures, however, is the creative process itself. She has also begun to explore the grounds on which works of art can be judged, a preoccupation that stems in part from the success of *The Autobiography* and is manifest in Stein's various recraftings of that text's creation.

CHAPTER 4

After the Tour: Naturalized Aesthetics and Systematized Contradictions

As Stein's lecture tour reached its conclusion and some of her newly published books continued to sell poorly, she fell under increasing pressure from her publisher to produce another memoir. Before beginning, however, she set out to formalize her ideas in what is perhaps best referred to as a philosophical treatise entitled *The Geographical History of America* (1936). Free from the formal confines of the lecture format and the pressures of an immediate audience, *The Geographical History* returns to the obscure, but playful, meditative style that characterizes many of Stein's earlier works, including *Four in America*. It also marks a return, though somewhat more tentatively, to the synthetic strategies Stein employed in that text. This book simplifies her previous formulations by recasting the opposition between "serving God" and "serving Mammon" into essentialized terms: "human nature" and the "human mind." All people contain varying degrees of both elements and can potentially operate from either impulse, much as Stein's earlier formulation posited that writers who understood the difference between "writing as it is written" and "writing as it is going to be written" could potentially have some control over their approach to art.

One significant consequence of Stein's new formulation is that it places a strong emphasis on the competing and irresolvable tension between these two states in any given person. Artists are always forced to wrestle with both impulses in the process of creation, regardless of their intentions or aims. Accordingly, tensions surface throughout Stein's text, permeating her discussions not only of human nature and the human mind but also of a whole range of related aesthetic issues. For instance, this book and another lecture she gave at the time—"What Are Master-pieces and Why Are There So Few of Them?"—show an increasing preoccupation with the logistics of creating a publicly recognized "masterpiece," which is to say a book that can be embraced by both elite and popular audiences. Stein's insistence on the link between textual value and the internal creative processes of the author, however, prevents her from making any prescriptive statements about the content or form of specific texts. Instead, she emphasizes the potential contradictions her theories raise for authors, an approach that allows her to navigate between her own detailed theories of textual production and the seemingly impossible task of setting out to create a "masterpiece." It is, finally, a stance that allows her to pursue and avoid directly addressing questions of textual evaluation and canonization.

These theories, and the complex formal experiments contained in *The Geographical History,* helped to lay the groundwork for Stein's second memoir, *Everybody's Autobiography* (1937), which foregrounds the contradictions inherent in presenting a supposedly private, internal self to a public audience. This approach allows Stein to claim a public voice while simultaneously distancing herself from celebrity media outlets, which insist on the production of stable and marketable personae. In lieu of such a persona, Stein inserts a contradictory voice that unsettles attempts to locate the author in the text. *Everybody's Autobiography* ultimately represents an attempt to create a new textual form that can embody the struggles of Stein's intellectual and creative processes while also remaining familiar and accessible to a wide range of readers.

On Theory and Practice: Laying the Groundwork for the Next Autobiography

Throughout the early stages of her U.S. tour, Stein continued to haggle with Alfred Harcourt over the publication of other books. Her agent, William Aspinwall Bradley, had proposed as early as February 1933 that Harcourt reprint *Three Lives* along with *The Autobiography* and distribute the leftover copies of books that Stein had attempted to sell under her own publishing imprint, the Plain Edition. Harcourt was less than enthusiastic about the idea and put off publishing anything else until after *The Autobiography* had been distributed.

Stein, however, was not willing to commit her entire publishing future to Harcourt simply because he had agreed to print *The Autobiography.* At the same time that her agent was pressing Harcourt to put out more works, Stein was working to cultivate a relationship with Bennett Cerf, one of the founders of Random

House. Their association began with the assistance of Carl Van Vechten, one of Stein's close friends who had published several books with Random House in the early 1930s. According to Cerf's memoirs, Van Vechten had first suggested that he seek out Stein in order to reprint some of her older works. After the initial success of *The Autobiography,* Cerf agreed and immediately added *Three Lives* to the Modern Library, a dollar reprint series put out by Random House. He also agreed to publish a new collection, *Portraits and Prayers,* in November, to coincide with the beginning of the lecture tour, and the libretto of *Four Saints in Three Acts.* The libretto came out in February 1934, at the time of the opera's New York debut.[1]

Cerf and Stein were on such good terms by the time of the lecture tour that, when Stein first arrived in New York, Cerf and Van Vechten were two of the first people to meet her at the dock. Cerf, speaking of the early weeks of the lecture tour, says that Stein "just took me over, and for the two or three weeks she was in New York, I was her slave. She ordered me around like a little errand boy."[2] Despite their budding relationship, Stein continued to offer proposals to Harcourt, who, largely to pacify Stein, finally agreed in October to put out an abridged version of *The Making of Americans.* (The day she signed the contract, Cerf wrote her offering to publish the work in its entirety.)

Donald Brace, Harcourt's partner, told Bradley that the sales of *The Making of Americans* were only one-quarter of those of *The Autobiography* and that the latter book had actually slowed the sales of her popular memoir.[3] Shortly thereafter, Harcourt cut ties with Stein, and Cerf stepped in to become her primary publisher in the United States. He promised to publish whatever she wanted to see in print, whether or not it had market potential.[4]

The first book Stein sent to Cerf after her tour was *The Geographical History.* Cerf, despite the unorthodox nature of this difficult text, remained true to his promise and published it to both lackluster reviews and low sales.[5] It was the last major work Stein would publish before beginning her second memoir, *Everybody's Autobiography.*

The Geographical History, like many of Stein's previous works, sets out through a series of examples, exploratory discussions, and digressions to examine the meaning of two primary terms, in this case, "human nature" and the "human mind." These two terms in large part restate the distinction Stein made between "serving God" and "serving Mammon." This book, however, takes Stein's previous examination of authorial intention and recharacterizes her two positions as essential features of all human beings. "Human nature," like an author who "serves Mammon," is repeatedly linked with constructs that distort knowledge of the immediate present, including memory and "identity." Stein uses the latter term to refer to the sense of self cultivated through the recognition of others, as opposed to one's own immediate self awareness. The "human mind" roughly equates to "serving God," in that it exists in a timeless present and simply writes what it is thinking without conscious reflection on external or historical considerations. One consequence of this formulation, already implicit in her *Narration* lectures, is that the human mind, and any text it produces, cannot be evaluated based on accuracy or correctness: "Write and right. Of course they have nothing to do with one another. Right right left right left he had a good job and he left, left right left."[6] This passage is important because it explicitly disconnects writing and being "right," and implicitly devalues the search for what is "right" by linking it with regimental militarism. The attempt to find such metaphysical truths stands in direct opposition to the spontaneous and playful actions of the human mind, a form of activity that generates its own knowledge in the process of writing.

While these ideas should all be familiar from Stein's earlier writings, her transposition of "serving God" into bodily terms shifts the emphasis away from the relationship between, as she said in the lectures, the "doer" and the "thing done." It also renders adjectives such as "direct" and "indirect," which Stein had previously used to describe this relationship, largely superfluous because "real" writing can now be simply defined as any writing emerging from the human mind. This formulation also allows Stein to elide many of her previous arguments, for "vitality" and the autonomy of the artwork to name just two relevant examples, by recharacterizing them as byproducts of the operation of the human mind. This does not mean that there is a contradiction or gap between her current and previous accounts. The new formulation simply traces the vitality of the text to its source in the human mind, a progression that allows her to impute the atemporal universality of that mind to the final text itself. In other words, Stein no longer needs to claim that a writer working in the correct frame of mind with total concentration on the present will impute vitality into a text that can be felt by all people. Instead, she can simply say, "The human mind is the mind that writes what any human mind years after or years before can read, thousand of years or no years it makes no difference."[7]

Yet, the cost of such simplicity is that the human mind often seems like little more than a mystification. Given the parameters that define this entity, it would be impossible to describe the human mind in any but the most abstract terms, and even these terms would ultimately prove to be inadequate. In her many attempts to characterize the human mind throughout *The Geographical History*, Stein can only defer to the present ("there is no knowing what the human mind is because as it is it is") and stress the process of perpetual change ("there is no such thing as the habit of the human mind...not even the habit of being the human mind of course not").[8] It becomes, in effect, the endpoint of rational analysis, a process that ultimately resists logical exploration.

Moreover, when Stein asks if the human mind can be glimpsed in the body of a text it has written, she dismisses the possibility by saying, "[writing] cannot sound like writing because if it sounds like writing than anybody can see it being written, and the human mind nobody sees the human mind while it is being existing."[9] Despite the seemingly obscure nature of this text, Stein's new position does not significantly alter her theories about the creative process. The human mind produces an autonomous text that can be recognized by other human minds even though it leaves no definable or analyzable trace of its existence in the words themselves.

Furthermore, Stein maintains a similar attitude toward the relationship between the author's mind and the external world. With regard to the audience, Stein is, again, quite explicit in her dismissal, saying, "When a great many hear you that is an audience and if a great many hear you what difference does it make." She also reiterates that the mind must create texts without regard for any potential readers: "The words spoken are spoken to somebody, the words written are except in the case of master-pieces written to somebody."[10]

And yet, while Stein's previous works provide a useful basis for explaining this book, her latter text cannot be entirely subsumed into the former ones, as Stein wryly asserts when she dismisses the idea of God: "It is the habit to say that there must be a god but not at all the human mind has neither time or identity and therefore enough said."[11] The author, according to this text, no longer needs to "serve God" because God, who has traditionally been characterized as an infallible, atemporal entity working beyond the reaches of human consciousness, has now been incorporated as a process that exists in every human brain. Moreover, the human mind has effectively usurped and naturalized what Stein had implicitly characterized as the higher calling of the "true" artist.

It would not even be entirely accurate to generalize "serving God" and the "human mind" as comparable steps in Stein's internalization of the aesthetic process because, in her later formulation, the individual always contains both the human mind and human nature. Stein does insist throughout *The Geographical History* that these two categories bear no relationship to each other, thereby securing creative independence for the human mind, but much of the tension in the book is generated by the fact that Stein cannot simply dismiss human nature.[12] Despite the relatively obvious conclusion that Stein wants to reach—namely, that the human mind creates great works of art—the book as a whole cannot shake the specter of human nature and ultimately ends on an ambivalent note. She concludes, "Identity is not there at all but it is oh yes it is...Do they put up with it. Yes they put up with it. They put up with identity. Yes they do that. And so anything puts up with identity."[13]

Stein, however, does not simply bemoan the ambivalent state of living between two contradictory poles. Throughout the text, she both emphasizes this condition and plays with the potential difficulties that it raises for her formulations. For instance, she has gone to great lengths to extrapolate a theory that supposedly covers all of human kind in her historical moment, and yet she also suggests that the literal content of her ideas is irrelevant. If this text is in fact the product of Stein's human mind, then other minds will recognize it as a valuable work regardless of what it actually says. This position frees Stein to assert, "It is so easy to be right if you do not believe what you say."[14] Similarly, Stein contradicts her own claim that "write" and "right" are unrelated by specifically defining a process for the human mind, giving it, if nothing else, a correct form of operation. She paradoxically enunciates a larger truth in the text, all the while using a repeated play on "write" and "right" to both clarify and draw attention to the problems inherent in her larger formulations: "The human mind has no resemblances if it had it could not write that is to say write right."[15]

In this way, Stein's text as a whole reflects her attitude toward the opposition she has established. In a section titled "Autobiography number one," Stein concludes, "Not to solve it but be in it, that is what one can say of the problem of the relation of human nature to the human mind, which does not exist because there is none there is no relation."[16] By placing this declaration under the heading of autobiography, Stein suggests that she is talking about her own experiences living with the human mind and human nature. The contradictory form of her statement emphasizes that, even though the two states may be entirely separate, a human being must always exist in their midst, or, perhaps more accurately, must endlessly vacillate between them.

Stein also emphatically declares that "autobiographies have nothing to do with the human mind," presumably because they involve memory and identity, which are both part of human nature.[17] Perhaps the heading then suggests that the entire section was constructed by Stein's human nature and should thus be considered metaphysically suspect. Yet Stein's larger categories are not, as we have seen, content distinctions, which leaves open the possibility that the passage does not have to be read under erasure. In short, Stein does not attempt to solve the contradictions she has created, nor does she attempt to minimize the difficulties of living with such contradictions. There is simply no resolution, and the human mind will continue to wander and play with little regard for resolution anyway.

I do not mean to suggest that this is the first time in Stein's major works from the 1930s that irony and contradiction play significant roles. Throughout the previous chapter, I argued that the contradiction between internalizing and universalizing value was a generative force behind Stein's writing in the 1930s. Moreover, even though I have not spent much time on Stein's linguistic games in my discussions of her works, a playful engagement with contradiction and irony is a feature of almost every Stein text. Yet, the change in Stein's formulations here foregrounds such complexities in a way that some other texts from the mid-1930s did not. She is not simply combining two equal and largely unproblematic terms as she did in *Four in America,* nor is she attempting to maintain the strict division of the lectures. She is, in effect, combining these approaches in a simultaneous embrace of two highly oppositional terms, creating a tense and playful meditation that dwells at the interstices of two states that perhaps never intersect.

* * *

After completing *The Geographical History,* Stein traveled to England and gave a lecture entitled "What Are Master-pieces and Why Are There So Few of Them?" before the English Clubs at both Oxford and Cambridge Universities. Critics have gravitated toward this work because it echoes the ideas that Stein had been playing with throughout the decade in a compact and direct form. In the terms I have outlined above, it largely reiterates Stein's ideas from

The Geographical History, which is not surprising given the chronology of its composition. The lecture juxtaposes human nature and the human mind as well as identity and entity. It also connects the latter categories with the creation of masterpieces, a move that pushes her lecture beyond some earlier formulations that did not explicitly link a particular form of writing to the production of great literature.

Yet this potentially arrogant formulation, which suggests that Stein possesses the key to creating great literature, is not, in practice, quite as bold as it sounds. At this point, Stein has so completely isolated her process of creation in the unknowable reaches of the human mind that such a claim entails little more than commitment to a few general creative principles. Moreover, Stein's insistently internal focus and the generality with which she must explain the operation of the human mind makes any discussion directed outside the author—say, on the qualities of texts themselves—much more problematic.

This problem appears in *The Geographical History* when Stein considers how masterpieces relate to their own historical period. In her 1926 lecture "Composition as Explanation," Stein suggested that true artists are defined by their ability to capture the essence of the contemporary moment in their work before anyone else has come to express such an understanding. A true masterpiece, however, cannot simply encapsulate one particular moment in time; it must, at least potentially, remain relevant to all readers through different ages, much as Homer and Shakespeare remain pertinent to contemporary readers.[18] Stein's new formulations, which emphasize only the wandering of the human mind in a perpetual present, leave little room for negotiating this difficulty and Stein ultimately acknowledges the contradiction: "Everybody says that is what a master-piece does but does it. Does it say what everybody sees, and yet it does but is not that what makes a master-piece not have it be that it is what it is."[19]

Stein raises similar issues in "What Are Master-pieces," but she seems no closer to mediating between theoretical processes and textual characteristics. For instance, she posits that the human mind remains in perpetual motion, but masterpieces, because of their textual nature, must begin and end. With no easy way to bridge this gap, Stein playfully concludes, "Well anyway anybody who is trying to do anything today is desperately not having a beginning and an ending but nevertheless in some way one does have to stop. I stop."[20] She also discusses, to give another example, the problem of temporal awareness. An author writing from the human mind must be working without a sense of time or identity, but must be elaborating on these very things in writing, a problem that folds back again into the tension between "timeliness" and timelessness in true works of art.

Stein enumerates these difficulties in part to reiterate the elusiveness of her objects. In this lecture, she has taken on the problematic position of explaining a process that exists outside the scope of rational analysis and a product that can only be deformed by interpretation. In addition, she highlights the problems faced by contemporary authors who are, if we are to believe Stein's formulations, consciously or unconsciously struggling with all these difficulties in their attempt to create lasting art. The sheer number of problems Stein attempts to express and consider provides ample justification for her insistence, even as she purports to be explaining the process of creating great literature, that there are in fact very few masterpieces.

This reading of *The Geographical History* and "What Are Masterpieces" again challenges interpretations of Stein's work that attempt to emphasize the communal nature of her writing. For instance, Harriet Scott Chessman only mentions this late lecture in a footnote, where she acknowledges that Stein sees herself as "constructing...'master-pieces' in pure isolation from an audience." Yet she goes on to dismiss the piece because "this late essay must be placed in the context of Stein's own difficulty with the fact of her sudden success from *The Autobiography of Alice B. Toklas,* which was written precisely from a position of 'identity.' Stein's defensiveness about the relatively small audience held by her more experimental texts seems to infuse this account of how unimportant audience has been to her."[21] It is unclear from Chessman's brief dismissal why Stein would only, in this one lecture three years after the publication of *The Autobiography,* have had difficulty with "the fact of her sudden success." Stein's texts throughout the 1930s posit an author working in isolation from an audience, and they directly link the value of literary works to that state of mental isolation. As Stein says in *The Geographical History,* "There is no connection no relation between reading and the human mind."[22] Perhaps she best summed up the centrality of subjectivity to her aesthetic theories in a letter to Edmund Wilson, where she claims, "All literature is to me me, that isn't as bad as it sounds."[23]

In addition, Stein did not simply dismiss *The Autobiography* as irrelevant, but in fact worked to cultivate theories that allowed her to claim this text as an original and important work just one year before delivering "What Are Master-pieces." To imply that Stein's struggles with fame led to a simple denunciation of *The Autobiography* and one reactionary lecture is, I think, to mischaracterize her work from the period. By the time of writing "What Are Master-pieces," Stein has forcefully reiterated that each consciousness is entirely isolated from every other consciousness and the only possible form of interaction is "contact." Moreover, Stein at this stage in her writing is far from a celebratory embrace of her audience. She has conceived of a world where people exist between an externally and historically imposed sense of identity and the unencumbered present moment. The practical difficulties that such a position creates loom large as Stein prepares to work on another autobiography, one that will attempt to avoid the pitfalls of human nature and become a "masterpiece."

Yet, in accordance with her recent theories, her text must reflect more than the human mind. It must embody the conflicted state of living between entity and identity. Along similar lines, she must also attempt to navigate the implicit challenge of her theories and create a text that is both aesthetically successful and "interesting" to a wide range of readers, regardless of their typical brow "level." Stein, as might be expected, was not ultimately successful in navigating this last divide. Despite the continued popularity of her first autobiography, sales of the second book were so poor that Random House printed only one edition of 3,000 copies.[24] Critics have traditionally responded to Stein's autobiographies in a similar way. *The Autobiography* has amassed a provocative and wide ranging critical literature, while *Everybody's Autobiography* has received relatively little attention. Many scholars treat it as if it were, at best, "a kind of postscript" to the first work and, at worst, a marginal effort designed to cash in on the success of her lecture tour.[25]

In the following section, I examine how *Everybody's Autobiography* might encourage such a critical response in its explicit invocation of the first book; however, I claim that it does so to deliberately distance itself from *The Autobiography* in range, scope, and formal intention. Beginning with a discussion of its unorthodox title, I examine specifically how *Everybody's Autobiography* simultaneously employs and works to undermine its connection with the first text in order to lay the groundwork for a more detailed assessment of the book's form and structure. I then move on to analyze Stein's account of the difficulties that arise from *The Autobiography*'s publication, in particular her characterization of celebrity as a threat to personal autonomy. Ultimately, I propose that she attempts to solve this problem by retreating, both formally and literally, to an insistently illogical space of contradiction where her work can deflect attention from a seemingly all-encompassing celebrity media apparatus to the unified, though never static, work of art itself.

My goal in providing this reading of Stein's second autobiography is, in part, to draw attention to the complexity of this neglected text. I would also like to provide a specific example of how Stein's theoretical work during the decade translated into a text that was ostensibly constructed for a mass audience. The text that emerges is, as Marianne DeKoven says of Stein's writing in the 1930s more generally, "not a repudiation of or release from experimental writing," but is instead a "rapprochement of the experimental with the conventional."[26] As DeKoven suggests, Stein's attempt to embrace both sides of a dichotomy is not new to her work in the late 1930s. It is not even limited to her work in the 1930s more generally. For instance, in "Arthur A Grammar," a poetic essay written in the late 1920s, Stein explores the tension between grammar as a rule-bound system that channels thought into predetermined patterns and writing in a way that confounds traditional grammatical systems. Throughout the article, Stein plays with the idea that she needs to employ grammatical constructions in order to critique grammar and, rather than simply promote a playful approach to language in the piece, she claims "Arthur a grammar can be both."[27]

Everybody's Autobiography, however, engages with a different series of practical and theoretical concerns than those that Stein frequently discussed earlier in her career. The issues that she deals with in this book have arisen from the specific context of her lecture tour and the general theoretical framework outlined in her earlier texts. It is, in many respects, an attempt to push the ideas she had developed in new directions and elaborate on the implications of the work she had accomplished over the previous four years.

GERTRUDE STEIN'S *EVERYBODY'S AUTOBIOGRAPHY* AND THE ART OF CONTRADICTIONS

Barbara Mossberg, in an essay exploring detachment in the work of Emily Dickinson and Gertrude Stein, claims, "The titles of Stein's autobiographies are oxymoronic, self-canceling and for that reason compelling."[28] Though "The Autobiography of Alice B. Toklas" only becomes "oxymoronic" when we take Stein's authorship of the text into account, Mossberg's unconscious association of title and literary gesture reflects the influence that this one trope has had on scholarly explorations of the book. From the earliest narrative studies to more recent analyses of identity and sexuality, critics have almost universally incorporated, and frequently constructed entire theories out of, Stein's playful authorial inversion.[29]

The pervasive influence of this move is also reflected in Mossberg's reading of the willfully ambiguous title "Everybody's Autobiography" as a reinscription of problematized authorship, even though many potentially productive readings could de-emphasize the phrase's apparent contradictions. For instance, "Everybody's" could be read as a contraction, which would relate it not only to the book's thematic concern with creation but also to contemporary autobiographical theories that explore the narrative construction of identity.[30] Alternatively, the title could be read as the articulation of a collective identity, presumably available to individuals through an exploration of the "self." Such a reading would draw useful connections between this book and some of Stein's other contemporaneous works, such as *The Geographical History of America.*

Grouping these two titles together under the assumption that they function in similar ways also obscures the hyperbolic tone that is unique to "Everybody's Autobiography." Taken literally, Stein is not only claiming to speak on behalf of all humanity but also purporting to embody and represent the consciousness of all people. From an opposing, and equally plausible, perspective, this title could be read as an attempt to decentralize the authority inherent in such a claim. Autobiography is traditionally defined, in part due to its dependence on language, as a solitary enterprise, that is, as the expression of an individual consciousness interacting with the material world.[31] Yet here, the subject of representation can be neither unified nor material. The reader begins, as it were, from the imagined space of a heterogeneous collectivity. It is this double movement, the projection of the self outward coupled with the consequent refinement of that projection into a problematically singular vision, that makes the title seem doubly self-canceling, first in its apparent negation of a literal, unified self, and second in its challenge to the premises of autobiographical form.

I emphasize the complexities that the title "Everybody's Autobiography" could potentially generate in part to set the stage for what I see as a text structured around contradictions. These ambiguities are also important because several recent critics have characterized Stein's book as a largely unproblematic attempt to tell the story of everybody. For instance, Juliana Spahr attempts to read *Everybody's Autobiography* as an explicitly inclusive work and a defense of Stein's earlier experiments with "open" poetry: "Stein attempts to write an autobiography that invokes this flexibility [of pronouns] by emptying out the self of autobiography to acknowledge and encourage instead the everybody of autobiography."[32] As suggested above, any one-dimensional approach to this work will necessarily elide many significant facets of the text. In fact, one of the biggest problems Stein faces in this autobiography is that no matter how much she attempts to fragment, abstract, or generalize her identity on a theoretical level, the cultural and economic capital that accrues from the expression of such theories will always come back to the author. Put differently, the autobiography of everybody will always be "by Gertrude Stein," an inequality Stein calls attention to explicitly throughout the text, as in her famous lines, "In America everybody is but some are more than others. I was more than others."[33]

When viewed from this perspective, the complex significations of Stein's title reflect the larger problems that pervade this book and offer a challenge to readers looking for a repeat performance of *The Autobiography*. "Everybody's Autobiography" does not just recall the problematized authorship of the first book but employs it as an ironic sign that may well undermine the very project it designates. Similarly, this contradictory trope raises a complex of identity-related issues, the very issues that have come to dominate critical readings of *The Autobiography*, while at the same time it undercuts any expectation for a repeat performance through both the visibility of the gesture and its literal impossibility.

This desire to avoid redundancy becomes a central thematic concern early in the text when Stein considers the concept of originality. In a discussion of Picabia's art, she claims, "I do not care about anybody's painting if I know what the next painting they are painting looks like. I am like any dog out walking, I want it to be the same and I want it to be completely unalike."[34] This passage and the larger discussion of which it is a part reflect Stein's tendency to speak of art in abstract or metaphorical terms.[35] Throughout the book, she discusses, criticizes, and evaluates painters, though never once does she physically describe either their technique or their work as a whole.[36] Here, Stein chooses to address Picabia's work not in terms of its literal content, which will always change from picture to picture, but in terms of the formative ideology behind the work itself. It is presumably this kind of theoretical redundancy that must be avoided in order to create interesting works of art repeatedly. Yet Stein undercuts the pretension of this intellectual posture by comparing her own sensibilities to those of a dog, suggesting that, despite appearances, her underlying tastes are at the very least common, if not altogether simple.[37] She merely wants more of what she likes, but if it is exactly the same, then it will ultimately be unsatisfying. "That," she says, generalizing at the end of the book, "is what they meant when they said that it turns to dust and ashes in your mouth."[38]

This difficult relationship between a text and its predecessors is, as we have seen, partially inscribed in *Everybody's Autobiography* through its title. It is a playful resignification that anticipates, addresses, and, perhaps most importantly, undermines the audience's expectations. The reversed phrasing of the title seems to function in a similar manner. *The Autobiography of Alice B. Toklas* is a passive construction that de-emphasizes Stein's ownership of the story in favor of the "autobiographical" text itself.[39] The converse, possessive form highlights both the subject and its claim on the text. So, if one reads the titles allegorically, the problematics of authority over image and the ownership of one's own life story seem to have moved from the thematic subtext of an otherwise "breezy" autobiography to a central literal position inside the story itself, a story that fittingly attempts to interrogate the relationship between image and identity in a rapidly evolving media culture.[40]

The book further draws attention to and simultaneously distances itself from *The Autobiography* by framing the text with references to it. The book opens with a brief anecdote about the difficulties of international publication: "In the first place she did not want it to be Alice B. Toklas, if it has to be at all it should be Alice Toklas and in the French translation it was Alice Toklas in French it just could not be Alice B. Toklas but in America and in England too Alice B. Toklas was more than Alice Toklas. Alice never thought so and always said so. That is the way any autobiography has to be written."[41] On a literal level, Stein again directs attention to the problematics of signification and the instability of autobiography by emphasizing the apparent gap between "external" significations and the "inner" self that is taken to be the object of representation. For Alice, the name is just an empty sign that has no bearing on her true identity, so the text should use her familiar appellation.

The intricacies of Stein's language also work to undercut the publishers' debate by drawing attention to the form of the passage. For example, the excessive repetition of Alice's name along with the homophonous link between "B" and "be" highlight the commodification of her identity and the resulting fetishization of her be-ing into a concrete and salable referent, here the letter B, but also, by extension, *The Autobiography* itself.

The importance of referentiality is further undermined through this passage's playful emphasis on the materiality of the signifier. First, translation itself focuses on material signs because, in an ideal communication system, that is the place where change is affected. The underlying referents themselves are never at issue. In this case, however, Alice Toklas "translated" into French remains simply Alice Toklas.[42] Second, Stein's use of the ambiguous word "more" allows her to engage with both the larger philosophical issues of identity and the materiality of the words themselves, as "Alice B. Toklas" is literally more than "Alice Toklas."

Finally, the demonstrative pronoun "that," severed from any specific referent, seems designed to symbolize, right at the beginning of the book, the overdetermined nature of the autobiographical form. The most immediate referent for "that" is the preceding paragraph, which could suggest that autobiography itself, according to the previous reading, is nothing more than a word game that is unable to capture any "true" identity.[43] Alternatively, "that" could refer specifically to the publisher's dilemma, emphasizing that all artistic endeavors are enmeshed in both textual histories and sociocultural processes that modify their final form.[44] It could also refer more generally to the discursive form of the opening, with the implication being that all autobiography is indebted to memory, another issue that Stein takes up repeatedly in the text.[45] Though the exact content of the referent cannot be determined, all of these possible readings point, in some form, to both the fundamental unreliability of autobiography and the elusiveness of language.

While *Everybody's Autobiography* begins by implicitly acknowledging its link to *The Autobiography*, particularly through an emphasis on their shared interest in the implications of traditional autobiographical form, it ends by very explicitly positioning itself in relation to its predecessor: "I would simply say what was happening [in *Everybody's Autobiography*] which is what is narration....And now I almost think I have the first autobiography was not that, it was a description and a creation of something that having happened was in a way happening not again but as it had been which is history which is newspaper which is illustration but is not a simple narrative of what is happening not as if it had happened not as if it is happening but as if it is existing simply that thing. And now in this book I have done it if I have done it."[46] This passage reflects Stein's long-standing commitment to undermining generic conventions, as is evidenced by her unusual categorical conflations (autobiography/history/newspaper/illustration) as well as her more conventional combination of description and creation. Yet she is also drawing a broad *formal* distinction between the two works in question. Literal content does not enter into this discussion at all. Instead, she wants to focus attention on the way that any given experience is transcribed in language.

Interestingly, some critics dismiss the issue of style in relation to Stein's prose autobiographies, in no small part because Stein herself occasionally differentiated them from her other work. For example, Ulla Dydo takes up the distinction Stein made, in correspondence with her agent, between her "audience writing" and her "real kind of books." Dydo, in order to characterize the difference between *The Autobiography of Alice B. Toklas* and *Stanzas in Meditation*, defines the latter category, and by extension the *Stanzas*, as "a literature of word compositions rather than a literature of subject matter." Her intention, however, is not simply to examine the formal elements of Stein's poetry, so the subject matter/formal compositions distinction must be slightly modified: "Not that the compositions lacked subject matter, but Stein believed that subject matter had no existence apart from its shape in compositions."[47] By suggesting that the complex interrelation of subject and form is relevant only in Stein's "compositions," Dydo is essentially erasing the boundaries that she claims distinguish the "real" works while at the same time attempting to maintain the integrity of the other category, "audience writing."[48]

I do not want to diminish the difference between Stein's different modes of writing, nor dismiss categories that she herself once employed, but, as her formal declaration at the end of *Everybody's Autobiography* demonstrates, Stein is evidently concerned with the "shape" of both these autobiographies. In fact, as Dydo herself notes, the difficult relation between audience and author "worried" Stein for the rest of her career and did much to shape her theories about narrative and writing.[49] Stein concludes her lecture "Poetry and Grammar" by saying, "I am working at [narrative] and what will it do this I do not know but I hope that I will know."[50] She then went on, after preparing her other talks for the American tour, to write four more addresses for the University of Chicago on the subject of narration.

Ten years later, in the "Transatlantic Interview," Stein reflects on these concerns: "The bulk of my work since [the mid-1930s] has been largely narration. I think *Paris France* and *Wars I Have Seen* are the most successful."[51] This quotation demonstrates not only the changing nature of Stein's narrative theories, which were still developing ten years after the *Lectures*, but also the importance of autobiographical works to her formal development.[52] Consequently, I agree with Dydo's claim that Stein sees form and content as inextricably linked, but I would apply this claim to all of her work, even the so-called audience writing. Moreover, in *Everybody's Autobiography*, Stein characterizes the success of her work specifically in terms of its ability to approach theoretical difficulties in a formally innovative way, which means, in this case, that she would like to readdress her theories of identity and language but avoid wholly replicating either the form or the ideological content of her previous works.

In order to examine Stein's complex position in this text, I begin with what, in a traditional autobiography, might have been one of its most emotionally charged moments: Stein's return to the site of her old family home in East Oakland, California. After summing up the entire trip in one sentence, Stein moves on to discuss a nameless interlocutor who had asked her whether or not she found America changed. In a typical move, she does not choose to speak directly about her old neighborhood, or even the landscape more generally, but instead focuses on larger theoretical issues: "Of course it had not changed what could it change to. The only thing that makes identity possible is no change but nevertheless there is no identity nobody really thinks they are the same as they remember."[53] For Stein, true identity is always an impossibility because it relies on the presumption of a static and knowable past that can be used as the basis for identity claims, a presumption that discounts the partial knowledge of an entity engaged in acts of definition and, in this particular case, the continuing existence of the thing being defined. Thus, any given designation is doubly incomplete because, even in the very moment of formulating an identity, a new being will have already emerged. From this perspective, "America" either represents a fixed and knowable concept that, by definition, cannot change, or it is simply an empty signifier that can potentially take on new meanings with each articulation. In either case, "America" does not ever fully encompass its object, leaving traditional communication systems with only one stable element: the materiality of the words themselves. As a result, the concrete signifier can be seen throughout Stein's text as a static object epistemologically unsuited to its fluid environment and as a larger symbol of linguistic insufficiency.[54]

This logical difficulty at the core of representation, an idea Stein had been playing with in different forms throughout her career, begins to raise serious concerns for her when, following the publication of *The Autobiography*, she becomes an object of media scrutiny. Entertainment marketers, including her own publicists, begin creating different and often competing versions of "Gertrude Stein" as they promote her upcoming lecture tour. Their threat is symbolized by the electric sign Stein encounters shortly after arriving in America: "It said Gertrude Stein has come and that was upsetting. . . . it does give me a little shock of recognition and nonrecognition. It is one of the things most worrying in the subject of identity."[55] Given Stein's theories of signification, this sign represents more than simply the publicists' ability to create and circulate images independently of her. The words themselves symbolize the media's need for a fixed and knowable "Gertrude Stein" that can be marketed to the reading public. As such, her name and likeness are being used to solidify a limited, and limiting, public identity that stands in direct opposition to the metaphysically unrepresentable person she had been attempting to fashion in her work.

Additionally, Stein's newfound audience begins to complicate her writing process, a situation that, interestingly, she also characterizes in terms of her sense of self: "When [the outside world] does put a value on you then it gets inside or rather if the outside puts a value on you then all your inside gets to be outside."[56] On the one hand, Stein fears that internalizing readers' impressions and expectations will inevitably modify her own self-conception, in effect allowing the "outside" to get "inside." Conversely, both her identity and the literary process that seems so central to it are now matters of concern for the general public, and thus are open to "outside" speculation and redefinition. Again, Stein's primary anxiety stems from the fact that she is losing control of her "self" amidst larger systems of public discourse, a situation she seems ill-equipped to deal with immediately following the publication of *The Autobiography*.

The point here is not just that external systems of representation constrain Stein, but that these systems have a particularly strong effect on her because she has theoretically renounced the ability to make accurate or enduring statements about her own identity. As such, she has no way of reclaiming the authority of self-representation without compromising her belief in a fluid self that exists beyond the "violence" of signification. Even autobiography does not offer an easy way out, as traditional forms of the genre simply reinforce the importance of public image management and its concomitant need for coherent and salable identities.

As the integrity and autonomy of Stein's "internal" world breaks down, she suffers from writer's block, one of the primary difficulties in *Everybody's Autobiography*.[57] Stein's loss of control also leads her to shun people who might influence either her public image or her writing. For example, Stein repeatedly rebuffs her agent's attempts to hire her a manager for the lecture tour, as she does not want "to go anywhere without...knowing where and doing there what anybody would want [her] to do there whether afterwards [she] wanted to or not." Eventually Stein fires him as a result of the ongoing dispute. Similarly, she mentions refusing to sign a contract promising another autobiography because she is unwilling to give up total creative control of her work. This dispute concludes with the blunt proclamation, "I would not sign a contract to do anything."[58] Stein's bravado seems slightly absurd, since we know that she did not single-handedly orchestrate her whole lecture tour, and she obviously did not refuse to write a second autobiography. Still, these gestures reinforce our sense of Stein as a woman struggling to maintain control over her life and writing.

And yet, even though Stein's pretense of authority does seem to return some semblance of the control she has lost, it does not by itself provide her text with the innovative perspective that would justify its creation. As noted above, Stein is not simply interested in presenting solutions to the problems she introduces in her text, but is equally concerned with how those solutions are incorporated into language itself. To understand one of the ways in which Stein attempts to formally address her difficulties, I would like to briefly examine the role of referentiality in *Everybody's Autobiography*, in part because it is one of the most commonly discussed features of Stein's work, and also because it is Dydo's primary point of distinction between "audience" and "real" writing.

As several of the quotations above suggest, representation in *Everybody's Autobiography* is a significantly more complex issue than it might appear at first glance. Nancy Blake provides a useful account of Stein's descriptive style in this book: "Stein banishes the adjective. She describes nothing. Or if she must do so, she will employ only the most banal of terms."[59] Such an approach is particularly striking given that the text is ostensibly an account of her first trip to America in thirty years. This is certainly not a typical "travel book," which David E. Johnson has called the form of "writing most preoccupied with sites and with...sight-seeing."[60] In fact, Stein spends more time cataloging the people and places she visits than she does describing them. Often, no physical descriptions are offered at all and, whenever something is described, Stein undercuts any distinctive details in the image.

For instance, early on in the autobiography, she begins a story about receiving a phone call from David Edstrom: "David Edstrom was the big Swede who was a sculptor and was thin when I first knew him and then enormously fat."[61] The only visual cues we receive relate to Edstrom's size and, without any further details, they do not even give us a clear picture of his physical dimensions. She also destabilizes the temporality of this description, which ultimately makes the reference significantly more obscure. First, Edstrom himself is not given a specific size at a particular moment in time but rather a range of sizes extending over years. Second, the authorial perspective complicates the sequence of events. Stein is speaking in the present, or at least the moment in which she is writing, but is reflecting back to a man she saw repeatedly in the past. Then she begins an anecdote from an indeterminate point during her trip to America, an altogether different moment in the past, which does not involve the sculptor's size in any way. In short, when the story begins, any direct reference to this man as another human body interacting with Stein has been stripped away and the reader is left with little more than the signifier "Edstrom" to mark the absence.[62]

This example is not intended to suggest that Stein discounts the importance of the human body. Stein's focus on Edstrom's stature serves to call attention to his form even as she disrupts its appearance in the text. Much as she challenges the signifying function of language, Stein refuses to reify the sculptor's mobile and changing body in order to fix his identity on the page. Moreover, she "remembers" him in the first place because "he used to complain so that I like everybody in character."[63] As such an attitude could potentially problematize her more recent theories of identity, Stein immediately dismisses this earlier position, claiming that character no longer "excites" her. Yet, again demonstrating her whimsical sensibility, she does not entirely refute this position and even implies that there may be some important truth in her earlier beliefs. She has simply chosen not to explore them anymore. So, while the repeated references to Edstrom's size might seem unrelated to a passing comment about Stein's earlier psychological theories, this juxtaposition serves to link the continuous development of the human body with both Stein's refusal to look for underlying identities and her own personal sense of play.

In addition to these bodily disruptions, Edstrom's appearance is further undermined by the overall pattern of repetition in the text. By the time he is described on page four of the book, Stein has already mentioned fourteen other individuals, not including herself, and she goes on to mention thirty-three different people in the first seven pages. Many critics have argued, with respect to *The Autobiography*, that Stein's repetitive use of proper names is designed to make her seem more prominent, "the focus of a coterie of luminaries."[64] In *Everybody's Autobiography*, the sheer number of people and the seeming lack of selectivity about who is included make individuation difficult. Unlike in *The Autobiography*, where insignificant characters are generally not given proper names, Stein adds to the sense of displacement in this text by identifying people much less systematically. After arriving at Bryn Mawr, for instance, she sums up the entire faculty by saying, "The male professors were bearded, one of them promised me a photograph."[65] Conversely, she spends a great deal of time in the early chapters detailing each of a long succession of servants that have worked for her, some of whom are named and some of whom are not. When coupled with the limited focus on individual characters and the temporal shifts that disrupt both chronology and continuity, many characters in the book, famous or not, appear much like David Edstrom, contextually detached and physically displaced.[66]

This flow of names through Stein's text can certainly be read as a reflection of her experiences on the lecture tour. She spent over six months traveling around America, all the while giving talks, attending dinners, and visiting with friends and strangers. Yet Stein suggests that the strange combination of connection and isolation she feels on her trip also results from the current state of the world: "The earth is all covered over with everyone there is really no relation between anyone and so if this *Everybody's Autobiography* is to be the Autobiography of everyone it is not to be of any connection between anyone and anyone because now there is none."[67] While the paradox of universal isolation is itself a fairly common modernist conception, Stein, unlike some other writers at the time, explicitly connects this idea to her aesthetic project. Such a condition, she claims, undermines traditional narrative strategies and fundamentally alters the focus of her work.

Yet even as Stein touts a radical shift in autobiographical writing and works to deny the reader any easy sense of "immersion" in the text, it is not entirely accurate to say that she rejects the referential function of language in this book. Many of the details that she gives are verifiable and thus would seem to point to a world outside of the text. David Edstrom is indeed a sculptor that Stein knew, and she did see him while in the United States. Moreover, Stein's work creates the appearance of a traditional, and thus supposedly referential, autobiography. The whole book is structured around her trip to America, an account that moves chronologically from "Chapter 1: What Happened after the Autobiography of Alice B. Toklas" through "Chapter 4: America" to "Chapter 5: Back Again," and though, as we have seen, her anecdotal accounts frequently create chronological ruptures in the text, the overall pattern of narration does roughly follow a chronological sequence.[68]

Finally, Stein creates the impression of a direct and coherent autobiographical account by employing a conversational style. Through simple language and a recurrent emphasis on the narrator in the process of speaking, Stein sets up this text like a conversation, situated in the present tense, between narrator and reader.[69] For example, she initially "remembers" Edstrom's story because of an anecdote about wooden umbrellas and disrupts her reminiscing to inform the reader that it "does remind me of David Edstrom but I have been reminded of him after I was reminded of Dashiell Hammett."[70] She then goes on to recount these anecdotes in the specified order, faithful to both her audience and a coherent, if not altogether temporal, arrangement.

Yet even this small degree of organization does not exist entirely without complications. While such simple language and a pattern of direct address might seem to give the reader a stable position in the present tense moment of the text, Stein never particularizes the location of this moment, nor does she directly attribute any actual presence to her narrative voice. As such, the "continuous present" operates not as a specific site within the text from which she can deploy her anecdotes, but rather as an elusive counterpoint that disrupts the temporal continuity of the past tense narrative and enhances the reader's alienation from the bulk of the narration. Moreover, the specific temporal location of the present tense is itself continuously changing with the passage of time, which only complicates the intricate tapestry of events that unfold throughout the text.

In short, a deliberate slippage occurs, as Stein employs conventions that suggest her book is a straightforward transcription of events while she simultaneously alienates readers by stripping words of context, specificity, and, to a certain extent, progression.[71] By embodying this contradiction in the very form of her text, Stein draws attention to both the words themselves and readers' assumptions about the referential function of language. Much like the seemingly absurd "America" quip discussed previously, Stein's formal presentation of people and events does not convey details so much as it foregrounds the ways in which language can fail to transmit conventional meanings.

I have elaborated Stein's approach to representation in part to bolster my previous claim that Stein, even in her "audience writing," is always concerned with the interplay of form and meaning. I have also chosen to emphasize the particular difficulties raised by her formal play in order to place these strategies within a larger pattern of contradictions that emerge throughout the text. Stein has, after all, written an autobiography in part to declare that the genre, as it has traditionally been conceived, is logically incoherent.

Such an approach characterizes Stein's attitude toward gender in the text as well. She guides the reader through the narrative as a disembodied voice, largely stripped of gender associations. Linda Wagner-Martin, in a discussion of Stein as a Jewish writer, contextualizes this strategy in terms of modernist authorship more generally: "The modernist writer aimed to be universal, above political alliances, washed clean in the purity of serious and innovative aesthetics, and Gertrude certainly wanted to play that game well. She would have gained nothing in high modernist Paris by describing herself as a Jewish American lesbian."[72] The irony, then, is that Stein, by stripping her narrator of overt gender markers throughout much of the text, actually aligns herself with a high modernist voice that was often implicitly figured as *male*, a gender association Stein emphasized throughout much of her career. G. F. Mitrano, for instance, claims that, during her lectures, "Stein played up her mannishness: her strong, austere features framed by her cropped hair unmistakably bespoke a command for the masculine position. Robed in a timeless loose silk tunic made for the occasion, she was in many ways the incarnation of a historical stereotype." In support of this claim, Mitrano notes the degree to which accounts of Stein's lectures emphasized her "masculine countenance," often over the content of the speeches themselves.[73]

This stance ironically led Stein to denounce the importance of gender throughout much of her work in the 1930s. In *The Geographical History,* she aligns gender with "identity" and explicitly dismisses it: "I think nothing about men and women because that has nothing to do with anything."[74] Similarly, in *The Autobiography,* Stein explains to an old friend that it is not "that she at all minds the cause of women or any other cause but it does not happen to be her business."[75]

Yet, particularly in *Everybody's Autobiography*, Stein acknowledges that she can escape neither identity nor the larger social structures connected with it. Accordingly, she does occasionally use her male-sanctioned high modernist voice to draw attention to her status as a female writer and she champions that position, at least in the abstract. In the opening pages of *Everybody's Autobiography*, for instance, Stein asks Dashiell Hammett why men in the nineteenth century could invent "a great number of men" while women only wrote about themselves, but in the twentieth century male writers could only write about themselves. Hammett replies, "In the nineteenth century men were confident, the women were not but in the twentieth century the men have no confidence and so they have to make themselves as you say more beautiful more intriguing more everything and they cannot make any other man because they have to hold on to themselves not having any confidence."[76] The unspoken point of this exchange is, of course, that confident women were creating the most imaginative literature in the twentieth century, a point that Stein made even more forcefully in *The Geographical History*: "In this epoch the only real literary thinking has been done by a woman."[77] Yet the importance of this work is predicated on women's ability to step outside of their own identities. In short, Stein implicitly acknowledges the challenges women face and elevates their role as authors even as she advocates transcending gender in a way that, ironically, aligns her with a male perspective.

In addition to gender and genre, Stein, alongside what are essentially a series of logical critiques of traditional linguistic systems, goes so far as to problematize the value of logic itself. She repeatedly suggests that causation is, if not impossible to trace, at least something far too complex for direct explanation. Lightning, with its connotations of ephemerality and apparent arbitrariness, becomes her symbol of the incomprehensible present moment. As Stein explains early in the text, "Lightning never strikes twice in the same place and that is because the particular combination that makes lightning come there has so many things make it that all those things are not likely to come together again." Following the logic of this statement, Stein frequently refuses to provide causal connections and often raises issues only to deny the reader any direct explanation. Just prior to her statement about lightning, she wonders why one of her friends became a painter and simply concludes, "There is no reason not and there is no reason to." She then goes on to claim that "generally speaking you have to be small" in physical size to be a painter, a claim that she does not attempt to justify or explain in any way.[78]

This denial, or perhaps more properly, this refusal of causation also leads Stein to dismiss the need for sequential order. My earlier discussion of representation reveals some of the ways she undercuts progression and causation in her anecdotal accounts of America.[79] Stein is, however, at several points in the text, even more direct in her insistence on disrupting sequence. In what is perhaps one of the most famous passages from *Everybody's Autobiography,* she claims that, when counting, "you should never say three or even two, you should keep strictly on a basis of one" and always count "one one one."[80] Stein's method of counting is analogous to her sense of temporality in the text, which is rooted in the idea that neither memory nor theories of cause and effect are sufficient to establish a connection between the present and other points in the past. Hence, each moment must ultimately be seen as a discrete point that is, in some sense, unrelated to any other instant in time.

This interpretation also reveals another potential contradiction with Stein's sense of time. If the current moment is unconnected to any previous point, then each instant is not only unique but also, in theory, equivalent to any other. So each new moment must repeatedly be signified with the same term "one," rather than a random array of numbers.

On one level, then, all of these various elements, including temporality, causation, sequence, representation, and even Stein's literal dismissal of authority help to create a sense of unlimited freedom in the textual space of *Everybody's Autobiography.* Yet, on another level, this supposed openness is beset by ironies and contradictions that only proliferate as the narrative progresses. Stein, for instance, needs to assert her own authority in order to denounce the influence of outside forces and thus must always reintroduce a delimiting power dynamic into the textual space. She must also erect a logical framework and marshal coherent, if often roundabout, arguments for establishing an alogical "narrative" that emphasizes the slipperiness of language itself. Finally, the arbitrary sense of time exists in relation to a series of deliberately placed organizational cues and the ultimately repetitive and predictable movement of the present, that is, Stein's "one one one."

In this web of contradictions and logical puzzles, "Gertrude Stein" becomes nearly impossible to locate throughout *Everybody's Autobiography.* She comes to exist as nothing more than a textual voice reverberating through past events reconstituted in a present moment that escapes definition or explanation. Amidst such contradictory significations, the narrator becomes a philosopher of riddles and offhand statements that seem to necessitate no proof because they are made without regard for causation, even as they collectively allude to an underlying logic that both justifies and threatens to undermine the whole project. Ultimately, it is an identity that is both fixed in language but never stable or definable, a linguistic flash of lightning that always exists in the present tense and is never logically bound by any accumulating "inside." In this way, Stein is able to dismiss the threat an audience poses to her creative "inside" because she has undermined the processes of unproblematically representing an historical self and theoretically evacuated, without altogether eliminating, the space where such a self may have existed.

The sense of ambivalence that comes to dominate *Everybody's Autobiography* creates a narrative full of recognizable words, arguments, and situations that somehow seem to deny readers their "real" meaning.[81] This difficult position has many metaphorical applications to the narrative, as Stein, who claims to be already in the midst of an identity crisis created by her new celebrity persona, finds herself in a country that is both familiar and radically different from anything she has ever seen before. Stein's approach is also a formal methodology, one designed to depict events as things "existing" and not "as they had been which is history." She does this both literally with an ambivalent narrative voice that presses relentlessly into the present and figuratively by utilizing contradictions that never seem to settle on the page. Trapped in a media environment where even the denial of autobiographical identity can be seen as an intervention in celebrity discourse, Stein attempts to confound the all-consuming logic of this system by incorporating both poles at the same time. In effect, Stein attempts to simultaneously adopt the role of avant-garde writer and popular author by creating a book that is both easy and difficult, equal parts celebrity autobiography, philosophical meditation, and formal language experiment.

In this way, Stein confounds not only those readers who would quickly relegate her to one side of the "great divide" but also those who might too easily dismiss the material and theoretical challenges she faces. Stein's textual strategies certainly afford her enough freedom to write this second autobiography, but they also leave her perpetually trapped between two poles in the literary marketplace. As a result, despite Stein's characteristically even tone, this book is significantly darker than her first autobiography. She repeatedly discusses the necessity of death and the inevitable downfall of civilizations. She talks, at some length, about several unsolved murders. She even brings up her estranged brother Leo, whom she had largely ignored in *The Autobiography.*

The ending of the book is also strikingly ambivalent. After traveling to England for a ballet adaptation of Stein's play *They Must. Be Wedded. To Their Wife.*, another triumph for the author, Stein and Toklas return to Paris, now a depressing city preoccupied with the possibility of war. On the flight home, Stein is overcome with fear at the sight of a mysterious fog that seems to run down the middle of the English Channel. Then, without any further discussion of either her fear or the fog, the plane lands and the book closes on a note of resigned affirmation: "Perhaps I am not I even if my little dog knows me but anyway I like what I have and now it is today."[82]

The fear and uncertainty that linger at the edges of Stein's otherwise playful autobiography, apparent in this last instance as she travels between a site of public acceptance and the private residence where her experimental texts are created, have received little critical attention, despite the fact that they recur in other works during the 1930s. As we have seen, one of Stein's most forceful theoretical meditations from this period, and not surprisingly the book she completed just prior to writing her second autobiography, *The Geographical History of America*, has a similarly ambivalent conclusion. In this work, Stein has a clear preference between the two poles, but knows that she can never escape entirely into the placid existence of the human mind.

Still, Stein is not simply the victim of her own ambivalent formulations as she manages to cultivate her multifaceted persona through the oppositions she explores. Kirk Curnutt, in an analysis of the trope of authenticity in *Everybody's Autobiography,* demonstrates how Stein feigns ignorance of common publicity techniques, as when she has a photographer define the term "layout," in order to depict herself as free from market influence.[83] I would add that Stein adopts a similar naive pose to insulate herself from charges of being a pretentious highbrow author, a very real danger for her when she first arrived in the United States. The wariness with which many approached Stein for the first time is evident in newspaper reports about her from the early days of the tour. For instance, Lansing Warren, who interviewed her for the *New York Times Magazine* shortly before she left for the United States, begins his piece by emphasizing popular preconceptions of the author. He refers to her repeatedly as a "Grecian sibyl" and discusses his own hesitancy to visit another "eccentric studio" typical of "Parisian bohemian life." His apprehensions, however, quickly fade in front of the "quiet comfort, neatness, and order" of her studio and the charms of the woman herself.[84] In *Everybody's Autobiography*, Stein attempts to cultivate the same sense of openness by blithely ignoring social customs that would set her apart from others and refusing to distinguish among the various people she encounters on her travels, whether they are professors or mechanics or police officers. She even requests to ride up front with the chauffeurs so that they can talk along the way.[85]

In short, Stein has constructed a persona that both insulates her from the corruption of crass materialism and distances her from the rarefied airs of the avant-garde. It is a complex construction that allows her to become, as Laurel Bollinger says, "the dual figure who writes the successful novel and also the solitary genius who writes the experiments in language. She need not choose one over the other."[86] Of course, as Stein reveals indirectly throughout her text, it is not always an easy position and it certainly comes with its own set of costs.

Nonetheless, it is her effort to write these contradictory notions of authorship into the form of an autobiography that supposedly gives her the inspiration to escape her writer's block and craft a sequel to *The Autobiography*. The threat of redundancy looms large over this book, in part because its subject matter, the lecture tour, is dependent on the popularity generated by her previous book and in part because she is elaborating on themes found in her last text. Yet, Stein's formal and theoretical innovations lead her to create a new textual space that embodies the seemingly irresolvable tensions generated by the publication of *The Autobiography* and draws attention, again and again, to the philosophical difficulties underlying conventional modes of representation.

Given this reading of the text, I would like to return one last time to the title and view it as equally bound up in the larger pattern of contradictions that structure this narration. "Everybody's Autobiography" is a productive disruption under which the text as a whole operates. It immediately raises a wide range of methodological issues that perhaps do not exist at all and, in its compelling refusal of resolution, helps to unify a work that rejects stasis on literal, narrative, and theoretical levels. It also draws attention to issues of image, power, and agency at the beginning of a text that relentlessly interrogates autobiography as a way of both reclaiming the authority of self-representation and transcending the need for it. Lastly, it represents Stein's attempt to create a new textual form, one that seems familiar and accessible, but is simultaneously a critique of the assumptions inherent in that familiarity. According to this reading, Stein's text does, after all, rely on the apparent difficulty of its title and, more particularly, the specifically oppositional form that these difficulties can take. Yet, before subsuming *Everybody's Autobiography* entirely into larger patterns in Stein's oeuvre or even just into the binary arrangements present in much of her work, I would also like to suggest that it is Stein's uncompromising use of contradiction that sets this text apart from the others and ultimately allows her to find a new space for writing in an environment that had suddenly embraced and also strangely impeded her production of complex "literary" texts.

PART III

The Crack-Up of F. Scott Fitzgerald

F. Scott Fitzgerald and His Critics

F. Scott Fitzgerald's short autobiographical sketch, "The Crack-Up," first appeared in the February 1936 issue of *Esquire* without advance publicity of any kind.[1] This silence is surprising in part because of the sensational nature of Fitzgerald's piece, which explores his psychological state in the period leading up to and immediately following what he obscurely refers to as a collapse of his "nervous reflexes."[2] The lack of publicity is also perplexing because Arnold Gingrich, the editor of *Esquire*, frequently used controversy to stimulate magazine sales. In one instance, he ran an announcement informing readers that Langston Hughes had submitted a short story called "A Good Job Done." The announcement explains that this piece is about a wealthy white man named Mr. Lloyd who falls in love with "one of these golden browns," which leads to a confrontation between Mr. Lloyd and "a tall black good looking guy." Just in case the inflammatory nature of racial conflict and potential miscegenation might be lost on some readers, Gingrich adds, "This is the kind of story that no commercial magazine would touch with a ten foot pole."[3] He then asks the largely affluent white male readership of *Esquire* to vote on whether or not such a work should be published.[4] Confrontational responses to this query appeared in the magazine for the next three months until the story was finally published in April 1934.[5]

Despite this flair for the sensational, Gingrich evidently did not see much commercial value in Fitzgerald's revelations. After having run six largely unremarkable and, more importantly, unremarked pieces by Fitzgerald over the previous two years, including two articles that offered fragmented and impressionistic details of his life with Zelda,[6] Gingrich explained to readers, "We thought the whole idea of a series of self-revelatory sketches was lacking in general interest."[7] In private correspondence, he was much more critical of Fitzgerald's public reputation, claiming that "at [the time of publishing "The Crack-Up"], sixteen years after [Fitzgerald's] fame, a lot of people thought he was dead."[8]

In spite of this apparent lack of interest in Fitzgerald's work, the response to his "Crack-Up" pieces was immediate and passionate. Fitzgerald was flooded with correspondence from old friends, writers, and even complete strangers, letters that covered a range of emotions from genuine sympathy to thinly veiled contempt.[9] *Esquire,* which had encouraged reader participation from the very first issue, was also inundated with responses. In the June 1936 issue, Gingrich recanted his initial skepticism about the articles and admitted, "Seldom has as much interest been aroused by anything printed in our pages."[10] Moreover, the discussion was not limited simply to Fitzgerald's acquaintances or readers of the magazine. Cultural critics and journalists from around the country remarked on the pieces, both publicly and privately. Perhaps the most incisive commentary came from E. B. White, who, in the *New Yorker*'s "Talk of the Town" column, glossed Fitzgerald's first piece as "picturesque despondency" and then placed it in the context of *Esquire*'s liquor, clothing, and automobile ads, all of which, White claimed, convey the message that "now if ever in the history of the world a man should be at peace in body and spirit."[11]

In addition to all of the attention these pieces received during Fitzgerald's lifetime, and no doubt as a direct result of it, they have also attracted a significant amount of attention from scholars. Since one of my concerns will be the relationship between Fitzgerald's work, particularly the "Crack-Up" essays, and public perceptions of them, I would like to begin by briefly outlining several major critical approaches to these pieces. This examination should help to make clear exactly where my own reassessment is positioned in relation to other scholarship in the field, and it will also establish several of the larger themes that will be important in my analysis.

Immediately after Fitzgerald's death in December 1940, critics were primarily concerned with reassessing his life and work. Following the 1945 publication of *The Crack-Up,* a collection of Fitzgerald's articles, select correspondence, and various entries from his notebooks edited by Edmund Wilson, critics primarily focused on how these autobiographical pieces could be fit into the larger narratives that were being constructed around the author. One of the most popular versions of Fitzgerald's story, a story that still circulates in various forms today, heralded him as a tragic hero. It goes something like this: Fitzgerald's first book, *This Side of Paradise,* published in 1920, catapulted him to fame as the voice of a younger generation disillusioned by the war and distanced from the seemingly outdated values of their parents. After several collections of short stories and another novel, Fitzgerald reached his artistic peak in 1925 with *The Great Gatsby*. After this point, life became increasingly difficult, as his nearly constant drinking grew more and more debilitating, his relationship with his wife Zelda worsened, and he was forced to pump out artistically worthless short stories to pay bills. Zelda's first hospitalization in 1930, for what was later diagnosed as schizophrenia, marked the end of Fitzgerald's golden years and the beginning of the final decade of his life, years marred by alcoholism, depression, and poverty.

In 1934, nine years after the appearance of *The Great Gatsby*, Fitzgerald finally published his fourth novel, *Tender Is the Night*. The novel had three printings, sold roughly 15,000 copies, and was not poorly reviewed by critics, but it was neither the critical darling nor the runaway success that the author needed to change his emotional and economic condition. Ultimately, he made only about $5,000 from *Tender Is the Night*, not nearly enough to pay back the debts he had accrued with his publishing house (Scribner's), his publisher (Max Perkins), his agent (Harold Ober), the many clinics that treated Zelda throughout the 1930s, the various people and institutions that took care of his daughter Scottie, and his mother. An overwhelming sense of failure sent Fitzgerald into an alcoholic depression for the next two years that culminated with the publication of "The Crack-Up" in February 1936. These essays marked a turning point, an admission of his failure and subsequent breakdown that allowed him to recommit himself to the craft of writing. He moved to Hollywood in 1937 and got a steady job as a scriptwriter for MGM. He sobered up, paid back some of his debts, got involved in a serious relationship with British columnist Sheilah Graham, and finally began work on a new novel about Hollywood, a book that he thought would be the crowning achievement of his career. Tragically, his magnificent comeback was cut short by the stroke that took his life in December 1940.

Perhaps the most famous piece written on Fitzgerald in the first phase of his critical reassessment, Lionel Trilling's "F. Scott Fitzgerald," supports precisely such a reading of the "Crack-Up" articles and of Fitzgerald's later years more generally.[12] Trilling claims that Fitzgerald's confessions reveal his "heroic awareness" of both "the lost and the might-have-been" as well as the "exemplary role" that he might strive to fulfill during what would turn out to be the last years of his life. In this view, the sheer spectacle of the writer's failures (Trilling avoids any direct reference to alcoholism) could only serve "to augment the moral force of the poise and fortitude which marked Fitzgerald's mind in the few recovered years that were left to him."[13] Trilling then goes on to systematically dismantle some of the most prevalent criticisms of Fitzgerald's writing, setting up his final effusive praise for *The Great Gatsby*, presumably the culmination of Fitzgerald's career and a lasting monument to his talent.

The appeal of this larger story seems obvious: spectacular success, a decadent fall, the triumphant return, which is engineered primarily through the exercise of an indomitable individual will,[14] and the final tragic death, a stroke that could be seen as just one more lingering punishment for, and a warning against, years of alcoholic waste. Such an arc makes for a good story, and it accords closely with a major historical paradigm frequently applied to the 1920s and 1930s. Marc Dolan, in *Modern Lives,* glosses this pattern as youthful exuberance, narcissistic decline, bored decadence, and finally the "nervous collapse" that was the Great Depression, a pattern that, not so coincidentally, he sees running through many of Fitzgerald's autobiographical pieces in the 1930s.[15]

As appealing as this dramatic and relatively linear narrative is, it has been resisted by many critics and biographers who have attempted to cull truth from the legend, primarily by showing the failures of Fitzgerald's later years alongside his successes.[16] For instance, after writing the "Crack-Up" essays in the winter of 1935, Fitzgerald's life remained relatively unchanged for over a year, as he continued to drink and actively resisted his agent's suggestions that he look for steady work in Hollywood. Then, after he finally signed a contract with MGM in July of 1937, he worked for eighteen months and received only one on-screen credit for his writing. His contract was not renewed at the end of 1938. Furthermore, Fitzgerald's "poise and fortitude" did fail him from time to time during his final years and he resorted to drinking on several occasions, often with disastrous consequences.[17]

These details, however, only appeared tangentially in the years immediately after Fitzgerald's death, when most critics took to debating his literary merit. William Troy, speaking of Fitzgerald's omissions from the "Crack-Up" essays, said, "In the etiology of the FSF case, as the psychologists would say, the roots run much deeper, and nobody cares to disturb them much at this early date."[18] Alfred Kazin pushes the issue further by suggesting that Fitzgerald employed the form of the guilty confession to emphasize his emotional revelation and draw attention away from the larger issues underlying his breakdown. Yet Kazin does not dwell on Fitzgerald's problems in the article, nor does he challenge the larger narrative of redemption that began to surround Fitzgerald during the 1940s. When discussing the "Crack-Up" essays, he comes to much the same conclusion as Trilling, claiming that these pieces mark the point at which "he who had never given himself freely to art now did."[19]

It was not until after the publication of Schulberg's *The Disenchanted* in 1950 and the first comprehensive biography of Fitzgerald, Arthur Mizener's *The Far Side of Paradise* in 1951, that the darker elements of Fitzgerald's final years began to appear regularly next to his successes, forcing many critics to reassess more sanguine readings of the "Crack-Up" essays. Increasingly during the 1950s and 1960s, these pieces came to be characterized as just another failed commitment from Fitzgerald's depression years.[20] Novelist Wright Morris, writing in 1958, says that, while Fitzgerald might have dedicated himself to his craft at the end of "Handle with Care," he ultimately "had been suckled too long on the sweet pap of life, and the incomparable milk of wonder, to be more than a writer in name only, resigned to the fact."[21] Similarly, James Miller, in his 1964 book exploring the craft of Fitzgerald's writing, claims that the "Crack-Up" essays must be seen as "embarrassing because [Fitzgerald] is obviously still keenly involved in a losing emotional struggle to become cured."[22]

For my purposes, the most interesting facet of this wide body of criticism is that it presents only one very literal reading of Fitzgerald's "Crack-Up" essays. Despite otherwise wide discrepancies in opinion, tone, and philosophical orientation, every one of these critics reads these pieces as a personal revelation of failure and a public declaration of change. Such uniformity of opinion might seem less surprising given that much of this work attempts to understand Fitzgerald's writing in relation to the biographical details of his life. Yet, even on the biographical terms in which most of these criticisms operate, there is ample evidence to suggest that Fitzgerald did not envision the essays as a straightforward confessional narrative.

In his own ledger, which lists both published writings, organized by year of publication, and the amount Fitzgerald was paid for each piece, he listed the "Crack-Up" essays under the heading of "Biography." Similarly, Arnold Gingrich notes that " 'sketches' was the [term] Scott always used to refer to such things as the now-famous Crack-Up series of 1936."[23] In his ledger, Fitzgerald employed the term "sketches," as opposed to stories or articles, to refer to pieces that outlined a specific type of person. Zelda, for instance, did a series of articles for *College Humor* magazine in 1929 that described different types of women, such as the "Poor Working Girl" or the "Girl with Talent." Fitzgerald listed these in his ledger under the heading

"Zelda's sketches." This label suggests that, while the "Crack-Up" essays might certainly have come out of his own personal experience and employed details from his life, he did not necessarily see them as a pure revelation of his character or as a simple transcription of his desires.

Moreover, the assumption that the Crack-Up articles were conceived as a declaration of action—that is, as a recommitment to writing serious literature—is belied by the very process of their construction. Fitzgerald wrote the first article at least a month before the second two, and, early on in "The Crack-Up," he dismisses the idea of extending his discussion further, saying, "What was to be done about [the crack-up] will have to rest in what used to be called the 'womb of time.' "[24] Moreover, Fitzgerald immediately denied in personal correspondence that these pieces reflected a major breakdown,[25] and, as soon as they began to receive attention, he approached *The Saturday Evening Post*, who paid contributors significantly more than *Esquire*, about doing a similar series for them.[26]

Fitzgerald's desire to spin his series off into a larger body of work was in no way unusual for him or for other writers in the 1930s, a time when editorial budgets were decreasing and a series of stories could guarantee a paycheck from month to month. These projects also created an extra source of income, as the stories could easily be put together and published in a collection. Between 1931 and 1932 alone, seven new series of short stories appeared in *The Saturday Evening Post* and several long-running audience favorites began showing up with greater frequency.[27] Fitzgerald himself had attempted to spin off both articles[28] and stories[29] into longer sequences, and often toyed with the idea of putting out more collections of his work. In March 1936, he even suggested grouping some of his autobiographical pieces into a collection to capitalize on interest in "The Crack-Up."[30] None of this historical information is meant to suggest that Fitzgerald was not emotionally invested in his essays, or that they did not reflect some aspect of his personal experience. Yet his casual treatment of these pieces and his willingness to revisit the grounds of what would seem to be a personal tragedy for money and public visibility clearly undermine the image of a writer recommitting to some set of pure artistic values.

Contemporary autobiographical critics in the United States, following the poststructural turn of the late 1960s, would seem to agree with Fitzgerald and largely ignore the biographical impetus of the early critical studies. Instead, these critics see autobiography as a socially constructed genre that deploys recognizable conventions to order the chaos of human experience. As a result, more recent studies of the "Crack-Up" essays tend to examine the rhetorical conventions employed by both Fitzgerald and the author persona that these pieces create. The relationship between author and text, along with the whole host of theoretical issues that positing such a relationship entails, has largely been left for biographers and literary historians.

Despite a thorough theoretical critique of previous approaches to the "Crack-Up" essays and a steadily increasing body of historical analysis detailing Fitzgerald's complex attitudes toward his writing, many contemporary critics draw similar conclusions about these pieces and thereby reinforce traditional understandings of Fitzgerald's life and work. A. Banerjee's performative reading of the "Crack-Up" essays, for instance, might differ in tone and theoretical perspective from Trilling's early homage, but the underlying assessment of Fitzgerald's life remains fundamentally unchanged.[31] Banerjee says, "Fitzgerald underwent a chastening experience [writing the Crack-Up articles] in the sense that he was able to analyse his past as a writer in the context of the demands of the present. He came to realize that he would have to change according to the changing circumstances of his life."[32] Here, the impetus for change and the vision of life on which it is based emerge in the process of writing rather than simply appearing in print as a fully formed product of consciousness. Moreover, Fitzgerald's supposed goal is characterized as a fluid target perpetually re-created in response to changing material conditions, not as a static ideal that would function as a beacon in the final years of his life. Both Trilling's and Banerjee's essays, however, ultimately work to perpetuate a larger vision of Fitzgerald's life that accords quite closely with the general narrative outlined above.

Kirk Curnutt takes a rhetorical approach to the "Crack-Up" essays but, again, his analysis begins with the assumption that Fitzgerald is employing the "clean break," a device predicated on an individual's supposedly autonomous "power of self-transformation."[33] Curnutt argues that the initial angry response to these articles stems from the fact that this device conflicts with the conventions of celebrity journalism, a form of writing requiring the construction of stable images that audiences can trust. As a critic focusing on the rhetorical strategies employed in the "Crack-Up" essays, his willingness to fashion an argument around a literal reading of the pieces seems surprising, especially since such a reading requires him to disregard many features of the text. He notes, for instance, that the narrator of "The Crack-Up" criticizes "Hollywood" endings, but he is subsequently forced to acknowledge that his own reading of the text, which concludes with the narrator asserting "total power of self-control and self-determination" through the clean break, posits an equally sensational conclusion. Fitzgerald only needs to commit to his new life and the previous failures will simply fall away. Curnutt dismisses the contradiction as "curious." He then writes off the stoic tone of the ending, which again directly contradicts a "triumphant" reading of the text and, Curnutt admits, was striking enough to draw commentary from the readers of *Esquire*.[34]

Similarly, Curnutt must dismiss the text's "relentless sarcasm" as an "emotional hedge" that allows Fitzgerald's persona to enact a search for authentic self-expression without having to commit to any of the modes he "briefly inhabit[s]." Thus, when the narrator spends too much time discussing contemporary affairs, he must parody "his own self-absorption by portraying himself [in parenthetical asides] as a pontificating public speaker who bores his audience." This reading is plausible up to a certain point. The narrator clearly wants to distance himself from the persona of a lecturer. Yet, from a rhetorical perspective, such a move does not simply clear the path for another voice, one that might be the "proper form of expression" that the narrator is seeking.[35] Instead, the denial itself, along with a noted proclivity for digressing into tedious lectures, must be seen as part of the larger figure being created in the "Crack-Up" essays.

In fact, Fitzgerald, who would later write his daughter that "he really just wanted to preach to people in some acceptable form," has constructed pieces that are, in many ways, quite different from conventional forms of celebrity confession. The narrator consistently refuses to reveal salacious details or assign blame for his breakdown. Moreover, he anticipates and actively resists potential autobiographical readings of the text. He claims, for instance, that alcoholism could not be the cause of his problems because he has not had a drink in six months. While this claim is not literally true, it does at the very least attempt to shift focus away from common associations with Fitzgerald's personal life and redirect attention to the specific claims being presented in the essays. To make this emphasis even more clear, the narrator repeatedly proposes various "theses" that he then explicitly tests against his own experiences.[36]

The organization of the pieces also enhances these more contemplative elements. The three articles as a whole are structured as a "brief history" that systematically explores the narrator's breakdown.[37] "The Crack-Up" begins with a few propositions and a brief history of the narrator's early life before moving on to draw a psychological portrait of him during the periods immediately preceding and following the crack-up. "Pasting It Together" picks up where the first essay left off, dealing primarily with a period of "vacuous quiet" following his immediate responses to the crack-up.[38] "Handle with Care" concludes the trilogy by explaining the narrator's supposed plan for moving forward in a world that now seems hostile and threatening to the author-figure.

It is important to make the systematic focus and argumentative nature of these pieces explicit in part because some critics, perhaps reflecting traditional literary disdain for such seemingly lowbrow, celebrity-driven texts, tend to dismiss precisely these elements of the "Crack-Up" essays. Milton Hindus, for instance, assumes these pieces are to be read entirely "as confession" and that they suffer because they are littered with so many "intellectual generalizations" that "rhetoric...seeps in whenever true feeling fails."[39] Alternatively, Henry Dan Piper disregards any structural trends that might emerge from the collective work by claiming that the latter two essays "covered pretty much the same ground as the first, but with more humor and detachment."[40]

By reading these pieces not simply as a sensationalized confession, but as an attempt to explore the psychological and theoretical undercurrents of a generalized nervous breakdown, what Marc Dolan calls the "quasi-Platonic standardized form of [the] 'crack-up'" begins to make more sense.[41] The narrator's distant tone and inclination for generalities are much better suited to reflection or interrogation than to tawdry revelation.[42] Similarly, his vague commentary on a past full of "too much anger and too many tears" should not necessarily call to mind the now quite detailed biographical picture we have of Fitzgerald in the 1930s.[43] Instead, it draws attention to the very absence of personal details and could be seen as a reference to any number of issues explicitly mentioned in the text, such as the narrator's anguish over America's rapidly changing cultural landscape or the sense of persecution he seems to feel in relation to his profession. While most critics read this phrase as an evasion on Fitzgerald's part, the sheer frequency with which it appears in discussions of these essays (James Mellow even uses it as a chapter title in his biography of Fitzgerald) indicates its suggestiveness, especially in light of the narrator's thesis, which he immediately reiterates after "too many tears" in the text. When it comes to breaking people down, "life has a varying offensive."[44]

The "Crack-Up" essays' lack of sensational self-revelation also allows them to de-emphasize the melodramatic emotional spectacle of the popular confession, even as they implicitly valorize public scrutiny of highly personal material. By rationalizing his "admissions," the narrator is able to adopt a hardened masculine pose, placing his own inner self as the object of an unflinching male gaze. He ultimately challenges stereotypical notions of stoic manhood, embodied in the essays by William Ernest Henley's paean to the "Unconquerable Soul." Such posturing seems designed to insulate Fitzgerald's work from charges of both effeminacy and triviality, and it reinforces the larger cultural and social criticisms in the essays by linking his very visible personal struggle with the larger conditions that engendered it.

Before elaborating further on the "Crack-Up" essays, I would like to briefly examine some of Fitzgerald's other autobiographical writings in order to provide a larger rhetorical context for my reading. I will begin by briefly surveying the young genius persona that appears in much of Fitzgerald's early publicity and then look at how this figure changed in the years leading up to the "Crack-Up" essays. This examination reveals that Fitzgerald's interrogation of struggle and failure is not so radical a departure from his other work as it might at first seem and, by itself, does not explain the animated responses that these pieces received from some readers. Instead, we must look at the gendered subtext of the narrator's specific attempts to negotiate with the difficulties of his profession and the particular form of masculine subjectivity he inhabits in order to understand why a predominantly middle-class white male readership and other white male professional writers would react so strongly to what most might normally have dismissed as celebrity fluff.

CHAPTER 5

On the Limitations of Image Management: The Long Shadow of "F. Scott Fitzgerald"

THE CONSTRUCTION OF A PERSONA (1920–1926)

Many critics have noted Fitzgerald's insistent attempts, particularly early in his career, to manage his image. A quick glance through any of his volumes of business correspondence will offer numerous examples of these efforts.[45] He was particularly concerned with production issues, making suggestions to his publishers about everything from layouts and fonts to bindings and the use of blurbs on dust jackets. He worried about the timing and manner of publication, including forms of serialization, the use of book clubs, and the size of his volumes. Finally, he suggested marketing tactics that would maximize the sale of his books, and he even wrote some of his own ad copy.[46] Beyond issues of production and distribution, Fitzgerald, especially early on in his career, appeared regularly in interviews, publicity blurbs, and personality sketches in major papers and magazines around the country. He also wrote numerous pieces about himself that were circulated, formally and informally, through the press.

Out of all of the public exposure Fitzgerald received during the early years of his career, several major themes emerge.[47] First, he is insistently associated with the "younger generation." This alignment stems, in part, from the enormous success of *This Side of Paradise,* a novel about the moral, social, and intellectual development of Amory Blaine, a Princeton student who is searching for the means to fulfill the rarefied destiny he is certain awaits him. The book, frequently noted for its unapologetic descriptions of the modern young women known as "flappers," received so much attention that its title was used in articles and interviews throughout the

1920s to identify Fitzgerald, a simple signifier that communicated both his success as an author and his connection with the youth of the United States.[48]

If this conflation of name and text was partially a journalistic expedient, it certainly helped Fitzgerald's publishers, who attempted to capitalize on both his youth and his youthful subject matter. When Scribner's began publishing *This Side of Paradise*, Fitzgerald was advertised as "the youngest writer for whom Scribners have ever published a novel," and, when he signed a contract with the Hearst Corporation, he and Zelda appeared on the cover of *Hearst's International* with a caption calling him the "best-loved author of the young generation."[49]

Fitzgerald, in a similar fashion, worked hard to strengthen the association between his name and the collegiate characters depicted in his first published book. This effort is particularly surprising given Fitzgerald's own tumultuous career at Princeton University. He first applied for admission in the fall of 1913, but was initially rejected because of low scores on the entrance exams.[50] He traveled to the university before the semester began for a personal interview and was able to convince administrators of his merit. He was ultimately enrolled on the condition that he pass makeup exams in four subjects (algebra, Latin, French, and physics).

For the next two years, Fitzgerald spent much of his time focusing on social and literary endeavors and only fell further behind in school. On January 3, 1916, he was finally required to withdraw because of "scholastic deficiencies," though he did later convince the Dean to place a notice of voluntary leave (for health reasons) in his record.[51] Fitzgerald returned for a second junior year in the fall of 1916, but he flunked two of six courses (history and chemistry) and was marked absent for a third (philosophy). He was spared a similar fate the next semester when, in April 1917, the United States entered World War I. Fitzgerald enlisted in a short training program that provided credit for the classes he did not complete, allowing him, for the first time in his college career, to pass all of his courses. He then took his officer's exam and spent the summer writing, reading, and drinking, until his commission finally arrived in October 1917. Fitzgerald did not complete his college education; he never received an undergraduate degree.

Despite this spotty academic record, Fitzgerald associated himself with the university throughout his career.[52] He discussed it during interviews and depicted it as a crucial part of his life in autobiographical reflections.[53] Fitzgerald even went back to Princeton in late February 1920 so that he could be on campus when *This Side of Paradise* was published.[54]

This association served several crucial purposes for Fitzgerald in the early decades of the twentieth century. At the time, college was becoming an increasingly important part of everyday life for white middle-class families, as new industries required a whole host of so-called brain workers to manage increasingly complex production and distribution processes. This new group of employees, frequently referred to as the professional-managerial class, included such professionalized workers as engineers, accountants, and midlevel corporate managers as well as their educated counterparts in government and other major institutions.[55] Richard Ohmann, in his detailed analysis of the professional-managerial class at the turn of the century, estimates that in 1880, about one-fifteenth of the workforce, or approximately 1 million people, filled such roles. By 1910, the number had risen to over 3.5 million, roughly one-tenth of all workers.[56] These trends did not abate: between 1910 and 1940, for example, the number of practicing accountants multiplied sevenfold, from 39,000 to 288,000, the ranks of engineers grew from 77,000 to 297,000, and the number of university professors rose from 16,000 to 77,000.[57]

As these professions expanded, members developed highly rationalized accrediting procedures that typically relied on specialized courses of education. In part as a result of these growth trends, formal schooling became an increasingly regular part of white middle-class life in America and the number of students attending college expanded rapidly. In 1870, only one in sixty men between the ages of eighteen and twenty-one was enrolled in college. By 1900, that number had risen to one in twenty-five.[58] The total number of undergrads rose from about 52,300 in 1870 to 237,600 in 1900, and there were nearly 600,000 college students by 1920.[59]

As a result, Fitzgerald's work can be seen to reflect the interests of a distinct group whose education and aspirations for professionalism distinguished them from other social classes. For these students, the university, which provided both a common base of knowledge and a distinct locus for shared experiences, became an increasingly important part of their lives.[60] This new faction of "youth" was increasingly visible to the public through both the attention of marketers, who wanted to capitalize on such a rapidly growing consumer group, and an array of public conversations covering everything from child development and moral upbringing to the shifting institutional structure of the United States.[61] Thus, Fitzgerald's own personal association with Princeton gave him credibility to represent the younger generation, and it made him valuable to those supposed "outsiders" looking for a symbolic means to understand the new subculture.

Fitzgerald, however, does not simply write about college life in general, nor does he specifically associate himself with an ascendant class of professional white men. Instead, he links himself primarily to elite Eastern universities, writing about Princeton in both *This Side of Paradise* and his own publicity materials. These aristocratic institutions, which admitted a significant number of students from expensive private prep schools, permitted Fitzgerald to write about student life with the authority of recent experience while also retaining an aura of personal distinction.[62] This difficult position helped Fitzgerald inhabit his seemingly contradictory public role as a representative example of the brash and vaguely immoral younger generation and as a brilliant young artist who was unique in his ability to capture the vicissitudes of contemporary youth.[63]

Fitzgerald helped to promote the impression that he was at the elite edge of the university set by dressing in what biographer Matthew Bruccoli has appropriately called the "Brooks Brothers collegiate style."[64] His outfits and general appearance were such an important part of his public image that, when photos could not accompany his press pieces, interviewers regularly described both his youthful appearance and his stylish clothes. They even occasionally went beyond the bounds of accurate reportage to capture Fitzgerald's stereotypical, but always remarkable, features. One journalist described the five feet seven-inch, 140-pound Fitzgerald as if he were a hulking young Adonis: "Tall, blond, broad-shouldered, he towers above his petite wife."[65]

While there is no way of knowing how much Fitzgerald influenced others' portrayals of him, Ruth Prigozy reads the repetitive pattern of his interviews as an indication that he did have some control over these pieces.[66] She also suggests that the format seems designed to promote the impression that Fitzgerald was a young genius. Each interview would begin with a few brief questions about flappers, setting the author up to deliver a seemingly spontaneous speech that, as one interviewer described it, "came in such a rush of words, in such a tumbling of phrase upon phrase that neither objection nor appeal was possible. It was a rush of words which only a powerful feeling could dictate."[67] These pieces not only reflect Fitzgerald's supposed authority as the spokesman of the younger generation, but, Prigozy argues, they also work to enhance his reputation as an "expert" on contemporary morals and lifestyles. So Fitzgerald's expertise is not merely rooted in his own personal experiences or his membership in a particular "youth" subculture. He is also distinguished by the keen intellect that allows him to discuss subjects as disparate as marriage, classical writers, the contemporary state of communism, and the future of the human race, with spontaneous ease (and supposed brilliance).

Even when Fitzgerald and Zelda moved back to his hometown, St. Paul, Minnesota, for the birth of their child in 1921, local interviews tended to follow much the same pattern. For example, Thomas Boyd wrote a piece on Fitzgerald for the St. Paul *Daily News* in March of 1922 that purports to go beyond "that which was appearing in the literary supplements and magazines."[68] He begins, however, by describing Fitzgerald's features and concludes, "His were the features that the average American mind never fails to associate with beauty. But there was a quality in the eye with which the average mind is unfamiliar."[69] He then goes on to mention a series of contemporary literary figures, allowing Fitzgerald to speak spontaneously on each one. Finally, he describes Fitzgerald's writing habits, emphasizing his sincerity, enthusiasm, and, of course, the power of his creative brain.

These details about Fitzgerald, recurring in interview after interview, all enhance his image as a brilliant young man trying to harness his genius. The speed and naive enthusiasm with which he supposedly speaks underscores the truthfulness of the image depicted and it serves to emphasize the immediacy of his thoughts. The Fitzgerald that emerges in these articles does not have time to reflect. He is simply a passionate young man explaining how he feels.

This attitude carries over to his writing as well. For instance, Boyd explains, "His writing is never thought out…Most of the time words come to his mind and then spill themselves in a riotous frenzy of song and color all over the page."[70] The subtext of this description is that Fitzgerald's work cannot simply be a mindless transcription of his own (drunken) youth, the kind of writing any hack could perform. It is as vibrant and alive as the young man himself.

While these articles provided an overwhelmingly positive depiction of Fitzgerald, the most forceful assertions of the author's genius appeared in his own writings. He began constructing his public narrative, along with the accompanying persona, as soon as *This Side of Paradise* was published. He scripted one interview with himself around the time of the book's publication and had it distributed to newspaper columnists through his publisher. Heywood Broun ran a portion of the piece in his "Books" column for the *New York Tribune,* attributing the interview to Carleton R. Davis.[71] Later that year, Fitzgerald excerpted the best lines from this interview and put them, along with a large picture of himself, on an insert that was distributed to the American Booksellers Association. Several of the lines from these pieces, which reflect the young genius persona discussed above, have been quoted often enough to enter Fitzgerald lore. Fitzgerald claims, "To write [*This Side of Paradise*] took three months; to conceive it—three minutes; to collect the data in it—all my life."[72] Fitzgerald also contributed to a column in *The Editor* that featured contemporary authors talking about their writing. This shift in focus from text to author suited Fitzgerald's publicity aims perfectly, and, in a typical moment of bravura, he uses the experience of writing "The Ice Palace" to explain his "theory that, except in a certain sort of naturalistic realism, what you enjoy writing [and thus write quickly] is liable to be much better reading than what you labor over."[73]

The most comprehensive elaboration of Fitzgerald's persona came in an autobiographical piece he did for a column in *The Saturday Evening Post* called "Who's Who—and Why." The article is essentially an outline of Fitzgerald's early years constructed to show his life as "the struggle between an overwhelming urge to write and a combination of circumstances bent on keeping me from it." At each phase of his development, Fitzgerald explains, his literary ambitions were thwarted by a different disruptive force, including secondary school teachers, World War I, and economic necessity. In each case, Fitzgerald refuses to accept blame for any of the delays that he implies prevented him from becoming a famous author more quickly, an approach that makes his ascension to fame seem inevitable and his character, faultless. He does not even mention Scribner's rejection of his first and second drafts of *This Side of Paradise*, only that he wrote a novel "on the consecutive week-ends of three months" while in the army. The revision of this draft, written several summers later in St. Paul, is treated separately. The only real rejection he receives in this account is when a handful of short stories, "the quickest written in an hour and a half, the slowest in three days," get repeatedly rejected by popular magazines. Fitzgerald is ultimately redeemed, however, when, after the publication of *This Side of Paradise*, he notes that one of his stories is accepted by the same magazine that had previously rejected it.[74]

In short, most of the major elements of the Fitzgerald legend seem to have fallen in place only six short months after the publication of *This Side of Paradise*. Over the next few years, as Fitzgerald's antics kept his face in the newspapers and reinforced his image as a debauched young man, many of the articles written about him reiterated the other elements of the legend: his quick mind, his impressive talent, and his profound understanding of American youth. Perhaps the most surprising element of Fitzgerald's publicity is that the stories changed so little. For years, "interviewers" took biographical details from Fitzgerald's original "Who's Who" article, sometimes almost verbatim, and published the author's own well-worn anecdotal accounts as if they were breaking news.[75]

As discussed in chapter 2, highbrow critics' responses to Fitzgerald's first two novels reveal the effectiveness of this media campaign. Many reviews of *The Beautiful and Damned* use strikingly similar language to describe the work, language that seems closely tied to the author's by then well-established public persona. Fitzgerald had a considerable talent, critics agreed, but he had not yet worked hard enough to master his abilities. The novel suffered as a result.

This attitude helps to explain why, when Fitzgerald published his next novel, *The Great Gatsby,* in 1925, critics were attracted to the notion of "double vision" as a way of explaining his artistic success. (Malcolm Cowley would later famously use this phrase to explain Fitzgerald's entire oeuvre.)[76] In this context, "double vision" refers to the way that Fitzgerald was supposedly able to participate in America's crass consumer culture and live a life of public revelry while still maintaining enough detachment to write insightfully about it. As William Rose Benét succinctly states, "For the first time Fitzgerald surveys the Babylonian captivity of this era unblinded by the bright lights."[77] The man and his text were linked closely enough at this point that critics came to understand *The Great Gatsby*'s effectiveness not simply in terms of literary devices, as, say, the consequence of using a removed narrator, but as a measure of personal development. The brash youth had finally gained the critical perspective necessary to harness his previously unwieldy talent. The end product is not just a triumph for literature, or even for Fitzgerald's art. It marks a great *personal* success and, according to Gilbert Seldes, proves that Fitzgerald has put "bad and half-bad things behind him."[78]

The Fallout of Celebrity (1926–1940)

Shortly after the publication of *The Great Gatsby,* Fitzgerald's personal and professional life as well as his pattern of publicity grew increasingly complex. From March 1920 until February 1926, Fitzgerald published three novels, three collections of short stories, and one play, *The Vegetable,* which was released in written form and then had a brief run at Nixon's Apollo Theater in Atlantic City. He published some forty stories, many of them in the most popular magazine of the period, *The Saturday Evening Post*. He wrote several dozen articles, book reviews, and a handful of poems, and he participated in dozens of interviews that ran in newspapers and supplements around the country. Of course, this list of Fitzgerald's activities does not include the countless articles about Fitzgerald and Zelda that were run during those years, detailing their wild, and presumably drunken, antics, nor does it count offshoots of Fitzgerald's work such as film and theatrical adaptations, the reproduction of his stories in collections or anthologies, and critical commentary on his work.

By way of contrast, in the eight years after *Gatsby*, Fitzgerald did not put out another novel, largely gave up reviewing, and wrote far fewer articles. His one consistent market during this time was *The Saturday Evening Post* and, by the late 1920s, it provided nearly all of his income.[79] Fitzgerald remained loyal to the *Post* in these years and made more money than he ever had in his career. As the Great Depression lingered on and Fitzgerald's near constant drinking made writing increasingly difficult, he appeared less frequently in the *Post* and the amount he was paid for each piece decreased significantly. By the time he published *Tender Is the Night* in 1934, he had gone from publishing seven or eight *Post* stories a year to publishing two or three, and by the end of the year, Fitzgerald's main supporters at the magazine had begun to disappear. George Horace Lorimer, who had run the *Post* since shortly after Cyrus Curtis bought it in 1897, liked much of Fitzgerald's work, but after Curtis died in 1933, he became increasingly involved in the *Post*'s parent company and in politics more generally. Also, Thomas Costain, an associate editor who had backed Fitzgerald's fiction, left in 1934 to work for Twentieth Century Fox. During the remaining six years of his life, Fitzgerald would sell only four more pieces to the *Post*.[80]

So, in 1934, when *Tender Is the Night* failed to revive his career, Fitzgerald had to seek out new markets for his talents. He approached Princeton about doing formal lectures on writing and tried selling several movie scripts, including a version of *Tender*. He experimented with ideas for a musical review and several plays. He began a short-lived story sequence about a ninth-century French count supposedly modeled on Ernest Hemingway. He also put together *Taps at Reveille*, a collection of previously published stories that would prove to be the last book he published during his lifetime. Scribner's ran one printing of *Taps*, totaling 5,100 copies.

The only steady source of income Fitzgerald could find in the mid-1930s turned out to be *Esquire*. Arnold Gingrich, who was referred to as a "headhunter" of celebrity writers, had grown up reading

Fitzgerald's fiction and believed that the author had enough name recognition left to be of value to his new magazine. Over the next six years, Gingrich would publish nearly everything Fitzgerald sent to him and, as a matter of policy, did very little editing.[81] From Fitzgerald's perspective, *Esquire* was also an excellent venue because it ran pieces that were typically 1,000 or 2,000 words, significantly less than the 6,000–7,000 word stories that the *Post* preferred. On the downside, Gingrich paid $250 per contribution and only 600,000 people regularly bought *Esquire* in 1935, which was significantly less than the 3 million subscribers the *Post* had during its peak years. Still, as other opportunities became more and more remote, Fitzgerald became a regular contributor to *Esquire* and, in the last six years of his life, would publish only a dozen stories in other places.

In short, Fitzgerald's visibility decreased throughout the 1930s, as he published less and less, and what he did publish circulated among fewer people. His two books from the decade, *Tender Is the Night* and *Taps at Reveille,* sold fewer copies than any he had written and he spent a large portion of the decade struggling to find viable new projects.[82] The resulting decrease in his income after 1931 coupled with his rapidly deteriorating family life also limited his public visibility. Zelda, first hospitalized in April 1930, was diagnosed with schizophrenia and spent the decade in and out of institutions, a situation that was both financially and emotionally difficult for Fitzgerald.[83] He also had charge of their daughter, Scottie, whom he was in no condition to raise alone. The string of nurses and friends who helped him take care of her sapped his resources even further.

Without Zelda, who had played a significant role in many of his public appearances, and with a growing pile of debts, Fitzgerald spent an increasing amount of time lost in alcoholic depression. There were no more wild antics or zany pictures to be splashed throughout the gossip columns, nor were there many interviewers waiting to get the inside scoop on the author's latest project. As Ruth Prigozy points out, when Fitzgerald managed to appear in the news at all, it was mostly small pieces run by local papers in the various towns and cities where he lived throughout the 1930s.[84]

In addition to Fitzgerald's gradual disappearance from the public spotlight, he also stopped writing the promotional pieces and topical articles on "flappers" that had helped to establish him in the early 1920s. Given the downward trajectory of his career, it might be easy to assume that public and editorial indifference were the main causes of this shift; however, there is no evidence to suggest that, after Zelda's illness, Fitzgerald even tried to write such pieces. He was commissioned by *McCall's* in 1929 to write an article on the current state of the flapper and he edited a few pieces, originally written by Zelda, about their own lives for publication in *Esquire*,[85] but the author seems to have largely moved away from such work after the publication of *Gatsby*. This change seems even more significant in light of the fact that Arnold Gingrich would publish whatever Fitzgerald submitted; so, if he had been interested in writing regular pieces about topical matters, especially gender or relationship issues, *Esquire* would most likely have been willing to publish them.

Fitzgerald moved away from such pieces partly for economic reasons, as he stopped writing them around the time his short stories began commanding prices of $1,500 to $2,000, far more than the $1,000 he was receiving for articles from magazines such as *Ladies' Home Journal* or *Woman's Home Companion*. Yet economics alone does not explain why Fitzgerald did not return to these types of pieces, especially when his visibility in the public sphere was decreasing and his income from short stories was rapidly shrinking. A quick glance over his business correspondence from the 1930s shows that he was no less concerned about other dimensions of his public presentation during the decade. He continued to assail Scribner's, through his friend and editor, Max Perkins, for everything from conservative advertising to the firm's disapproval of inexpensive editions, and he attempted to control as many of the aesthetic details of his books as he could. In the months before publication of *Tender Is the Night*, he worried about everything from advertising and review copies to the dust jacket, which he complained should not be in red and white, as those colors evoked the Italian Riviera and not the Cote d'Azur.[86]

Instead of seeing this shift away from certain forms of writing and particular venues for nonfiction work as further evidence of Fitzgerald's slow decline, a perspective premised on the dubious assumption that he was casually dismissing mechanisms that had proven to be effective publicity tools in the past, this trend seems to be part of a larger move toward a more restrained public persona in the 1930s. I do not mean to suggest that Fitzgerald was completely happy and in control of both himself and his writing during the decade. His bouts of depression are well documented, as is his near-constant drinking throughout much of the decade.

These problems do not imply, however, that his writing can simply be reduced to a reflection of some "essential" depressed inner self. Such an approach deprives Fitzgerald of agency and disregards the fairly stable image that emerges in his nonfiction writing over the course of the decade. It also overlooks both the various ways in which he shaped the particular materials at hand and the complex source material that underlay much of his writing. The latter issue became a bone of contention between Fitzgerald and Hemingway following the publication of *Tender Is the Night*. Hemingway, who disliked the book in part because he felt it was an unfair depiction of their mutual friends Sara and Gerald Murphy, wrote Fitzgerald insisting that he needed to "write truly" and not create "damned marvelously faked case histories."[87] Fitzgerald, in his six-page reply, points out that his characters are composites, not attempts to "truly" capture the Murphys and that writers since before Shakespeare have been successful in creating imaginary fusions. Several months later, he made a similar point to Sara Murphy herself, claiming that "it takes half a dozen people to make a synthesis strong enough to create a fiction character."[88]

The issue would surface again with the publication of the "Crack-Up" essays, which Hemingway dismissed as "whin[ing] in public."[89] In reality, the historical antecedents of these essays are incredibly complex and can be traced throughout Fitzgerald's life. As with *Tender Is the Night*, the author tended to draw heavily on his experiences with Zelda and her doctors for information about mental illness, and many of the couples' letters from the early 1930s reveal interesting parallels with Fitzgerald's later pieces. Throughout her confinement, Zelda wrote to Fitzgerald about her struggle to preserve a sense of identity and maintain an emotional investment in her life, two major characteristics of the narrator in the "Crack-Up" essays.[90] Zelda also wrote to him several times about her inability to tolerate the presence of other people,[91] a problem prevalent in Fitzgerald's essays and an issue he had already been considering for over a decade. When Fitzgerald's close friend Monsignor Cyril Sigourney Webster Fay died of pneumonia in 1919, he wrote a letter to their mutual friend Shane Leslie, claiming that as a result of the death he was "beginning to have a horror of people."[92] Biographer Matthew Bruccoli sees this letter, in which Fitzgerald claims he wants to follow Monsignor Fay's path and join the priesthood, as "mostly a pose for Leslie's benefit."[93]

Given that the historical and personal antecedents for Fitzgerald's "Crack-Up" essays are extraordinarily complex, I think it is crucial to move beyond simplistic readings of these pieces as an expression of his internal state to see how they operate rhetorically as part of a larger persona being created throughout his nonfiction writing in the 1930s. In fact, Fitzgerald frequently expressed a desire for a new public image, one free of the complications generated by all his past publicity work.

In one famous story about the genesis of the "Crack-Up" essays, editor Arnold Gingrich says he visited Fitzgerald to ask about new work when the author's debt to the magazine became so large that the accountants began asking questions. He found Fitzgerald drunk and depressed, upset because he no longer wanted to write what he called "stories of young love" for *The Saturday Evening Post.* Gingrich, in a desperate attempt to get the author writing again, suggested that he do a piece about his inability to produce this kind of text. The next piece he received was "The Crack-Up."[94]

While elements of this story are certainly questionable, Fitzgerald's complaint was a common one. Toward the end of his life, he even talked Gingrich into running his work under the pseudonym Paul Elgin, so, he claimed, he could see readers react to his writing and not his name. His professed goal was to write a story so good that Elgin would receive a fan letter from his daughter Scottie.[95] In a similar attempt to break with the past, Fitzgerald told his editor Max Perkins that *Tender Is the Night* would be his last work on the boom years. He also suggested the book's publicity emphasize that, compared to his *Post* work, this is "quite definitely...a horse of another color."[96]

Fitzgerald's desire for change is also reflected in the new autobiographical persona that he constructed throughout the decade. Many critics have commented on the apparent rhetorical shift in his later nonfiction writing, but few efforts have been made to specify the nature of the changes. The words "introspective" and "retrospective" are frequently used to characterize his later work; however, many of his most topical pieces had already adopted precisely these poses to enhance their effectiveness. Most of his articles on male and female flappers, for example, involve a historical analysis that is not much different from more critically acclaimed pieces such as "Echoes of the Jazz Age" or "My Lost City." One article published shortly after *The Great Gatsby*—titled "What Became of Our Flappers and Sheiks?"— even employs a removed narrative persona to comment on the action from a more detached perspective. He also frequently reflected on his own life, or at least what he presented as such, in his early work. Articles such as "Wait Till You Have Children of Your Own!"—in which Fitzgerald looks back on the child-raising techniques of his parents' generation and outlines his own plan for parenting—gain emotional force from the narrator's personal investment in the topic at hand.

In other words, the apparent shift many critics note in Fitzgerald's later writings does not stem from any radical deviation from his early work. Instead, it seems to be a by-product of the sheer consistency evinced by his later nonfiction texts. While he did appear melancholy, reflective, and introspective in some of his early work, by the early 1930s, his autobiographical writing would consistently adopt these characteristics. From "Echoes of the Jazz Age," an article written in 1931 that examines the previous decade through the perspective of someone who feels he has left a piece of himself behind, to "Early Success," one of his last autobiographical pieces and another wistful recollection of the early 1920s, Fitzgerald repeatedly assumes the pose of someone who is trying to assess the present through an understanding of the past. Just as he had previously presented a unified portrait of himself as a genius writer, Fitzgerald now seems to have adopted a new pose, one that is predicated on its very distance from the earlier persona.

Scott Donaldson, reviewing Fitzgerald's nonfiction, characterizes the later writings similarly, claiming they are different in part because the speaker drops the air of expertise so prevalent in early articles and interviews.[97] While this assessment captures the sense of remove noted above, it does not quite encapsulate the difference. Certainly, the brazen "Fitzgerald" of 1923 who could proclaim, "all women over thirty-five should be murdered," is a different character than the narrator of "Echoes of the Jazz Age," who circumspectly asserts, "the general decision to be amused that began with the cocktail parties of 1921 had more complicated origins."[98] The latter speaker, however, still claims the authority to pass judgment on a decade, even if from the more removed space of a nostalgic historian. Denying that agency feeds into the larger vision of Fitzgerald in the decade as a man mired in sadness and loss. It also misrepresents the rhetorical position that the author is constructing for himself. When Fitzgerald claimed to possess "the authority of failure" in his notebooks, he was not simply berating himself for being unsuccessful. He was claiming a particular position from which he could continue to assert his "authority."[99]

Shortly before writing the "Crack-Up" essays, supposedly his most profound admission of failure, Fitzgerald could still tell his typist and confidant Laura Guthrie, "I have no patience and when I want something I *want* it. I break people. I am part of the break-up of the times."[100] This unusual ending juxtaposition links Fitzgerald's perverse pride in his ability to inflict harm on others with the pervasive "break-up" of the Great Depression as well as, presumably, a larger moral collapse that connects him with the "times." Fitzgerald is placing himself in the position of one who is cracking up, but his collapse is not passive, nor can it be called a "failure" in any simple sense of the word.

This new sense of authority becomes an essential part of Fitzgerald's larger attempt to distance himself from the past. For instance, "Echoes of the Jazz Age," first published in 1931, examines what Fitzgerald sees as the significant cultural events of the 1920s, but it also declares the Jazz Age "as dead as were the Yellow Nineties in 1902."[101] Following this opening proclamation, the narrator links this period with historical events (the May Day riots in 1919 to the stock market crash in October 1929) and charts the unfolding chronology of the decade, from the "peak of the younger generation" in 1922 to the "orgy" of the elders in 1923 through the "wide-spread neurosis" of 1927.[102] These dates not only underscore the supposed knowledge and authority of the narrator, but they give concrete boundaries to the period. Hence, "the utter confidence which was [the Jazz Age's] essential prop" can be said to pass as certainly as an October afternoon, creating a sense of finality absolute enough to admit some nostalgic rumination, even though, as the narrator points out, this piece is being written only two years after the supposed close of the Age. The periodizing title itself works in much the same way, simultaneously delimiting a particular period of time and emphasizing its difference from the hardship and deprivation of the early Depression.

Besides telling his readers about the specific contours of the past decade, the narrator also frames the text with commentary about his own sense of personal loss, effectively distancing the present speaker from his previous self. He begins, "The present writer already looks back to [the Jazz Age] with nostalgia. It bore him up, flattered him and gave him more money than he had dreamed of, simply for telling people that he felt as they did."[103] Perhaps the most surprising element of this quote, in light of Fitzgerald's previous publicity efforts, is the way in which it trivializes the narrator's early self. The work that once seemed to be the product of brilliant insight and a powerful natural intellect, now, eleven years later, appears to be not much more than a well-crafted expression of his own emotions, emotions that happened to resonate with a larger public.[104]

This pose of an older, more mature self dispelling the illusions of naive youth works to frame a larger historical analysis that operates in much the same way, with a knowledgeable narrator setting the record straight on a decade that is both too close and too far removed from present concerns for most to assess. The narrator then concludes the essay by returning attention to both his own longing for and current remove from the Jazz Age, claiming, "it all seems rosy and romantic to us who were young then, because we will never feel quite so intensely about our surroundings any more."[105] This position, among other things, works to emphasize his distance from the passionate, and naive, days of his youth, and it helps to establish a mature voice whose supposed experience buttresses the previous discussion.

Fitzgerald's next major autobiographical piece, "My Lost City," takes his rhetorical distance from the impudent young genius further by recasting the original myth of *This Side of Paradise*. The narrator is no longer bragging about how fast he writes novels or laying down proclamations about contemporary literature. Instead, he glosses over writing his first book, an episode central to his early persona, with an ellipsis and does not even mention the title: "Hating the city, I got roaring, weeping drunk on my last penny and went home. . . . Incalculable city. What ensued was only one of a thousand success stories of those gaudy days."[106] This omission essentially erases Fitzgerald's justification for his own celebrity, and it helps to create the impression of a far more random series of events. Success, no longer a natural outgrowth of his unique genius, has become so commonplace that the narrator nearly attributes it directly to the "gaudy days" of the early 1920s.

Moreover, he does not appear in the guise of the spontaneous, quick-witted celebrity, but as a reticent, even confused outsider, uncertain about both the role he was previously asked to play and the duties that such a role entailed. The narrator explains, "For just a moment, before it was demonstrated that I was unable to play the role, I, who knew less of New York than any reporter of six months standing. . . was pushed into the position not only of spokesman for the time but of the typical product of that same moment."[107] This rhetorical positioning subtly stretches the speaker's distance from his old persona because he is not only demonstrably removed from his naive young self, but that self, it turns out in retrospect, was always remote from his persona as well.

One advantage of creating such distance is that the speaker can simultaneously exploit the lingering value of Fitzgerald's previous publicity and, at the same time, distance himself from it. Throughout the article, he discusses a host of scandalous antics, from disrobing in public to a fight with a police officer to his famous ride with Zelda through the streets of New York on the roof of a taxi. He also wryly suggests that, even at the time, he rarely remembered doing the things he read about in the papers. Whether the stories were publicity stunts or simply drunken escapades is never specifically addressed, but, in either case, the triple layering of present speaker, past speaker, and public persona works to emphasize the relative maturity, as well as the intellectual development, of the current narrator.[108]

The persona that emerges from Fitzgerald's autobiographical works in the 1930s is an intensely introspective figure searching the past to help clarify and explain the losses of the present. The narrator also has an aura of authority that does not emanate from his innate genius but from the hard-learned lessons of experience. Along similar lines, Fitzgerald frequently depicts himself as an ordinary man struggling with the problems of his craft. In 1934, he wrote an introduction to the Modern Library edition of *The Great Gatsby* that claims, "The present writer has always been a 'natural' for his profession, in so much that he can think of nothing he could have done as efficiently as to have lived deeply in the world of imagination. There are plenty other people constituted as he is."[109] Unlike in his early years, when words simply spilled from his brain to the page, Fitzgerald's "talent" here is no longer directly connected to writing. It is predicated on an active imagination. Moreover, this supposed ability, already undermined by the quotation marks around "natural," does not even set him apart from other writers.

Surprising as this modesty is in the context of an introduction to a reprinted novel, it seems even more out of place, given Fitzgerald's history of bravado, in interviews. In one conversation with a reporter from the *Montgomery Advertiser*, Fitzgerald makes an offhand comment about, as the interviewer characterizes it, the "foolish gesture" of prohibition and the potential problems this law raised for the government. While his comment itself is reminiscent of the brash young man of the previous decade, what sets this statement apart is that it is immediately followed by a series of qualifications: "Understand now, I'm purely a fiction writer and do not profess to be an earnest student of political science...and all the writers, keenly interested in human welfare whom I know, laugh at the prohibition law....All of my writer friends think and say the same thing."[110] Here, Fitzgerald is no longer the natural genius with license to discourse on any topic that crosses his mind. He is merely a writer who is, in a notable admission, perhaps less than qualified to pass judgments on "political science." A few mildly inflammatory opinions, once the staple of any Fitzgerald interview, now require far more corroboration than personal experience alone can provide. The collective authority of his "writer friends" must be summoned, and reiterated, before the next slightly provocative topic, "communism," can be addressed in equally qualified terms.

Perhaps the most direct depiction of Fitzgerald's new position as a writer appears in "One Hundred False Starts," a humorous piece detailing the various unfinished projects that fill his notebook. This article takes as its subject the countless pages he must write or, in the racing metaphor that dominates the piece, the "days and days" he must "crouch" in order to create the mere handful of publishable stories attributed to his name. The overriding irony of the piece—that is, Fitzgerald's ability to take these failures and create a highly amusing story out of them—enhances its humor and helps to undercut the darker implications that could be read into Fitzgerald's many "false starts." He is not a washed-up alcoholic stuck in a pattern of failure, but a fairly typical writer struggling with the difficulties of his craft. After reiterating that he is "in every sense a professional," Fitzgerald concludes the piece by praising both hard work and the extensive experience, gained through false starts as well as successful writing, necessary to make that work productive.[111]

Ultimately, the narrator of "One Hundred False Starts" suggests that this new outlook has changed both the writer himself and the kind of pieces he is capable of writing. One of his notebook entries, "Article: Unattractive Things Girls Do, to pair with counter article by woman: Unattractive Things Men Do," recalls an earlier set of pieces he did with Zelda for *McCall's* in response to the question, "Does a Moment of Revolt Come Sometime to Every Married Man?"[112] From his current position, the narrator cannot even put the topic into proper perspective and he narrows the title from universal female characteristics to those reflecting "a great majority" of women to "a strong minority." He finally gives up the article fragment as a remnant of a distant "gilded age," a decision that takes on even greater significance in light of the fact that Fitzgerald rarely attempted anything like his earlier pieces in the 1930s.[113] So, much like in his other supposedly nonfictional pieces from the decade, this narrator is not only distancing himself from a recognizable past but also formulating that gap as an uncrossable boundary. He is, by extension, depicting himself as a fundamentally different figure from the one who previously appeared in the popular magazines.

Again, this perspective, while prevalent in many of Fitzgerald's nonfiction pieces from the 1930s, cannot be used to mark a distinct shift in his work. Fitzgerald had been fascinated by both the potential benefits and the dangers inherent in a doctrine of fundamental change from the earliest days of his career. He often characterized his own life in terms of irrevocable shifts, as when, in his ledger entry for the year 1919, he wrote, "The most important year of my life. Every emotion and my life work decided."[114] The finality of this judgment is as striking in scope as it is myopic in vision, and it reflects a perspective that would recur in Fitzgerald's work until the end of his life, when he characterized Monroe Stahr, the hero of his final, posthumously published novel, as the last tycoon.[115]

These continuities in some of Fitzgerald's later work help to characterize the change that so many critics have glossed or subsumed into the larger narrative of his life. Instead of attributing the difference to the emergence of some specific characteristics or merely to Fitzgerald's declining capabilities, his autobiographical writing in the 1930s can be far more easily characterized by the *consistency* of several elements, particularly in relation to the narrative persona he develops across the body of his work. He seemed to be cultivating a new persona as a wholly different kind of writer, one far more devoted to his craft than the youth who effortlessly turned out pages for an adoring fan base.

Given that the marketplace for fiction was becoming increasingly less stable as the Depression wore on and Fitzgerald himself was producing fewer salable pages of material, these efforts to reinforce the elements of his image that suggest he is a competent writer make a certain kind of commercial sense. In comparison with his early publicity blitz, however, a handful of articles published in magazines with relatively small circulations did little to change larger perceptions of the author. His very inability to promote himself as a more "serious" writer through many of the methods that helped circulate his name and image in the first place hindered the recuperation of his reputation in the 1930s, even if it may have ultimately contributed to his later revival. Despite a fairly consistent effort to cultivate the persona of a more serious and sedate writer, the image of the young genius from Princeton would follow Fitzgerald, in various forms, for the rest of his life.

Many of the interviews Fitzgerald conducted throughout the 1930s document this conflict between the new writer and the old persona. Most of these pieces still associate him directly with *This Side of Paradise* and organize their discussions around questions about "flappers" and "youth" in America. Yet many of Fitzgerald's comments pertain directly to writing and, in place of the flip comments of his youth, he now offers sedate advice. In one interview, he lectures, "The American people are just beginning to wake up to the fact that success comes hard."[116] He then goes on to chastise writers for getting caught up in larger struggles and leaving behind their "detached viewpoint," an ironic comment for an author who cultivated a reputation in part by portraying *This Side of Paradise* as more or less a record of his immediate experiences. This commitment to a disciplined writing process is also reflected in the comments Fitzgerald makes about his own work ethic. He talks, for instance, about spending fifteen consecutive nights in the emergency room of a hospital in order to write one short story, "Zone of Accident."[117]

In interviews where he does discuss topical matters, Fitzgerald's commentary is equally far removed from the outspoken proclamations of his youth. One piece, published in 1935, provides a brief commentary on the six different generations that have, by his count, supposedly existed since 1916. Fitzgerald—in direct opposition to some of his earlier comments from "Wait Till You Have Children of Your Own!"—concludes by advising parents to teach children the "old truths" and infuse them with traditional "character."[118]

The inability to develop a new image was not entirely negative for Fitzgerald, in part because his name occasionally resurfaced in popular references to the Jazz Age. If such mentions often ignored his continuing existence and referred only to a handful of early accomplishments, they did help him remain visible to the larger public.[119] However remote this success may have seemed, Fitzgerald was also able to cash in on these old associations in times of desperate need. In July 1937, a time when he was regularly earning only $250 for a short story and had made less than $3,500 in six months, Fitzgerald was still able to land a contract with MGM paying $1,000 a week. His first job, not surprisingly, was to help patch up the script for *A Yank in Oxford,* a movie about a young American student in England.

The flip side of Fitzgerald's lingering association with the past was that many of his contemporaries dismissed him. As Budd Schulberg, who worked with Fitzgerald on *Winter Carnival,* later said, "My generation thought of F. Scott Fitzgerald as an age rather than as a writer, and when the economic strike of 1929 began to change the sheiks and flappers into unemployed boys and underpaid girls, we consciously and a little belligerently turned our backs on Fitzgerald."[120] Moreover, when Schulberg, who had long been an admirer of Fitzgerald's fiction, first learned they would be collaborating together, he was surprised to learn Fitzgerald was still alive.[121] And Schulberg was not alone. As noted previously, Arnold Gingrich, despite his personal dislike of the "Crack-Up" essays, thought any publicity could help a man most people thought was dead. Even Fitzgerald's future partner Sheilah Graham would claim that she had, at first, associated his name only with the 1920s.[122]

Those who still read Fitzgerald's writing in the 1930s did not frequently have a much higher opinion of him. In part because Fitzgerald had forged such a close relationship between his person and his writing, and in part because of the retrospective viewpoint adopted in much of his later work, many people began to see him not as a serious writer struggling with his craft but as a literary failure. The "Crack-Up" essays would, as we have seen, prompt many such readings of Fitzgerald's life during the period, and the publicity they generated only enhanced the view that he was little more than a washed-up rummy. This attitude took its most public, and its most scandalous, form several months after the final "Crack-Up" essay appeared in *Esquire*.

In September 1936, journalist Michel Mok traveled to the Grove Park Inn in Asheville, North Carolina, where Fitzgerald had been staying since July, to do a piece on the author. Fitzgerald was in no condition to do an interview. In July, he had broken his arm in a diving accident and had to spend ten weeks in a body cast. To make matters worse, he fell in the bathroom late at night and, as a result of the fall, developed a form of arthritis in the arm. The cast also largely prevented him from going, or at least provided him with an excuse for not going, to visit Zelda, who was institutionalized nearby at Highland Hospital in the nearby town of Asheville. Her immediate presence served as yet another reminder of how far he had fallen from his early years of easy money and widespread publicity. Finally, Fitzgerald's mother, with whom he had had an ambivalent relationship throughout much of his life, died in early September. Fitzgerald was medicated, drinking heavily, depressed, and possibly ill when Mok came to his hotel room for the interview, which, not incidentally, was on September 24, the author's fortieth birthday.[123]

As might be expected, the piece Mok wrote reads like a nightmare version of Fitzgerald's early interviews.[124] In the first half of the article, Mok describes Fitzgerald's current state, referring to his incessant drinking, "his twitching face with its pitiful expression of a cruelly beaten child," and his addled conversation. This man is no longer, Mok explicitly informs readers, the spontaneous genius spouting off witticisms and prophecy for an adoring audience. He refers to Fitzgerald as "an actor," pointing out the transparency of the author's poses, and glosses over much of his "long, rambling, disjointed talk," which sounds like the "Crack-Up" essays but is "not nearly as poetic." Then, the second half of the article has Fitzgerald recounting, in that same rambling, disjointed fashion, the legend of his youth, including many of the same events that had circulated since his early "Who's Who" piece. The contrast is devastating, and, by Fitzgerald's own account, he swallowed an overdose of morphine after reading it.

The association of Fitzgerald with drunken failure would come to dominate criticism of his work in the 1930s. Yet, as much as Mok's article attempts to highlight changes in the author, it does, when viewed from the perspective of Fitzgerald's reputation, point to the lingering interest in his earlier persona. Mok's overt maliciousness is not directed at Fitzgerald the man, nor does he attempt to criticize any of the author's books. Instead, he attacks Fitzgerald's image and, in the sheer force of the attack, he reveals that nearly two decades after the publication of *This Side of Paradise,* this image was still relevant enough to invite a public flogging. Mok's piece, which originally ran in the *New York Post,* generated enough interest to be picked up and excerpted in *Time* magazine's "People" column a week later.[125]

In the context of this complex blending of stability and fluctuation, of uncritical praise and unapologetic condemnation, of success and failure, the "Crack-Up" essays take on an added poignancy. Throughout the 1930s, Fitzgerald looked to recast his career outside the confines of the Jazz Age from the position of one reflecting on the nature of change itself. These essays are at once a meditation on his profession and an exploration of the enormous psychological costs that often accompany such major shifts in perspective and positioning. In a larger theoretical sense, they are about how a "life" can be shaped within the dictates of celebrity discourse and a changing cultural marketplace. On a much smaller level, they are simply one more part of F. Scott Fitzgerald's ongoing project to manage his own reputation by whatever means were available to him.

CHAPTER 6

The "Crack-Up" Essays: Masculine Identity, Modernism, and the Dissolution of Literary Values

The "Crack-Up" essays occupy an important symbolic position in critical and biographical assessments of Fitzgerald's later years. Many contemporary readers took these essays literally and interpreted them as a straightforward account of Fitzgerald's nervous breakdown. Quite a few respondents, including other male writers, various figures involved in the publication of Fitzgerald's works, and many readers of *Esquire,* found such an open and public admission of personal problems contemptible.

These initial responses differ greatly from the critical accounts that appeared after Fitzgerald's death five years later, and they diverge even further from the relatively reasoned assessments that accompanied the essays' republication in Edmund Wilson's collection *The Crack-Up.* The early emphasis on Fitzgerald's nervous collapse lessened as critics shifted their focus from the breakdown to the author's resolution to make a "clean break" at the end of the pieces. This change allowed later readers to reinterpret these essays not as, in Ernest Hemingway's words, "whining in public," but as a heroic recommitment to the creation of great art.

Despite the change in outlook after Fitzgerald's death, few subsequent commentators questioned the literal message of these pieces. Both sets of responses, while widely divergent in tone and content, were essentially predicated on the same basic interpretation of the texts: Fitzgerald had a nervous breakdown and decided to make a "clean break" with his old life by recommitting to a new existence as a "writer only." What this means is that any attempt to understand the underlying shift in attitudes cannot be predicated simply on differences of interpretation.

In order to decenter the seemingly authoritative literal reading of these texts, I begin the following chapter by positing an alternate interpretation through an examination of the narrative persona that emerges in the essays. While the narrator is in most important respects similar to the figure that emerges in other autobiographical works during this period, I argue that Fitzgerald recasts the divide between his current identity and his past persona. Unlike his earlier essays from the 1930s, which depict the young Fitzgerald as naive and out of place, the narrator of the "Crack-Up" essays idealizes many aspects of his earlier self. The gap between the two figures, then, is not a mark of the current narrator's maturity, but is instead a reflection of the negative impact society has had on him in the intervening years.

If an alternate interpretation of these texts seems plausible, then the consistency with which certain commentators have approached them deserves more consideration. To understand particular responses to these pieces, the final section will examine the rhetorical function that particular interpretations served for readers. Some of Fitzgerald's male contemporaries focus on the confessional aspect of the "Crack-Up" essays in a way that short-circuits potential challenges to conventional notions of masculinity imbedded in the pieces. Later readings, which emphasized Fitzgerald's resolution to make a "clean break," pick up on the narrator's efforts to imagine his breakdown in terms of the struggling male artist; however, they do not by and large pursue the challenge to conventional notions of masculinity implicit in this stance. Instead, they use the narrator's rhetoric to bolster more traditional conceptions of the heroic male embracing art as the highest calling.

THE CRACK-UP, CONTRADICTIONS, AND THE CHALLENGES OF "MODERN" AUTHORSHIP

In November of 1935, Fitzgerald left the cold Baltimore winter behind and traveled to North Carolina. He had visited the state several times during the past year, partly because the weather was more favorable for his health. On this particular trip, he went to the Skyland Hotel in Hendersonville. A frequently cited passage from his notebooks describes the initial conditions of his stay: "Monday and Tuesday I had two tins of potted meat, three oranges and a box of Uneedas and two cans of beer. For the food that totaled 18 cents a day...It was funny coming into the hotel and the very deferential clerk not knowing that I was not only thousands, nay tens of thousands in debt, but had less that 40 cents cash in the world and probably a $13. deficit at my bank."[1] It was in this condition that Fitzgerald sat down to write "The Crack-Up." The next two essays in the series were probably written a month later, shortly before the author returned home to Baltimore and checked into Johns Hopkins, another semiregular stop for Fitzgerald at the time. He went to the hospital over a half dozen times in the mid-1930s to manage tuberculosis and to reduce his alcohol consumption.

It would not be improbable to suggest that these bleak circumstances provided Fitzgerald with material for the persona he would construct in the "Crack-Up" essays. The narrator, who claims to be suffering "a crack-up of all values," spends the first several pages of the opening piece attempting to explain his "thesis that life has a varying offensive," meaning that life can destroy individuals in any number of ways.[2] He discusses external and internal blows; attacks on the nerves, the mind, and the body; and the difference between sudden damages and lingering effects. He talks about both "common ills" and larger metaphysical difficulties, going as far as to assert the fundamental "futility of effort" (CU, 70). He even illustrates compensatory mechanisms that neither correct problems nor prevent further damage from occurring.[3]

To simply dismiss this bleak outlook as the by-product of a real alcoholic depression, however, is to ignore the larger rhetorical uses that Fitzgerald makes of this perspective. Fitzgerald's narrator does not merely indulge in the details of his own impotence for the readers' voyeuristic pleasure, but he instead posits several related theses as a way of generalizing about his "revelations." At the beginning of the first essay, after a description of the ways in which life assaults the individual, the narrator pauses to make what he calls "a general observation." He says, "The test of a first-rate intelligence is the ability to hold two opposed ideas in the mind at the same time, and still retain the ability to function. One should, for example, be able to see that things are hopeless and yet be determined to make them otherwise" (CU, 69). Here, the narrator implicitly constructs a worldview that hinges on contradictions. He does not mention the possibility of living without logical difficulties or seem to hold out hope for any kind of resolution. Instead, he posits as an ideal the consciousness that can function despite irresolvable difficulties.

Such a perspective suggests that these meditations will provide no easy solution to the larger problems of life. Neither logic nor strength nor sheer determination will be enough to save the narrator from the many unpredictable assaults on his mind, his body, and his spirit. The best he can hope for is to "retain the ability to function" in a hostile and unyielding world. This view, presented in the very opening passages of these essays, complicates any easy reading of the last essay, "Handle with Care," wherein the narrator claims to make a clean break with his past and press on as a "writer only." The supposed solution, at least in the context of the narrator's opening comments, hardly seems to address the underlying problem, a type of mental paralysis caused by the sheer complexity of the world and its assaults on the body.

Given this opening perspective, the narrator's seemingly inexplicable reactions to adversity in the essays make some sense. When the narrator receives bad news, his first response is to retreat from the outside world and impose some semblance of order on his life. The most obvious withdrawal occurs after the narrator realizes he has "cracked" and he travels "a thousand miles to think it over. I took a dollar room in a drab little town where I knew no one" (CU, 80). Central as this episode may be, the escape is only one of several significant retreats that occur throughout the essays. In the first piece, shortly before the narrator realizes that he has cracked, his doctor reports what he vaguely describes as a "grave sentence" (CU, 71). As a result of this random and unpredictable blow, the narrator withdraws from the world he knows to an isolated spot where he alternates between sleeping and making "hundreds of lists."[4]

These lists provide another means of organization and control for the narrator, who, ironically, does not simply discuss his tendency but replicates it in the text, saying he made lists "of cavalry leaders and football players and cities, and popular tunes and pitchers, and happy times, and hobbies and houses lived in and how many suits since I left the army and how many pairs of shoes..." (CU, 71–72). The excerpt does not reproduce even half the text he devotes to this particular list, but it provides a representative sample of the random events and objects that the narrator tries to organize upon learning that he is seriously ill. The irony of creating a list out of his lists also draws attention to the way in which these essays as a whole participate in a similar process of organization. All three essays contain various catalogs that ultimately reflect the narrator's need to bring order to a life threatened by the dissolution of a psychological crack-up. The presence of these lists also reflects the difficulty of the narrator's "solution," which cannot entail a reprieve from the complexities of life but must end in a standoff with them. Even the "recovered" author of these pieces must continue to search for an impossible order.

This reading suggests that the chaos plaguing the narrator is a function of existence itself, which is both a crucial issue in the text and a recurring motif throughout Fitzgerald's work. After Ring Lardner's death in September 1933, Edmund Wilson commissioned Fitzgerald, who had become good friends with Lardner in the early 1920s, to write a piece about him for *The New Republic*. Fitzgerald concluded that Lardner was incredibly talented but never achieved greatness as a writer because he had spent his formative years working as a sports reporter. This occupation left him with a very narrow view of the world and a limited standard by which to judge it. As a result, Lardner was unable "to apply that standard to the horribly complicated mess of living, where nothing, even the greatest conceptions and work-ings and achievements, is else but messy, spotty, tortuous" (CU, 37). Fitzgerald used a similar vision of life to good dramatic effect in an article he wrote the following year called "Sleeping and Waking." In this piece, he describes his own difficulties with insomnia, a descrip-tion that rests on his vision of sleep as a biological mechanism so complex that it "can be spoiled by one infinitesimal incalculable ele-ment" such as a change in the weather, a bodily adjustment, or even a small fly (CU, 65).

William Troy, in an article reassessing Fitzgerald's work after the release of Wilson's *The Crack-Up* in 1945, has perhaps best captured the implications of this problem for Fitzgerald's writing. He says, "There was Fitzgerald's exasperation with the multiplicity of modern human existence—especially in his own country. 'It's under you, over you, and all around you,' he protested, in the hearing of the pres-ent writer, to a young woman who had connived at the slow prog-ress of his work. 'And the problem is to get hold of it somehow.' It was exasperating because for the writer, whose business is to extract the unique quality of his time, what Baudelaire calls the quality of modernité, there was too much to be sensed, to be discarded, to be reconciled into some kind of order."[5] In these terms, Fitzgerald's dif-ficulties with the "multiplicity" of life make him seem profoundly more troubled than the typical struggling author, in that he is not just fighting to pare down his text and create an organic work of art. He is mired in the elements of his life that will ultimately become the content of his next work.

Troy also aligns Fitzgerald's struggle with a larger tendency dur-ing the period to valorize artistic originality. Writers who aspired to create "high" art were encouraged to develop new styles and forms to capture the particular essence of the current moment. So Fitzgerald's task was not simply to harness the complexity of his world and turn it into art, but also, in the process, to develop a new mode of expression that would adequately embody his vision. In a testament to the importance of the concept of "newness" in this particular moment, the narrator of the "Crack-Up" essays does not attempt to rehabilitate his struggle with contemporary life by challenging the importance of originality. Instead, he insists that his own alienation might ironically be a hallmark of the new era: "My self-immolation was something sodden—dark. It was very distinctly not modern—yet I saw it in others . . . I had watched when another, equally eminent, spent months in an asylum unable to endure any contact with his fellow men. And of those who had given up and passed on I could list a score" (CU, 81). The narrator's anxieties about becoming obsolescent may not literally be "modern," but it is precisely this sense of existing out of time, of being trapped between two incompatible ages, that connects him with others. The state of modernity might be, he implies, to be constantly in danger of being unmodern, a condition fraught with the anxieties documented in these essays.

The Past and the Present: Fitzgerald's Narrator as Literary Man

The narrator's sense of obsolescence suggests something interesting about the "Crack-Up" essays, especially in light of Fitzgerald's previous nonfiction work from the 1930s. The author's young counterpart is no longer being cast in a nostalgic frame but is being repositioned in a complex and somewhat idealistic manner. This speaker is not the narrator of "Echoes" for whom the past "seems rosy and romantic . . . because [he] will never feel quite so intensely about [his] surroundings any more" (CU, 22). The sadness that emerges in these final lines stems from the gap between the more worldly speaker and his young self, a figure who lived life with gusto and was foolishly convinced that the younger generation was about to take over the world. The narrator of "My Lost City" adopts a similar attitude. He concludes by lamenting the loss of his "splendid mirage," a phrase that suggests the appeal of his former life while also emphasizing the illusory nature of his earlier beliefs (CU, 33). In each of these pieces, the speaker has outgrown his previous attitudes and so often treats his past self as naive, foolish, or out of place.

In the "Crack-Up" essays, Fitzgerald adopts a similar pose, reflecting on a past that no longer seems tenable. The problem, however, is not that the narrator's attitude has changed significantly in the intervening years but that he has been worn down in the interim. As a result, his younger self is often treated positively in the text. For instance, after the narrator proposes that a "first-rate intelligence" can function while fully aware of the contradictions inherent in any course of action, he goes on to say, "this philosophy fitted on to my early adult life, when I saw the improbable, the implausible, often the 'impossible,' come true." Rather than surrender to life's unpredictability, his younger self chose to believe that "life was something you dominated if you were any good" (CU, 69). In sharp contrast to the sense of entitlement present in many of his early publicity pieces, Fitzgerald suggests that he was always alert to the precariousness of his own position. And his previous confidence, he now claims, always existed in tension with an awareness of its improbability.

While Fitzgerald's persona in the "Crack-Up" essays can be distinguished in some ways from the figures that appear in his other Depression-era autobiographical writings, this narrator does still have much in common with them. He adopts, for instance, the now-familiar guise of the committed artist. In the opening page of the first essay, readers are informed that this figure is both a serious professional and a "successful literary man," two details that stand largely unchallenged throughout the essays (CU, 69). Even after the narrator decides that the only way to deal with his crack-up is by making a "clean break" from obsolete aspects of his life, he still summarily declares, "I must continue to be a writer because that was my only way of life" (CU, 81–82).

From a contemporary position nearly seventy years after Fitzgerald's death, on the far side of several dozen biographies, such a commitment might seem like a positive decision. By 1936, the author was a nearly bankrupt alcoholic whose avenues of publication were rapidly disappearing. For contemporaneous readers, however, many of whom might have known little more about Fitzgerald than what they had read in newspapers during his heyday as a celebrity author, this claim would certainly have lacked some of the weight it contains in hindsight.

Additionally, the Fitzgerald figure that appears in much contemporary scholarship differs significantly from the narrator of these essays. The speaker provides surprisingly little information about his current position in the profession, an elision that could lead readers to associate the contemporary author with what, from a biographical perspective, would have to be considered past successes. He also puts a relatively positive spin on his current material circumstances. Readers learn early on that *This Side of Paradise* thrust Fitzgerald into the "leisure class." The narrator also mentions his servants, a notable detail in the midst of the Great Depression, and speaks rather casually about traveling "a thousand miles" to find a peaceful place to think (CU, 80).

Given these details, Fitzgerald's desire to downplay his alcoholism in the pieces makes sense.[6] Such a move underscores the seriousness of the essays. Charles Sweetman takes this point a step further and suggests that Fitzgerald may have dismissed his own drinking out of a "fear of harming his reputation among magazine editors and Hollywood producers."[7] While there is little direct evidence to support such a claim, it is a logical conclusion to draw, especially when considering the contrast between Fitzgerald's condition throughout much of the decade and the image that he promoted in many of his nonfiction writings.

Michael Nowlin summarizes the appeal of the professional persona for writers striving to attain elite status. He says, "[literary] professionalism could connote, in effect, the masculine career and possession of special knowledge and competence justly conferring prestige, stability, and a salary not necessarily reflective of competitive market values."[8] For Fitzgerald, whose cultural capital was steadily decreasing throughout the 1930s, the persona of a competent and knowledgeable professional was useful both to counter attacks on his personal habits and to isolate aesthetic value from the operations of the marketplace. Nowlin, however, ultimately downplays the appeal of this position for Fitzgerald, claiming that the author "seldom characterized himself as a professional." In support of this statement, he cites the late essay, "Early Success," where Fitzgerald explicitly refers to himself as a "professional" and claims "no decent career was ever founded on a public," as an exceptional example. These statements were, Nowlin claims, designed to bolster the author's reputation after he had signed a contract with MGM.[9]

In contrast, I would assert that Fitzgerald repeatedly depicted himself as an author committed to the production of quality fiction and referred to himself as a literary "professional," explicitly or implicitly, in nearly every nonfiction essay he wrote during the 1930s. From his claim to be "in every sense a professional" in "One Hundred False Starts," to the typical "sedentary work-and-cigarette day" of "Sleeping and Waking," to his depiction of the frail author struggling to find the energy to work on his story in "Afternoon of an Author," Fitzgerald insistently creates narrators that are committed to the craft of writing and struggle, sometimes against great odds, to continue producing good stories. While such depictions are relatively few in number when compared with the publicity pieces done on and by

Fitzgerald in the 1920s, the consistency with which he emphasized his commitment to writing in the 1930s suggests that he relied a bit more heavily on notions of literary "professionalism" than previous commentators have acknowledged.

One element makes the "Crack-Up" essays stand out within this larger pattern: the narrator suggests that his earlier self was equally committed to the craft of writing. This young man did not fritter away his collegiate years in drunken escapades or neglect his studies for extracurricular pursuits. He "took a beating on poetry" and, after learning all he could, he "set about learning to write" (CU, 76). Moreover, Fitzgerald's struggles at Princeton are here chalked up to the early onset of tuberculosis, a claim that both distances his recurring illness from his current drinking habits and relieves him of responsibility for his academic troubles. In this version of the story, the narrator loses his position at the university simply because he needed too much time for recuperation. As usual, the conclusion of his college career is not mentioned at all.

When examining his life after college, the narrator places a similar emphasis on writing. Reflecting on the years between his first novel and the crack-up, the narrator says that he largely ceased to consider the outside world, opting instead to rely on the guidance and expectations of others. The one area he exempts from this judgment, however, is his writing. He claims that, in the previous twenty years, he "had done very little thinking, save within the problems of [his] craft" (CU, 79). This depiction of Fitzgerald, as a young man who is largely torpid except when animated to work through the technical difficulties of his "craft," is vastly different from, say, the figure in "Who's Who," who could care less what he is doing as long as he can make a "mark" on the world. In this piece, written during the earliest period of Fitzgerald's career, the young author decides to publish a book of poetry because "I had read somewhere that every great poet had written great poetry before he was twenty-one." Far from struggling to "learn what it was all about," as he says in the "Crack-Up" essays, this man spends one year fixating on poetry because he wants to be considered a "great poet." The previous year he had been obsessed with musical comedies and the following year he decides to write an "immortal novel."[10] Such a figure, concerned as he is with creating a lasting reputation, could hardly be bothered to worry about the craft of fiction, much less the specific form of the novel, which the Crack-Up narrator reveres as "the strongest and supplest medium for conveying thought and emotion from one human being to another" (CU, 78).

In short, there is little trace of the brash but talented youth churning out 7,000 words a day between parties. The new version of the young Fitzgerald is confident but alert to the contradictions inherent in his attitudes and actions. This depiction is important in part because it marks a subtle change from the persona Fitzgerald constructs in nonfiction pieces early in the decade, even as it reiterates many key elements of that public identity. It is also significant because the tragedy of the "clean break" arises from his lingering desire to retain elements of this previous life. As a result, the distance between the contemporary narrator and his former self serves as a useful measure of the crack-up's effects and thereby provides a frame through which to view the conclusions reached in these essays.

"BEING A WRITER ONLY": SOLUTIONS AND CONTRADICTIONS

In contrast to the complex rhetorical position that the narrator outlines during these essays, a position that is fraught with contradictions arising from the "multiplicity" of existence, he proposes a relatively simple solution in the final essay, "Handle with Care": "sheer" away the past self, along with all ideals that conflict with the modern world, and focus on "being a writer only." This new figure, the narrator claims, will look out only for himself and will not waste any time helping others unless doing so will forward his career in some way.

The final essay concludes with a long description of what such a transformation would entail for the narrator. He claims that he will hire a lawyer to teach him how to speak with a "polite acerbity that makes people feel that far from being welcome they are not even tolerated and are under continual and scathing analysis at every moment." He will also work on developing a slavish smile and a vocal tone that "will show no ring of conviction except the conviction of the person I am talking to." The narrator then concludes the essays by referring to himself as a "correct animal" who "may even lick your hand," if, that is, "you throw [him] a bone with enough meat on it" (CU, 82–84).

As the heavy sarcasm of this description should suggest, such an approach to the world hardly seems like a viable solution. One of the ironies of the narrator's final position is that, rather than correct or improve the nightmarish state of isolation he bemoans in the first essay, the "solution" effectively embraces it as a necessary condition of existence. The final essay even closes with a passage that echoes an earlier description of his illness. In the first essay, he explains, "I saw that for a long time I had not liked people and things...that even my love for those closest to me was become [sic] only an attempt to love, that my casual relations—with an editor, a tobacco seller, the child of a friend, were only what I remembered I *should* do, from other days" (CU, 72). In "Handle with Care," he describes his new life as "a writer only": "I do not any longer like the postman, nor the grocer, nor the editor, nor the cousin's husband, and he in turn will come to dislike me" (CU, 84).

Another one of the ironies of the narrator's final position is that a man who is supposedly committing himself wholeheartedly to a difficult craft has very little to say about that craft. Instead, the entire concluding rant is about the narrator conniving for advancement in the *business* of authorship, a view that directly opposes the heroic author-figure some later critics have found in this essay. Moreover, all of the traits the narrator must shed in order to survive have positive connotations. He can no longer be kind, just, or generous. He will not strive to emulate St. Francis of Assisi any more. He must give up the dream of being an "entire man." In short, the reader is being rhetorically positioned against the figure that emerges at the end of "Handle with Care," a point that is underscored by the progression of the essays' titles. From "The Crack-Up" to "Pasting It Together" to "Handle with Care," these names reveal the final figure to be a pastiche so poorly assembled that he may actually be dangerous, both in the sense that he could collapse at any moment and in the sense that this self-described "correct animal" could lash out unpredictably if not handled correctly. The implicit contrast to this sniveling misanthropic figure is, of course, the narrator's former self. He was strong enough to oppose such cynicism and to strive for completeness while remaining fully aware of the futility of his efforts.

Another important element of the narrator's hypothetical description in "Handle with Care" is the effect that the process of describing has on him. The narrator begins by wondering how "my enthusiasm and my vitality had been steadily and prematurely trickling away." He then reenacts the return of his vitality over the course of the next several pages. First, the narrator decides to "outlaw" all giving, a decision that leaves him feeling exuberant. Then, after listing many of the mundane responsibilities that currently dominate his life, he imagines himself as a "beady-eyed," self-absorbed careerist who could easily refuse such menial labors, a thought that prolongs his "heady villainous feeling" (CU, 82). Before the narrator even gets to the most open and direct attacks on the personality he is supposedly adopting, both the satirical nature of his pronouncements and his growing enthusiasm should be obvious. The narrator's strength is returning, but not directly as a result of his commitment to art. It stems from his critique of the position he is describing.

So the narrator of these pieces does not seem committed to the "clean break" as a way of overcoming his problems. The life he would lead as a conniving materialistic writer seems almost as abhorrent as his previous existence.[11] Yet, in the highly satirical portrayal of the "pure" writer that he is supposed to become, at least according to the Fitzgerald mythology, the narrator derives a new strength of purpose. In other words, he is reasserting himself as a serious writer, but not, ironically, in the literal manner most critics would like to suggest. He is contending to *remain* the devoted professional author he has always been, at least according to these particular pieces. When viewed from such a perspective, the narrator's opening "observation" about contradictions comes to seem much more like an epigraph for his former/new mode of existence than an epitaph for the young man who once faced the world with strength and courage. The narrator has accepted that his own case may be hopeless, but he continues to write.

CREATIVE FREEDOM AND MASCULINE CRISIS

This analysis of the "Crack-Up" essays can serve as a counterpoint to conventional interpretations. It does not, however, provide a clear indication of why particular groups of readers were attracted to alternate readings, some of which neglect crucial aspects of Fitzgerald's pieces. In order to understand the purchase of the most unsympathetic early interpretations, it is necessary, as will become apparent in the final section of the chapter, to situate the author-figure outlined above within a specifically gendered context.

The figure that Fitzgerald valorizes in the "Crack-Up" essays is strong enough to maintain a place in the world and preserve his individuality despite a constant barrage of "common ills-domestic, professional, and personal" (CU, 70). He is, in effect, free to cultivate his own personality, at least within the framework of a literary text, while remaining fully aware of all the contradictions and difficulties that will inevitably surface. It is precisely this sense of creative freedom that characterizes the profession of authorship in the "Crack-Up" essays. At two separate points that effectively bookend these pieces, he compares his line of work with other occupations and concludes that writing is distinguished, at least in part, by its lack of boundaries. The opening of the first essay includes a brief explanation of the "romantic" appeal of authorship. The narrator says, "You were never going to have the power of a man of strong political or religious convictions but you were certainly more independent" (CU, 70). In his concluding remarks, which are ironically given at the exact same point that he is submitting to the dictates of the literary marketplace by becoming a "beady-eyed" careerist, he says that doctors commit to helping people and soldiers fight to enter Valhalla, but "a writer need have no such ideals unless he makes them for himself" (CU, 84). In both cases, writing is distinguished from other professions because it depends only on the creativity of the author. There are no larger convictions or expectations to limit one's production.

Given this idealization of the writing process, it is not surprising that Fitzgerald repeatedly figures his breakdown as the gradual erosion of personal freedoms. In "Pasting It Together," the narrator fears that the cinema, a "mechanical and communal art," is usurping the space of literature in American cultural life. Such a shift relegates true literary talents, presumably like Fitzgerald himself, to dependent roles on scriptwriting teams or, even worse, editorial jobs fixing the work of others. In addition to these larger cultural constraints, the narrator describes his profession as little more than a series of personal obligations. He does not talk about the actual act of writing at all, even after he has committed himself to being "a writer only." Instead, he merely complains about others who want his help: "As a sort of beginning there was a whole shaft of letters to be tipped into the waste basket when I went home, letters that wanted something for nothing—to read this man's manuscript, market this man's poem, speak free on the radio, indite notes of introduction, give this interview, help with the plot of this play, with this domestic situation, perform this act of thoughtfulness or charity" (CU, 82).

Beyond cultural and professional obligations, the social roles that the narrator is required to play have become an increasing burden on him as, he realizes in retrospect, he runs out of emotional capital. Unable to fully participate in his world and yet initially unwilling to cast off his obligations, the narrator is trapped by routines that further drain his assets: "I realized that in those two years...I had weaned myself from all the things I used to love—that every act of life from the morning tooth-brush to the friend at dinner had become an effort. I saw that for a long time I had not liked people and things, but only followed the rickety old pretense of liking. I saw that even my love for those closest to me was become only an attempt to love, that my casual relations...were only what I remembered I *should* do, from other days" (CU, 72).

The narrator's desire for a freedom beyond the constraints of American culture, his profession, and his current social location reaches its endpoint in his anxieties about the essentially random nature of existence itself. He wants to occupy a position that is radically free, but he constantly appeals to the predefined roles that exist within larger sets of prescribed values. Alternatively, the narrator compulsively orders the fragments of his own existence while also bridling at any larger orders imposed on him, though these orders have conditioned his agency in the first place. In short, the narrator wants to avoid the contemporary social obligations of being a writer, but he is unwilling to admit too much relativity into his life. He cannot conceive of himself in any other profession, nor does he attempt to reimagine his profession in a more acceptable form.

These struggles can be characterized as two opposing forces. On one hand, the narrator faces the random, ever-proliferating universe that threatens to invalidate any rational activity. On the other, he faces the danger of overly systematized human activity, which itself threatens to smother or enslave the otherwise distinct, independent individual. As many critics have pointed out about the era's larger debates over standardization and individuality, such discussions are typically written in strikingly gendered terms. In the current context, Andreas Huyssen's important work on gender, technology, and aesthetics in *After the Great Divide* proves to be particularly useful. Huyssen argues that not only are autonomous individuals opposed to a feminized culture of mass production, but that industrialized production in the nineteenth and early twentieth centuries was often connected more specifically with maternal forces run wild. This seemingly counterintuitive metaphor emphasizes the danger inherent in such degraded cultural forms, which threaten to erode the boundaries distinguishing mass culture from the sacred work of art and undermine the control of the male subject. So artists distanced themselves from feminized mass culture as a way of both reinforcing the difference of the individuated subject and asserting their authority as elite figures removed from such degraded cultural forms.[12]

Huyssen's analysis helps to explain why Fitzgerald could so easily alternate between what appears to be two opposing problems: the underlying "multiplicity" of existence and the gradual standardization/ degradation of contemporary culture. Both problems could be subsumed under a larger opposition between the rational masculine individual and the boundless/constraining female impulse, an opposition that appears throughout Fitzgerald's nonfiction work. In some cases, Fitzgerald directly connects the feminine with the difficulty of rational containment. In an interview with Harry Salpeter in the mid-1920s, Fitzgerald claims that Americans were traveling to France because America is "too big to get your hands on. Because it's a woman's country. Because its very nice and its various local necessities have made it impossible for an American to have a real credo." He then goes on at some length about how people in the United States have not been able to think enough in order to have "great dreams."[13]

This conflation of the feminine, the overwhelming nature of contemporary life, and people's inability to develop coherent principles creates an ominous backdrop for Fitzgerald's final statement of hope. He wishes that the country could be saved by the birth of a new hero, one who is explicitly male and will certainly "not be educated by women teachers." Moreover, the new hero will be both independent and inherently masculine enough, if he can avoid being corrupted by feminine teachings, to need no father.[14] This refiguring of the Christ story, which posits the new "hero" emerging from a lowly "immigrant class" to a mother who knows the special destiny of her hypermasculine son, suggests that the true evil from which contemporary Americans must be saved is the suffocating feminine impulse, a force barely controlled enough to maintain the integrity of the country. The true inheritance of this fatherless boy, the essential godliness bestowed upon him at conception, seems to be masculinity itself.

While this example may be more elaborate than most, its quasi-hysterical tone was not altogether uncommon in Fitzgerald's publicity pieces during the 1920s. In one of his last articles of the decade, "Girls Believe in Girls," published in the February 1930 issue of *Liberty*, Fitzgerald makes an equally strong case for the danger of standardized feminine culture. He says, "The man of intelligence either runs alone or seeks amusement in stimulating circles—in any case, he is rarely available [to women]; the business man brings to social intercourse little more than what he reads in the papers...so that, in the thousand and one women's worlds that cover the land, the male voice is represented largely by the effeminate and the weak, the parasite and the failure."[15] Here, the independent, rational man remains separate from both the standardized ideas emerging from widely available newspapers and ominously pervasive "women's worlds."

This phrase refers to the rapid expansion of cultural spaces for women in the early twentieth century, spaces that Ezra Pound, in a similar diatribe, saw as receptacles for an American literature bereft of the masculinity inherent in true poetic "virtu." Such effeminate writing is, Pound claimed, "left to the care of ladies' societies, and of 'current events' clubs, and is numbered among the 'cultural influences.'"[16] Fitzgerald's broad reference figures the rapid expansion of such spaces as symptomatic of the larger danger inherent in a sprawling, suffocating feminine force.

Furthermore, the effeminate man, already rendered parasitical and weak for his association with the noncreative world of "business," lacks even the little bit of intellect necessary to sort through the information in newspapers. Such a position locates him intellectually in the same sphere as the women in Pound's book and "current event" clubs, who lack the penetrating masculine insight to glean true knowledge from literature. Again, Fitzgerald ultimately associates this rise of the feminine, in both its distinct cultural forms and its infiltration of the masculine sphere, with the larger disintegration of a society characterized by "its confusion and its wide-open doors," a place that "no longer offers the stability of thirty years ago."[17]

Fitzgerald's references to the uncontainable and smothering evil of the feminine sphere lost some of their intensity in his nonfiction work during the 1930s, as his new persona seemed to necessitate a less frenzied tone. The twin dangers conflated and somewhat confused under the larger banner of the feminine, however, continue to reappear throughout the decade, as in his idolization of the mellow monasticism of Edmund Wilson's study in "My Lost City," the contemptible rise of feminized culture depicted in "Echoes of the Jazz Age," and his opposition between the "beautiful muscular organization" of masculine sports and the "horribly complicated mess of living" in "Ring" (CU, 25–26, 19, 37). In the "Crack-Up" essays, Fitzgerald implicitly positions himself against both faces of the pernicious feminine threat by insisting on his role as a professional male writer.

The masculine subtext that surfaces immediately in the first essay could suggest that Fitzgerald began the piece with his male audience specifically in mind. Given *Esquire*'s unusual publication standards, it seems reasonable to assume that Fitzgerald knew who would ultimately be reading his work.[18] First, he sets out to shock the sensibilities of presumably privileged males with his brazen opening line ("Of course all life is a process of breaking down"). Then he associates himself with his male audience by adopting both a tone of familiarity and a second person point of view ("[the big blows] you remember and blame things on and, in moments of weakness, tell your friends about"). He finishes the opening passage by identifying his generalized subject as a male and aligning his concerns specifically with the condition of the male psyche ("you realize with finality that in some regard you will never be as good a man again") (CU, 69).

Following this series of general observations, the essay moves into a broad portrait of the narrator's background, a description that marks him explicitly as a "literary man." Writing is also repeatedly compared to other respectable male professions. Doctors, soldiers, politicians, and religious leaders are just a few of the predominantly male circles to figure into these essays. The narrator even draws attention to the ongoing struggle of his day-to-day responsibilities, one area where smothering feminine dependence directly intrudes on his creative freedom. This topic was a particularly difficult one for Fitzgerald, who had, in both personal exchanges and nonfiction writing, repeatedly emphasized the implicitly male burden of being financially responsible for a household. In one early piece for *McCall's* where both he and Zelda were asked to respond to the question "Does a moment of revolt come sometime to every married man?" Fitzgerald bemoans "that ghastly moment once a week when you realize that it all depends on you—wife, babies, house, servants, yard and dog. That if it wasn't for you, it'd all fall to pieces like an old broken dish. That because of those things you must labor all the days of your life."[19] The "cracked plate" metaphor so neatly links Fitzgerald's professional endeavors with the pressing exigencies of the domestic sphere, which could shatter irreparably without sufficient male support, that he used it several times throughout his career.

Most notably in this context, the narrator employs it as a focal image at the beginning of "Pasting It Together," the second of the three "Crack-Up" essays. Here, the narrator himself has become a "cracked plate" that can still be used but is no longer fit for company. He goes on to claim that such an unvarnished lament, free of any redemptive heroics, is necessary because "there weren't any Euganean hills that I could see" (CU, 75). As Ronald Gervais persuasively argues, this passage most immediately refers to Percy Bysshe Shelley's "Lines Written Among the Euganean Hills," a poem in which the narrator bemoans the misery of life but is inspired by the beauty of the hills to imagine a redeemed society. For Fitzgerald's narrator, there is no idyllic retreat from the agonies of life, not even through the poetic imagination.[20] So the image of the cracked plate, which substitutes a single domestic object for grandiose heroic idealizations, succinctly encapsulates the reduced aspirations and the diminished vision of Fitzgerald's narrator. He cannot even begin to imagine something as large as a redeemed society. It is enough for him to face himself, honestly and openly, and admit whatever he happens to find there.

It is important to note, given the narrator's insistence in these essays on his ability to continue writing, that he does not seem to seriously entertain the idea of running away from his vaguely defined "responsibilities," nor does he finally question his ability to serve. He is still fit to hold "crackers" and "leftovers," perhaps the metaphorical equivalent of the short texts he had been working on since completing *Tender Is the Night* two years earlier. Moreover, while he has unquestionably been worn down by experience, it is ironically the damage suffered that provides him with material to continue working, just as his supposed breakdown provides the subject matter for these particular pieces.

It is around precisely such notions of masculine responsibility that other macho professional figures such as Arnold Gingrich were able to rally in support of the author. In his introduction to the collected Pat Hobby stories, all of which were originally published in *Esquire,* Gingrich dismisses the claim that these pieces are inferior because they were done for money. Rather than simply argue for the merit of these stories, however, he outlines Fitzgerald's demanding work habits and his scrupulous attention to detail. The defense concludes with the claim that all of Fitzgerald's work was done for money, the good and the bad, and so to distinguish these particular pieces on that basis seems absurd. Of course, the obligations driving Fitzgerald in Gingrich's account all stem from his wife, Zelda: "From 1920 on [Fitzgerald] wrote for money—enough to marry Zelda in the first place and to afford her, and the wild life they led together until 1930. And after that, he wrote for money enough to meet the strain of her fantastically expensive treatments for mental illness."[21]

As should now be apparent, Fitzgerald's attitude toward women was not altogether atypical for the time. His comments often veered into open misogyny and he certainly employed the gendered constructions common to his age. He was, however, often wary of relatively extreme forms of masculine posturing, which were, in the literary field, regularly associated with his onetime friend and lifelong acquaintance, Ernest Hemingway. In "Echoes," published shortly before Gertrude Stein and Hemingway's personal dispute received public attention through the pages of Stein's memoir *The Autobiography of Alice B. Toklas,* Fitzgerald approvingly quotes Stein's commentary on an unnamed "he-man": " 'And what is a He-man?' demanded Gertrude Stein one day. 'Isn't it a large enough order to fill out to the dimensions of all that 'a man' has meant in the past? A *He*-man!' " (CU, 17).

This quote takes on particular importance in the context of the "Crack-Up" essays, where Fitzgerald is struggling to live up not only to his own idealistic vision of his past self but also to a larger male intellectual tradition. As Scott Donaldson points out, these essays, perhaps more than anything else Fitzgerald had ever written, are littered with references to famous writers and thinkers, ranging from Descartes to Wordsworth to Tolstoy to Lenin. Donaldson interprets these myriad references as a symptom of the author's desire to find a suitable model on which to base his essays.[22] More importantly for my purposes, Fitzgerald is also implicitly connecting his own struggle to a long male tradition. He is not simply wallowing in a shamefully revelatory celebrity exposé, but is joining a line that goes back at least as far as St. John of the Cross.

Fitzgerald takes up this underlying conflict between the stoic he-man impulse in the literary field and his own revelatory discourse at several points during the "Crack-Up" essays. For instance, the previous reference to Shelley's "Lines Written Among the Euganean Hills" is couched in a larger dismissal of "those to whom all self-revelation is contemptible, unless it ends with a noble thanks to the gods for the Unconquerable Soul" (CU, 75). The narrator's reference to an "Unconquerable Soul" specifically recalls William Ernest Henley's "Invictus," a poem that may have been written immediately before Henley, who had already had one foot amputated, underwent treatment to save his other leg. The narrator of Henley's poem repeatedly asserts his resilience to adversity, from an opening paean to the gods for his "unconquerable soul" to the concluding lines, "I am the master of my fate: / I am the captain of my soul."[23]

For Fitzgerald's narrator, Henley's idealistic retreat into the refuge of the "unconquerable soul," similar to Shelley's romantic elevation of the Euganean hills, is an explicit refusal to face what Henley calls "this place of wrath and tears."[24] The narrator asserts, to the contrary, that a man must be able to look unflinchingly at the suffering of life and press on anyway, a rhetorical move that turns the tables on a reigning standard of masculinity while simultaneously appealing to that standard. The narrator is, in effect, implying that he is manlier than his stoic counterparts precisely because he is willing to face, and display, his own losing struggle against the world as it happens, without recourse to any heroic idealizations.

In addition to his implicit declaration of masculinity, the narrator weaves a series of masculine metaphors throughout the essays, relying in particular on images that refer to sports and war, as when he refers to his ego as an "arrow shot" or compares the silence following his crack-up to "standing at twilight on a deserted range, with an empty rifle in my hands and the targets down" (CU, 70, 77–78). At the same time, the two major disappointments of his life are, as he tells us at both the beginning of the first essay and the end of the last, failing at football in college and not going overseas during World War I. These references, appearing within a broader framework of failure, do not simply point to masculine rites of passage but also function as a potentially emasculating reminder of the narrator's inability to secure his status through conventional paths. Yet when this reversal is combined with the narrator's larger reassertion of masculinity, itself embodied in the text that represents his willingness to continue writing in the face of unbeatable odds, this series of metaphors again twists into a reflection of the narrator's larger claim to manhood. The primary difference is that the assertion of masculinity is now rooted in the narrator's willingness to reveal past failures and anxieties.

This complex rhetorical strategy, which entails employing a familiar set of masculine tropes only to challenge and then ironically reaffirm their social significance, also helps the narrator to avoid the connotations of standardization often linked with his particular models, war and sports. He invokes these two arenas as culturally sanctioned spaces in which a man, through strong will power and a commitment to discipline, can prove his mettle. Both arenas, however, potentially suggest a perverse form of over-discipline that turns men into mindless cogs in a larger machine. The narrator, who both rails against standardization and insists on the importance of conscious reflection, avoids such charges by openly insisting on his failure in these traditional domains, even as he hedges his bets by simultaneously implying, through his own pain at losing out in these arenas, that he desires to be blessed with the laurels of conventional masculinity.

Again, the narrator's desire to recoup his manhood is most readily apparent in his own self-descriptions. He is a rifleman, a lone warrior, a single arrow. These are, not surprisingly, terms Fitzgerald employed elsewhere in the 1930s, particularly in connection with his work as a writer. He used a similar description the previous year in an introduction to *The Great Gatsby*. In a brief passage that explicates what it means to be a writer, which he defines as "giving expression to intimate explorations," he suggests that all writers "have a pride akin to a soldier going into battle; without knowing whether there will be anybody there, to distribute medals or even to record it."[25] Fitzgerald suggests that a writer shares many attributes with a soldier but is more manly because the act of creation is always a struggle one begins alone, with, as he says in "Handle with Care," "no such ideals [as a soldier has] unless he makes them for himself" (CU, 84).

MASCULINITY AND THE NEGATIVE RESPONSE TO THE CRACK-UP

Following conventional readings of the "Crack-Up" essays, it is surprising that the trilogy managed to cause so much controversy, especially among Fitzgerald's fellow writers. The essays' larger vision of a professional author struggling simultaneously against life and the dictates of his craft was nothing new in Fitzgerald's work. As we have seen, this persona was part of a larger pattern that connected much of his nonfiction work in the 1930s. Even the overriding emphasis on failure could also be found in a piece such as "One Hundred False Starts," which addresses, albeit in a somewhat lighter tone, the countless failures that accompany any notable success.

Similarly, Fitzgerald's vague challenge to crass materialism did not pose a problem for other writers, as many of his acquaintances were, in the 1930s at least, actively critical of the larger economic and social systems that had brought the world to a crisis point. Finally, the troubled view of life that unfolds throughout the "Crack-Up" essays was not significantly different from the despondent view expressed by many other writers at the time. Hemingway, who was highly critical of the essays, outlined a similar vision in a letter to Fitzgerald that commented on *Tender Is the Night*: "Forget your personal tragedy. We are all bitched from the start and you especially have to be hurt like hell before you can write seriously. But when you get the damned hurt use it—don't cheat with it. Be as faithful to it as a scientist."[26] Hemingway insists on the inevitability of death and failure, the importance of professional integrity, and the necessity of maintaining an unflinching, implicitly masculine, rational gaze in the face of intense personal struggles, all of which feature centrally in Fitzgerald's essays.

When read in terms of the gendered aesthetic hierarchies that suffused literary discussions in the early twentieth century, however, Fitzgerald's essays do pose a significant challenge to other men working in the literary field. Not only do the articles directly attack those "to whom all self-revelation is contemptible," the unnamed people who idolize "Henley's familiar heroics," but by extension they attempt to reconstitute a celebrity confession, that notorious instrument of America's feminized mass culture, in a sensational mass-market magazine as a valid expression of literary masculinity. In short, Fitzgerald's essays challenge the boundaries of what it is acceptable for a man to say under the banner of a culturally sanctioned masculinity. This reading of the Crack-Up will help to explain the opinions expressed by some of Fitzgerald's contemporaries, opinions that strongly contrasted with those of critics writing after his death.

Few, if any, contemporary responses, from readers of *Esquire* to fans of Fitzgerald's work to his associates and friends, show admiration for the author's "heroic awareness," to use Trilling's phrase. Instead, readers tended to take his declarations of psychological and spiritual crises at face value, by turns supporting, cajoling, urging, and criticizing him. Perhaps more directly, the two men most involved in the business of selling Fitzgerald's work, Max Perkins and Harold Ober, both came to feel the essays had a significant *negative* impact on his reputation. In a letter to Fitzgerald, Ober initially commented, "No one who had cracked up and stayed that way could possibly write as well as this."[27] Then, after spending several months struggling to convince the representatives of various Hollywood studios that Fitzgerald could still perform adequately as a scriptwriter, Ober wrote Fitzgerald another note that concluded with the blunt assertion, "I think those confounded *Esquire* articles have done you a great deal of harm and I hope you won't do any more."[28]

This judgment reflects the larger trajectory of Fitzgerald's career in the mid-1930s. The author was repeatedly connected with the distant glamour of the 1920s and did not produce enough work, or grab enough headlines, to significantly modify the public's opinion of him. In such a context, Fitzgerald's scattered meditations on his past persona and the difficulties of producing quality writing only worked to reinforce the sense that the author's best writing was behind him. By 1936, even those critics and writers who knew that Fitzgerald possessed a keen literary mind had a hard time seeing the "Crack-Up" essays as anything more than an embarrassing admission of failure or a desperate grab for attention.

John Dos Passos, for instance, wrote late in 1936 to ask about a shoulder injury that had been troubling Fitzgerald since July. After a brief series of pleasantries, he launches into a page-long diatribe about the "Crack-Up" essays, opening with, "Christ, man, how do you find time in the middle of the general conflagration [of the Depression] to worry about all that stuff? If you don't want to do stuff on your own, why not get a reporting job somewhere" (CU, 311). Dos Passos's continued willingness to impugn these pieces, which had begun appearing on newsstands at least nine months before this letter was written, suggests something of the ire the "Crack-Up" essays provoked, particularly among white male professionals and contemporary male writers. Fitzgerald's editor, Max Perkins, who referred to the essays as the author's "indecent invasion of his own privacy," disliked the pieces so much that when Edmund Wilson tried to get Scribner's to publish them in collected form ten years later, in part as a way to keep Fitzgerald's name available to the literary public five years after his death, Perkins refused.[29] Despite the fact that Scribner's had published every book Fitzgerald put out during his lifetime as well as Wilson's posthumous collection containing the extant fragments of Fitzgerald's final, uncompleted novel *The Last Tycoon*, Wilson had to go to New Directions in order to get *The Crack-Up* published.

Such responses were not atypical. Most literary professionals writing to Fitzgerald in the early months of 1936 focused not on the author's supposedly resilient conclusion, as many later critics would do, but on his declaration of illness. Figures as various as Ernest Hemingway, John O'Hara, John Dos Passos, Burton Rascoe, Gilbert Seldes, and Julian Street all wrote letters encouraging Fitzgerald to get past his difficulties and continue writing. To give just one particularly direct example, Dos Passos, in an earlier letter, wrote, "I...wish like hell you could find some happy way of getting that magnificent writing apparatus of yours to work darkening paper; which is its business."[30] Read on its simplest level, such a comment neglects the developments in the final essay of Fitzgerald's "Crack-Up" trilogy and it misses, as many respondents at the time did, the larger irony that this depressed persona had become a potent new source of material for Fitzgerald. The first three essays alone managed to generate enough publicity that Simon and Schuster attempted to pull the author away from Scribner's to do an autobiographical collection with them.

Given both the melancholy tone present throughout much of the "Crack-Up" essays and Fitzgerald's supposedly depressed mind-set while writing, Dos Passos's phrase, "some happy way" can easily be interpreted as a dismissal of these pieces. Such a reading would suggest that Dos Passos is not simply encouraging Fitzgerald to write, but is instead urging him to produce something different from the "Crack-Up" essays. This interpretation is borne out by Dos Passos's other comments at the time, including the previously cited letter in which he launches a much more direct attack on the "Crack-Up" essays. What makes this assessment interesting, and relevant to many of the other negative responses Fitzgerald received in the months after publishing the "Crack-Up" essays, is not simply its more overt invocation of conventional aesthetic categories, but the insistently gendered terms used to elaborate them. After writing off Fitzgerald's essays as little more than an admission of impotence ("If you don't want to do stuff on your own ...''), Dos Passos describes the contemporary state of authorship in terms of a violent, if largely abstract, combat, where the ideal soldier/writer must enter the "general conflagration" to struggle against both the "murderous forces of history" and "the big boys," who, he claims, are constantly threatening to "close down on us" (CU, 311).

In such a charged, masculine environment, Fitzgerald's work, which amounts to little more than "go[ing] to pieces" in print, represents the kind of mindless popular work that should be avoided by serious artists. It is, to use Dos Passos's vaguely sexual terminology, equivalent to "spilling" one's creative energies, which is even more abhorrent given that Fitzgerald is willing to waste his energy "for Arnold Gingrich." Dos Passos does not press this connection further, but the link serves to connect Fitzgerald's work with both vaguely homosexual and materialistic impulses, positioning him as an author working to please other men and not pursuing the imperatives of his creative vision. In contrast, Dos Passos champions "do[ing] stuff on your own," which is to say, creating literary texts beyond the reaches of, and thus as an implicit challenge to, the "big boys'" efforts at ideological control.

Somewhere in between these two extremes lies journalism, a suggestion that carries much rhetorical baggage in the early decades of the twentieth century. As Christopher Wilson has argued in *The Labor of Words,* the "ideal of reportage" began to take over the literary field during the early twentieth century in direct opposition to what was frequently characterized as an effeminate and attenuated literary writing. Authors increasingly strove to distance themselves from associations with an effete bookishness by adopting the pose of uncompromising reporters dredging through "the muck of American life," and many male writers from the period, including Crane, James, Dreiser, Hemingway, and Dos Passos himself, spent time working as reporters in their youth.[31] So Dos Passos's suggestion, part of what he fittingly refers to as his "locker room pep talk," can be read as a call to a specifically masculine form of engagement, one that would allow Fitzgerald to employ his talent in a more direct, if somewhat less artful, challenge to the powers that be.

What is particularly interesting about the aesthetic structure Dos Passos sets up in his letter to Fitzgerald is that it places a significant amount of emphasis on the *form* of Fitzgerald's essays. He even concludes his discussion by suggesting that Fitzgerald could safely use the same material, as long as he fictionalizes it: "If you want to go to pieces I think it's absolutely O.K. but I think you ought to write a first rate novel about it" (CU, 311). While Dos Passos does not specifically distinguish between autobiography and the superficially revelatory style of the "Crack-Up" essays, other people picked up the same charge more directly.

When Fitzgerald began toying with the idea of creating an autobiographical compilation that would include the "Crack-Up" essays, Max Perkins immediately discouraged the project. Instead, he suggested that Fitzgerald begin work on "a reminiscent book—not autobiographical, but reminiscent." Perkins then goes on to flatter Fitzgerald by saying that critic Gilbert Seldes approves of the idea, before he finally closes in on the true target of his criticism: "I do not think the *Esquire* pieces ought to be published alone. But as for an autobiographical book which would comprehend what is in them, I would be very much for it."[32] In the last instance, Perkins, like Dos Passos, is willing to accept a work that uses the underlying ideas of the "Crack-Up" essays and he is even willing, in direct contradiction to his initial judgment, to accept a book that is fundamentally autobiographical, as long as it is ultimately a reflective assessment and not an embarrassing confessional revelation like "The Crack-Up."

These two examples elaborate many of the ideas that remain implicit in other critiques of Fitzgerald's essays. Professionals in the literary field, from critics to writers to members of the managerial class, implicitly leveled charges that Fitzgerald had violated both his masculinity, by complaining about life in an autobiographical format, and his artistic integrity with these pieces. Hemingway's numerous references to the essays have perhaps garnered the most attention. He once characterized the works as "whin[ing] in public" and he repeatedly referred to Fitzgerald's disgraceful "shamelessness of defeat" in correspondence. One such reference was even followed by the assertion that Fitzgerald simply needs to do some "noncommercial, honest work."[33] All of Hemingway's animosity culminated with the now-famous reference to Fitzgerald in his short story, "The Snows of Kilamanjaro," which ran in *Esquire* the same month that Fitzgerald published "Afternoon of an Author," another semi-autobiographical piece about a physically and mentally exhausted writer.[34]

As dramatic as Hemingway's references are, similar comments appeared in a wide variety of places, from the *San Francisco Chronicle*'s charge that Fitzgerald was "being a bit too sorry for himself" to the pages of *Esquire,* where one respondent openly scoffed at Fitzgerald's weakness: "His pearl: VITALITY. I agree with him. It's too darn bad he hasn't got it!"[35] Even Gilbert Seldes, who was far more sympathetic to popular culture than most, had a hard time accepting Fitzgerald's confessions as significant pieces of work. In response to Fitzgerald's desire to publish a collection of autobiographical works featuring "The Crack-Up," Seldes wrote Fitzgerald advocating, like Perkins, a reminiscent collection. After several paragraphs that explain the value of an integrated text, the letter concludes with an uncharacteristically rambling paragraph that attempts to deal with the "Crack-Up" pieces directly. Seldes begins by praising the essays for their "thoughtfulness," but then suggests that this virtue is the very reason they should not be included in a collection, as Fitzgerald could use his newfound creative energy to start a reflective autobiography. Such a work, he claims encouragingly, would be "of supreme importance," presumably in a way that the "Crack-Up" essays are not.[36]

Not everyone responded similarly to Fitzgerald's essays. Yet the consistency with which such gendered criticisms appear among a subset of male respondents and the extent to which these arguments dominate the more extreme negative responses suggest their importance for understanding the controversy surrounding the "Crack-Up" essays. Kirk Curnutt, whose article "Making a 'Clean Break'" is perhaps the most sustained attempt to assess the reception of "The Crack-Up" in historical terms, advances this argument by working somewhat counterintuitively to connect Fitzgerald's pieces with a decidedly feminized form of confessional writing popular during the 1920s and 1930s.

The confessional form in question, though it had existed long before the twentieth century, returned to prominence through *True Story Magazine,* first published by Bernarr MacFadden in 1919. MacFadden's magazine contained first-person accounts, always under the pretext that they were true stories, about the various misfortunes that befell young women. What links these stories, Curnutt argues, with something as seemingly different as Fitzgerald's "Crack-Up" essays is the form that both types of writing take. The salacious narratives of the confessional magazines were presented as cautionary tales, with narrators who had supposedly learned from their mistakes and had come to renounce the past indiscretions that ultimately constituted the bulk of their stories. So both the typical confessional tale and Fitzgerald's essays are structured around the idea of a "clean break," that is, "the determined abandonment of a self-image that one no longer chooses to perpetuate." The appeal of these stories, Curnutt claims, is that they promote the "illusion that we can purify ourselves of undesirable behavioral tendencies through resolution and will power."[37]

While Curnutt's article uses this historical connection to examine some of the implications of Fitzgerald's formal choices, he never addresses the specifically gendered nature of the confessional magazines. *True Story* magazine was, from the outset, edited to appeal to a working-class female audience by using heroines that these readers could identify with and by depicting events that could have occurred in their lives. In short, it attempted to recreate a young woman's world, though always with an emphasis on the more sensational aspects of life. As one magazine historian tersely stated, it repeatedly highlighted "violence, overpowering sex drives, and broken homes."[38]

It is perhaps telling of the specifically female dimension of this world as well as the gossipy tone of these stories, which one confession writer characterized as "the warm breathlessness of a girl confiding to a friend across the table," that Mary Macfadden, Bernarr's wife, ultimately received credit for creating *True Story*. She presents her account in a book written about her husband, *Dumbbells and Carrot Strips: The Story of Bernarr Macfadden*. She claims that the idea came from reading the confessional letters sent in by readers of Macfadden's *Physical Culture* magazine. Realizing that these letters were entertaining and salable in their own right, she supposedly approached Bernarr, saying, "These are true stories. They come from the following you have attracted.... Let's get out a magazine to be called *True Story*, written by its own readers in the first person. This has never been done before."[39]

True or not, the story certainly conforms to the magazine's image as an entertaining but, at least initially, honest look at the lives of working-class women. This basic perspective turned out to be so successful that *True Story* quickly spawned a number of imitators, all publishing comparable stories under suggestively similar titles such as *True Experiences* and *Intimate Stories*. Despite the increased competition, *True Story* was selling 850,000 copies per issue within five years and, by 1927, was challenging *Ladies' Home Journal* and *McCall's* for leadership in the women's field by selling over 2 million copies of each issue. By 1950, the field had grown so much that eighteen separate confession magazines sold over 7 million copies per issue.[40]

As might be expected, the rapidly increasing market for such magazines coupled with their often salacious content led many, even in the mainstream press, to disparage both this lowbrow fodder and those people foolish enough to read it. *The Saturday Evening Post* once referred to the audience for such magazines as "Macfadden's anonymous amateur illiterates."[41] Public opinion was so negative that, despite impressive sales numbers, publishers had an incredibly difficult time procuring advertising. The problem arose in part because advertisers had little respect for a lower-class female readership and because few businesses wanted their goods linked in the larger public mind with so contemptible a product. Publishers, as a result, had to convince advertisers not that they offered the best available market for certain products, but that their audience should be considered a viable market in the first place. A quick glance at titles of trade publications, such as *The Women That Taxes Made; An Editor's Intimate Picture of a Large but Little Understood Market,* put out by the editor-in-chief of *True Story* Women's Group, or "On the Subject of Social Class and Its Relation to Magazines," written by the director of research for Macfadden Publications, suggests just how far such magazines were from being considered legitimate advertising outlets.[42]

Given that one of the most popular forms of public confession in the 1920s and 1930s was an explicitly feminized, widely disdained lowbrow product, it is not surprising that Fitzgerald's own first-person revelations attracted similar associations, especially from those men whose very occupations potentially placed them outside, or on the edges of, traditional spheres of masculinity.[43] To make matters worse, the success of confession magazines led advertisers to employ the form as an alternative to more traditional sloganeering. By the late 1920s, ads for everything from condensed milk to pens to dress shoes ran scandalous headlines over pseudoconfessions that revealed the virtues of everyday items.[44] So Fitzgerald's use of the confessional form ran the added risk of associating his work directly with ad copy and indirectly with the feminized banality of the mass market, a connection that E. B. White made explicit in his critique of the "picturesque despondency" of Fitzgerald's pieces.

Yet, if, as Curnutt argues, the central connection between Fitzgerald's work and confessional discourse resides in their formal similarities, particularly in their shared use of the "clean break," then my own reading of these essays allows us to interpret Fitzgerald's pieces as a critique of the confessional form, or at least the larger claim to total self-control that underlies it.[45] As George Gerbner points out in his early study of confession magazines, such stories counteract the subversive potential of having a sympathetic lower-class woman rebel against social norms by insistently "making her act of defiance a crime or a sin; [by] making her suffer long and hard; [by] making her, not society, repent and reform; [by] permitting her only to come to terms, and not to grips, with the 'brutal world' in which she lives."[46] In contrast, Fitzgerald's essays draw strength from their willingness to critique the world that the narrator feels has, in many ways, victimized him. It is only through his relentless search for answers and solutions, sustained by the endless multiplicity of the very environment he seeks to understand, that he can finally achieve some sense of authority in the world.

Similarly, by folding a critique of traditional masculinity into the confessional form, Fitzgerald's pieces challenge the masculine boundaries that have been drawn around the literary sphere while implying that such a challenge is, in turn, a reflection of his manly resolve. It is a move that could potentially recoup the very position he overturns, only in a somewhat more complex fashion. His form suggests that the psychological and emotional recesses of the self should remain open to the penetrating masculine gaze of the scientist and, furthermore, that this unflinching examination of life is no less worthy of textual space than any of the other areas of life that writers, partially under the rubric of a masculine reportage, found worthy of print.

The subheadings run under the titles of each piece in *Esquire* underscore the emphasis on both the manliness of the narrator ("Handle with Care/Vivisection of a hardening soul by one who had no use for anesthesia") and the literary pretense of the pieces ("Shoring up the fragments against the ruin left in the wake of that psycho-physical storm: a crack-up"). The reference to T. S. Eliot's "The Waste Land," which was already implicit, if slightly less direct, in Fitzgerald's title, also works to compliment Fitzgerald's troubled vision of both contemporary America and himself.

Finally, it is Fitzgerald's tendency to turn his personal revelation into a study of abstract theses, in a variety of different forms, that formally distances his pieces from the feminized lowbrow products they in other ways resembled. By retaining some semblance of analysis throughout his pieces, Fitzgerald bolsters the implicit claim that such work is not simply a cheap grab for attention or an egotistical exercise. It is, at least in part, a serious exploration of the circumstances surrounding his emotional collapse.

To see that Fitzgerald himself at times invested these essays with the seriousness I have read into them takes little more than a look at his correspondence, particularly in the months shortly after they were written. Yet nowhere is his purpose more evident than in the plan for his autobiographical collection. In a letter written to Max Perkins in April 1936, Fitzgerald revisited his proposal for a compilation and outlined the pieces he would include. His list, which begins with the promotional "Who's Who" and a short piece on Princeton from *College Humor* magazine, progresses toward more reflective essays, such as "My Lost City" and "Echoes of the Jazz Age." This organization suggests, as Marc Dolan points out, "a redemptive passage from prior callowness into a wider, wiser consciousness."[47] The proposed book would conclude/culminate with the "Crack-Up" essays.[48]

Despite the possibility of reading these pieces as a thoughtful meditation, most of Fitzgerald's contemporaries interpreted them as a relatively straightforward expression of emotion, hence the outpouring of both sympathy and contempt as readers measured the appropriateness of his public revelations. Many readers accepted the new persona they saw in the "Crack-Up" essays even as they disagreed over the exact nature of the changes Fitzgerald was supposedly attempting to document. Of course, the term "new" is a bit misleading in such a context, given that "Fitzgerald" did not simply spring into existence as a product of the author's most recent rhetorical constructions. The dominant image of Fitzgerald-the-failing-author that emerged in discussions of "The Crack-Up," an image that had been slowly developing throughout the decade, was as dependent on his early fame and other contemporaneous writings as it was on the content of these much-debated essays. Moreover, the somewhat pathetic Fitzgerald that emerges in these discussions, a figure alternatively pitied and scoffed at by friends and strangers alike, is quite different in many respects from both the narrative persona outlined above and the Fitzgerald image that would emerge in later analyses of these articles.

Ultimately, the canonization of Fitzgerald in the 1940s would entail revising earlier accusations of effeminacy and triviality, in large part by rereading Fitzgerald's essays as a display of his "heroic awareness." Interestingly, this appeal to a particular form of masculine strength, already explicit in Fitzgerald's essays, was coupled not with Fitzgerald's own emphasis on self-scrutiny but with a fairly blatant misreading of his claim to be "a writer only." This move enabled critics to elevate Fitzgerald while also supporting a certain construction of the male intellectual, one that Fitzgerald's essays could be said to challenge, by selectively reading his pieces in a way that supported their claims to authority.

This rereading of Fitzgerald's work suggests the lingering attraction of a particular form of elite male authorship in the 1940s and it reflects the failure of the "Crack-Up" essays to galvanize resistance to the boundaries that such a form of authorship entailed. Fitzgerald's use of the public confession, a traditionally feminized form, ultimately undermined his effort to find a marketable new persona through which he could continue working. The form of the "Crack-Up" essays also challenged a subset of male professionals in a way that led them to disregard many salient features of the pieces. While Fitzgerald's persona was ultimately forged out of the contradictions inherent in widely circulated conceptions of the literary field itself, along with many of the misogynist associations that these conceptions entailed, he did, in these particular works, open the way for a new synthesis by positing a space in which such contradictions could exist in simultaneity. This conception did not specifically admit the feminine as much as it posited a form of masculinity strong enough to venture into traditionally feminine spheres. Yet even this subtle challenge proved enough to disturb Fitzgerald's contemporaries and affect the image of the man who would be canonized in subsequent decades by predominantly white male critics.

Epilogue

Gertrude Stein and F. Scott Fitzgerald both engaged with various elements of the mass media during the Depression in order to influence public responses to their work. Over the course of the decade, Stein attempted to construct a theoretical framework that would simultaneously explain and dictate the proper way to approach a modern work of art. These theories, which were often equivocal about her own promotional activities, finally paved the way for her to return to the supposedly subliterary genre of the memoir. Fitzgerald, through a handful of autobiographical meditations and publicity pieces, cultivated the image of a serious literary professional in order to distance himself from an outmoded earlier persona. His efforts culminated in the "Crack-Up" essays, a series of pieces that adopted a cynical attitude, but, when viewed outside the confines of contemporary biographical narratives, potentially promoted a similar image of the author.

One thing these two analyses make clear is that, even as the literary market fragmented under the economic pressures of the Depression and new forms such as the middlebrow became increasingly prominent, some authors continued to employ traditional binaries with regard to the literary market. Stein and Fitzgerald, however, did not simply or slavishly adhere to such dichotomies. Both writers used them tactically and, in an increasingly media-saturated culture, they often pursued cultural capital through strategic interventions in the mass market itself. Based on these examples, modernists' allegiance to elite culture comes to seem less like a defining element of a particular aesthetic faction and more like a contingent and increasingly residual strategy tied to developments in the market itself.

More importantly, given the focus of the present study, such terms must not be seen simply in relation to a large and generic "marketplace," a view that emerges in part from writers' own rhetoric, but is equally bound up in a range of cultural shifts taking place in the early twentieth century. The use of terms such as high/low, for instance, is intimately connected with developments in celebrity media. As noted earlier, even our most conventional assessments of modernist authors operating in texts as "style" are implicitly dependent on the increasing importance of public personae in the early decades of the twentieth century. Writers were forced to consider the divide between often-profitable lowbrow hack work and aesthetically valuable highbrow creation. Yet, they also had to assess the ways in which they would position themselves along that continuum. If standardized lowbrow texts excluded the personality of the author, a situation that modernist "geniuses" certainly wanted to avoid, too much personality would undermine the value of the sacred artwork and undercut, in turn, a writer's claim to public visibility. Alternatively, too little publicity in an era of increasingly international media would leave a writer's persona and the public reception of his or her work entirely in the hands of others.

In addition to such local revisionary gestures, critical assessments of aesthetic value must be reconsidered in relation to the image and perceived intentions of an author. For instance, as John Kuehl and Jackson R. Bryer have suggested, many facets of Fitzgerald's novels could be described in typically modernist terms: "Fitzgerald, who respected the single word and the single line, fought against 'fatal facility.' And he sought ways to convey personal subject matter objectively; hence, the theory of 'composite' characterization practiced in the books following *The Beautiful and Damned* and the technique of the observer-narrator employed in *Gatsby* and *The Last Tycoon*. His insistence on 'shaping' and 'pruning' and his tendency to render experience dramatically are reflected in his sympathy toward Hemingway and his antipathy for [a more spontaneous and autobiographical writer like Thomas] Wolfe."[1] Yet, the term "modernism" is rarely used, even with qualifications, in relation to Fitzgerald's work. Instead, he is typically called, as he has been since the first publicity blitz that helped to shape his public persona, the "spokesman of the Jazz Age." It is hardly surprising that Fitzgerald, near the end of his life, would write in his notes for *The Last Tycoon*, "There are no second acts in American lives."[2]

Similarly, recent Stein critics rely in part on her distance from the male heterosexist centers of modernist literary production, and her supposed "opposition" to figures such as James Joyce, in their reconstructions of her aesthetic program. Stein's difference from her contemporaries has become an implicit factor that underlies many discussions of her work, often at the expense of some obvious, and important, connections between them. Stein, of course, encourages such readings through an insistent emphasis on her own unique "genius" and her subtle and, often times incongruous, attempts to shape her own public image.

Such efforts suggest, at the very least, that authorial self-fashioning in the context of America's burgeoning celebrity culture is a far more complex subject than some previous studies have acknowledged. While the terms under which authors cultivated personae for certain kinds of elite audiences differed from those for larger publics, both types of work required writers to promote their own visibility and develop some type of public face, one that would, for the most successful authors, be forced to mediate between different fields of production and seemingly opposed sets of values. In the works examined above, Stein and Fitzgerald employ a similar strategy in their attempt to overcome such difficulties. Both writers use a high/low opposition, a move that allows them to organize and, in many ways, simplify the complexities of the literary market. At the same time, they structure their texts around the tense and always tentative traversal of such contradictory poles. This strategy allows them to maintain associations with elite modes of artistic production even as they promote themselves in the market. It also enables them to claim an elevated status for forms of writing that might otherwise be dismissed as insignificant.

The similarities that can be found between Stein's and Fitzgerald's auto-biographical writing during this period constitute a significant shift in traditional understandings of modern(ist) self-representation. It is important to note, however, that there are subtle differences in the way each writer engages with the idea of contradiction. Stein uses the tension between two poles, in conjunction with her performative conception of identity, to emphasize the ever-shifting nature of reality. Much as Stein's narrator in *Everybody's Autobiography* is always disappearing into the present, the reader is never allowed to choose between presence and absence, rationality and irrationality, high and low. Each pole works to undercut its opposition in a difficult text that challenges answers as quickly as it provides them. Fitzgerald's essays do acknowledge the impossibility of final resolution, but they also draw attention to the narrator's ability to imaginatively insert himself into apparent contradictions. The "Crack-Up" essays, then, leave us not with a ghostly presence retreating into the ever-mobile present but with an angry and declarative voice, one that asserts the "unmodern" Romantic self as modernist or, perhaps more directly, the struggling author as a potential literary genius.

This difference also helps to explain the complex deployment of gender in each work. The "Crack-Up" essays do not simply upset prevailing notions of literary masculinity; they replace them with new, somewhat more subtle, formulations. Similarly, Fitzgerald's narrator engages with aspects of experience that have traditionally been dismissed as "feminine," but he refigures them as part of a new masculine project. Stein, on the other hand, works through the tense textual space between presence and absence, a strategy that does in some ways prefigure the poststructural aporia. She approaches the reigning masculine paradigm by stripping away gender markers from her performative voice, leaving a narrator that can tactically align herself with women even as she implicitly embraces supposedly male forms of creativity and rationality.

These complex responses to rapidly changing conditions in the literary field, and the various ways in which they have been assessed by readers and critics, raise many important questions for modernist scholars, questions that cannot be answered without a better understanding of how perceptions of literature in the early twentieth century were transformed by the expansion of celebrity media outlets. Stein and Fitzgerald wrestled throughout their careers with the meaning that such changes had for traditional conceptions of authorship even as they expended great effort promoting themselves and their work to as many people as possible.

So, while two intelligent and savvy writers such as Gertrude Stein and F. Scott Fitzgerald are certainly not representative of the increasingly fragmented state of the literary field in the early twentieth century (what two or three or four writers would be?), they do provide a useful perspective on the changes that were taking place. Both authors reflect and, to a certain extent, revel in these transformations, reinforcing older ideals even as they explore opportunities for change. Their work during this period helps to shed light on the ways in which experienced authors approached the new literary conditions of the Great Depression. These pieces also clearly demonstrate the important, if not central, role that celebrity played for both writers at the time.

NOTES

PART I   CONTEXTS: LITERARY MODERNISM IN THE AGE OF CELEBRITY

1   CRITICAL HISTORIES: THE CHANGING FACE OF LITERATURE, 1870–1920

1. A. Scott Berg, *Max Perkins: Editor of Genius* (New York: E. P. Dutton, 1978), 12–14; Matthew J. Bruccoli, *Some Sort of Epic Grandeur*, 2nd rev. ed. (Columbia: University of South Carolina Press, 2002), 97–100.

2. "Publisher's Note," in *Everybody's Autobiography* (Cambridge, MA: Exact Change, 1993).

3. The rapidly proliferating volumes of celebrity studies have been accompanied in the last several years by an explosion of celebrity "readers," a total output far too vast to summarize in one note. A few works that have remained significant in the scholarship are Daniel Boorstin, *The Image: A Guide to Pseudo-Events in America* (New York: Harper & Row, 1964); Richard Dyer, *Stars* (London: BFI Publishing, 1979); Richard Schickel, *Intimate Strangers: The Culture of Celebrity in America* (Chicago: Ivan R. Dee, 1985); Joshua Gamson, *Claims to Fame: Celebrity in Contemporary America* (Berkeley: University of California Press, 1994); Leo Braudy, *The Frenzy of Renown: Fame and Its History* (New York: Vintage Books, 1997); P. David Marshall, *Celebrity and Power: Fame in Contemporary Culture* (Minneapolis: University of Minnesota Press, 1997). A few other works that have had a significant impact on my thinking about celebrity include Thomas Baker, *Sentiment and Celebrity: Nathaniel Parker Willis and the Trials of Literary Fame* (New York: Oxford University Press, 1999); John G. Cawelti, "The Writer as a Celebrity: Some Aspects of American Literature as Popular Culture," *Studies in American Fiction* 5 (1977); Neal Gabler, *Winchell: Gossip, Power, and the Culture of Celebrity* (New York: Knopf, 1995); Loren Glass, *Authors Inc.: Literary Celebrity in the Modern United States, 1880–1980* (New York: New York University Press, 2004); Tom Mole, ed., *Romanticism and Celebrity Culture, 1750–1850* (New York: Cambridge University Press, 2009); Joe Moran, *Star Authors: Literary Celebrity in America*

(Sterling, VA: Pluto Press, 2000). Some of these works deal with literature and authors, but the relationship between literary celebrity and forms of celebrity in other fields remains largely unexplored. This notable omission potentially undermines attempts to generalize across media.

4. David Hochfelder, "The Communications Revolution and Popular Culture," in *A Companion to 19th-Century America*, ed. William L. Barney (Oxford: Blackwell Publishers, 2001); Elmo Scott Watson, *A History of Newspaper Syndicates in the United States, 1865–1935* (Chicago: Publisher's Auxiliary, 1936).

5. Frank Luther Mott, "The Magazine Revolution and Popular Ideas in the Nineties," in *American History: Recent Interpretations*, ed. Abraham Eisenstadt (New York: Crowell, 1969), 231; David R. Spencer, *The Yellow Journalism: The Press and America's Emergence as a World Power* (Evanston, IL: Northwestern University Press, 2007).

6. John F. Kasson, *Houdini, Tarzan, and the Perfect Man: The White Male Body and the Challenge of Modernity in America* (New York: Hill & Wang, 2002), 15; Theodore Peterson, *Magazines in the Twentieth Century* (Urbana: University of Illinois Press, 1956), 46. For more on the development of newspapers in the United States, see James L. Crouthamel, *Bennett's New York Herald and the Rise of the Popular Press* (Syracuse: Syracuse University Press, 1993); Dan Schiller, *Objectivity and the New: The Public and the Rise of Commercial Journalism* (Philadelphia, PA: Temple University Press, 1981); Michael Schudson, *Discovering the News: A Social History of American Newspapers* (New York: Basic Books, 1978); Mitchell Stevens, *A History of News* (New York: Viking, 1988).

7. George H. Douglas, *The Smart Magazines* (Hamden, CT: Shoe String Press, 1991); Frank Luther Mott, *A History of American Magazines: 1865–1885*, 5 vols., vol. 3 (Cambridge, MA: Harvard University Press, 1966), 7–12; John William Tebbel and Mary Ellen Zuckerman, *The Magazine in America, 1741–1990* (New York: Oxford University Press, 1991), 68.

8. Mott, *History of American Magazines*, 20.

9. William R. Leach, "Transformations in a Culture of Consumption: Woman and Department Stores, 1890–1925," *Journal of American History* 71, no. 2 (1984): 321–30; Susan Strasser, *Satisfaction Guaranteed: The Making of the American Mass Market* (New York: Pantheon Books, 1989), 206–11.

10. Tebbel and Zuckerman, *Magazine*, 140–46.

11. Richard Ohmann, *Selling Culture: Magazines, Markets, and Class at the Turn of the Century* (New York: Verso, 1996), 176–85.

12. Jennifer Wicke, *Advertising Fictions: Literature, Advertising, and Social Reading* (New York: Columbia University Press, 1988), 22.

13. Alex Groner and the Editors of *American Heritage* and *Business Week*, *The American Heritage History of American Business and Industry* (New York: American Heritage Publishing, 1972), 250.

14. In 1870, 121 trademarks were registered with the U.S. patent office, though the relatively unsophisticated state of the market at this date means there were probably many more unregistered trademarks in use. By 1906, more than 10,000 were registered, an increase that suggests the importance of branding at the turn of the century as well as the increasing legal complexity of expanding consumer markets in the United States. See Ibid.

15. Mott, "Revolution," 240; Tebbel and Zuckerman, *Magazine*, 140–46.

16. Strasser, *Satisfaction*, 150.

17. For more on the middle class at the turn of the century, see Stuart Blumin, *The Emergence of the Middle Class: Social Experience in the American City, 1760–1900* (Cambridge: Cambridge University Press, 1989).

18. Robert Wiebe, *The Search for Order* (New York: Hill & Wang, 1967), 12.

19. For more on masculinity in the late nineteenth century, see Gail Bederman, *Manliness and Civilization: A Cultural History of Gender and Race in the U.S., 1880–1917* (Chicago: University of Chicago Press, 1996); Mark C. Carnes and Clyde Griffen, eds., *Meanings for Manhood: Constructions of Masculinity in Victorian America* (Chicago: University of Chicago Press, 1990); Ann Douglas, *The Feminization of American Culture* (New York: Anchor Press, 1977); Michael Kimmel, *Manhood in America: A Cultural History* (New York: Free Press, 1996); Anthony Rotundo, *American Manhood: Transformations in Masculinity from the Revolution to the Modern Era* (New York: Basic Books, 1994).

20. Kasson, *White Male Body*, 39–41.

21. Richard Brodhead, *Cultures of Letters: Scenes of Reading and Writing in Nineteenth Century America* (Chicago: University of Chicago Press, 1994), 156–59.

22. For more on the emergence of a high/low division in American art, see Lawrence Levine, *Highbrow/Lowbrow: The Emergence of Cultural Hierarchy in America* (Cambridge, MA: Harvard University Press, 1988); Ohmann, *Selling Culture*, 149–60; Janice Radway, *A Feeling for Books: The Book-of-the-Month-Club, Literary Taste, and Middle-Class Desire* (Chapel Hill: University of North Carolina Press, 1997), 127–53. The shift to distinct aesthetic categories was, needless to say, not wholly new or unprecedented in the latter half of the nineteenth century, as many of these authors readily note. For a reading of these developments as a refinement and elaboration of earlier beliefs, see Joan Shelley Rubin, *The Making of Middlebrow Culture* (Chapel Hill: University of North Carolina Press, 1992), 1–33.

23. Radway, *Feeling*, 367.
24. For more on cheap book production during this period, see Michael Denning, *Mechanic Accents: Dime Novels and Working-Class Culture in America* (London: Verso, 1987); Hellmut Lehmann-Haupt, *The Book in America: A History of the Making and Selling of Books in the United States* (New York: R. R. Bowker Company, 1952); Raymond Shove, *Cheap Book Production in the United States, 1870–1891* (Urbana: University of Illinois Library, 1937); John William Tebbel, *A History of Book Publishing in the United States: The Expansion of an Industry, 1865–1919*, 4 vols., vol. 2 (New York: R. R. Bowker Company, 1972–1981).
25. Radway, *Feeling*, 129–47.
26. Kasson, *White Male Body*, 240 fn. 28.
27. Frank Lentricchia, *Modernist Quartet* (Cambridge: Cambridge University Press, 1994), ix–xiii.
28. Mary Kelley, *Private Woman, Public Stage: Literary Domesticity in Nineteenth-Century America* (New York and Oxford: Oxford University Press, 1984), 180. Kelley's book contains statistics and select publication details for a number of nineteenth-century female authors, including Gilman, Southworth, Stowe, and Warner. See especially pp. 3–27.
29. Andreas Huyssen, *After the Great Divide: Modernism, Mass Culture, Postmodernism* (Bloomington: Indiana University Press, 1986), 47.
30. Glass, *Authors*, 18.
31. Bluford Adams, *E Pluribus Barnum: The Great Showman and the Making of U.S. Popular Culture* (Minneapolis: University of Minnesota Press, 1997), 1–10; Neil Harris, *Humbug: The Art of P. T. Barnum* (Boston: Little, Brown & Company, 1973), 20–23.
32. Fred Kaplan, *Dickens: A Biography* (London: Hodder & Stoughton, 1988), 126; Moran, *Authors*, 18. For other studies that examine American literature and celebrity in the early nineteenth century, see Michael Newbury, *Figuring Authorship in Antebellum America* (Stanford, CA: Stanford University Press, 1997); R. Jackson Wilson, *Figures of Speech: American Writers and the Literary Marketplace, from Benjamin Franklin to Emily Dickinson* (Baltimore, MD: Johns Hopkins University Press, 1989).
33. Levine, *Highbrow*, 78–79.
34. Charles L. Ponce de Leon, *Self-Exposure: Human Interest Journalism and the Emergence of Celebrity in America* (Chapel Hill: University of North Carolina Press, 2002), 206–10.
35. For more on Sullivan, see Michael Isenberg, *John L. Sullivan and His America* (Urbana: University of Illinois Press, 1988); Adam J. Pollack, *John L. Sullivan: The Career of the First Gloved Heavyweight Champion* (Jefferson, NC: McFarland & Company, 2006); John L. Sullivan, *Life and Reminiscences of a Nineteenth Century Gladiator* (London: Routledge, 1892).

36. This passage was quoted in Mark Caldwell, "New York's School for Scandal Sheets," *International Herald Tribune*, April 22, 2006. For more on the history of gossip, particularly as it emerges from the British press, see Roger Wilkes, *Scandal: A Scurrilous History of Gossip* (London: Atlantic, 2002).

37. For more on Mann and *Town Topics*, see Douglas, *Smart Magazines*; Andy Logan, *The Man Who Robbed Robber Barons* (New York: W. W. Norton, 1965).

38. Samuel D. Warren and Louis D. Brandeis, "The Right to Privacy," *Harvard Law Review* 4, no. 5 (1890): 196, 205–07. For a more detailed discussion of this opinion in the context of celebrity, see Glass, *Authors*, 8–11. For more on the right to privacy in a legal context, see Darien A. McWhirter and Jon D. Bible, *Privacy as a Constitutional Right* (New York: Quorum Books, 1992); Don R. Pember, *Privacy and the Press: The Law, the Mass Media, and the First Amendment* (Seattle: University of Washington Press, 1972).

39. Peterson, *Magazines*, 10–11.

40. S. S. McClure, *My Autobiography* (New York: F. Ungar Publishing Company, 1963), 221.

41. Ohmann, *Selling Culture*, 242.

42. Don C. Seitz, *Joseph Pulitzer: His Life and Letters* (New York: Simon & Schuster, 1924), 422.

43. Charles L. Ponce de Leon's *Self-Exposure* provides the most detailed survey of "human-interest" journalism at the turn of the century. See especially pp. 42–105.

44. Richard deCordova, *Picture Personalities: The Emergence of the Star System in America* (Urbana and Chicago: University of Illinois Press, 1990), 50–116.

45. Ibid., 117.

46. While such reporting was relatively new for the film industry press, depicting the "moral transgression[s] and social unconventionality" of celebrities was not a new phenomena in the early twentieth century. The theater press, to give just one example, was revealing private details about actors and actresses before the mid-nineteenth century.

47. Karen Leick, "Popular Modernism: Little Magazines and the American Daily Press," *PMLA* 123, no. 1 (2008): 125–30.

48. Louis Kaplan, *A Bibliography of American Autobiographies* (Madison: University of Wisconsin Press, 1961), 327–72.

49. George H. Doran, *Chronicles of Barabbas: 1884–1934* (New York: Harcourt Brace, 1935), 267. For other examples, see David Welky, *Everything Was Better in America: Print Culture in the Great Depression* (Urbana and Chicago: University of Illinois Press, 2008), 153.

50. Quoted in Glass, *Authors*, 20; Henry Holt, "The Commercialization of Literature," *Atlantic Monthly* (1905): 578.

51. Wyndham Lewis, *The Art of Being Ruled*, ed. Reed Way Dasenbrock (Santa Rosa, CA: Black Sparrow Press, 1989), 181.

52. Quoted in Humphrey Carpenter, *A Serious Character: The Life of Ezra Pound* (London: Faber & Faber, 1988), 236.

53. Matthew J. Bruccoli and Jackson R. Bryer, eds., *F. Scott Fitzgerald in His Own Time: A Miscellany* (Kent, OH: Kent State University Press, 1971), 273.

54. Samuel M. Steward, *Dear Sammy: Letters from Gertrude Stein and Alice B. Toklas* (Boston: Houghton Mifflin Company, 1977), 26.

2 CRITICAL REASSESSMENTS: CELEBRITY, MODERNISM, AND THE LITERARY FIELD IN THE 1920s AND 1930s

1. Fredric Jameson, "Reification and Utopia in Mass Culture," *Social Text* 1 (1979): 133–34.

2. As many contemporary scholars note, theorists in the 1930s had already advanced the idea that no cultural product exists outside of market relations. Richard Keller Simon, for instance, has pointed out an influential exchange between Clement Greenberg and Dwight Macdonald in the late 1930s that led them to advocate a dialectical approach to high and mass cultural forms. See Richard Keller Simon, "Modernism and Mass Culture," *American Literary History* 13, no. 2 (2001): 345–48. Andreas Huyssen also finds the idea in the work of Theodor Adorno, whom he ironically notes is a "key theorist of the [aesthetic] divide." Andreas Huyssen, "High/Low in an Expanded Field," *Modernism/modernity* 9, no. 3 (2002): 367.

3. See Daniel Borus, *Writing Realism: Howells, James, and Norris in the Mass Market* (Chapel Hill: University of North Carolina Press, 1989); Patrick Brantlinger and James Naremore, eds., *Modernism and Mass Culture* (Bloomington: Indiana University Press, 1991); John Xiros Cooper, *Modernism and the Culture of Market Society* (Cambridge: Cambridge University Press, 2004); Kevin J. H. Dettmar and Stephen Watt, eds., *Marketing Modernisms: Self-Promotion, Canonization, Rereading* (Ann Arbor: University of Michigan Press, 1996); Andreas Huyssen, *After the Great Divide: Modernism, Mass Culture, Postmodernism* (Bloomington: Indiana University Press, 1986); Mark S. Morrisson, *The Public Face of Modernism: Little Magazines, Audiences, and Reception, 1905–1920* (Madison: University of Wisconsin Press, 2001); Lawrence S. Rainey, *Institutions of Modernism: Literary Elites and Public Culture* (New Haven, CT: Yale University Press, 1998); Jani Scandura and Michael Thurston, *Modernism, Inc.: Body, Memory, Capital* (New York: New York University Press, 2001); Thomas Strychacz, *Modernism, Mass Culture and Professionalism* (Cambridge: Cambridge University

Press, 1993); Catherine Turner, *Marketing Modernism between the Two World Wars* (Amherst and Boston: University of Massachusetts Press, 2003); Joyce Piell Wexler, *Who Paid for Modernism?: Art, Money, and the Fiction of Conrad, Joyce, and Lawrence* (Fayetteville: University of Arkansas Press, 1997); Jennifer Wicke, *Advertising Fictions: Literature, Advertising, and Social Reading* (New York: Columbia University Press, 1988); Ian Willison, Warwick Gould, and Warren Chernaik, eds., *Modernist Writers and the Marketplace* (New York: St. Martin's Press, 1996); Christopher Wilson, *The Labor of Words: Literary Professionalism in the Progressive Era* (Athens: University of Georgia Press, 1985).

4. Douglas Mao and Rebecca L. Walkowitz, "The New Modernist Studies," *PMLA* 123, no. 3 (2008): 744.

5. Aaron Jaffe, *Modernism and the Culture of Celebrity* (Cambridge: Cambridge University Press, 2005), 10.

6. Ibid., 20.

7. F. Scott Fitzgerald, *F. Scott Fitzgerald on Authorship*, ed. Matthew J. Bruccoli (Columbia: University of South Carolina Press, 1996), 37.

8. F. Scott Fitzgerald, *Afternoon of an Author*, ed. Arthur Mizener (New York: Charles Scribner's Sons, 1957), 85.

9. Jackson R. Bryer, ed., *F. Scott Fitzgerald: The Critical Reception* (New York: Burt Franklin & Co., 1978), 22–23, 28; H. L. Mencken, "Untitled Review," *The Smart Set* 62 (1920); R.V.A.S., "Untitled Review," *New Republic* 22 (1920).

10. Seldes says, "He is this side...of a full respect for the medium he works in; his irrelevance destroys his design." The work, he claims, suffers from the author's "carelessness about structure and effect." Jackson R. Bryer, *The Critical Reputation of F. Scott Fitzgerald: A Bibliographical Study* (Hamden, CT: Archon Books, 1967), 109.

11. Bryer, *Critical Reception*, 129–30.

12. Ibid., 71–74.

13. I do not mean to suggest that Fitzgerald's publicity exerted a simple deterministic force on critics. It was only one of many factors that helped a particular reading of Fitzgerald's life and work gain purchase in this particular historical context. It would, however, be difficult to examine the critical reception of Fitzgerald's works without taking his public persona into account.

14. Perhaps the most famous account from this period came from another of Fitzgerald's Princeton acquaintances, Edmund Wilson, who said that *The Beautiful and Damned* was "animated with life" and acknowledged that Fitzgerald had "an instinct for graceful and vivid prose." He also claimed, "[Fitzgerald] has been given imagination without intellectual control of it; he has been given the desire for beauty without an aesthetic ideal; and he has been given a gift for expression without very many ideas to express." Edmund Wilson, *The Shores of Light* (New York: Farrar, Straus & Young, 1952), 27.

Less than a year before, Wilson wrote Fitzgerald a letter criticizing America's "commercialism" and the "ease with which a traditionless and half-educated [American] public…can be impressed, delighted, and satisfied." Edmund Wilson, *Letters on Literature and Politics, 1912–1972*, ed. Elena Wilson (New York: Farrar, Straus & Giroux, 1977), 64.

15. Janice Radway, *A Feeling for Books: The Book-of-the-Month-Club, Literary Taste, and Middle-Class Desire* (Chapel Hill: University of North Carolina Press, 1997), 127–86.

16. Gertrude Stein, *Everybody's Autobiography* (Cambridge, MA: Exact Change, 1993), 6.

17. Turner, *Marketing Modernism*, 30–33.

18. For more on Harcourt's marketing of *The Autobiography*, see Ibid., 111–26. This discussion is much indebted to her analysis. For perspectives on the conflict between genteel literary notions and modern culture, see Frank Lentricchia, *Modernist Quartet* (Cambridge: Cambridge University Press, 1994), ix–xiii, 47–77; Joan Shelley Rubin, *The Making of Middlebrow Culture* (Chapel Hill: University of North Carolina Press, 1992), 1–33.

19. Ann Douglas, *Terrible Honesty: Mongrel Manhattan in the 1920s* (New York: Farrar, Straus & Giroux, 1995), 71.

20. T. S. Eliot, "Tradition and the Individual Talent," in *Selected Essays, 1917–1932* (New York: Harcourt, Brace & Company, 1932), 10–11.

21. Ibid., 7, 11.

22. Ibid., 4.

23. Ibid., 10.

24. Charles Tomlinson, ed., *Marianne Moore: A Collection of Critical Essays* (Englewood Cliffs, NJ: Prentice-Hall, 1969), 48.

25. T. S. Eliot, "London Letter," *The Dial* LXXIII, no. 6 (1922): 370–72. The piece later appeared in a shorter form in Eliot's *Criterion*. In the later version, several of the references to Marie Lloyd's upbringing have been cut, but Eliot's argument in the piece remains unchanged. Such modifications suggest many interesting avenues for the study of Eliot's own self-presentation. For a useful reassessment of Eliot's relationship to mass culture, which positions the Marie Lloyd article as a precursor to Eliot's own attempts to connect with a "popular" audience through dramatic verse, see David E. Chinitz, *T. S. Eliot and the Cultural Divide* (Chicago: University of Chicago Press, 2003). For the *Criterion* reprint, see T. S. Eliot, "Marie Lloyd." For a readily available version of Eliot's original text from *The Dial*, see T. S. Eliot, *London Letter, 1922* (Rickard A. Parker, December 3, 2004 [cited March 11, 2009]); available from http://world.std.com/~raparker/exploring /tseliot/works/london-letters/london-letter-1922–12.html .

26. Michael Nowlin, *F. Scott Fitzgerald's Racial Angles and the Business of Literary Greatness* (Basingstoke and New York: Palgrave Macmillan, 2007), 10.

27. F. Scott Fitzgerald and Maxwell Perkins, *Dear Scott/Dear Max: The Fitzgerald-Perkins Correspondence*, ed. John Kuehl and Jackson R. Bryer (New York: Charles Scribner's Sons, 1971), 47.

28. Ulla E. Dydo, *Gertrude Stein: The Language That Rises, 1923–1934* (Evanston, IL: Northwestern University Press, 2003), 419–20.

29. Daniel Joseph Singal, "Towards a Definition of American Modernism," *American Quarterly* 39, no. 1 (1978): 12.

30. Ibid., 15.

31. Rainey, *Modernism*, 3.

32. Robert Scholes, *Paradoxy of Modernism* (New Haven and London: Yale University Press, 2006), xi–xii.

33. For more on the emergence of the middlebrow, see Janice Radway, "The Scandal of the Middlebrow: The Book-of-the-Month Club, Class Fracture, and Cultural Authority," *South Atlantic Quarterly* 89, no. 4 (1990); Rubin, *Making*. For more on *Vanity Fair* as a form of middlebrow production, see Michael Murphy, " 'One Hundred Per Cent Bohemia': Pop Decadence and the Aestheticization of Commodity in the Rise of the Slicks," in *Marketing Modernisms: Self-Promotion, Canonization, Rereading*, ed. Kevin J. H. Dettmar and Stephen Watt (Ann Arbor: University of Michigan Press, 1996).

34. Van Wyck Brooks, *America's Coming-of-Age* (New York: B. W. Huebsch, 1915), 4–7, 112.

35. For several different versions of this argument, see Jean-Christophe Agnew, "Coming up for Air: Consumer Culture in Historical Perspective," *Intellectual History Newsletter* 12 (1990); Stuart Ewen, *All Consuming Images: The Politics of Style in Contemporary Culture* (New York: Basic, 1988); Terry Smith, *Making the Modern: Industry, Art and Design in America* (Chicago: University of Chicago Press, 1993).

36. Roland Marchand, *Advertising the American Dream: Making Way for Modernity, 1920–1940* (Berkeley: University of California Press, 1985), 285–301.

37. Warren Susman, *Culture and Commitment, 1929–1945* (New York: G. Braziller, 1973), 82–83. In part as a result of these shifts, Jean-Christophe Agnew notes, Americans came to see their lives more and more in terms of the commodities they purchased, so that, by the 1940s, the United States could go to war on "conspicuously private, consumptionist themes." As one wartime GI was reported to have said, "I am in this damn mess...to help keep the custom of drinking Cokes." Agnew, "Air," 14.

38. John William Tebbel, *A History of Book Publishing in the United States*, vol. 4 (New York: R. R. Bowker, 1981), 1, 721–25.

39. Quoted in David Welky, *Everything Was Better in America: Print Culture in the Great Depression* (Urbana and Chicago: University of Illinois Press, 2008), 149.

40. Linda Wagner-Martin, *The Mid-Century American Novel* (New York: Twayne, 1997), ix–x, 1–15.

41. Alfred Kazin, *Starting Out in the Thirties* (Boston: Little, Brown & Company 1965), 15.

42. Mark Conroy, *Muse in the Machine: American Fiction and Mass Publicity* (Columbus: Ohio State University Press, 2004), 10.

43. Ibid.

44. For a detailed examination of writers in Hollywood during the 1930s, see Richard Fine, *Hollywood and the Profession of Authorship, 1928–1940.* (Washington, D.C.: Smithsonian Institution, 1993).

PART II   FROM TOKLAS TO EVERYBODY: GERTRUDE STEIN BETWEEN AUTOBIOGRAPHIES

3   THE CELEBRITY SPEAKS: GERTRUDE STEIN'S AESTHETIC THEORIES AFTER *THE AUTOBIOGRAPHY OF ALICE B. TOKLAS*

1. Stein's biographers have traced her earliest works to the winter of 1902. For example, see John Malcolm Brinnin, *The Third Rose: Gertrude Stein and Her World* (New York: Addison-Wesley Publishing Company, 1987), 41, 44–45; James R. Mellow, *Charmed Circle: Gertrude Stein and Company* (New York: Praeger, 1974), 115; Linda Wagner-Martin, *"Favored Strangers": Gertrude Stein and Her Family* (New Brunswick, NJ: Rutgers University Press, 1995), 57. For an account of Stein's early publishing history, see Bryce Conrad, "Gertrude Stein in the American Marketplace," *Journal of Modern Literature* XIX (1995).

2. Laurel Bollinger, " 'One as One Not Mistaken but Interrupted': Gertrude Stein's Exploration of Identity in the 1930s," *Centennial Review* 43, no. 2 (1999): 255 fn. 1.

3. Ulla E. Dydo, *Gertrude Stein: The Language That Rises, 1923–1934* (Evanston, IL: Northwestern University Press, 2003), 551–53.

4. Gertrude Stein, "And Now," in *Vanity Fair: Selections from America's Most Memorable Magazine, a Cavalcade of the 1920s and 1930s*, ed. Cleveland Amory and Frederic Bradlee (New York: Viking Press, 1934), 280.

5. Dydo discusses the publication of Stein's manuscript in some detail. See Dydo, *Rises*, 543–50. For relevant correspondence, see Donald Gallup, ed., *The Flowers of Friendship: Letters Written to Gertrude Stein* (New York: Alfred A. Knopf, 1953), 259–63.

6. Stein, "And Now," 280.

7. Gertrude Stein, *Everybody's Autobiography* (Cambridge: Exact Change, 1993), 86.

8. Pierre Bourdieu, *The Field of Cultural Production: Essays on Art and Literature*, ed. Randal Johnson (New York: Columbia University Press, 1993), 115.

9. Loren Glass, *Authors Inc.: Literary Celebrity in the Modern United States, 1880–1980* (New York: New York University Press, 2004), 1.

10. G. F. Mitrano, *Gertrude Stein: Woman without Qualities* (Burlington, VT: Ashgate Publishing Company, 2005), 58.

11. Wagner-Martin, *"Favored Strangers"*, 108–09, 40.

12. For a useful discussion of Stein parodies, see Kirk Curnutt, "Parody and Pedagogy: Teaching Style, Voice, and Authorial Intent in the Works of Gertrude Stein," *College Literature* 23, no. 2 (1996). For a more general discussion of Stein's reception, see Karen Leick, *Gertrude Stein and the Making of an American Celebrity* (New York: Routledge, 2009).

13. T. S. Eliot, "Charleston, Hey! Hey!" *The Nation & Athenaeum* xl, no. 17 (1927): 595; "The Ten Dullest Authors: A Symposium," in *Vanity Fair*, Amory and Bradlee, 76.

14. Bennett Cerf, *At Random: The Reminiscences of Bennett Cerf* (New York: Random House, 1977), 102.

15. Gertrude Stein, *Lectures in America* (New York: Vintage Books, 1975), 312.

16. Ibid., 147.

17. Gertrude Stein, *What Are Masterpieces* (New York: Pitman Publishing Corporation, 1970), 29.

18. Neil Schmitz, "Gertrude Stein as Post-Modernist: The Rhetoric of 'Tender Buttons,'" *Journal of Modern Literature* 3, no. 5 (1974): 1217.

19. Stein, *Lectures*, 17.

20. Charles Caramello, "Reading Gertrude Stein Reading Henry James, or Eros Is Eros Is Eros Is Eros," *Henry James Review* 6 (1985): 188.

21. Gertrude Stein, *The Making of Americans* (New York: Something Else, 1966), 212.

22. Juliana Spahr, *Everybody's Autonomy: Connective Reading and Collective Identity* (Tuscaloosa: University of Alabama Press, 2001), 6.

23. Ibid., 32.

24. Barbara Will, *Gertrude Stein, Modernism, and the Problem of "Genius"* (Edinburgh: Edinburgh University Press, 2000), 9.

25. Stein, *Masterpieces*, 86. Stein did make another reference to "myself and strangers" in her short article for *Cosmopolitan*, "I Came and Here I Am," which was published in February 1935. This is the latest reference I have found that employs the phrase as a useful descriptor. This particular instance, however, does not entirely fit with the others because she is referring to broadcasting and not her own writing. She says, "In writing in *The Making of Americans* I said I write for myself

and strangers and this is what broadcasting is. I write for myself and strangers." Gertrude Stein, *How Writing Is Written: Volume 2 of the Previously Uncollected Writings of Gertrude Stein*, ed. Robert Bartlett Haas (Los Angeles: Black Sparrow Press, 1974), 71.

26. Stein, *How Writing Is Written*, 62.
27. Stein, *Everybody's*, 104.
28. Ibid., 102.
29. Gertrude Stein, *Four in America* (New Haven, CT: Yale University Press, 1947), xxi–xxii.
30. Stein, *How Writing Is Written*, 61.
31. Stein, *Primer*, 19.
32. Henry McBride's remark about the success of *The Autobiography* provides an interesting counterpoint: "It was apparent, with the very first chapter in the *Atlantic*, that the book was doomed to be a best seller." Gallup, *Flowers*, 270–71.
33. Stein, *How Writing Is Written*, 61.
34. Harcourt, Brace & Company, who had published *The Autobiography* and an abridged version of *The Making of Americans*, rejected *Four in America* in May of 1934. Even though no other publisher would put it out in time for the American tour, as Stein wanted, she remained committed to the work. For example, see her comments to Carl Van Vechten in Edward Burns, ed., *The Letters of Gertrude Stein and Carl Van Vechten, 1913–1946*, 2 vols., vol. I (1913–1935) (New York: Columbia University Press, 1986), 329.
35. Stein, *Four in America*, 66, 193. Grant, Wright, James, and Washington all exhibit more or less the same characteristics in both Stein's "lives" and in their real lives, even though these characteristics do not necessarily guarantee them the same degree of success in their fictional professions. For instance, Hiram Grant might prove to be a religious *leader*, but Wilbur Wright will not be "remarkable" as a painter. Stein, *Four in America*, 97. So, while fame itself might prove to be ephemeral or unpredictable, internal characteristics seem relatively stable in the text. Such a perspective may have been comforting for Stein, who worried about both what her sudden fame meant for all of the previous, and unrecognized, books she had written, and also what effect that fame might have on her writing in the future.
36. Stein, *Four in America*, 130.
37. While Stein's linking of familiarity and positive audience reception might open the way for theorizing something like Benjamin's shock aesthetic, her own term is far less confrontational and does not rise to the level of ideological critique. Her focus is on establishing an arational form of value that will ultimately allow her to deem her own works to be timeless masterpieces.
38. Stein, *Four in America*, 131.
39. Ibid., 122–23.

40. Quoted in Donald Gallup, "Gertrude Stein and the *Atlantic*," *Yale University Library Gazette* XXVIII (1954): 124.

41. Stein, *Four in America*, xxiii.

42. I do not mean to suggest that Stein came to fixate on the process of artistic creation for the first time in the wake of *The Autobiography* or that she developed this approach to writing entirely as a result of her celebrity. Stein had, throughout her career, emphasized the importance of the artist's mind in the process of writing. Nevertheless, her public declarations of these ideas in the early 1930s, and the particular forms that these declarations took, do seem related to her changing circumstances.

43. Stein, *Four in America*, 127–28.

44. Bob Perelman, *The Trouble with Genius: Reading Pound, Joyce, Stein, and Zukofsky* (Berkeley and Los Angeles: University of California Press, 1994), 150.

45. Stein, *How Writing Is Written*, 53.

46. Stein, *Primer*, 30.

47. Cf. "It can easily be realized that after these years of faith that there is and was a public and that sometime I would come in contact with that public." Stein, *How Writing Is Written*, 62.

48. This interpretation elucidates many of Stein's seemingly cryptic statements about art in the text. She says, for example, that Shakespeare's sonnets and his plays "not being the same is not due to their being different in their form or in their substance. It is due to something else." Stein, *Four in America*, 119.

49. Ibid., 130.

50. It is possible to read Stein's position in *Four in America* as an elaboration of her famous quip from *The Autobiography*: "No artist needs criticism, he only needs appreciation. If he needs criticism, he is no artist." Gertrude Stein, *The Autobiography of Alice B. Toklas* (New York: Vintage Books, 1990), 235.

51. Stein, *Four in America*, 89.

52. Harriet Scott Chessman, *The Public Is Invited to Dance: Representation, the Body, and Dialogue in Gertrude Stein* (Stanford: Stanford University Press, 1989), 2, 8.

53. Stein, *Four in America*, 125.

54. Ibid., 124–25.

55. Ibid., 130.

56. The following brief history of "And Now" is heavily indebted to Ulla Dydo's analysis of Stein's manuscripts in *Rises*. See especially pp. 569–606.

57. The difficulty Stein had writing this article, not to mention the "Confessions" as a whole, is suggested by her inclusion of an anecdote about Cézanne, who, after his first "serious public recognition" at an autumn salon, supposedly produced a series of canvases that were "more than ever covered over painted and painted over" (280).

58. Stein, "And Now," 280.

59. Ibid.
60. Ibid.
61. Ibid., 281.
62. The only major exception to this dating is "The Gradual Making of *The Making of Americans*." Stein had written the first half of this lecture several months earlier, when she was invited by the American Women's Club in Paris to speak about the abridged version of *Making* that had been published by Harcourt in February. Her speech was given on March 23, 1934.
63. Stein, *Lectures*, 23–24.
64. Ibid., 54.
65. Quoted in Dydo, *Rises*, 626.
66. Stein, *Lectures*, 54.
67. Conrad, "American Marketplace," 228 fn. 37.
68. Stein, *Lectures*, 204–05.
69. Ibid., 205–06.
70. Ibid., 24.
71. Ibid., 79.
72. Ibid., 44.
73. Michael Szalay, "Inviolate Modernism: Hemingway, Stein, Tzara," *Modern Language Quarterly* 56, no. 4 (1995): 470.
74. Stein, *Lectures*, 90.
75. Stein, *Four in America*, 126.
76. Stein, *Masterpieces*, 26.
77. Stein, *Lectures*, 61.
78. Gertrude Stein, *Narration* (Chicago: University of Chicago Press, 1935), 53.
79. Ibid., 55–56.
80. Ibid., 56.
81. Stein, *Lectures*, 135.
82. Stein, *Narration*, 53–54, 56. Stein also addresses a third option, reading aloud what one has written, but she suggests that this process, too, is complicated by the physical act of presentation: "If you are reading what you are lecturing then you have a half in one of any two directions, you have been recognizing what you are writing when you were writing and now in reading you disassociate recognizing what you are reading from what you did recognize as being written while you were writing. In short you are leading a double life." Stein, *Narration*, 57.
83. Stein, *Narration*, 60.
84. Stein plays on the relationship between one and two during the lecture, particularly in reference to the split between the creative and audience functions of consciousness. For instance, in reference to writers, she says, "One is not one because one is always two that is one is always coming to a recognition of what the one who is one is writing that is telling." Ibid., 57.

85. Ibid., 61.
86. Ibid., 62.
87. Stein's previous, and future, ambivalence about the artistic merit of *The Autobiography* obviously undercuts the claim that she achieved an immediate recognition in the moment of writing.
88. Marjorie Perloff, *21st-Century Modernism: The 'New' Poetics* (Malden, MA: Blackwell Publishers, 2002), 26.
89. The following discussion owes a debt to the work of Jennifer Ashton, even though, as will become apparent, I disagree with Ashton on several points. See Jennifer Ashton, *From Modernism to Postmodernism: American Poetry and Theory in the Twentieth Century* (Cambridge: Cambridge University Press, 2005); "Gertrude Stein for Anyone," *ELH* 64, no. 1 (1997); "Modernism's 'New' Literalism," *Modernism/modernity* 10, no. 2 (2003); " 'Rose Is a Rose': Gertrude Stein and the Critique of Indeterminacy," *Modernism/modernity* 9, no. 4 (2002).
90. Perloff is more concerned with tracing the "indeterminate" tradition in her earlier book and spends more time detailing the specific modes and methods involved. In particular, see Marjorie Perloff, *The Poetics of Indeterminacy: Rimbaud to Cage* (Princeton: Princeton University Press, 1981), esp. 4–44.
91. Quoted in Ashton, "Literalism," 388.
92. Ibid., 7.
93. Ashton, "Critique."
94. Lisa Siraganian, "Out of Air: Theorizing the Art Object in Gertrude Stein and Wyndham Lewis," *Modernism/modernity* 10, no. 4 (2003): 665.
95. Ibid.

4   AFTER THE TOUR: NATURALIZED AESTHETICS
AND SYSTEMATIZED CONTRADICTIONS

1. Bennett Cerf, *At Random: The Reminiscences of Bennett Cerf* (New York: Random House, 1977), 101–08.
2. Ibid., 102.
3. Catherine Turner, *Marketing Modernism between the Two World Wars* (Amherst and Boston: University of Massachusetts Press, 2003), 125.
4. Janet Hobhouse, *Everybody Who Was Anybody: A Biography of Gertrude Stein* (New York: G. P. Putnam's Sons, 1975), 176. My account of Stein's publishing history has been drawn from a variety of sources. For useful secondary accounts of these events, and Stein's lecture tour more generally, see Ulla E. Dydo, *Gertrude Stein: The Language That Rises, 1923–1934* (Evanston, IL: Northwestern University Press, 2003), 543–50; James R. Mellow, *Charmed Circle: Gertrude Stein and Company* (New York: Praeger, 1974), 379–415; Linda

Wagner-Martin, *"Favored Strangers": Gertrude Stein and Her Family* (New Brunswick, NJ: Rutgers University Press, 1995), 208–20. For published correspondence pertaining to the tour, see Edward Burns, ed., *The Letters of Gertrude Stein and Carl Van Vechten, 1913–1946*, 2 vols., vol. 1 (1913–1935) (New York: Columbia University Press, 1986), 265–432; Edward Burns, Ulla E. Dydo, and William Rice, eds., *The Letters of Gertrude Stein and Thornton Wilder* (New Haven and London: Yale University Press, 1996), 3–26; Donald Gallup, ed., *The Flowers of Friendship: Letters Written to Gertrude Stein* (New York: Alfred A. Knopf, 1953), 280–99.

5. For several examples of the negative criticism that *The Geographical History* received, see Kirk Curnutt, ed., *The Critical Response to Gertrude Stein* (Westport, CT: Greenwood Press, 2000), 100–03.

6. Gertrude Stein, *The Geographical History of America or the Relation of Human Nature to the Human Mind*, ed. Catharine R. Stimpson and Harriet Chessman, 2 vols., vol. 2, *Gertrude Stein: Writings 1932–1946* (New York: Random House, 1936), 483.

7. Ibid., 407.

8. Ibid., 15, 421.

9. Ibid., 450.

10. Ibid., 384, 465.

11. Ibid., 451.

12. Stein begins *The Geographical History* by questioning whether there is a relationship between the two primary terms and, early on in the book, she poses the same question many times. Yet, about halfway through the book, Stein's interrogative mode gives way to a series of relatively straightforward assertions: there is no relationship between human nature and the human mind. For relevant examples, see pages 422, 427, 430, 449, 455, and 457.

13. Stein, *Geographical History*, 488.

14. Ibid., 457.

15. Ibid., 396.

16. Ibid., 455.

17. Ibid., 389.

18. It is during a discussion of masterpieces and timelessness in *The Geographical History* that Stein makes her famous proclamation, "Think of the Bible and Homer think of Shakespeare and think of me." Ibid., 407.

19. Ibid., 459.

20. Gertrude Stein, *What Are Masterpieces* (New York: Pitman Publishing Corporation, 1970), 89. Michel Foucault's comments on beginnings in his lecture, "The Discourse on Language," provide an interesting comparison with Stein's formulations. Stein's mistrust of beginnings arises from her belief in the ahistorical nature of the human mind. According to her formulation, any material or historical necessity, such as the necessity to begin or end, is a distortion of this entity.

Foucault, in a similar fashion, bemoans the process of beginning, but he uses these statements to elaborate on anxieties about the historical nature of discourse, anxieties implicitly present in Stein's text. See Michel Foucault, "The Discourse on Language," in *Critical Theory since 1965*, ed. Hazard Adams and Leroy Searle (Tallahassee: Florida State University Press, 1986), 148.

21. Harriet Scott Chessman, *The Public Is Invited to Dance: Representation, the Body, and Dialogue in Gertrude Stein* (Stanford: Stanford University Press, 1989), 209 fn. 57.

22. Stein, *Geographical History*, 389.

23. Quoted in Dydo, *Rises*, 7.

24. "Publisher's Note," in *Everybody's Autobiography* (Cambridge: Exact Change, 1993), viii.

25. Estelle C. Jelinek, *The Tradition of Women's Autobiography: From Antiquity to the Present* (Boston: Twayne Publishers, 1986), 145.

26. Marianne DeKoven, *A Different Language: Gertrude Stein's Experimental Writing* (Madison: University of Wisconsin Press, 1983), 150.

27. Gertrude Stein, "Arthur A Grammar," in *How to Write* (Los Angeles: Sun & Moon Press, 1995), 81. Stein employs a similar approach in "Patriarchal Poetry," where she juxtaposes her own playful poetic language with patriarchal language, but ultimately concludes that some elements of patriarchal poetry could be salvaged. For a more extended reading of this piece, see Laurel Bollinger, " 'One as One Not Mistaken but Interrupted': Gertrude Stein's Exploration of Identity in the 1930s," *Centennial Review* 43, no. 2 (1999): 231–42. Susan Schultz makes this argument again with respect to "Stanzas in Meditation," which she reads as a necessarily failed attempt to eliminate the audience from writing. See Susan M. Schultz, "Gertrude Stein's Self-Advertisement," *Raritan* 12, no. 2 (1992). Many critics also read *The Autobiography* as a text that negotiates a wide variety of contradictions. For one provocative example, see James Breslin, "Gertrude Stein and the Problems of Autobiography," *Georgia Review* 33 (1979).

28. Barbara Mossberg, "Double Exposures: Emily Dickinson's and Gertrude Stein's Anti-Autobiographies," *Women's Studies: An Interdisciplinary Journal* 16, no. 1–2 (1989): 245.

29. For an early, predominantly theoretical, exploration of Stein's autobiographies, see S. C. Neuman, *Gertrude Stein: Autobiography and the Problem of Narration* (Victoria, B.C.: English Literary Studies, 1979). For provocative readings of Stein's lesbianism, see Karin Cope, " 'Moral Deviancy' and Contemporary Feminism: The Judgment of Gertrude Stein," in *Feminism Beside Itself*, ed. Diane Elam and Robyn Wiegman (New York: Routledge, 1995); Catharine R. Stimpson, "Gertrice/Altrude, Stein Toklas and the Paradox of the Happy Marriage," in *Mothering the Mind, Twelve Studies of Writers*

and Their Silent Partners, ed. Ruth Perry and Martine Watson Brownley (New York: Holmes & Meier, 1984).

30. See Paul John Eakin, "What Are We Reading When We Read Autobiography?" *Narrative* 12, no. 2 (2004).

31. Philippe Lejeune's famous definition of autobiography shows a particularly strong individualistic bias: "Definition: Retrospective prose narrative written by a real person concerning his own existence, where the focus is his individual life, in particular the story of his personality." See Philippe Lejeune, "The Autobiographical Pact," in *On Autobiography*, ed. Paul John Eakin (Minneapolis: University of Minnesota Press, 1989), 4. Only recently have critics begun to explore the theoretical implications of joint authorship. For example, see Paul John Eakin, *The Ethics of Life Writing* (New York: Cornell University Press, 2004).

32. Juliana Spahr, *Everybody's Autonomy: Connective Reading and Collective Identity* (Tuscaloosa: University of Alabama Press, 2001), 38.

33. Gertrude Stein, *Everybody's Autobiography* (Cambridge: Exact Change, 1993), 173. Barbara Will reads *Everybody's Autobiography* in a similar fashion, claiming that "[Stein's] story, the story of a 'genius,' is potentially the story of 'everybody.'" Will's reading is far more attuned to the nuances of Stein's text and devotes slightly more attention to what she sees as Stein's "anxiety about the de-personalizing and de-hierarchizing effects of the story which [she] is engaged in telling." Barbara Will, *Gertrude Stein, Modernism, and the Problem of "Genius"* (Edinburgh: Edinburgh University Press, 2000), 9, 154. My own reading differs in that I see Stein as profoundly aware of the complexities of her own position and *Everybody's Autobiography* as her attempt to work with such difficulties.

34. Stein, *Everybody's*, 100.

35. Coincidentally, it is precisely this tendency to treat art abstractly that allowed Stein to make the now famous comparison between her own writing and Picasso's early Cubist paintings. Of all the work done analyzing her comparison, Marianne DeKoven has provided some of the most consistently insightful and provocative analyses in this area. For example, see Marianne DeKoven, "Gertrude Stein and Modern Painting: Beyond Literary Cubism," *Contemporary Literature* 22, no. 1 (1981).

36. Cf. "There has just been recently an exhibition of Spanish painting here…they do do more than can be done, which carries them so far that they are not there, but certainly twentieth-century painting is Spanish, they do it but it is never begun. That is what makes the painting Spanish today." Stein, *Everybody's*, 32.

37. Stein frequently uses dogs to examine the nature of human behavior, both in this book and in other works of the period. She addresses the metaphorical value of dogs at the end of *Everybody's Autobiography*

when describing a conversation with Thornton Wilder: "We talked about the passage of time about the dogs and what they did and was it the same as we did." Ibid., 310.

38. Ibid., 325.

39. For an examination of ownership and identity in *The Autobiography of Alice B. Toklas*, see Leigh Gilmore, "A Signature of Lesbian Autobiography: "Gertrice/Altrude,"" *Prose Studies* 14, no. 2 (1991).

40. "Publisher's Note," vii.

41. Stein, *Everybody's*, 1.

42. Ironically, it is only in her native language that Alice Toklas must be modified to achieve an appropriate degree of presence, perhaps a subtle indication of Stein's own feelings about their return trip to America.

43. Mossberg reads this sentence in a similar way and argues that "autobiography is a process of transforming objective truths." Mossberg, "Double Exposures," 246. While the general sentiment of this passage may be comparable to my reading, I have difficulty with its metaphysical implications because it seems to suggest that some definable self exists prior to its autobiographical representation, a self that is consequently being deformed in the process of signification.

44. For a discussion of cultural difference in *Everybody's Autobiography*, see Shawn H. Alfrey, " 'Oriental Peaceful Penetration': Gertrude Stein and the End of Europe," *Massachusetts Review* 38, no. 3 (1997).

45. Cf. "You are never yourself to yourself except as you remember yourself and then of course you do not believe yourself. That is really the trouble with an autobiography." Stein, *Everybody's*, 70.

46. Ibid., 312.

47. Ulla E. Dydo, "*Stanzas in Meditation*: The Other Autobiography," *Chicago Review* 35, no. 2 (1985): 4–5.

48. Dydo maintains this difficult position throughout the essay and, in her concluding remarks, reiterates it by saying, "Again and again in the *Stanzas* [Stein] describes what she sees, trying not to turn her back to it. In the *Autobiography* she renders the appearance and the public image, with the sort of peace-loving statements an audience likes to hear." Ibid., 18. In other words, Stein's poetry attempts to capture the difficulties of "really" seeing through formal innovation, whereas the autobiographical work is designed to convey information in a direct and straightforward way.

49. Ibid., 19.

50. Gertrude Stein, *Lectures in America* (New York: Vintage Books, 1975), 246.

51. Gertrude Stein, *A Primer for the Gradual Understanding of Gertrude Stein*, ed. Robert Bartlett Haas (Los Angeles: Black Sparrow Press, 1971), 103.

52. Both *Paris France* and *Wars I Have Seen* have traditionally been considered part of Stein's autobiographical oeuvre, and most

commentators consider *Wars* to be her third major autobiography. For example, see Wagner-Martin, *"Favored Strangers,"* 243–44.

53. Stein, *Everybody's*, 72.
54. For a more detailed theoretical discussion of Stein's theories of representation, see Alan R. Knight, "Explaining Composition: Gertrude Stein and the Problem of Representation," *English Studies in Canada* 13, no. 4 (1987). For provocative arguments about Stein's language in the context of her early experimental texts, see Cyrena N. Pondrom, "An Introduction to the Achievement of Gertrude Stein," in *Geography and Plays* (Madison: University of Wisconsin Press, 1993); Wendy Steiner, *Exact Resemblance to Exact Resemblance* (New Haven, CT, 1978).
55. Stein, *Everybody's*, 180.
56. Ibid., 48.
57. Stein tellingly uses the same internal/external opposition to explain both the limiting effect of her audience and the onset of her writer's block: "I had written and was writing nothing. Nothing inside me needed to be written. . . . there was no word inside me that could not be spoken and so there was no word inside me. And I was not writing. I began to worry about identity." Ibid., 66.
58. Ibid., 33, 127.
59. Nancy Blake, "Everybody's Autobiography: Identity and Absence," *RANAM* 15 (1982): 138.
60. David E. Johnson, "'Writing in the Dark': The Political Fictions of American Travel Writing," *American Literary History* 7, no. 1 (1995): 2.
61. Stein, *Everybody's*, 4.
62. Though I have discussed only one example, almost any reading from the text would underscore both the generality of Stein's language and the lack of sustained narrative. For instance, Stein sums up their entire trip to Cleveland by saying, "Well we went on to Cleveland and that was pleasant too and it was the first American city where the streets were messy they said there was a reason but I do not remember the reason." Ibid., 236.
63. Ibid., 4.
64. Lynn Z. Bloom, "Gertrude Is Alice Is Everybody: Innovation and Point of View in Gertrude Stein's Autobiographies," *Twentieth Century Literature* 24, no. 1 (1978): 84.
65. Stein, *Everybody's*, 187.
66. For a more detailed examination of Stein's attitude toward embodiment, see Susan McCabe, "'Delight in Dislocation': The Cinematic Modernism of Stein, Chaplin, and Man Ray," *Modernism/modernity* 8, no. 3 (2001).
67. Stein, *Everybody's*, 102.
68. S. C. Neuman, following Stein's own theoretical formulations, claims, "The entire thrust of [Stein's] literary theory and practice was

towards the elimination of consciousness of time and particularly of the past." Neuman, *Problem of Narration*, 19–20. This statement, employed in various forms by many critics, seems hyperbolic in light of the various temporal markers that appear throughout *Everybody's Autobiography*. While Stein herself might claim to be unaware of history and work to confuse narrative sequence in this text, her explicit organizational cues certainly evoke the past and could potentially provoke a totally different awareness of time for her readers.

69. Though many critics have commented on the theoretical premises underlying Stein's use of the "continuous present," much less attention has been paid to the specific ways in which this style shapes her texts. For a theoretical account of the "continuous present" in Stein's autobiographies, see Shirley Swartz, "The Autobiography as Generic 'Continuous Present': Paris France and Wars I Have Seen," *English Studies in Canada* 4, no. 2 (1978). For an examination of Stein's "continuous present" in relation to twentieth-century scientific thought, see Robert Chodat, "Sense, Science, and the Interpretations of Gertrude Stein," *Modernism/modernity* 12, no. 4 (2005).

70. Stein, *Everybody's*, 2.

71. Many critics have examined Stein's detachment from a psychoanalytic perspective; however, it would be interesting for such a reading to consider not only the effects of certain textual moves but also Stein's broader linguistic theories, as the emotional distance she creates works to highlight the artificiality of representation as well. Moreover, Stein's larger tendency to subsume interpersonal issues into aesthetic and formal theories deserves more serious consideration.

72. Linda Wagner-Martin, "Gertrude Stein," in *Jewish American Women Writers: A Bio-Bibliographical and Critical Sourcebook*, ed. Ann Shapiro (London: Greenday Press, 1994), 436.

73. G. F. Mitrano, *Gertrude Stein: Woman without Qualities* (Burlington, VT: Ashgate Publishing Company, 2005), 136–37.

74. Stein, *Geographical History*, 469.

75. Gertrude Stein, *The Autobiography of Alice B. Toklas* (New York: Vintage Books, 1990), 83.

76. Stein, *Everybody's*, 4.

77. Stein, *Geographical History*.

78. Stein, *Everybody's*, 16–17.

79. Kirk Curnutt, drawing on a similar sense of Stein's disruptive narrative techniques, refers to this autobiography as a "haphazard picaresque." Kirk Curnutt, "Inside and Outside: Gertrude Stein on Identity, Celebrity, and Authenticity," *Journal of Modern Literature* 23, no. 2 (1999): 304.

80. Stein, *Everybody's*, 157–58.

81. Stein's awareness of the potential obscurity of everyday language could offer another useful connection between her work and that of Ernest

Hemingway, who was briefly a member of her artistic circle. For useful accounts of Stein's influence on Hemingway, see Charles Harmon Cagle, "'Cezanne Nearly Did': Stein, Cezanne, and Hemingway," *Midwest Quarterly: A Journal of Contemporary Thought* 23, no. 3 (1982); Susan J. Wolfe, "Insistence and Simplicity: The Influence of Gertrude Stein on Ernest Hemingway," *South Dakota Review* 35, no. 3 (1997).

82. Stein, *Everybody's*, 328.

83. Curnutt, "Inside and Outside," 305–06.

84. Lansing Warren, "Gertrude Stein Views Life and Politics," *New York Times Magazine*, May 6, 1934, 9.

85. Stein, *Everybody's*, 221. Stein adopted a similar stance throughout the mid-1930s. In an interview with the *New York Herald Tribune*, for instance, Stein said, "I like ordinary people who don't bore me. Highbrows, you know, always do." Quoted in Mellow, *Charmed Circle*, 409.

86. Bollinger, "Interrupted," 254–55. Laurel Bollinger also sees Stein as embracing duality in the wake of *The Autobiography*. Yet she glosses over much of Stein's work during the 1930s, including *Everybody's Autobiography,* and claims that this shift culminates with the novel *Ida* in 1941.

Part III The Crack-Up of F. Scott Fitzgerald

5 On the Limitations of Image Management: The Long Shadow of "F. Scott Fitzgerald"

1. Fitzgerald's "The Crack-Up" was the first of a three-part autobiographical series. The next two pieces, "Pasting It Together" and "Handle with Care," were published in March and April of 1936, respectively. I will follow scholarly convention in referring to the three-part series collectively as the "Crack-Up" essays. I will also follow scholarly convention in pointing out that when Edmund Wilson first collected these three pieces in *The Crack-Up,* he transposed the titles, and only the titles, of the last two pieces. In subsequent printings of Wilson's book, however, the error was corrected, a point overlooked by some scholars who have noted the change and then incorrectly reversed the corrected titles in their work.

2. Edmund Wilson, ed., *The Crack-Up* (New York: New Directions, 1945), 71.

3. Arnold Gingrich, "Three Characters in Search of a Magazine That Is Unhampered by the Old Taboos," *Esquire*, February 1934.

4. For information about *Esquire*'s circulation, see Arnold Gingrich, *Nothing but People: The Early Days at Esquire, a Personal History, 1928–1958* (New York: Crown Publishers, 1971), 140. For scholarly analyses of these numbers, see Hugh Merrill, *Esky: The Early Years*

at Esquire (New Brunswick, NJ: Rutgers University Press, 1995), 51, 54, 58–60; Tom Pendergast, *Creating the Modern Man: American Magazines and Consumer Culture, 1900–1950* (Columbia: University of Missouri Press, 2000), 220–21.

5. In order to give a sense of this "debate," I would like to provide one set of examples from the February 1934 issue, which was the issue immediately following the initial call for responses. One reader, citing Voltaire, implies that freedom of speech is worth dying for and characterizes any man who feels otherwise as "effete." In opposition, a man from Oklahoma claims, "The World War gave negroes delusions of equality and strength that culminated in a race riot in this town and it took the city incinerator days to burn the black bodies...Don't you think having the only nigger in Congress is enough of an embarrassment to the administration without Chicago starting something that it may cost men and millions to stop?" "The Sound and the Fury," *Esquire*, February 1934.

6. The two articles explicitly about Fitzgerald and Zelda were "Show Mr. and Mrs. F. to Number-" (published during May and June 1934) and "Auction-Model 1934" (July 1934). Both were run with a joint byline crediting Fitzgerald and Zelda. I have chosen to emphasize Fitzgerald's authorship above because his name would have been more recognizable to the male readers of *Esquire*. Scholars agree, however, that Zelda was the primary author of these pieces, which were revised by Fitzgerald prior to publication. In his biography of Fitzgerald, Matthew J. Bruccoli compares a portion of Zelda's original text to Fitzgerald's revised version in order to show how he "polished" her prose and worked to make larger thematic points more explicit for readers. See Matthew J. Bruccoli, *Some Sort of Epic Grandeur*, 2nd rev. ed. (Columbia: University of South Carolina Press, 2002), 385.

7. Arnold Gingrich, "Backstage with *Esquire*," *Esquire*, June 1936, 28.

8. Quoted in James L. W. West, "Fitzgerald and *Esquire*," in *The Short Stories of F. Scott Fitzgerald: New Approaches in Criticism*, ed. Jackson R. Bryer (Madison: University of Wisconsin Press, 1982), 155.

9. Scott Donaldson's article, "The Crisis of Fitzgerald's 'Crack-Up,'" provides a detailed summary of published and unpublished responses to the "Crack-Up" essays. Much of this article is also incorporated into his provocative biography of Fitzgerald, *Fool for Love: F. Scott Fitzgerald*.

10. Gingrich, "Backstage," 28. Gingrich's confession seems designed to spark interest in Fitzgerald's second series of autobiographical pieces that began running in the next issue. (The above quote is followed by the line, "So there'll be more soon.") Gingrich, however, expressed similar sentiments in a variety of other places as well. In a letter to his father, who disliked the first two pieces, Gingrich says, "I felt very much as you did about the Scott Fitzgerald series but this is a

case where my misgivings proved to be wrong as these articles have been enormously popular. I myself saw no sense in such a parade of futility." Arnold Gingrich to John Gingrich, March 25, 1936, Box I: Personal Correspondence, Arnold Gingrich Papers, Bentley Historical Library, University of Michigan.

11. E. B. White, "Talk of the Town," *New Yorker*, March 14, 1936, 11.

12. I am citing from the essay that appears in *The Liberal Imagination* because it is the most readily available. This text, however, published in 1950, uses material from two earlier pieces Trilling had written on Fitzgerald, an introduction he wrote for the New Directions edition of *The Great Gatsby* in 1945 and a review of *The Crack-Up*, also from 1945, published in *The Nation*. For more information on this article, and other secondary materials on Fitzgerald, see Jackson R. Bryer, *The Critical Reputation of F. Scott Fitzgerald: A Bibliographical Study* (Hamden, CT: Archon Books, 1967).

13. Lionel Trilling, "F. Scott Fitzgerald," in *The Liberal Imagination* (New York: Viking, 1950), 243–44.

14. Trilling praises Fitzgerald's individualism and admiringly cites his willingness "to blame himself...even though at the time when he was most aware of his destiny it was fashionable with minds more pretentious than his to lay all personal difficulty whatever at the door of the 'social order.'" Ibid., 245.

15. Marc Dolan, *Modern Lives* (West Lafayette, IN: Purdue University Press, 1996), 134.

16. Such efforts to challenge this narrative have only served to perpetuate its appearance in the critical literature. And while I too have resurrected this story in my work, I do not simply mean to endorse or discredit it, but to emphasize the political and rhetorical functions it has served for critics from both camps.

17. Perhaps the most famous of Fitzgerald's relapses took place during a freelance film job in early 1939. He was hired by United Artists to help improve the script for a movie called *Winter Carnival*. The plot revolved around the winter carnival at Dartmouth, and in February he traveled to the university with fellow scriptwriter Budd Schulberg. On the plane, Budd convinced Fitzgerald to share a bottle of champagne with him, which led to a three-day bender that got both writers fired. The whole experience was later memorialized in Schulberg's novel, *The Disenchanted*, a book based, in part, on their trip to Dartmouth. For an account of Fitzgerald's difficulties during his final years, see Bruccoli, *Epic Grandeur*, 432–94. For a concise history of Fitzgerald's work in Hollywood, see Alan Margolies, "Fitzgerald and Hollywood," in *The Cambridge Companion to F. Scott Fitzgerald*, ed. Ruth Prigozy (New York: Cambridge University Press, 2002). Sheilah Graham, Fitzgerald's partner during his final years, has also written extensively of her time with him. In particular, see Sheilah Graham, *Beloved Infidel: The Education of a Woman*

(New York: Holt, 1958); *The Rest of the Story* (New York: Coward-McCann, 1964).

18. William Troy, "F. Scott Fitzgerald: The Authority of Failure," in *F. Scott Fitzgerald*, ed. Harold Bloom (New York: Chelsea House Publishers, 2006), 28.

19. Alfred Kazin, "An American Confession," in *F. Scott Fitzgerald: The Man and His Work*, ed. Alfred Kazin (Cleveland, OH: The World Publishing Company, 1951), 180. Kazin's depiction of *The Crack-Up* is certainly darker and more tentative than Trilling's portrayal. For instance, he reads "Handle with Care" literally and suggests that Fitzgerald's ultimate commitment to art is a means of survival only, not a "heroic" revelation. His piece does, however, ultimately accord with the larger "tragic hero" story outlined above.

20. I think it is important to note here that the availability of knowledge about Fitzgerald does not seem to be an overriding factor in the critical positions I am laying out. That is, I do not believe a critic such as Trilling would have been less laudatory had he been privy to more negative details about Fitzgerald's life. The letters collected in *The Crack-Up* alone contain enough information to suggest that the end of Fitzgerald's life was not necessarily "heroic." And a critic such as Edmund Wilson, who attended Princeton with Fitzgerald, probably knew enough about these final days to challenge such a view if he felt so inclined.

21. Wright Morris, "The Function of Nostalgia: F. Scott Fitzgerald," in *F. Scott Fitzgerald: A Collection of Critical Essays*, ed. Arthur Mizener (Englewood Cliffs, NJ: Prentice-Hall, 1963), 29.

22. James E. Jr. Miller, *F. Scott Fitzgerald: His Art and His Technique* (New York: New York University Press, 1964), 128.

23. Arnold Gingrich, "Introduction," in *The Pat Hobby Stories* (New York: Scribner, 1962), xi–xii.

24. Wilson, *Crack-Up*, 72.

25. He wrote to a former lover, Beatrice Dance, in March 1936, "For myself don't take that little trilogy in *Esquire* too seriously." See Matthew J. Bruccoli and Margaret M. Duggan, eds., *Correspondence of F. Scott Fitzgerald* (New York: Random House, 1980), 427–28.

26. Henry Dan Piper, *F. Scott Fitzgerald: A Critical Portrait* (New York: 1965), 240. The *Post* ultimately declined, but he did write another set of melancholy reflections for *Esquire*. The three pieces, "An Author's House," "Afternoon of an Author," and "An Author's Mother," were published in July, August, and September of 1936, respectively.

27. Stephen W. Potts, *The Price of Paradise: The Magazine Career of F. Scott Fitzgerald* (San Bernardino, CA: Borgo Press, 1993), 74.

28. Fitzgerald spun off the success of his "How to Live on $36,000 a Year," first published in 1924, into two other articles, "How to Live on Practically Nothing a Year" and "The High Cost of Macaroni." The latter article, alternatively titled "What Price Macaroni" in

correspondence with his agent, ultimately went unpublished. For the short history of "Macaroni," see Matthew J. Bruccoli, ed., *As Ever, Scott Fitz-: Letters between F. Scott Fitzgerald and His Literary Agent Harold Ober, 1919–1940* (Philadelphia, PA: J. B. Lippincott Company, 1972), 67n, 78, 79n, 81, 89, 91.

29. Fitzgerald wrote a story sequence in 1928, a series for *The Saturday Evening Post* about a young man named Basil Duke Lee who appears similar in many respects to a young Fitzgerald. He followed these stories with a series about Josephine Perry, a young woman roughly based on Ginevra King, one of his early love interests. Throughout the 1930s, Fitzgerald attempted to publish another series, but failed repeatedly. His attempts included story sequences about an intern (1932), a French count in the ninth century (1934), a single father and his daughter (1935), and a nurse nicknamed Trouble (1936). The only series he was able to extend to any length, seventeen short pieces about a studio hack named Pat Hobby, was published by *Esquire,* which accepted nearly everything Fitzgerald submitted.

30. See John Kuehl and Jackson R. Bryer, eds., *Dear Scott/Dear Max: The Fitzgerald-Perkins Correspondence* (New York: Charles Scribner's Sons, 1971), 227–30.

31. While Trilling and Banerjee's approach may seem the same when viewed from the larger perspective of the biographical narrative, I do not mean to suggest that these two critics are employing this narrative for the same reason or to attain similar effects. Elaborating on the particular tactics and aims of critics writing nearly fifty years apart, however, would take me far outside the scope of my argument.

32. A. Banerjee, "A Move towards Maturity: Scott Fitzgerald's 'the Crack-up,'" *Revista Alicantina de estudios Ingleses* 8 (1995): 48.

33. Kirk Curnutt, "Making a 'Clean Break': Confession, Celebrity Journalism, Image Management and F. Scott Fitzgerald's 'the Crack-up,'" *Genre: Forms of Discourse and Culture* 32, no. 4 (1999): 299.

34. Ibid., 307–08.

35. Ibid., 307 fn. 10.

36. Cf. "Moreover, to go back to my thesis that life has a varying offensive, the realization of having cracked was not simultaneous with a blow, but with a reprieve" Wilson, *Crack-Up*, 71.

37. As noted above, these pieces were probably not conceived initially as a single unit, but the larger pattern of the pieces suggests that Fitzgerald did consider their overall structure when writing the last two articles.

38. Wilson, *Crack-Up*, 76.

39. Milton Hindus, *F. Scott Fitzgerald: An Introduction and Interpretation* (New York: Holt, Rinehart & Winston, 1968), 90.

40. Piper, *Critical Portrait*, 237.

41. Dolan, *Modern*, 143.

42. Occasional asides, as in the aforementioned "lecturer" comments, also work to distance the narrating voice from the immediacy of the "crack-up." The first essay in particular is full of present tense commentary, such as the narrator's repeated insistence that the "story" is over, though the essay continues, and his willingness to judge the situation as it unfolds in the text ("All rather inhuman and undernourished, isn't it?") Wilson, *Crack-Up*, 72–73.

43. Ibid., 71.

44. Ibid.

45. The two main published collections of Fitzgerald's business letters are Bruccoli, *As Ever* and Kuehl and Bryer, *Dear Scott*. Several other collections of Fitzgerald's correspondence have important letters left out of these collections. For example, *The Correspondence* contains a much quoted letter to Max Perkins, not included in *Dear Scott*, where Fitzgerald complains that reporters "twist [my words] to make an idiot out of me." Bruccoli and Duggan, *Correspondence*, 92. See also Matthew J. Bruccoli, ed., *F. Scott Fitzgerald: A Life in Letters* (New York: Charles Scribner's Sons, 1994); Andrew Turnbull, ed., *The Letters of F. Scott Fitzgerald* (New York: Charles Scribner's Sons, 1963), 137–291, 391–408.

46. During the months just prior to the publication of any of his books, many of the letters he wrote to Max Perkins contained suggestions about publishing or marketing. His letter on February 5, 1934, shortly before the book publication of *Tender Is the Night,* provides a particularly elaborate example. First, he reminds Perkins that the indentations and the layout of his name on the cover should correspond with all of his other books. Then, he warns against playing up the fact that the book is largely set in resorts on the Riviera, as it would only feed misconceptions of his work as trivial. He also discourages the use of blurbs, as "the public is very, very, very weary of being sold bogus goods." Finally, he suggests mentioning that several scenes were cut in the magazine serialization, to entice people who already read the abridged version in *Scribner's* magazine. See Kuehl and Bryer, *Dear Scott*, 191–92.

47. Several scholars have done excellent work examining the publicity surrounding Fitzgerald's early career, and the first half of this section is indebted to their research. In particular, Kirk Curnutt, Scott Donaldson, and Ruth Prigozy, whose works will be cited throughout this chapter, have provided the foundation upon which my reflections are based.

48. For examples of several interviews from the late 1920s where Fitzgerald is identified primarily by his "flapper" novel, see Matthew J. Bruccoli and Jackson R. Bryer, eds., *F. Scott Fitzgerald in His Own Time: A Miscellany* (Kent, OH: Kent State University Press, 1971), 274–81.

49. A. Scott Berg, *Max Perkins: Editor of Genius* (New York: E. P. Dutton, 1978), 19; Curnutt, "Clean Break," 316.

50. For more detailed accounts of Fitzgerald's years at Princeton, see Bruccoli, *Epic Grandeur*, 41–79; Andre Le Vot, *F. Scott Fitzgerald: A Biography*, trans. William Byron (Garden City, NY: Doubleday & Company, 1979), 30–55.

51. Quoted in Bruccoli, *Epic Grandeur*, 60.

52. Though there is certainly evidence to suggest that Princeton played a crucial role in Fitzgerald's own self-conceptions, I am primarily concerned here with its elaboration in relation to the larger persona Fitzgerald attempted to construct.

53. Fitzgerald was insistent enough about his relationship to Princeton that one writer, summarizing important facts about the author in 1928, still listed Princeton as one of his "greatest interests in life." See Bruccoli and Bryer, *Miscellany*, 281–84.

54. Bruccoli, *Epic Grandeur*, 111.

55. Much work has been done analyzing and debating the emergence of the professional-managerial class. For Barbara and John Ehrenreich's article, "The Professional-Managerial Class," as well as a series of articles discussing the evolution of the middle class at the turn of the century, see Pat Walker, ed., *Between Labour and Capital* (Boston: South End Press, 1979). See also Stuart Blumin, *The Emergence of the Middle Class: Social Experience in the American City, 1760–1900* (Cambridge: Cambridge University Press, 1989).

56. Richard Ohmann, *Selling Culture: Magazines, Markets, and Class at the Turn of the Century* (New York: Verso, 1996), 119.

57. Michael Augspurger, *An Economy of Abundant Beauty: Fortune Magazine and Depression America* (Ithaca, NY: Cornell University Press, 2004), 14.

58. John F. Kasson, *Houdini, Tarzan, and the Perfect Man: The White Male Body and the Challenge of Modernity in America* (New York: Hill & Wang, 2002), 240, fn. 28.

59. Janice Radway, "Research Universities, Periodical Publication, and the Circulation of Professional Expertise: On the Significance of Middlebrow Authority," *Critical Inquiry* 31, no. 1 (2004): 213.

60. Many critics have argued that the rise of the university system was central to the development of the concept of "youth" around the turn of the century. For more on the emergence of a "youth" sub-culture in America, see Dolan, *Modern*; Joseph F. Kett, *Rites of Passage: Adolescence in America 1790 to the Present* (New York: Basic Books, 1973), 245–72. For an interesting application of this work to Fitzgerald's writing, see Kirk Curnutt, "F. Scott Fitzgerald, Age Consciousness, and the Rise of American Youth Culture," in *The Cambridge Companion to F. Scott Fitzgerald*, ed. Ruth Prigozy (New York: Cambridge University Press, 2002).

61. For the standard work on the development of advertising in the early twentieth century, see Roland Marchand, *Advertising the American Dream: Making Way for Modernity, 1920–1940* (Berkeley: University of California Press, 1985). For a work that treats earlier decades, primarily the 1880s through the 1920s, see Daniel Pope, *The Making of Modern Advertising* (New York: Basic Books, 1983). See also Ohmann, *Selling Culture*, 81–117.

62. Fitzgerald even went as far as to claim himself an alumnus of the university. See Bruccoli and Bryer, *Miscellany*, 167.

63. Fitzgerald was certainly not the first author to write about young adults in the early decades of the twentieth century, though the various reasons for his own ascendant rise as the spokesman of the younger generation are far too complex to begin speculating about here. In any case, his own association with this group is important both because it helped to generate an aura of authority around his work and because it allowed him to speak with authority outside of his fiction.

64. Bruccoli, *Epic Grandeur*, 115.

65. Bruccoli and Bryer, *Miscellany*, 258.

66. Ruth Prigozy, "Introduction: Scott, Zelda, and the Culture of Celebrity," in *The Cambridge Companion to F. Scott Fitzgerald*, ed. Ruth Prigozy (New York: Cambridge University Press, 2002), 7.

67. Bruccoli and Bryer, *Miscellany*, 274.

68. Ibid., 245. Fitzgerald became good friends with Thomas Boyd and recommended his first novel, *Through the Wheat*, to Max Perkins. Scribner's published it in 1923. Extant correspondence suggests that their relationship was largely professional at the time Boyd published his piece.

69. Ibid., 247.

70. Ibid., 253.

71. The piece, along with a brief note about its publication history, is collected as "An Interview with F. Scott Fitzgerald" in Matthew J. Bruccoli, ed., *F. Scott Fitzgerald on Authorship* (Columbia: University of South Carolina Press, 1996), 33–35. This "interview" follows the typical pattern of Fitzgerald publicity. First, the "interviewer" describes Fitzgerald's appearance, which he finds unexpectedly striking. Then, he poses a few simple questions that Fitzgerald answers with spontaneous wit. Finally, as Fitzgerald's enthusiasm takes over, the interviewer fades into the background to document the author's passionate burst of words.

72. Ibid., 35. This statement is not literally true. Fitzgerald redrafted the novel two times over a period of several years before Scribner's finally accepted it for publication.

73. Ibid., 37.

74. Arthur Mizener, ed., *Afternoon of an Author* (New York: Charles Scribner's Sons, 1957), 83–85.

75. For one example from 1924, four years after "Who's Who," see Bruccoli and Bryer, *Miscellany*, 267–70.
76. I am indebted to Bryer's "Introduction" for pointing out the emergence of this idea in *Gatsby* criticism. See page xix for more elucidation and examples of this point. Also, see Malcolm Cowley, "Third Act and Epilogue," *New Yorker* XXI (1945).
77. Quoted in Jackson R. Bryer, ed., *F. Scott Fitzgerald: The Critical Reception* (New York: Burt Franklin & Co, 1978), xix.
78. Ibid., 241.
79. In calculating Fitzgerald's earned income, I deducted both Zelda's earnings and advances against his future novel, which functioned more like loans than payments on future earnings. In 1927, Fitzgerald's earned income was $22,935.81, of which $15,300 came from *Post* fiction, amounting to roughly 67 percent. In 1928, that proportion rose, as his income increased slightly to $23,423.93, but his *Post* earnings shot up to $22,050, or 94 percent of the total. For the next four years, the *Post* would dominate Fitzgerald's earnings. In 1929, total earned income was $30,018.18, with $27,000 from *Post* fiction (90 percent). 1930: $25,638.13 total, $25,200 from *Post* fiction, or about 98 percent. 1931: $37,554.85 total, $28,800 from *Post* fiction (77 percent). 1932: $15,343.40 total, $14,605 from *Post* (95 percent). 1933: $16,208.03 total, $7,650 from *Post* (47 percent). 1934: $13,550.35 total, $8,100 from *Post* (60 percent). 1935: $16,503.13 total, $5,400 from *Post* (32.7 percent). 1936, the last year he sold stories to the *Post:* $10,180.97 total, $5,000 from *Post* (49.1 percent). For more details, see F. Scott Fitzgerald, *F. Scott Fitzgerald's Ledger* (Washington, D.C.: NCR/Microcard Editions, 1972).
80. The best source of information on Fitzgerald's short story writing is Potts, *Magazine Career*. For historical information on *The Saturday Evening Post*, see John William Tebbel, *George Horace Lorimer and the Saturday Evening Post* (Garden City, NY: Doubleday, 1948). For a more recent cultural history, see Jan Cohn, *Creating America: George Horace Lorimer and the Saturday Evening Post* (Pittsburgh, PA: University of Pittsburgh Press, 1989).
81. The best source on *Esquire*'s early years is still Gingrich's *Nothing but People*. For several contemporary accounts that add a few details to Gingrich's book, see George H. Douglas, *The Smart Magazines* (Hamden, CT: Shoe String Press, 1991); Merrill, *Esky*.
82. Fitzgerald's novels, as was typical at the time, sold far better than his short story collections. *This Side of Paradise* and *The Beautiful and Damned* each sold approximately 50,000 copies in their first year of publication. *The Great Gatsby* sold its initial run of 20,870 copies and had a second printing of 3,000 in the same span of time. By contrast, *Tender Is the Night* sold only about 15,000 copies. Fitzgerald's first collection of short stories, *Flappers and Philosophers*, sold more than 15,000 copies in its first several months of publication, but sales

slowed quickly. *Tales of the Jazz Age* quickly sold its first 8,000 copies and ran through two smaller printings in its first year. *All the Sad Young Men* sold 16,170 copies in the same amount of time. In contrast, *Taps at Reveille* sold less than 5,100 copies. For more information on Fitzgerald's sales, see James L. W. West, "F. Scott Fitzgerald, Professional Author," in *A Historical Guide to F. Scott Fitzgerald*, ed. Kirk Curnutt (Oxford: Oxford University Press, 2004), 56–61. Also, see Bruccoli, *Epic Grandeur*, 31, 45, 62, 68, 133, 217, 391.

83. For an interesting examination of Zelda's life and illness that problematizes this diagnosis, see Linda Wagner-Martin, *Zelda Sayre Fitzgerald: An American Woman's Life* (New York: Palgrave Macmillan, 2004), 120–96.

84. Prigozy, "Culture of Celebrity," 13.

85. The flapper piece titled "Girls Believe in Girls" was ultimately rejected by *McCall's* and sold to *Liberty* for $1,500. For more information about the series of events surrounding this story, see Bruccoli, *As Ever*, 156–62.

86. For some more of Fitzgerald's specific complaints, see Kuehl and Bryer, *Dear Scott*, 186–95.

87. For more on the exchange between Fitzgerald and Hemingway, see Matthew J. Bruccoli, *Fitzgerald and Hemingway: A Dangerous Friendship* (New York: Carroll & Graf, 1994), 171–75.

88. Bruccoli, *Life in Letters*, 288.

89. Carlos Baker, ed., *Ernest Hemingway: Selected Letters 1917–1961* (New York: Charles Scribner's Sons, 1981), 438.

90. In one of her more despairing, though not altogether atypical, moments, Zelda wrote, "I am sorry too that there should be nothing to greet you but an empty shell. The thought of...the suffering this nothing has cost would be unendurable to any save a completely vacuous mechanism. Had I any feelings they would all be bent in gratitude to you and in sorrow that of all my life there should not even be the smallest relic of the love and beauty that we started with to offer you at the end...I love you anyway—even if there isn't any me or any love or even any life." Bruccoli, *Life in Letters*, 285.

91. For example, in late 1930, Zelda wrote, "I was nervous and half-sick but I didn't know what was the matter. I only knew that I had difficulty standing lots of people." Jackson R. Bryer and Cathy W. Barks, eds., *Dear Scott, Dearest Zelda: The Love Letters of F. Scott and Zelda Fitzgerald* (New York: St. Martin's Press, 2002), 71.

92. Quoted in Bruccoli, *Epic Grandeur*, 92.

93. Ibid.

94. Gingrich retells this story in several places. For several widely available examples, see Arnold Gingrich, *Nothing but People*, 241–43; "Scott, Ernest, and Whoever," *Esquire*, December 1966, 322–25.

95. For Gingrich's version, see West, *Nothing but People*, 288–89. Also, see West, "Esquire," 157–58.

96. Kuehl and Bryer, *Dear Scott*, 187.
97. Scott Donaldson, "Fitzgerald's Nonfiction," in *The Cambridge Companion to F. Scott Fitzgerald*, ed. Ruth Prigozy (New York: Cambridge University Press, 2002), 174.
98. The first quote comes from an interview Fitzgerald did with B. F. Wilson for *Metropolitan Magazine*. It is collected in a slightly abridged form under the title "All Women Over Thirty-Five Should Be Murdered," in Bruccoli and Bryer, *Miscellany*, 263–66.
99. F. Scott Fitzgerald, in *The Notebooks of F. Scott Fitzgerald*, ed. Matthew J. Bruccoli (New York: Harcourt Brace Jovanovich/ Bruccoli Clark, 1978), 318. For a similar reading of this phrase, see Morris Dickstein, "Fitzgerald: The Authority of Failure," in *F. Scott Fitzgerald in the Twenty-First Century*, ed. Jackson R. Bryer, Ruth Prigozy, and Milton R. Stern (Tuscaloosa: University of Alabama Press, 2003), 313.
100. Quoted in Andrew Turnbull, *Scott Fitzgerald* (New York: Charles Scribner's Sons, 1962), 265.
101. Wilson, *Crack-Up*, 13.
102. Ibid., 15, 19.
103. Ibid., 13.
104. Later in the essay, the narrator will explicitly scoff at the naïveté of an age that treated writers, such as Fitzgerald himself, as "geniuses on the strength of one respectable book or play." Ibid., 22.
105. Ibid.
106. Ibid., 26. Author's ellipsis.
107. Ibid., 27. The narrator goes on to dismiss his public interviews and articles, saying that he and Zelda "were quoted on a variety of subjects we knew nothing about. Actually our 'contacts' included half a dozen unmarried college friends and a few new literary acquaintances." Wilson, *Crack-Up*, 27.
108. The narrator refers to his early self as acting with "theatrical innocence" because he was the observed but not the observer. This sense of acting but never really being in control, as one who is merely playing a role, aptly characterizes the young narrator in the piece. A similar emphasis on both public visibility and lack of a certain type of agency appears in another crucial description of his early years: "I had as much control over my own destiny as a convict over the cut of his clothes." Wilson, *Crack-Up*, 25, 29.
109. Bruccoli, *On Authorship*, 140.
110. Bruccoli and Bryer, *Miscellany*, 285.
111. Mizener, *Afternoon*, 131.
112. For the original articles, see F. Scott Fitzgerald and Zelda Fitzgerald, "Does a Moment of Revolt Come Sometime to Every Married Man?" *McCall's* 51 (1924): 21, 36, 82. The pieces are also collected separately. Scott's reply was included in Bruccoli and Bryer, *Miscellany*, 184–86. Zelda's version is collected in Zelda Fitzgerald,

The Collected Writings of Zelda Fitzgerald, ed. Matthew J. Bruccoli (Tuscaloosa and London: University of Alabama Press, 1991), 395–96.

113. Mizener, *Afternoon*, 128.

114. Quoted in Bruccoli, *Epic Grandeur*, 98.

115. Fitzgerald's notes for the novel contain many titles, including *Stahr: A Romance* and *The Last of the Tycoons*. The novel was originally published, under Edmund Wilson's hand, in 1941 as *The Last Tycoon: An Unfinished Novel Together With "The Great Gatsby" and Selected Stories*. Matthew Bruccoli later reedited Fitzgerald's final passages and notes under another of Fitzgerald's titles, *The Love of the Last Tycoon: A Western*.

116. Bruccoli and Bryer, *Miscellany*, 288.

117. Ibid., 292.

118. Ibid., 294.

119. Any discussion of Fitzgerald's personal feelings about these references would take me far outside the scope of my argument. I will merely say that evidence suggests he was quite ambivalent about his lingering persona. On one hand, he still clearly felt pride in these notices and kept collecting such clippings, many of which recalled his ability to capture the mood of the younger generation in *This Side of Paradise*, until his death. For relevant selections from Fitzgerald's scrapbooks, see Matthew J. Bruccoli, Scottie Fitzgerald Smith, and Joan P. Kerr, eds., *The Romantic Egoists* (Columbia: University of South Carolina Press, 1974), 204–05. On the other hand, Fitzgerald was not always pleased by these mentions, in part because they conflicted with his efforts to construct a more "literary" image. In a semiautobiographical piece published in late 1936, "Afternoon of an Author," the narrator stops to listen to music and bitterly remarks, "So long since he had danced, perhaps two evenings in five years, yet a review of his last book had mentioned him as being fond of night clubs; the same review had also spoken of him as being indefatigable. Something in the sound of the word in his mind broke him momentarily and feeling tears of weakness behind his eyes he turned away. It was like in the beginning fifteen years ago when they said he had 'fatal facility,' and he labored like a slave over every sentence." F. Scott Fitzgerald, *Afternoon of an Author*, ed. Arthur Mizener (New York: Charles Scribner's Sons, 1957), 181.

120. Quoted in Prigozy, "Culture of Celebrity," 15.

121. Bruccoli, *Epic Grandeur*, 449.

122. I am indebted to the work of Ruth Prigozy for this point. For other examples and quotes about Fitzgerald's growing obscurity, see Prigozy, "Culture of Celebrity," 13–15.

123. For more on the events leading up to the interview, see Bruccoli, *Epic Grandeur*, 404–07.

124. For a slightly condensed version of Mok's article, see Bruccoli and Bryer, *Miscellany*, 294–99. For the original article, see Michel Mok, "The Other Side of Paradise: Scott Fitzgerald, 40, Engulfed in Despair," *New York Post*, September 25, 1936.

125. Fitzgerald, in correspondence with Marie Hamm, one of his early love interests from St. Paul, claimed that the article was "an entirely faked-up picture of me as I was at forty. None of the remarks attributed to me did I make to him. They were taken word by word from the first 'Crack-Up' article." Turnbull, *Letters*, 545–47.

6 The "Crack-Up" Essays: Masculine Identity, Modernism, and the Dissolution of Literary Values

1. F. Scott Fitzgerald, in *The Notebooks of F. Scott Fitzgerald*, ed. Matthew J. Bruccoli (New York: Harcourt Brace Jovanovich/ Bruccoli Clark, 1978), #1598.

2. Edmund Wilson, ed., *The Crack-Up* (New York: New Directions, 1945), 71, 80. Henceforth abbreviated in text as CU.

3. For a meditation on the difficulty of approaching such a text from a removed critical perspective, see Gilles Deleuze, *The Logic of Sense* (New York: Columbia University Press, 1969), 154–61.

4. In an interesting biographical parallel, many scholars have noted Fitzgerald's lifelong tendency to keep records and lists. As early as age fourteen, he began keeping the *Thoughtbook of Francis Scott Fitzgerald Key*, a diary of his romantic and social adventures. He also had a habit of making lists out of random events in his life. Critic and Fitzgerald biographer Arthur Mizener notes that Fitzgerald used to keep lists of the various "snubs" he had suffered. F. Scott Fitzgerald, *Afternoon of an Author*, ed. Arthur Mizener (New York: Charles Scribner's Sons, 1957), 169. The latter list is also addressed in Edward J. Gleason, "Going toward the Flame: Reading Allusions in *Esquire* Stories," in *F. Scott Fitzgerald: New Perspectives*, ed. Jackson R. Bryer, Alan Margolies, and Ruth Prigozy (Athens: University of Georgia Press, 2000), 220. For more on Fitzgerald's tendency to make lists, see Matthew J. Bruccoli, *Some Sort of Epic Grandeur*, 2nd rev. ed. (Columbia: University of South Carolina Press, 2002), 27, 143, 220.

5. William Troy, "F. Scott Fitzgerald: The Authority of Failure," in *F. Scott Fitzgerald*, ed. Harold Bloom (New York: Chelsea House Publishers, 2006), 29.

6. Early on in the first essay, the narrator mentions writer William Seabrook's alcoholism and says, "The present writer was not so entangled—having at the time not tasted so much as a glass of beer in six months." F. Scott Fitzgerald, *The Crack-Up*, 71.

7. Charles Sweetman, "Sheltering Assets and Reorganizing Debts: Fitzgerald's Declaration of Emotional Bankruptcy in *the Crack-Up*," *Proteus: A Journal of Ideas* 20, no. 2 (2003): 13.

8. Michael Nowlin, *F. Scott Fitzgerald's Racial Angles and the Business of Literary Greatness* (Basingstoke and New York: Palgrave Macmillan, 2007), 6. Nowlin acknowledges the alternative negative connotations of literary "professionalism" as well: "The label 'professional writer'...could readily connote something all-too-ordinary-one's membership in a class of largely white, middle-class, well-salaried mental-laborers working in the service of the state or big business." Nowlin, *Racial Angles*, 7.

9. Nowlin, *Racial Angles*, 6.

10. Fitzgerald, *Afternoon*, 84.

11. In a letter to Mrs. Laura Feley on July 20, 1939, Fitzgerald provides a similar gloss on the essays, though with far more retrospective melancholy than can be read into "Handle with Care." He says, "I don't know whether those articles of mine in *Esquire*—that 'Crack-Up' series—represented a real nervous breakdown. In retrospect it seems more of a spiritual 'change of life'—and a most unwilling one—it was a protest against a new set of conditions which I would have to face and a protest of my mind at having to make the psychological adjustments which would suit this new set of circumstances." Andrew Turnbull, ed., *The Letters of F. Scott Fitzgerald* (New York: Charles Scribner's Sons, 1963), 589. Of course, these comments are only one of a wide range of positions Fitzgerald took on these essays in his final years.

12. Andreas Huyssen, *After the Great Divide: Modernism, Mass Culture, Postmodernism* (Bloomington: Indiana University Press, 1986), 65–81.

13. Matthew J. Bruccoli and Jackson R. Bryer, eds., *F. Scott Fitzgerald in His Own Time: A Miscellany* (Kent, OH: Kent State University Press, 1971), 276–77.

14. Ibid.

15. Ibid., 208.

16. Quoted in Frank Lentricchia, *Modernist Quartet* (Cambridge: Cambridge University Press, 1994), 185.

17. Bruccoli and Bryer, *Miscellany*, 210.

18. As noted earlier, *Esquire* published stories that were significantly shorter than those accepted by the other leading magazines of the day. Gingrich also provided relatively little editorial oversight, which was unusual for such a popular publication. Stephen W. Potts, in his study of Fitzgerald's short fiction, claims that Fitzgerald did not typically "write down" to the standards of a particular magazine, but he did have to adapt his style to the different editorial demands of *Esquire*. See Stephen W. Potts, *The Price of Paradise: The Magazine Career of F. Scott Fitzgerald* (San Bernardino, CA: Borgo Press, 1993), 82–90.

19. Bruccoli and Bryer, *Miscellany*, 185.
20. Ronald J. Gervais, "Fitzgerald's 'Euganean Hills' Allusion in 'the Crack-up,'" *American Notes and Queries* 21, no. 9–10 (1983): 139–40.
21. Arnold Gingrich, "Introduction," in *The Pat Hobby Stories* (New York: Scribner, 1962), xxii–xxiii. Fitzgerald's male friends and acquaintances frequently blamed his problems on Zelda, which led early biographers to depict her in quite unflattering terms. For one particularly scathing depiction of Zelda's effect on her husband, see Ernest Hemingway, *A Moveable Feast* (New York: Scribner, 1964), 147–93. For a more balanced assessment of the relationship between the two, see Linda Wagner-Martin, *Zelda Sayre Fitzgerald: An American Woman's Life* (New York: Palgrave Macmillan, 2004).
22. Scott Donaldson, "The Crisis of Fitzgerald's 'Crack-up,'" *Twentieth Century Literature* 26, no. 2 (1980): 180–81.
23. William Ernest Henley, "Invictus," in *Modern British Poetry*, ed. Louis Untermeyer (New York: Harcourt, Brace & Howe, 1920), www.bartleby.com/103/7.html (accessed August 10, 2010), ll. 15–16.
24. Ibid., ll. 9.
25. Matthew J. Bruccoli, ed., *F. Scott Fitzgerald on Authorship* (Columbia: University of South Carolina Press, 1996), 140–41.
26. Matthew J. Bruccoli, *Fitzgerald and Hemingway: A Dangerous Friendship* (New York: Carroll & Graf, 1994), 172.
27. Matthew J. Bruccoli, ed., *As Ever, Scott Fitz-: Letters between F. Scott Fitzgerald and His Literary Agent Harold Ober, 1919–1940* (Philadelphia: J. B. Lippincott Company, 1972), 245.
28. Ibid., 279–80.
29. Matthew J. Bruccoli, "The Perkins-Wilson Correspondence," *Fitzgerald/Hemingway Annual 1978* (1979): 65.
30. Quoted in Donaldson, "Crisis," 174.
31. Christopher Wilson, *The Labor of Words: Literary Professionalism in the Progressive Era* (Athens: University of Georgia Press, 1985), 17.
32. John Kuehl and Jackson R. Bryer, eds., *Dear Scott/Dear Max: The Fitzgerald-Perkins Correspondence* (New York: Charles Scribner's Sons, 1971), 228.
33. The relationship between Fitzgerald and Hemingway has been well documented in Matthew Bruccoli's *Fitzgerald and Hemingway*. For their relationship during "The Crack-Up" period, see esp. 179–207. The above references can also be found in Carlos Baker, ed., *Ernest Hemingway: Selected Letters 1917–1961* (New York: Charles Scribner's Sons, 1981), 44, 437–8.
34. In Hemingway's story, a dying writer "remembered poor Scott Fitzgerald and his romantic awe of [the rich] and how he had started a story once that began, 'The very rich are different from you and me.' And how someone had said to Scott, Yes they have more money.

But that was not humorous to Scott. He thought they were a special glamorous race and when he found they weren't it wrecked him just as much as any other thing that wrecked him." For more about this reference, including Maxwell Perkins's claim that Hemingway borrowed the put-down in "The Snows of Kilamanjaro" from a comment directed at Hemingway himself, see Bruccoli, *Dangerous*, 189–92.

35. Quoted in Donaldson, "Crisis," 172; Robert Alan Green, "Advice at Twenty," *Esquire*, April 1936.

36. Matthew J. Bruccoli and Margaret M. Duggan, eds., *Correspondence of F. Scott Fitzgerald* (New York: Random House, 1980), 436.

37. Kirk Curnutt, "Making a 'Clean Break': Confession, Celebrity Journalism, Image Management and F. Scott Fitzgerald's 'the Crack-up,'" *Genre: Forms of Discourse and Culture* 32, no. 4 (1999): 299.

38. Theodore Peterson, *Magazines in the Twentieth Century* (Urbana: University of Illinois Press, 1956), 10.

39. Mary Macfadden and Emile Gauvreau, *Dumbbells and Carrot Strips: The Story of Bernarr Macfadden* (New York: Holt, 1953), 218–19.

40. Roland Marchand, *Advertising the American Dream: Making Way for Modernity, 1920–1940* (Berkeley: University of California Press, 1985), 53–54.

41. Quoted in George Gerbner, "The Social Role of the Confession Magazine," *Social Problems* 6 (1958): 29.

42. Ibid., 30–31.

43. Fitzgerald himself at times associated his literary talent with femininity, as when he told confidante Laura Guthrie, "I don't know why I can write stories. I don't know what it is in me or that comes to me when I start to write. I am half feminine—at least my mind is." Turnbull, *Scott Fitzgerald*, 259.

44. Kirk Curnutt cites one ad that boasts the headline, "Because I confessed, I found the way to happiness." The accompanying copy reveals that the confession in question pertains to the narrator's ineptitude in the kitchen, an admission that led her to receive a copy of the Eagle-Brand Condensed Milk cookbook, which, in turn, helped her land a husband. Curnutt, "Clean Break," 313. Curnutt's example and the support for his point in general are drawn from Roland Marchand's book, *Advertising the American Dream*. See esp. 56–58.

45. Fitzgerald maintained a complex attitude toward the trope of the "clean break" throughout his writing career. While any kind of general survey of the topic is far too complicated to go into here, it is relevant to my argument that his fascination with the idea of absolute shifts carried itself over into a related interest in the proletariat revolution central to early Marxism. While Fitzgerald did often refer approvingly to Marxist philosophy, in the "Crack-Up" essays he repeatedly dismisses, much as he dismisses the easy escape of the "clean break," the relevance of Marxism. For instance, he concludes

the second essay with the ominous declaration, "I have the feeling that someone, I'm not sure who, is sound asleep—someone who could have helped me to keep my shop open. It wasn't Lenin, and it wasn't God" (CU, 79–80).

46. Gerbner, "Social Role," 35.

47. Marc Dolan, *Modern Lives* (West Lafayette: Purdue University Press, 1996), 206 fn. 10.

48. Kuehl and Bryer, *Dear Scott*, 228–30.

EPILOGUE

1. John Kuehl and Jackson R. Bryer, eds., *Dear Scott/Dear Max: The Fitzgerald-Perkins Correspondence* (New York: Charles Scribner's Sons, 1971), 11.

2. F. Scott Fitzgerald, *Last Tycoon: An Unfinished Novel Together with "The Great Gatsby" and Selected Stories*, ed. Edmund Wilson (New York: Scribner, 1941), 163.

BIBLIOGRAPHY

Adams, Bluford. *E Pluribus Barnum: The Great Showman and the Making of U.S. Popular Culture*. Minneapolis: University of Minnesota Press, 1997.

Agnew, Jean-Christophe. "Coming up for Air: Consumer Culture in Historical Perspective." *Intellectual History Newsletter* 12 (1990): 3–21.

Alfrey, Shawn H. "'Oriental Peaceful Penetration': Gertrude Stein and the End of Europe." *Massachusetts Review* 38, no. 3 (1997): 405–16.

Ashton, Jennifer. *From Modernism to Postmodernism: American Poetry and Theory in the Twentieth Century*. Cambridge: Cambridge University Press, 2005.

———. "Gertrude Stein for Anyone." *ELH* 64, no. 1 (1997): 289–331.

———. "Modernism's 'New' Literalism." *Modernism/modernity* 10, no. 2 (2003): 381–90.

———. "'Rose Is a Rose': Gertrude Stein and the Critique of Indeterminacy." *Modernism/modernity* 9, no. 4 (2002): 581–604.

Augspurger, Michael. *An Economy of Abundant Beauty: Fortune Magazine and Depression America*. Ithaca, NY: Cornell University Press, 2004.

Baker, Carlos, ed. *Ernest Hemingway: Selected Letters 1917–1961*. New York: Charles Scribner's Sons, 1981.

Baker, Thomas. *Sentiment and Celebrity: Nathaniel Parker Willis and the Trials of Literary Fame*. New York: Oxford University Press, 1999.

Banerjee, A. "A Move towards Maturity: Scott Fitzgerald's 'The Crack-Up.'" *Revista Alicantina de Estudios Ingleses* 8 (1995): 47–56.

Bederman, Gail. *Manliness and Civilization: A Cultural History of Gender and Race in the U.S., 1880–1917*. Chicago: University of Chicago Press, 1996.

Berg, A. Scott. *Max Perkins: Editor of Genius*. New York: E. P. Dutton, 1978.

Blake, Nancy. "*Everybody's Autobiography*: Identity and Absence." *RANAM* 15 (1982): 135–45.

Bloom, Lynn Z. "Gertrude Is Alice Is Everybody: Innovation and Point of View in Gertrude Stein's Autobiographies." *Twentieth Century Literature* 24, no. 1 (1978): 81–93.

Blumin, Stuart. *The Emergence of the Middle Class: Social Experience in the American City, 1760–1900*. Cambridge: Cambridge University Press, 1989.

Bollinger, Laurel. "'One as One Not Mistaken but Interrupted': Gertrude Stein's Exploration of Identity in the 1930's." *Centennial Review* 43, no. 2 (1999): 227–58.

Boorstin, Daniel. *The Image: A Guide to Pseudo-Events in America.* New York: Harper & Row, 1964.

Borus, Daniel. *Writing Realism: Howells, James, and Norris in the Mass Market.* Chapel Hill: University of North Carolina Press, 1989.

Bourdieu, Pierre. *The Field of Cultural Production: Essays on Art and Literature.* Edited by Randal Johnson. New York: Columbia University Press, 1993.

Brantlinger, Patrick, and James Naremore, eds. *Modernism and Mass Culture.* Bloomington: Indiana University Press, 1991.

Braudy, Leo. *The Frenzy of Renown: Fame and Its History.* New York: Vintage Books, 1997.

Breslin, James. "Gertrude Stein and the Problems of Autobiography." *Georgia Review* 33 (1979): 901–13.

Bridgman, Richard. *Gertrude Stein in Pieces.* New York: Oxford University Press, 1970.

Brinnin, John Malcolm. *The Third Rose: Gertrude Stein and Her World.* New York: Addison-Wesley Publishing Company, 1987.

Brodhead, Richard. *Cultures of Letters: Scenes of Reading and Writing in Nineteenth Century America.* Chicago: University of Chicago Press, 1994.

Brooks, Van Wyck. *America's Coming-of-Age.* New York: B. W. Huebsch, 1915.

Bruccoli, Matthew J. *Fitzgerald and Hemingway: A Dangerous Friendship.* New York: Carroll & Graf, 1994.

———. "The Perkins-Wilson Correspondence." *Fitzgerald/Hemingway Annual 1978* (1979).

———. *Some Sort of Epic Grandeur.* 2nd rev. ed. Columbia: University of South Carolina Press, 2002.

———, ed. *As Ever, Scott Fitz-: Letters between F. Scott Fitzgerald and His Literary Agent Harold Ober, 1919–1940.* Philadelphia, PA: J. B. Lippincott Company, 1972.

———, ed. *F. Scott Fitzgerald on Authorship.* Columbia: University of South Carolina Press, 1996.

———, ed. *F. Scott Fitzgerald: A Life in Letters.* New York: Charles Scribner's Sons, 1994.

Bruccoli, Matthew J., and Jackson R. Bryer, eds. *F. Scott Fitzgerald in His Own Time: A Miscellany.* Kent, OH: Kent State University Press, 1971.

Bruccoli, Matthew J., and Margaret M. Duggan, eds. *Correspondence of F. Scott Fitzgerald.* New York: Random House, 1980.

Bruccoli, Matthew J., Scottie Fitzgerald Smith, and Joan P. Kerr, eds. *The Romantic Egoists.* Columbia: University of South Carolina Press, 1974.

Bryer, Jackson R. *The Critical Reputation of F. Scott Fitzgerald.* Hamden, CT: Archon Books, 1967.

————, ed. *F. Scott Fitzgerald: The Critical Reception*. New York: Burt Franklin & Co., 1978.

Bryer, Jackson R., and Cathy W. Barks, eds. *Dear Scott, Dearest Zelda: The Love Letters of F. Scott and Zelda Fitzgerald*. New York: St. Martin's Press, 2002.

Burns, Edward, ed. *The Letters of Gertrude Stein and Carl Van Vechten, 1913–1946*. 2 vols. Vol. I (1913–1935). New York: Columbia University Press, 1986.

Burns, Edward, Ulla E. Dydo, and William Rice, eds. *The Letters of Gertrude Stein and Thornton Wilder*. New Haven and London: Yale University Press, 1996.

Cagle, Charles Harmon. "'Cezanne Nearly Did': Stein, Cezanne, and Hemingway." *Midwest Quarterly: A Journal of Contemporary Thought* 23, no. 3 (1982): 268–79.

Caldwell, Mark. "New York's School for Scandal Sheets." *International Herald Tribune*, April 22, 2006.

Caramello, Charles. "Reading Gertrude Stein Reading Henry James, or Eros Is Eros Is Eros Is Eros." *Henry James Review* 6 (1985): 182–203.

Carnes, Mark C., and Clyde Griffen, eds. *Meanings for Manhood: Constructions of Masculinity in Victorian America*. Chicago: University of Chicago Press, 1990.

Carpenter, Humphrey. *A Serious Character: The Life of Ezra Pound*. London: Faber & Faber, 1988.

Cawelti, John G. "The Writer as a Celebrity: Some Aspects of American Literature as Popular Culture." *Studies in American Fiction* 5 (1977): 161–74.

Cerf, Bennett. *At Random: The Reminiscences of Bennett Cerf*. New York: Random House, 1977.

Chessman, Harriet Scott. *The Public Is Invited to Dance: Representation, the Body, and Dialogue in Gertrude Stein*. Stanford, CA: Stanford University Press, 1989.

Chinitz, David E. *T. S. Eliot and the Cultural Divide*. Chicago: University of Chicago Press, 2003.

Chodat, Robert. "Sense, Science, and the Interpretations of Gertrude Stein." *Modernism/modernity* 12, no. 4 (2005): 581–605.

Cohn, Jan. *Creating America: George Horace Lorimer and the Saturday Evening Post*. Pittsburgh, PA: University of Pittsburgh Press, 1989.

Conrad, Bryce. "Gertrude Stein in the American Marketplace." *Journal of Modern Literature* XIX (1995): 215–33.

Conroy, Mark. *Muse in the Machine: American Fiction and Mass Publicity*. Columbus: Ohio State University Press, 2004.

Cooper, John Xiros. *Modernism and the Culture of Market Society*. Cambridge: Cambridge University Press, 2004.

Cope, Karin. "'Moral Deviancy' and Contemporary Feminism: The Judgment of Gertrude Stein." In *Feminism Beside Itself*, edited by Diane Elam and Robyn Wiegman, 155–78. New York: Routledge, 1995.

Cowley, Malcolm. "Third Act and Epilogue." *New Yorker* XXI (1945): 53–58.

Crouthamel, James L. *Bennett's New York Herald and the Rise of the Popular Press*. Syracuse: Syracuse University Press, 1993.

Curnutt, Kirk. "F. Scott Fitzgerald, Age Consciousness, and the Rise of American Youth Culture." In *The Cambridge Companion to F. Scott Fitzgerald*, edited by Ruth Prigozy, 28–47. New York: Cambridge University Press, 2002.

———. "Inside and Outside: Gertrude Stein on Identity, Celebrity, and Authenticity." *Journal of Modern Literature* 23, no. 2 (1999): 291–308.

———. "Making a 'Clean Break': Confession, Celebrity Journalism, Image Management and F. Scott Fitzgerald's 'the Crack-up.'" *Genre: Forms of Discourse and Culture* 32, no. 4 (1999): 297–328.

———. "Parody and Pedagogy: Teaching Style, Voice, and Authorial Intent in the Works of Gertrude Stein." *College Literature* 23, no. 2 (1996): 1–24.

———, ed. *The Critical Response to Gertrude Stein*. Westport, CT: Greenwood Press, 2000.

deCordova, Richard. *Picture Personalities: The Emergence of the Star System in America*. Urbana and Chicago: University of Illinois Press, 1990.

DeKoven, Marianne. *A Different Language: Gertrude Stein's Experimental Writing*. Madison: University of Wisconsin Press, 1983.

———. "Gertrude Stein and Modern Painting: Beyond Literary Cubism." *Contemporary Literature* 22, no. 1 (1981): 81–95.

Deleuze, Gilles. *The Logic of Sense*. New York: Columbia University Press, 1969.

Denning, Michael. *Mechanic Accents: Dime Novels and Working-Class Culture in America*. London: Verso, 1987.

Dettmar, Kevin J. H., and Stephen Watt, eds. *Marketing Modernisms: Self-Promotion, Canonization, Rereading*. Ann Arbor: University of Michigan Press, 1996.

Dickstein, Morris. "Fitzgerald: The Authority of Failure." In *F. Scott Fitzgerald in the Twenty-First Century*, edited by Jackson R. Bryer, Ruth Prigozy, and Milton R. Stern, 301–16. Tuscaloosa: University of Alabama Press, 2003.

Dolan, Marc. *Modern Lives*. West Lafayette, IN: Purdue University Press, 1996.

Donaldson, Scott. "The Crisis of Fitzgerald's 'Crack-up.'" *Twentieth Century Literature* 26, no. 2 (1980): 171–88.

———. "Fitzgerald's Nonfiction." In *The Cambridge Companion to F. Scott Fitzgerald*, edited by Ruth Prigozy, 164–88. New York: Cambridge University Press, 2002.

———. *Fool for Love: F. Scott Fitzgerald*. New York: Congdon & Weed, 1983.

Doran, George H. *Chronicles of Barabbas: 1884–1934*. New York: Harcourt Brace, 1935.

Douglas, Ann. *The Feminization of American Culture*. New York: Anchor Press, 1977.

———. *Terrible Honesty: Mongrel Manhattan in the 1920s*. New York: Farrar, Straus & Giroux, 1995.

Douglas, George H. *The Smart Magazines*. Hamden, CT: Shoe String Press, 1991.

Dydo, Ulla E. *Gertrude Stein: The Language That Rises, 1923–1934*. Evanston, IL: Northwestern University Press, 2003.

———. "*Stanzas in Meditation*: The Other Autobiography." *Chicago Review* 35, no. 2 (1985): 4–20.

Dyer, Richard. *Stars*. London: BFI Publishing, 1998.

Eakin, Paul John. *The Ethics of Life Writing*. New York: Cornell University Press, 2004.

———. "What Are We Reading When We Read Autobiography?" *Narrative* 12, no. 2 (2004): 121–32.

Eliot, T. S. "Charleston, Hey! Hey!" *The Nation & Athenaeum* xl, no. 17 (1927): 595.

———. "London Letter." *The Dial* LXXIII, no. 6 (1922): 659–63.

———. "London Letter." In *Exploring T. S. Eliot*, Rickard A. Parker, http://world.std.com/~raparker/exploring/tseliot/works/london-letters/london-letter-1922-12.html (accessed March 11, 2009).

———. "Marie Lloyd." In *T. S. Eliot: Selected Essays, 1917–1932*, 369–72. New York: Harcourt, Brace & Company, 1932.

———. "Tradition and the Individual Talent." In *Selected Essays, 1917–1932*, 3–11. New York: Harcourt, Brace & Company, 1932.

Ewen, Stuart. *All Consuming Images: The Politics of Style in Contemporary Culture*. New York: Basic, 1988.

Fine, Richard. *Hollywood and the Profession of Authorship, 1928–1940*. Washington, D.C.: Smithsonian Institution, 1993.

Fitzgerald, F. Scott, and Zelda Fitzgerald. "Does a Moment of Revolt Come Sometime to Every Married Man?" *McCall's* 51 (1924): 21, 36, 82.

Fitzgerald, F. Scott. *Afternoon of an Author*. Edited by Arthur Mizener. New York: Charles Scribner's Sons, 1957.

———. *F. Scott Fitzgerald's Ledger*. Washington: NCR/Microcard Editions, 1972.

———. *The Last Tycoon: An Unfinished Novel Together with "The Great Gatsby" and Selected Stories*. Edited by Edmund Wilson. New York: Scribner, 1941.

———. *The Love of the Last Tycoon: A Western*. Edited by Matthew J. Bruccoli. New York: Cambridge University Press, 1978.

———. *The Notebooks of F. Scott Fitzgerald*. Edited by Matthew J. Bruccoli. New York: Harcourt Brace Jovanovich/Bruccoli Clark, 1978.

Fitzgerald, Zelda. *The Collected Writings of Zelda Fitzgerald*. Edited by Matthew J. Bruccoli. Tuscaloosa and London: University of Alabama Press, 1991.

Foucault, Michel. "The Discourse on Language." In *Critical Theory since 1965*, edited by Hazard Adams and Leroy Searle, 148–62. Tallahassee: Florida State University Press, 1986.

Gabler, Neal. *Winchell: Gossip, Power, and the Culture of Celebrity*. New York: Knopf, 1995.

Gallup, Donald. "Gertrude Stein and the *Atlantic*." *Yale University Library Gazette* XXVIII (1954): 109–28.

———, ed. *The Flowers of Friendship: Letters Written to Gertrude Stein*. New York: Alfred A. Knopf, 1953.

Gamson, Joshua. *Claims to Fame: Celebrity in Contemporary America*. Berkeley: University of California Press, 1994.

Gerbner, George. "The Social Role of the Confession Magazine." *Social Problems* 6 (1958): 29–40.

Gervais, Ronald J. "Fitzgerald's 'Euganean Hills' Allusion in 'the Crack-up.'" *American Notes and Queries* 21, no. 9–10 (1983): 139–41.

Gilmore, Leigh. "A Signature of Lesbian Autobiography: 'Gertrice/Altrude.'" *Prose Studies* 14, no. 2 (1991): 56–75.

Gingrich, Arnold to John Gingrich, March 25, 1936, Box I: Personal Correspondence. Arnold Gingrich Papers. Bentley Historical Library, University of Michigan.

Gingrich, Arnold. "Backstage with *Esquire*." *Esquire*, June 1936, 26B, 28.

———. "Introduction." In *The Pat Hobby Stories*, ix–xxiii. New York: Scribner, 1962.

———. *Nothing but People: The Early Days at Esquire, a Personal History, 1928–1958*. New York: Crown Publishers, 1971.

———. "Scott, Ernest, and Whoever." *Esquire*, December 1966, 322–25.

———. "Three Characters in Search of a Magazine That Is Unhampered by the Old Taboos." *Esquire*, February 1934, 15.

Glass, Loren. *Authors Inc.: Literary Celebrity in the Modern United States, 1880–1980*. New York: New York University Press, 2004.

Gleason, Edward J. "Going toward the Flame: Reading Allusions in *Esquire* Stories." In *F. Scott Fitzgerald: New Perspectives*, edited by Jackson R. Bryer, Alan Margolies, and Ruth Prigozy, 216–30. Athens: University of Georgia Press, 2000.

Graham, Sheilah. *Beloved Infidel: The Education of a Woman*. New York: Holt, 1958.

———. *The Rest of the Story*. New York: Coward-McCann, 1964.

Green, Robert Alan. "Advice at Twenty." *Esquire*, April 1936, 8.

Groner, Alex, and the Editors of *American Heritage* and *Business Week*. *The American Heritage History of American Business and Industry*. New York: American Heritage Publishing Co., 1972.

Harris, Neil. *Humbug: The Art of P. T. Barnum*. Boston: Little, Brown & Company, 1973.

Hemingway, Ernest. *A Moveable Feast*. New York: Scribner, 1964.

Henley, William Ernest. "Invictus." In *Modern British Poetry*, edited by Louis Untermeyer. New York: Harcourt, 1920. Bartleby.com, 1999. www.bartleby.com/103/7.html. (accessed August 10, 2010).

Hindus, Milton. *F. Scott Fitzgerald: An Introduction and Interpretation*. New York: Holt, Rinehart & Winston, 1968.

Hobhouse, Janet. *Everybody Who Was Anybody: A Biography of Gertrude Stein*. New York: G. P. Putnam's Sons, 1975.

Hochfelder, David. "The Communications Revolution and Popular Culture." In *A Companion to 19th-Century America*, edited by William L. Barney. Oxford: Blackwell Publishers, 2001.

Holt, Henry. "The Commercialization of Literature." *Atlantic Monthly* (1905): 578–600.

Huyssen, Andreas. *After the Great Divide: Modernism, Mass Culture, Postmodernism*. Bloomington: Indiana University Press, 1986.

———. "High/Low in an Expanded Field." *Modernism/modernity* 9, no. 3 (2002): 363–74.

Isenberg, Michael. *John L. Sullivan and His America*. Urbana: University of Illinois Press, 1988.

Jaffe, Aaron. *Modernism and the Culture of Celebrity*. Cambridge: Cambridge University Press, 2005.

Jameson, Fredric. "Reification and Utopia in Mass Culture." *Social Text* 1 (1979): 130–48.

Jelinek, Estelle C. *The Tradition of Women's Autobiography: From Antiquity to the Present*. Boston: Twayne Publishers, 1986.

Johnson, David E. " 'Writing in the Dark': The Political Fictions of American Travel Writing." *American Literary History* 7, no. 1 (1995): 1–27.

Kaplan, Fred. *Dickens: A Biography*. London: Hodder & Stoughton, 1988.

Kaplan, Louis. *A Bibliography of American Autobiographies*. Madison: University of Wisconsin Press, 1961.

Kasson, John F. *Houdini, Tarzan, and the Perfect Man: The White Male Body and the Challenge of Modernity in America*. New York: Hill & Wang, 2002.

Kazin, Alfred. "An American Confession." In *F. Scott Fitzgerald: The Man and His Work*, edited by Alfred Kazin, 172–81. Cleveland, OH: The World Publishing Company, 1951.

———. *Starting Out in the Thirties*. Boston: Little, Brown & Company 1965.

Kelley, Mary. *Private Woman, Public Stage: Literary Domesticity in Nineteenth-Century America*. New York and Oxford: Oxford University Press, 1984.

Kett, Joseph F. *Rites of Passage: Adolescence in America 1790 to the Present*. New York: Basic Books, 1973.

Kimmel, Michael. *Manhood in America: A Cultural History*. New York: Free Press, 1996.

Knight, Alan R. "Explaining Composition: Gertrude Stein and the Problem of Representation." *English Studies in Canada* 13, no. 4 (1987): 406–19.

Kuehl, John, and Jackson R. Bryer, eds. *Dear Scott/Dear Max: The Fitzgerald-Perkins Correspondence.* New York: Charles Scribner's Sons, 1971.

Le Vot, Andre. *F. Scott Fitzgerald: A Biography.* Translated by William Byron. Garden City, NY: Doubleday & Company, 1979.

Leach, William R. "Transformations in a Culture of Consumption: Woman and Department Stores, 1890–1925." *Journal of American History* 71, no. 2 (1984): 319–42.

Lehmann-Haupt, Hellmut. *The Book in America: A History of the Making and Selling of Books in the United States.* New York: R. R. Bowker Company, 1952.

Leick, Karen. *Gertrude Stein and the Making of an American Celebrity.* New York: Routledge, 2009.

———. "Popular Modernism: Little Magazines and the American Daily Press." *PMLA* 123, no. 1 (2008): 125–39.

Lejeune, Philippe. "The Autobiographical Pact." In *On Autobiography,* edited by Paul John Eakin, 3–30. Minneapolis: University of Minnesota Press, 1989.

Lentricchia, Frank. "Lyric in the Culture of Capitalism." In *Modernist Quartet,* 47–76. Cambridge: Cambridge University Press, 1994.

———. *Modernist Quartet.* Cambridge: Cambridge University Press, 1994.

Levine, Lawrence. *Highbrow/Lowbrow: The Emergence of Cultural Hierarchy in America.* Cambridge, MA: Harvard University Press, 1988.

Lewis, Wyndham. *The Art of Being Ruled.* Edited by Reed Way Dasenbrock. Santa Rosa, CA: Black Sparrow Press, 1989.

Logan, Andy. *The Man Who Robbed Robber Barons.* New York: W. W. Norton, 1965.

Macfadden, Mary, and Emile Gauvreau. *Dumbbells and Carrot Strips: The Story of Bernarr Macfadden.* New York: Holt, 1953.

Mao, Douglas, and Rebecca L. Walkowitz. "The New Modernist Studies." *PMLA* 123, no. 3 (2008): 737–48.

Marchand, Roland. *Advertising the American Dream: Making Way for Modernity, 1920–1940.* Berkeley: University of California Press, 1985.

Margolies, Alan. "Fitzgerald and Hollywood." In *The Cambridge Companion to F. Scott Fitzgerald,* edited by Ruth Prigozy, 189–208. New York: Cambridge University Press, 2002.

Marshall, P. David. *Celebrity and Power: Fame in Contemporary Culture.* Minneapolis: University of Minnesota Press, 1997.

McCabe, Susan. "'Delight in Dislocation': The Cinematic Modernism of Stein, Chaplin, and Man Ray." *Modernism/modernity* 8, no. 3 (2001): 429–52.

McClure, S. S. *My Autobiography.* New York: F. Ungar Publishing Company, 1963.

McWhirter, Darien A., and Jon D. Bible. *Privacy as a Constitutional Right*. New York: Quorum Books, 1992.

Mellow, James R. *Charmed Circle: Gertrude Stein and Company*. New York: Praeger, 1974.

Mencken, H. L. "Untitled Review." *The Smart Set* 62 (1920): 140.

Merrill, Hugh. *Esky: The Early Years at Esquire*. New Brunswick, NJ: Rutgers University Press, 1995.

Miller, James E. Jr. *F. Scott Fitzgerald: His Art and His Technique*. New York: New York University Press, 1964.

Mitrano, G. F. *Gertrude Stein: Woman without Qualities*. Burlington, VT: Ashgate Publishing Company, 2005.

Mok, Michel. "The Other Side of Paradise: Scott Fitzgerald, 40, Engulfed in Despair." *New York Post*, September 25, 1936, 1, 15.

Mole, Tom, ed. *Romanticism and Celebrity Culture, 1750–1850*. New York: Cambridge University Press, 2009.

Moran, Joe. *Star Authors: Literary Celebrity in America*. Sterling, VA: Pluto Press, 2000.

Morris, Wright. "The Function of Nostalgia: F. Scott Fitzgerald." In *F. Scott Fitzgerald: A Collection of Critical Essays*, edited by Arthur Mizener, 25–31. Englewood Cliffs, NJ: Prentice-Hall, 1963.

Morrisson, Mark S. *The Public Face of Modernism: Little Magazines, Audiences, and Reception, 1905–1920*. Madison: University of Wisconsin Press, 2001.

Mossberg, Barbara. "Double Exposures: Emily Dickinson's and Gertrude Stein's Anti-Autobiographies." *Women's Studies: An Interdisciplinary Journal* 16, no. 1–2 (1989): 239–50.

Mott, Frank Luther. *A History of American Magazines, 1885–1905*. 5 vols. Vol. 4. Cambridge, MA: Harvard University Press, 1966.

———. *A History of American Magazines: 1865–1885*. 5 vols. Vol. 3. Cambridge, MA: Harvard University Press, 1966.

———. "The Magazine Revolution and Popular Ideas in the Nineties." In *American History: Recent Interpretations*, edited by Abraham Eisenstadt. New York: Crowell, 1969.

Murphy, Michael. "'One Hundred Per Cent Bohemia': Pop Decadence and the Aestheticization of Commodity in the Rise of the Slicks." In *Marketing Modernisms: Self-Promotion, Canonization, Rereading*, edited by Kevin J. H. Dettmar and Stephen Watt, 61–89. Ann Arbor: University of Michigan Press, 1996.

Neuman, S. C. *Gertrude Stein: Autobiography and the Problem of Narration*. Victoria, B.C.: English Literary Studies, 1979.

Newbury, Michael. *Figuring Authorship in Antebellum America*. Stanford, CA: Stanford University Press, 1997.

Nowlin, Michael. *F. Scott Fitzgerald's Racial Angles and the Business of Literary Greatness*. New York: Palgrave Macmillan, 2007.

Ohmann, Richard. *Selling Culture: Magazines, Markets, and Class at the Turn of the Century*. New York: Verso, 1996.

Parke, Catherine N. "'Simple through Complication': Gertrude Stein Thinking." *American Literature* 60, no. 4 (1988): 554–74.

Pember, Don R. *Privacy and the Press: The Law, the Mass Media, and the First Amendment.* Seattle: University of Washington Press, 1972.

Pendergast, Tom. *Creating the Modern Man: American Magazines and Consumer Culture, 1900–1950.* Columbia: University of Missouri Press, 2000.

Perelman, Bob. *The Trouble with Genius: Reading Pound, Joyce, Stein, and Zukofsky.* Berkeley and Los Angeles: University of California Press, 1994.

Perloff, Marjorie. *21st-Century Modernism: The 'New' Poetics.* Malden, MA: Blackwell Publishers, 2002.

———. *The Poetics of Indeterminacy: Rimbaud to Cage.* Princeton: Princeton University Press, 1981.

Peterson, Theodore. *Magazines in the Twentieth Century.* Urbana: University of Illinois Press, 1956.

Piper, Henry Dan. *F. Scott Fitzgerald: A Critical Portrait.* New York, 1965.

Pollack, Adam J. *John L. Sullivan: The Career of the First Gloved Heavyweight Champion.* Jefferson, NC: McFarland & Company, 2006.

Ponce de Leon, Charles L. *Self-Exposure: Human Interest Journalism and the Emergence of Celebrity in America.* Chapel Hill: University of North Carolina Press, 2002.

Pondrom, Cyrena N. "An Introduction to the Achievement of Gertrude Stein." In *Geography and Plays,* vii–lv. Madison: University of Wisconsin Press, 1993.

Pope, Daniel. *The Making of Modern Advertising.* New York: Basic Books, 1983.

Potts, Stephen W. *The Price of Paradise: The Magazine Career of F. Scott Fitzgerald.* San Bernardino, CA: Borgo Press, 1993.

Prigozy, Ruth. "Introduction: Scott, Zelda, and the Culture of Celebrity." In *The Cambridge Companion to F. Scott Fitzgerald,* edited by Ruth Prigozy, 1–27. New York: Cambridge University Press, 2002.

"Publisher's Note." In *Everybody's Autobiography,* vii–x. Cambridge, MA: Exact Change, 1993.

R.V.A.S. "Untitled Review." *New Republic* 22 (1920): 362.

Radway, Janice. *A Feeling for Books: The Book-of-the-Month-Club, Literary Taste, and Middle-Class Desire.* Chapel Hill: University of North Carolina Press, 1997.

———. "Research Universities, Periodical Publication, and the Circulation of Professional Expertise: On the Significance of Middlebrow Authority." *Critical Inquiry* 31, no. 1 (2004): 203–28.

———. "The Scandal of the Middlebrow: The Book-of-the-Month Club, Class Fracture, and Cultural Authority." *South Atlantic Quarterly* 89, no. 4 (1990): 703–36.

Rainey, Lawrence S. *Institutions of Modernism: Literary Elites and Public Culture.* New Haven, CT: Yale University Press, 1998.

Rotundo, Anthony. *American Manhood: Transformations in Masculinity from the Revolution to the Modern Era.* New York: Basic Books, 1994.

Rubin, Joan Shelley. *The Making of Middlebrow Culture.* Chapel Hill: University of North Carolina Press, 1992.

Scandura, Jani, and Michael Thurston. *Modernism, Inc.: Body, Memory, Capital.* New York: New York University Press, 2001.

Schickel, Richard. *Intimate Strangers: The Culture of Celebrity in America.* Chicago: Ivan R. Dee, 1985.

Schiller, Dan. *Objectivity and the New: The Public and the Rise of Commercial Journalism.* Philadelphia, PA: Temple University Press, 1981.

Schmitz, Neil. "Gertrude Stein as Post-Modernist: The Rhetoric of 'Tender Buttons.'" *Journal of Modern Literature* 3, no. 5 (1974): 1203–18.

Scholes, Robert. *Paradoxy of Modernism.* New Haven and London: Yale University Press, 2006.

Schudson, Michael. *Discovering the News: A Social History of American Newspapers.* New York: Basic Books, 1978.

Schulberg, Budd. *The Disenchanted.* New York: Random House, 1950.

Schultz, Susan M. "Gertrude Stein's Self-Advertisement." *Raritan* 12, no. 2 (1992): 71–88.

Seitz, Don C. *Joseph Pulitzer: His Life and Letters.* New York: Simon & Schuster, 1924.

Shove, Raymond. *Cheap Book Production in the United States, 1870–1891.* Urbana: University of Illinois Library, 1937.

Simon, Richard Keller. "Modernism and Mass Culture." *American Literary History* 13, no. 2 (2001): 343–53.

Singal, Daniel Joseph. "Towards a Definition of American Modernism." *American Quarterly* 39, no. 1 (1978): 7–26.

Siraganian, Lisa. "Out of Air: Theorizing the Art Object in Gertrude Stein and Wyndham Lewis." *Modernism/modernity* 10, no. 4 (2003): 657–76.

Smith, Terry. *Making the Modern: Industry, Art and Design in America.* Chicago: University of Chicago Press, 1993.

Spahr, Juliana. *Everybody's Autonomy: Connective Reading and Collective Identity.* Tuscaloosa: University of Alabama Press, 2001.

Spencer, David R. *The Yellow Journalism: The Press and America's Emergence as a World Power.* Evanston, IL: Northwestern University Press, 2007.

Stein, Gertrude. "And Now." In *Vanity Fair: Selections from America's Most Memorable Magazine, a Cavalcade of the 1920s and 1930s,* edited by Cleveland Amory and Frederic Bradlee, 280–81. New York: The Viking Press, 1934.

———. "Arthur A Grammar." In *How to Write,* 33–108. Los Angeles: Sun & Moon Press, 1995.

———. *The Autobiography of Alice B. Toklas.* New York: Vintage Books, 1990.

———. *Everybody's Autobiography.* Cambridge, MA: Exact Change, 1993.

———. *Four in America.* New Haven, CT: Yale University Press, 1947.

Stein, Gertrude. *The Geographical History of America or the Relation of Human Nature to the Human Mind.* Edited by Catharine R. Stimpson and Harriet Chessman. 2 vols. Vol. 2, *Gertrude Stein: Writings 1932–1946.* New York: Random House, 1998.

———. *How Writing Is Written: Volume II of the Previously Uncollected Writings of Gertrude Stein.* Edited by Robert Bartlett Haas. Los Angeles: Black Sparrow Press, 1974.

———. *Lectures in America.* New York: Vintage Books, 1975.

———. *The Making of Americans.* New York: Something Else, 1966.

———. *Narration.* Chicago: University of Chicago Press, 1935.

———. *A Primer for the Gradual Understanding of Gertrude Stein.* Edited by Robert Bartlett Haas. Los Angeles: Black Sparrow Press, 1971.

———. *What Are Masterpieces.* New York: Pitman Publishing Corporation, 1970.

Steiner, Wendy. *Exact Resemblance to Exact Resemblance.* New Haven, CT, 1978.

Stevens, Mitchell. *A History of News.* New York: Viking, 1988.

Steward, Samuel M. *Dear Sammy: Letters from Gertrude Stein and Alice B. Toklas.* Boston: Houghton Mifflin Company, 1977.

Stimpson, Catharine R. "Gertrice/Altrude, Stein Toklas and the Paradox of the Happy Marriage." In *Mothering the Mind, Twelve Studies of Writers and Their Silent Partners,* edited by Ruth Perry and Martine Watson Brownley, 122–39. New York: Holmes & Meier, 1984.

Strasser, Susan. *Satisfaction Guaranteed: The Making of the American Mass Market.* New York: Pantheon Books, 1989.

Strychacz, Thomas. *Modernism, Mass Culture and Professionalism.* Cambridge: Cambridge University Press, 1993.

Sullivan, John L. *Life and Reminiscences of a Nineteenth Century Gladiator.* London: Routledge, 1892.

Susman, Warren. *Culture and Commitment, 1929–1945.* New York: G. Braziller, 1973.

———. *Culture as History: The Transformation of American Society in the Twentieth Century.* Washington D.C.: Smithsonian Institution Press, 2003.

Swartz, Shirley. "The Autobiography as Generic 'Continuous Present': *Paris France* and *Wars I Have Seen.*" *English Studies in Canada* 4, no. 2 (1978): 224–37.

Sweetman, Charles. "Sheltering Assets and Reorganizing Debts: Fitzgerald's Declaration of Emotional Bankruptcy in *the Crack-Up.*" *Proteus: A Journal of Ideas* 20, no. 2 (2003): 10–14.

Szalay, Michael. "Inviolate Modernism: Hemingway, Stein, Tzara." *Modern Language Quarterly* 56, no. 4 (1995): 457–85.

———. *New Deal Modernism: American Literature and the Invention of the Welfare State.* Durham, NC: Duke University Press, 2000.

Tebbel, John William. *George Horace Lorimer and the Saturday Evening Post.* Garden City, NY: Doubleday, 1948.

———. *A History of Book Publishing in the United States.* Vol. 4. New York: R. R. Bowker, 1981.

———. *A History of Book Publishing in the United States: The Expansion of an Industry, 1865–1919.* 4 vols. Vol. 2. New York: R. R. Bowker Company, 1972–1981.

Tebbel, John William, and Mary Ellen Zuckerman. *The Magazine in America, 1741–1990.* New York: Oxford University Press, 1991.

"The Ten Dullest Authors: A Symposium." In *Vanity Fair: Selections from America's Most Memorable, a Cavalcade of the 1920s and 30s,* edited by Cleveland Amory and Frederic Bradlee, 76–77. New York: The Viking Press, 1960.

Tomlinson, Charles, ed. *Marianne Moore: A Collection of Critical Essays.* Englewood Cliffs, NJ: Prentice-Hall, 1969.

Trilling, Lionel. "F. Scott Fitzgerald." In *The Liberal Imagination,* 243–54. New York: Viking, 1950.

Troy, William. "F. Scott Fitzgerald: The Authority of Failure." In *F. Scott Fitzgerald,* edited by Harold Bloom, 25–30. New York: Chelsea House Publishers, 2006.

Turnbull, Andrew. *Scott Fitzgerald.* New York: Charles Scribner's Sons, 1962.

———, ed. *The Letters of F. Scott Fitzgerald.* New York: Charles Scribner's Sons, 1963.

Turner, Catherine. *Marketing Modernism between the Two World Wars.* Amherst & Boston: University of Massachusetts Press, 2003.

Wagner-Martin, Linda. *"Favored Strangers": Gertrude Stein and Her Family.* New Brunswick, NJ: Rutgers University Press, 1995.

———. "Gertrude Stein." In *Jewish American Women Writers: A Bio-Bibliographical and Critical Sourcebook,* edited by Ann Shapiro, 431–39. London: Greenday Press, 1994.

———. *The Mid-Century American Novel.* New York: Twayne, 1997.

———. *Zelda Sayre Fitzgerald: An American Woman's Life.* New York: Palgrave Macmillan, 2004.

Walker, Pat, ed. *Between Labour and Capital.* Boston: South End Press, 1979.

Warren, Lansing. "Gertrude Stein Views Life and Politics." *New York Times Magazine,* May 6, 1934, 9, 23.

Warren, Samuel D., and Louis D. Brandeis. "The Right to Privacy." *Harvard Law Review* 4, no. 5 (1890).

Watson, Elmo Scott. *A History of Newspaper Syndicates in the United States, 1865–1935.* Chicago: Publisher's Auxiliary, 1936.

Welky, David. *Everything Was Better in America: Print Culture in the Great Depression.* Urbana and Chicago: University of Illinois Press, 2008.

West, James L. W. "F. Scott Fitzgerald, Professional Author." In *A Historical Guide to F. Scott Fitzgerald,* edited by Kirk Curnutt. Oxford: Oxford University Press, 2004.

———. "Fitzgerald and *Esquire.*" In *The Short Stories of F. Scott Fitzgerald: New Approaches in Criticism,* edited by Jackson R. Bryer, 149–66. Madison: University of Wisconsin Press, 1982.

Wexler, Joyce Piell. *Who Paid for Modernism? Art, Money, and the Fiction of Conrad, Joyce, and Lawrence.* Fayetteville: University of Arkansas Press, 1997.

White, E. B. "Talk of the Town." *New Yorker,* March 14, 1936, 11.

Wicke, Jennifer. *Advertising Fictions: Literature, Advertising, and Social Reading.* New York: Columbia University Press, 1988.

Wiebe, Robert. *The Search for Order.* New York: Hill & Wang, 1967.

Wilkes, Roger. *Scandal: A Scurrilous History of Gossip.* London: Atlantic, 2002.

Will, Barbara. *Gertrude Stein, Modernism, and the Problem of "Genius."* Edinburgh: Edinburgh University Press, 2000.

Willison, Ian, Warwick Gould, and Warren Chernaik, eds. *Modernist Writers and the Marketplace.* New York: St. Martin's Press, 1996.

Wilson, Christopher. *The Labor of Words: Literary Professionalism in the Progressive Era.* Athens: University of Georgia Press, 1985.

Wilson, Edmund, ed. *The Crack-Up.* New York: New Directions, 1945.

———. *Letters on Literature and Politics, 1912–1972.* Edited by Elena Wilson. New York: Farrar, Straus & Giroux, 1977.

———. *The Shores of Light.* New York: Farrar, Straus & Young, 1952.

Wilson, R. Jackson. *Figures of Speech: American Writers and the Literary Marketplace, from Benjamin Franklin to Emily Dickinson.* Baltimore, MD: Johns Hopkins University Press, 1989.

Wolfe, Susan J. "Insistence and Simplicity: The Influence of Gertrude Stein on Ernest Hemingway." *South Dakota Review* 35, no. 3 (1997): 95–111.

Index